A
CAINSVILLE
NOVEL

# Also by Kelley Armstrong

A CAINSVILLE NOVEL

# KELLEY ARMSTRONG
# OMENS

sphere

SPHERE

First published in Great Britain in 2013 by Sphere

Copyright © 2013 K.L.A. Fricke Inc.

The moral right of the author has been asserted.

*All characters and events in this publication, other than
those clearly in the public domain, are fictitious
and any resemblance to real persons,
living or dead, is purely coincidental.*

A CIP catalogue record for this book
is available from the British Library.

HB ISBN 978-1-8474-4511-7
C FORMAT ISBN 978-0-7515-5346-8

Printed and bound in Great Britain by
Clays Ltd, St Ives plc

Papers used by Sphere are from well-managed forests
and other responsible sources.

MIX
Paper from
responsible sources
FSC® C104740

Sphere
An imprint of
Little, Brown Book Group
100 Victoria Embankment
London EC4Y 0DY

An Hachette UK Company
www.hachette.co.uk

www.littlebrown.co.uk

**FOR JEFF,**
who knew I needed a new story to tell
and encouraged me to take the leap.

The town of Cainsville has many secrets, and it is loath to part with them a moment sooner than necessary. Understandably, though, readers may wish to solve some of those mysteries before Olivia does. As a former computer programmer, I'm happy to oblige with some literary Easter eggs. Peppered throughout the book, you'll find foreign words and phrases that are not defined or easily interpreted in context. You can simply ignore them and travel on Olivia's journey with her, uncovering the secrets as she does and, yes, I hope that's the route you'll choose. But if you're impatient, I'm sure the Internet would provide translation help . . . and a few early answers.

# PROLOGUE

Eden crawled into the living room, the rough carpet burning her chubby knees and hands. As boots slapped the hall floor, she went still, holding her breath.

Had he heard her?

The footsteps stopped. She leaned back around the doorway and peeked down the dark hall. There was no sign of him. Not yet. But he'd come for her. He always did.

She crept a little farther, resisting the urge to leap to her feet and run. He'd hear her if she ran.

Once she was past the big chair, she stopped and looked around. The long table in front of the sofa had a cupboard. She opened the door, wincing at the click. The space was big enough to squeeze into, but it was full of books and magazines.

She glanced back at the big chair. It was too far from the wall. If she hid behind it, he'd see her as soon as he came around the corner. But the sofa? Yes! She flattened onto her stomach. Then she wriggled backward until her legs were all the way under and—

Her bum hit the frame and stopped her. She tried again, squirming madly, but she couldn't get under. Maybe if she went in headfirst. She tugged herself forward and—

She was stuck. She wiggled as hard as she could, the carpet burning her knees, but she couldn't get loose, and she was sure any moment now he'd—

She popped out. She took a second to catch her breath. Then she turned around to go in headfirst and—

Her head wouldn't fit under, either.

What about *behind* the sofa? If she could move it out a little, she could get in there. She grabbed the leg with both hands and pulled. It wobbled but didn't move.

The footsteps started again, slow and steady. Coming her way? She swallowed and tried to listen, but her heart was pounding so hard she could barely hear.

She skittered from between the table and sofa and glanced at the hall leading to the bedrooms. Lots of hiding places back there. Better hiding places. If she could—

"Eden?"

She dove for the sofa and pushed it forward just enough so she could squish in behind. She tried to look back to make sure her feet were hidden, but she couldn't tell. She wiggled in a little farther, and then she pressed her hands to her mouth. If she made any noise—any at all—he'd find her. She lay on the carpet, trying not to sniff the old cat pee as she made herself as small as possible.

Footsteps thudded into the room. And stopped. When Eden squeezed her eyes shut, she could hear the slight rasp of his breathing. She pictured him there, brushing his shaggy blond hair from his eyes as he scanned the empty room.

"Eden?" he called.

His boots swished on the carpet as he took a few more steps. He sucked in a breath. "She's gone. Oh my God, Pammie, our baby's gone!"

Eden pressed her fist into her mouth to stifle a laugh. Mommy's soft sigh wafted from the kitchen as she told Daddy—again— not to use language like that in front of their daughter.

"But she's disappeared!" he said. "Call the police! Call the fire department! Call the clown brigade!"

"Speaking of clowns . . ." her mother teased.

Eden's body shook with silent giggles.

"Our baby is gone! All that's left is this shoe." He dropped to his knees by the sofa. "Wait, there's a foot in it."

Eden twisted around, pulling her leg in.

"Oh, no! Now she's completely disapp—"

Eden backed out of her hiding place and launched herself into Daddy's arms. He scooped her up and twirled her around. She closed her eyes as the air whipped past, smelling of Daddy's spicy aftershave. Much better than the cat pee from the old owners, but when she was spinning, the smell made her tummy spin, too. She didn't tell him to stop, though. She'd never tell him to stop.

Daddy tossed her onto the sofa. The bright red pillows scattered as she landed. He picked up one and tucked it under her. Then he bent on one knee.

"I'm sorry, sweetheart, but I have to leave. I've got a big day ahead of me, helping a special girl celebrate her half birthday."

"Me!" Eden bounced on the cushions, singing, "Me! Me! Me!"

"Really? Are you sure?"

More shouting. More bouncing.

Today she turned two and a half. Last night, she'd barely slept, just curled up under the covers and stared at the mural Mommy had painted on the ceiling, a carousel of horses and swans and lions. Usually, if she couldn't sleep, she pictured herself on the black horse with the white mane, and she'd go around and around until she drifted off. That hadn't worked for a long time last night.

Then, when Mommy came to wake her up, Eden heard an owl hooting outside her window, and her tummy had started to hurt. She didn't like the owl—not in the daytime. It sounded scary, and it made her worry that Mommy and Daddy would forget it was her half birthday. But that had been silly. They'd never forget.

"Is it time?" she said, still bouncing. "Is it time?"

"It is. We have a big surprise planned. Do you know what it is?"

"No, she does not," Mommy said as she walked in. "That's the concept of a surprise, Todd."

Daddy leaned down to Eden's ear and whispered, "Pony ride!"

Eden shrieked. Her mother rolled her eyes and pretended to be mad, but she couldn't stop smiling.

"Let's get your hair brushed," Mommy said as Eden jumped into her arms. "We'll want to take lots of pictures when you get your big surprise."

"Pony ride!" Daddy said.

"I think we should put *him* on a pony," Mommy whispered in Eden's ear.

When Mommy finished brushing her hair, Daddy grabbed Eden again and swung her up onto his shoulders. "I think I'd *make* a good pony."

He snorted and pawed the ground. Mommy laughed and slapped him on the bum.

Then the door crashed in.

It happened so fast that nobody moved. Not Mommy. Not Daddy. Eden heard the crunch of breaking wood, and she saw the door fly right off its hinges, and she thought it was a storm like in the movie with the girl and her dog. Only it wasn't a storm. It was monsters.

Huge monsters, all in black, with helmets on their heads and masks over their faces. They swarmed through the broken door. They shouted and yelled and waved black things in their hands.

Eden screamed then, and Daddy stumbled back and Eden started to slip off his shoulders. Mommy caught her before she fell.

One of the monsters shouted. Eden couldn't understand him. Mommy and Daddy did, though. They stopped moving. Then Daddy backed up, arms going wide, shielding Mommy and Eden. Two monsters grabbed him by the shoulders and threw him to the floor.

Eden screamed again. Screamed as loud as she could, her mouth open so wide that her eyes squished shut and she couldn't see. When Mommy's arms wrapped around her, she could feel Mommy's heart pounding. Heard her panting. Smelled something bad and sour that was not like Mommy's smell at all.

"It's okay," Mommy whispered. "Don't look, baby. Just don't look."

Then Mommy shrieked and everything spun. Eden's eyes flew open. One of the monsters had Mommy. Another yanked Eden away. Mommy grabbed for Eden, her nails raking Eden's arm as she tried to get her back. Eden fought just as hard to get to her, kicking and screaming and clawing.

One of the monsters said Mommy and Daddy's names, then started saying other names, a whole bunch of them. Mommy stopped fighting then. So did Daddy, who was pinned to the floor under two monsters.

"Wh-what?" Mommy said, her voice so squeaky it hurt Eden's ears. "Those poor couples in the papers?" She glanced at Daddy. "What's going on?"

"I-I don't know." He looked at Eden. "It's okay, sweetheart. I know this is scary, but it's just a mistake. A bad, bad mistake."

A woman appeared then. A normal woman, dressed in a jacket and a skirt, like the kind Grandma Jean wore to work. Only it didn't matter if she was smiling and talking in a nice voice. Not when she took Eden away from Mommy and Daddy.

Eden struggled and kicked and howled.

"Enough of that, now," the woman said. "You're going to hurt yourself—"

Eden bit her. Chomped down on the lady's arm as hard as she could, tasting something bad and hot filling her mouth. The woman shrieked and let go, and Eden tumbled to the floor, then ran toward Mommy and Daddy as the monsters hauled them away.

Mommy twisted around and reached out. Eden threw herself at her, but a monster grabbed her dress and held her back as another dragged Mommy out the door.

# CHAPTER ONE

I waited in the shelter drop-in center for my next appointment. The murmur of children's voices wafted in from the play area. Low murmurs, hesitant, fractured. Guilty giggles, cut short, as if the children weren't sure they had anything to giggle about.

The faint smell of bleach from the toys, washed nightly, was almost overpowered by the sickly sweet smell of lilies. Vases on every table. A hundred dollars' worth of flowers. Money better spent on shampoo and baby wipes. But the donor meant well. They always did.

People say that volunteer work is rewarding in ways no paid job can match. I wouldn't know about the paid part. Barely a year out of college, I've never held a paying position. I know what I get out of volunteering, though, and it isn't the usual sanctimonious thrill of helping the less fortunate. It's the mirror they provide, reflecting me in ways that aren't always comfortable.

My 2:15 appointment was Cathy, who apologized for being late even as I assured her she wasn't. She'd slid into the room with her head down, prodding her two-year-old ahead of her.

"Hey, Joey," I said. "Are those new boots? Spider-Man, huh? Very cool."

A furtive glance my way. A quick nod. I like kids. Can't say they feel the same about me. I think they can sense I was an only child, only grandchild, too, growing up in a world of adults.

Cathy headed for a rickety wooden chair, but I patted the spot beside me on the sofa. She perched on the edge of the worn red vinyl. Not the prettiest piece of furniture, but it was bright and cheery and washable. Did the clients look at all the vinyl and wood and plastic, and imagine us after hours, bleaching down everything in sight, cleaning off the contagion of their desperate lives?

"Did you leave Amy in the playroom?" I asked.

Cathy stiffened. "Yes. The lady said it was okay—"

"I was just asking. They're doing crafts at two thirty and I know she loves crafts."

She relaxed and nodded. She had two children under the age of four. Another on the way. And she was three months younger than me. Not that she looked it. If I saw her on the street, I'd have added ten years. She certainly had that extra decade of life experience. Kicked out of the house at sixteen. Married by eighteen and divorced by twenty-one. A dozen jobs on her résumé, often more than one at a time.

Nothing could be further removed from my own experience. I live with my mother in a house bigger than the entire shelter. I have a master's degree from Yale. I work as a volunteer, and I don't even need to do that. Do I appreciate it? No. On good days, it chafes, like a dress with a scratchy tag. On bad ones, I feel like a bobcat caught in a trap, ready to gnaw my foot off to escape. Then I look at someone like Cathy, and a wave of guilt and shame stifles the restlessness.

"Thank you for seeing me, Miss Jones," she said.

"Olivia, please. And I'm here whenever you need me. You know that."

Cathy nodded and wound a lock of hair around her finger. Hair dyed blond almost a year ago, dark roots now to her ears; she'd refused to color it again because the dye job had been *his* idea. The guy who'd left her with those blond ends, a missing tooth, and another baby in her belly.

"So, Melanie has been helping you look for a job," I said. "How's that going?"

"Fine."

Her gaze stayed fixed on my chin. It always did, unless she got worked up enough, like when she'd declared unbidden that she wasn't fixing her hair. Brief shows of defiance. Achingly brief. Frustratingly brief.

There was more in that lowered gaze than deference, though. I could sense it. Feel it, thrumming through the air between us.

"Did—?" I began.

Joey raced past wearing a tattered backpack in the shape of an owl. It reminded me of the one that hooted outside my window that morning. A bad omen. If you believed in omens.

"Joey!" Cathy said. "Stop running and sit down." Then, to me, "Sorry, Miss Jones."

"No, he's fine. I was just admiring his backpack." I tore my gaze away. "Did the bakery ever give you that reference?"

She shook her head. I cursed under my breath. Cathy's last job had been at a bakery. Owned by the cousin of the man who'd left her pregnant. Her old boss now couldn't seem to recall how good an employee she'd been and thus sadly could not give a reference.

I had the name of the bakery in my wallet. More than once, I'd been tempted to help the woman remember Cathy. I had a few ideas for how to accomplish that. It's a satisfying image to contemplate, and it would be so much more feasible if I wasn't Olivia Taylor-Jones, daughter of Lena Taylor, renowned

Chicago philanthropist, and Arthur Jones, owner of the iconic Mills & Jones department store. But I am, and as such, I have other avenues of attack, equally effective, if somewhat lacking in drama.

"Let's leave that for now. I'm sure she'll change her mind." *Very sure.* "We'll grab a coffee and have a look through job postings."

After Cathy left, I flipped through the stack of job printouts. I told myself I was making sure I hadn't missed a suitable one for Cathy, but I was really looking for myself. Pointless, of course. In so many ways.

My mother had always expected me to follow her example. Marry well and devote myself to volunteerism and philanthropy. Leave paid work for those who need it. Dad had been more amenable to the idea that a young woman in my position could have a career beyond organizing fund-raisers. My mother came from money—she was the daughter of minor nobility, raised in English society. Dad had been brought up in the business world, where you were expected to work until you couldn't. Or until you had a fatal heart attack at the age of sixty-one, leaving behind a daughter who, ten months later, couldn't look at your picture without missing you so desperately it hurt.

I always thought I'd work for Dad someday. Take over the family business eventually. It didn't matter if the store bored me to tears. I'd be working with him and that would make him so happy. Except now he was gone, and I couldn't bear to step through the store's front doors.

For now, I intended to go back to school in the fall and get my doctorate in Victorian lit. No idea what I'd use that for in the real world, but it would give me time to figure out what I wanted.

I hadn't told my mother my plans. No use stressing her out

when her dream was about to come true—her only child married, and married well. As for my fiancé, James . . . I hadn't told him, either. First I was checking out my options for local schools. Once that was set—and before the wedding—I'd tell him. He'd be fine with it. He didn't expect me to sit home and keep house for him. Not unless I wanted to. I most certainly did not want to.

When I finished tidying up, I stepped outside the front doors, and the city hit me. The screech of tires and growl of engines. The stink of exhaust and the tang of roast pork. The flash of colors—bright shirts, neon signs, blinding blue sky.

Our family doctor used to blame my hypersensitivity on my upbringing, raised in a quiet house in the suburbs. But years of city exposure didn't seem to help. I'd walk onto a busy street and every sight, sound, and smell assaulted me, my brain whirring as if trying to make sense of it all. I'd learned to adjust—it was part of my life. Usually it passed in a moment, as it did now. I took a deep breath and headed to the gym.

*The photographer stepped back into the shadowy doorway as the young woman approached. Once she was abreast of him, he lifted his camera and held down the shutter button, silently snapping photos.*

*Amazing how much she looked like her mother.*

# CHAPTER TWO

"You're lucky I love you," I whispered as I leaned over. "Or I would be so out of here."

He smiled, a blazing grin that had every woman at the table swooning. CEO of Chicago's fastest growing tech firm, and son of a former senator, James Morgan isn't gorgeous, but that grin had landed him a spot on the city's most eligible bachelors list for three years running. Sadly, he wouldn't be eligible next year. Well, sadly for everyone else.

"Another hour," he whispered. "Then Penny has instructions to phone me with an urgent message."

Good. As charity dinners went, this one ranked about average, which meant somewhere between uncomfortable and excruciating. The cause was excellent—New Orleans reconstruction. The food was just as good—Creole by someone who obviously knew how to cook it, which meant it was heavy on the spices and not nearly as appreciated by the older crowd. Most of it got left on the plates, which had me looking around the sea of tables, mentally calculating how far that wasted food would go in some Chicago neighborhoods. But they'd paid handsomely for it, eaten or not, and that was the point.

James's father had been asked to give a speech tonight. James was doing it in his stead. That happened a lot lately, as his father aged, to the point where the organizers would be surprised—and probably disappointed—if James Senior showed up instead.

So James was a guest of honor, which meant everyone at this table wanted to make his acquaintance, and he couldn't spend the meal chatting to his fiancée. While he conversed with everyone in turn, I entertained the others. Every few minutes, his hand would brush my leg, sometimes a flirtatious tickle but usually just a pat or squeeze, a reminder that he appreciated me being there.

Finally dessert was served: Doberge cake, a New Orleans specialty, a half-dozen layers of chocolate cake with lemon and chocolate pudding between them. The meal was coming to an end, and conversation was hitting the stage of desperation.

"So how did you two meet?" asked the woman on my left.

"Their families know each other." A man across the table answered before we could. "Mills & Jones department stores. James Mills Morgan and Olivia Taylor-Jones." He sat back, looking smug, as if he'd just uncovered a secret—and somewhat shady—connection.

"Our grandfathers founded the company," James said. "Mine sold our shares to Liv's dad before I was born, but our families still get together a few times a year. Liv was always there. Usually getting into trouble."

A round of obliging laughter.

The woman on my left patted my arm. "I bet you had a secret crush on him."

"Er, no," James said. "She was seventeen before she remembered my name."

"Only because you look like your cousin," I said.

"Who's a half foot shorter than me and fifty pounds heavier." James turned to the others. "Let's just say Liv's complete lack of interest kept my ego in check."

"You were older," I said. Then hurried to add, "Out of my league."

"Nice save, darling. Truth is, by the time she was old enough to notice me, I'd gone from a gawky teenager to a boring businessman. Liv prefers fighter pilots."

I sputtered a laugh. "He was a computer tech in the air force."

"Close enough. The point is, she was not easily wooed. I've launched hostile takeovers that were easier."

James spoke after dinner, making an impassioned plea for donations. I would say it was a lovely speech, but that would be arrogant, considering I wrote it. I could point out that a master's degree in Victorian literature hardly qualifies me to write speeches about contemporary disasters, but I never did. If James was going to be my husband, I was going to be more than a bauble on his arm.

I hadn't planned to marry so young. I'm not sure if I planned to marry at all. My parents had a great relationship but, well, it lacked what is to me an essential component of a partnership. Namely the partnership. Dad ran the business, Mum did her charity work. Never the twain shall meet. James has let me into the business side of his life from the start, and I appreciate that. So if he asks me to write him a speech, I do.

I will say, then, only that the speech was successful. Checkbooks opened. As they did, James made his way through the crowd, with me at his side. Then, so deftly that even I hardly noticed, we ended up in the back hall.

"I think the party is that way," I said.

"Which is why we're going this way. You looked like you needed a break." He swung me into an alcove. "And I wanted to thank you for the speech. Perfect, as always."

He pressed me back against the wall, lips coming to mine in

the kind of deep, hungry kiss that had, a year ago, made me decide James Morgan was a lot more interesting than he looked.

When I finally needed oxygen, I pulled back and whispered in his ear, "If you want to thank me properly, I noticed the east wing was cordoned off."

He chuckled. "Dare I ask how you noticed that when we came in the *west* doors?"

"I wander."

The chuckle deepened, and he lowered his hands to my rear, pulling me against him as he kissed my neck.

"But it should probably wait," I said. "You are a guest of honor, and it would be most improper—"

"I like improper."

He let me down and we zipped along the hall toward the east wing.

I leaned against the wall, skirt hiked up my hips, legs still wrapped around him.

"I definitely need to write you more speeches," I said.

A rough laugh. "I definitely need to find more occasions for you to write me speeches."

We rested there. It was peaceful—the white walls, the distant voices blending into a monotone murmur, the stomach-churning mix of perfume and cologne reduced to the spicy scent of his aftershave. I buried my face against his neck, inhaled, and relaxed.

He kissed my hair. "Speaking of speeches . . ."

I lifted my head. He adjusted his stance, lowering me to the ground.

"I need to ask you something." He cleared his throat. "This isn't quite how I planned it. I was going to take you to a fancy dinner and pop the question . . ."

"Uh-huh. While I'm flattered that the sex was so good it caused temporary amnesia, we're already engaged."

He smiled. "Yes, I know. This is a proposal of another sort. Equally terrifying in its own way. Neil Leacock came to see me today. My dad's former campaign manager. He—*they*—the team and its supporters—would like me to consider running."

A moment passed before I could find my voice. "For junior senator?"

"Yes, but not right away. They want to wait until I'm thirty-five. For now, they'd just like me to start heading in that direction. Grooming me." He took my face in his hands. "I don't want to hit you with this after the wedding, Liv. I know you might not want a life of endless speeches and endless dinners."

A senator's wife? I swore I could hear the trap snap shut on my leg. I leaned against James, hiding my reaction.

*Just relax. Don't say anything. You need time to think this through. Play along for now.*

It took a moment, but I found a smile that would fool James. I'd minored in drama in my undergrad years. My instructors always said I was a natural. No big surprise there. Sometimes I felt as if I'd spent my life faking it.

I smiled up at him. "In other words, no more sex in the back hall?"

"Er, no . . . Actually, I was hoping that if I promised *more* sex in the back halls it might make the rest more tolerable."

I put my arms around his neck. "If you're willing to make such difficult concessions, then I can probably make some, too."

"Because it *is* difficult."

"I know, and I appreciate it."

He laughed and kissed me.

# CHAPTER THREE

We'd just made it back to the party when my cell phone beeped. My mother hates to text, but if the alternative is having me do something as crass as talk on my phone at a charity event, she'll make an exception.

*I need to speak to you, Olivia. Will you be coming home after the dinner?* Mum never lowers herself to text speak.

"What's up?" James asked.

"Mum needs to talk to me about something."

"Meaning you're not staying at my place."

"Sorry. You know how she gets."

When my dad died, I'd been home from college and planning to move into my own apartment. But then my mother needed me at home. I'd expected that. I hadn't expected the nonstop frantic calls to resolve every curve ball life threw at her. Last week, she'd called me home from James's place at 2 a.m. because she'd "heard something." It turned out to be a raccoon on the back deck. I would have been a lot more sympathetic if the housekeeper hadn't been right downstairs, as she was every night I stayed with James.

We'd already arranged for the housekeeper to move in permanently after I got married. We'd also decided to hire a full-time chauffeur to double as a security guard. I still wasn't sure it would be enough.

"Go on," James said. "I'll call a car to the back. I hear something's going on around front."

"A protest?"

He shook his head. "Just a couple of paparazzi. There must be a media personality here."

He lifted his cell phone then stopped. "Are you okay with going out the back? It's not the door you came in."

I shot him a glare.

He grinned. "Sorry. I'm just checking, because I know it's bad luck—"

"Once," I said, lifting my finger. "It was one time, and you're never going to let me forget it, despite the fact we just celebrated our engagement with a bottle of Cristal, and I could barely *find* the door."

"And the time in Cozumel, when you insisted on turning our pillows around so we wouldn't have nightmares?"

"Tequila."

"Alcohol isn't the cause. It just reveals your adorably superstitious self."

I don't know where my superstitions come from. A nanny, I suppose. It really does take alcohol—in copious quantities—for me to mention one. James thinks it's adorable. The only thing I can do is to change the subject fast, which I did.

Twenty minutes later, I slipped into the car's leather backseat, feeling faintly ill. James wanted to run for senator. I should have seen that coming. Soon after we'd started dating, I'd asked whether he had any plans to follow his dad into politics. He'd laughed it off but never really answered, and I hadn't pursued it. I hadn't dared. I'd been falling for James Morgan, and I didn't want to hear anything that might interfere with that.

I could fake a lot of things. A politician's wife, though? I might be able to pull it off for a month or two. Years? Maybe even a lifetime? Never. I'd grown up in these circles. I knew what came with the position. What would be expected of me. I could not do that. It was like masquerading as a paramedic and then suddenly being promoted to chief of surgery.

As the town car headed into the suburbs, I called James.

"I'm going back to school," I said when he answered.

A long pause. "You're going . . . ?"

"Back to school. For my doctorate. In the fall if I can."

"Okay."

That's all he said. *Okay.* My heart rate slowed.

"Where did this come from?" he asked.

"I've been thinking about it for a while. I was going to tell you after I looked into it some more, but now with your news . . ." I took a deep breath. "I wanted to be upfront about my plans, too. I'd really like to go back to school. Get my PhD in English."

"Okay."

I leaned back against the seat, eyes closing in relief.

"There's no reason you can't, Liv. Like I said, it'll be a few years before the campaign starts. I won't need you full time until then."

My eyes opened. "But I'm going back to school for a job. I want a career."

"With an English doctorate?"

"*Yes*, with an *English* doctorate," I snapped.

"Sorry," he said. "Of course you could do something. Maybe you could write."

"Write?"

"Mysteries. I know you love mysteries. You could be the next Arnold Conan Doyle."

I resisted the urge to correct him. *Arthur* Conan Doyle had been the subject of my master's thesis. James hadn't read a novel since college, but when he'd discovered my area of study, he'd read two volumes of the Sherlock Holmes stories, just for me.

"Fiction writing isn't really my thing," I said.

"Don't be modest, Liv. You're a great writer."

I'd meant that I had no interest in it as a career. I wanted to get out and do things, not tell stories about other people doing them. But at least he understood I needed a job. It was a start.

After we hung up, I relaxed into the seat again. I'd been overreacting. Even if he did run for senator, there was nothing to say he'd win. He wouldn't even run for five years anyway. Lots of time for me to persuade him this wasn't the path for us.

I was lost in my thoughts when the driver said, "Is this it, miss?"

I looked out the side window at the familiar gates. Manicured flowering shrubs softened the "keep out" message of the fence. My mother's touch. Dad always said if you're uncomfortable with the message a massive fence sends, then you damned well shouldn't put one up.

"Yes, this is it."

"Nice place."

Our house was actually modest for the neighborhood. The driver was impressed, though, which meant I had to give him a generous tip in addition to the standard gratuity on James's bill or he'd whine about the "cheap Mills & Jones brat."

As the driver did his paperwork, I walked to the front door. The rich scent of lilacs floated past, and I took a moment to enjoy it, the smell prompting memories of evening garden parties and late-night swims.

I glanced up at the sky. A perfect May evening, warm and clear. Still time for a swim if I could resolve Mum's problem fast enough. I might even get her into the pool if I promised to wear my suit.

I was still digging out my keys when our family lawyer flung open the door and practically dragged me inside, not an easy feat for a man who looks like Ichabod Crane, so pale and gaunt he breaks into a sweat climbing stairs.

"Howard?" I said as I escaped his grip. I sighed. "Let me guess. The board of directors wants Mum's feedback on something, and she's in a tizzy. How many times have we told them not to bother her?"

"It's not that. This is . . . a personal matter, Olivia."

My mother appeared in the study doorway.

"Olivia," she said in her soft British accent. "I hope my message didn't bring you home early."

"No," I lied. "James needed to leave, and I wouldn't stay without him."

Normally she'd have gently praised me for making the socially correct choice, which wasn't always my default. But she only nodded absently. She looked exhausted. I walked over to give her a hug, but she headed for the front door, double-checking the lock.

"What's wrong?" I said.

"Come into the sitting room."

As I was following her down the hall, the doorbell rang. I glanced down the hall to see a tall, capped figure silhouetted by the porch light.

"The driver's back," I murmured. "What did I leave in the car this time?"

My mother sighed. "You really need to be more careful."

"I know, I know."

As I reached for the handle, Howard hurried over.

"Olivia, allow me—"

"Got it."

I swung open the door to see, not the driver, but a middle-aged man in a fedora. Behind him was a woman with a camera.

"Eden," the man said. "I'd like to ask you a few questions."

# CHAPTER FOUR

lifted my hands to shield my face as the camera flashed.

"There's no Eden here," I said. "You've got the wrong house."

"No, I don't." He lifted a recorder. "Tell me, Miss Larsen, how does it feel to be the long-lost daughter of America's most notorious—"

Howard slammed the door and shot the bolt.

"What just . . . ?" I began. "Did they say what I thought they said?"

Howard tugged the sidelight curtains shut. Before I could ask my mother if we had a neighbor named Eden, she said, "I need to talk to you, Olivia."

"Okay," I said as I let her lead me into the sitting room. "We'll ignore the crazy folks at the door. What's up?"

Howard stayed in the doorway. I sat on the love seat and patted the spot beside me, but she was already heading for "her" chair—a very pretty antique so hard it felt like sitting on a rock. She hated the love seat, which didn't match anything in the room. But it was comfortable. Some of my earliest memories were of being curled up on it with Dad as he read to me.

"What's up?" I repeated.

"There's something I need to tell you. Something we probably should have told you years ago."

"Okay . . ."

She paused a moment, then blurted, "You're adopted."

"I'm . . . ?"

She nodded. Didn't say the word again. Just nodded.

I stared at her. That wasn't possible. I looked just like my parents. Everyone said so. I had my mother's ash-blond hair and green eyes, and my dad's height, wide mouth and strong jaw.

"Did you say I'm . . . adopted?"

I waited for her to stare at me in confusion. Maybe even laugh. Clearly that was not what she'd said.

Instead, she paused for at least five seconds and then nodded.

I thought of the reporter at the door. "So he didn't get the wrong place. Someone found out I'm adopted. They went to the press. You wanted to warn me *before* someone showed up on our doorstep."

She nodded again.

"And now they're saying I'm the daughter of America's most notorious . . . what? Actor? Rock star? Politician? Oh God, please tell me it isn't a politician."

She said nothing. As we sat there in silence, her words finally sank in. Forget whose child I was. I was someone else's. Not hers. Not my dad's.

"I'm sorry," she said at last. "You shouldn't have had to find out about it this way."

"No, I shouldn't."

I looked over at her and the shock cleared, pain seeping in. Hard, angry pain. "You had no intention of telling me I was adopted until you were forced to."

Howard stepped forward. "Olivia, your parents were unable

to have children of their own. They decided to give a wonderful, loving home to a child in need."

"I'm not questioning their motives," I said. "It's the part about not telling me for twenty-four years that I'm having trouble with."

"Twenty-one, actually. You—" Howard stopped. His sallow cheeks flushed. Then he cleared his throat, and stepped back. "I'm sorry. This really isn't my place."

"No shit," I muttered.

My mother didn't tell me to watch my language. Didn't even flinch.

"So I'm *not* twenty four?" I said.

"You are," Mum said. "It's just that you weren't an infant when we first got custody of you. You were a little over two and a half. I wanted a toddler. Everyone wants a baby and there are so many older children who need a home."

And it was much easier to find an older child who looked like you. Shame plucked at the edges of my anger, telling me I was being unfair.

We sat in silence. I didn't want silence. I wanted to rage and shout and throw everything within reach.

I wanted Dad. If he was here, I *could* rage and shout and throw things. He'd expect no less. But with Mum's worried eyes fixed on me, there was no way I could give in to a temper tantrum. Sitting there quietly hurt, though. Physically hurt.

"Okay," I said finally. "So I'm not your daughter—"

"Of course you are. Don't be melodramatic, Olivia. I only wanted to keep it a secret because I feared how others would treat you. When you live in a world of privilege, everyone wants to believe you don't deserve it. I had a younger cousin who was adopted and people always behaved as though she didn't really belong. I made your father swear that wouldn't happen to you."

"All right." I took a deep, ragged breath that seared my lungs. "So now the word is out, and the press is making a big deal out of it. Must be a slow news day. We're going to have to counter with a statement. I take it you know who my parents are?"

Silence. I looked at Mum. Then at Howard. Neither would meet my gaze.

"So you do know," I said. "You just don't want me knowing, because I might contact them. Well, clearly the press knows so you're going to have to—"

"That's not it," Mum said. "Neither your father nor I had any idea who your biological parents were when we adopted you. I only found out tonight. According to Howard"—she shot a look his way—"your father learned the truth two years ago. He decided to keep it from both of us."

"He *paid* a great deal to keep it from you," Howard added.

Mum nodded, and they looked at me expectantly, as if I should be grateful for this, when all I could think was, *My dad paid blackmail money to hide something from me.* My *father*. Who'd never coddled me. Never shielded me from the darker side of life. I'd loved him for that. Pay *blackmailers*? No, that wasn't possible. Not from a man who would thunder and lecture me when I argued for leniency dealing with young shoplifters at the store.

"I . . . don't understand," I said finally.

Howard answered. "Your father was the victim of a black-mailer who now seems to have realized he could get more money selling his story to the online tabloids."

More money than he could get from my wealthy family? How big of a story was it?

I swallowed. "Who are my birth parents?"

Howard watched my mother for a moment, silently pleading with her to answer. When she didn't, he cleared his throat.

"Pamela and Todd Larsen. The names will likely mean nothing to you—"

"I know who they are." The words came as a whisper, forced out past lungs that seemed to have collapsed, like I'd been hit in the chest with a five iron.

"Did you say . . . ?" Howard began.

"I know who they are. Everyone knows who they are."

Deep breaths. In and out. Don't think. Just breathe.

I shifted my gaze to my mother. She looked away.

*She looked away.*

Oh God. My own mother couldn't bear to look at me.

"So it's . . . ?" I shook my head and turned to Howard. "No, that's who they're *alleging* are my parents. It's a rumor. It has to be proven. I need to submit DNA and compare it to the records of these . . . people."

Howard shook his head. "Do you think your father didn't demand proof when this was first brought to him? The blackmailer provided test results and it wasn't enough. Your father took hair from your brush and had an independent lab test your DNA against the Larsens' DNA from their samples taken as evidence in their trial. There is no doubt. They are your biological parents."

"It means nothing, Olivia," my mother sniffed. "You are our daughter. Not theirs."

Not Pamela and Todd Larsen's. Not the child of . . . Oh God. My stomach heaved.

"I . . . I need a minute," I said and ran from the room.

# CHAPTER FIVE

*T*he names will likely mean nothing to you.

Right. No one living in the Midwest hadn't heard of Pamela and Todd Larsen.

Husband and wife. Serial killers.

I was the daughter of two sociopaths.

I stared at my laptop. I knew who the Larsens were, but not a lot about them. I should look it up.

For what?

They were killers. Convicted serial killers. Did I want to torture myself with the details of their crimes? Or was I hoping it wasn't as bad as I'd heard? *Oh, they only killed six people, not eight like I thought. Well, that's not so bad.*

I turned away from the laptop.

A knock at the door. "Olivia?"

When I didn't answer, my mother went away, and I lay there, wondering if she'd actually wanted me to open the door. Or if she'd just come up because it was what a mother was supposed to do.

I thought of how she'd acted downstairs. She'd seemed anxious, and I wanted to say she'd been worried about me, but then I remembered how she evaded me when I'd gone to hug her. I remembered tapping the love seat for her to sit with me . . . and watching her move to the chair.

Damning evidence. Except that we'd never been close. It was my dad who'd curled up on the love seat with me. My dad who'd given me bear hugs and piggyback rides and swirled me off my feet, long after I was too big to be swirled. My mother was kind and she was caring. She was just . . . distant, with everyone. Raised to show her love in other ways.

I went into my bathroom and flipped the sink faucets on to cold, to give myself a jolt, get back on track. As I wet the cloth, I looked up and caught my reflection. I stopped. For the first time in my life, I didn't see that comforting blend of Arthur Jones and Lena Taylor. I saw—

I yanked my gaze away, ripped off my dress, stepped into the shower, and cranked the water up as hot as I could stand it.

When I got out, I avoided the mirror. I left my dress pooled on the bathroom floor and grabbed my jeans and jersey from earlier. I walked into my room to get fresh underwear and socks. Stopped when I reached my dresser.

There was no mirror here. Just reflections of another kind: photos, crowded across the dresser top in mismatched frames. The clutter drove my mother crazy. She was forever straightening them, trying to bring order to the chaos.

My photos. A record of my life. Of what mattered in it. Nana, gone four years now, the only grandparent I'd known, my dad's father long dead. My maternal grandparents' interest in me had never extended beyond the obligatory annual Christmas and birthday gifts. Impersonal gifts for a child they didn't know.

A child they'd *never* known, I realized now. Growing up, I'd been told my parents and I had lived in England until I was three, when my grandfather died and Dad had to return to take over the business. Not true. The Larsens were American. So my parents had adopted me when they moved back here. A convenient way to pretend that I'd been their child all along. Only I hadn't been. My mother's family knew that and they wanted nothing to do with me.

I turned back to the photos. There were more pictures of my parents than anyone else, yet no more than the number they had of me scattered throughout the house. The three of us, our perfect little family.

There were photos of friends, too. Childhood friends. College friends. No best friend—I never felt the need for such a thing, preferring quantity over quality. Did that mean something? An inability to form truly close bonds of friendship?

My gaze slid to the photos on the far right. The most recent, the others inched aside to give way to the new phase of my life.

James.

I hurried to the desk and grabbed my cell phone. I went to hit the speed dial, then stopped.

How would he react?

I shook my head. Was I actually questioning that? This wouldn't be easy, but we'd get through it. First, though, I had to tell him before anyone else did.

I hit the key. The call went straight to voice mail.

I checked the clock. Just past midnight. He'd probably gone to bed. I left a message saying I needed to speak to him. Then I hung up and walked to the window.

A half-moon shone through the star-studded inky black of the clear night sky. I opened the window. The breeze fluttered in, rich with the smell of wood fire from the neighbor's yard, the faint glow of an extinguished bonfire still visible over the hedge.

A beautiful night for a bonfire. A beautiful night for a swim, too, as the moon shimmered across the ripples in our pool.

Maybe I could still do that. Maybe I *should*. Slice through the cool water, feel it wash over me, carry everything else away.

I pressed my fingers to the glass. Light flashed from the back of the yard. I blinked and shaded my eyes to peer out. Another flash. Then another. The staccato blinks of a camera shutter. I yanked the curtains so hard the rod popped free. I left it hanging, stalked to my bed, and dropped onto it.

"Olivia?" My mother was at my door again. "There are people outside. More media people."

I sat up and instinctively glanced toward the mirror, to make sure I looked calm and collected. When I caught my reflection, my stomach clenched so hard I winced.

"Olivia? I know this is a shock, but you need to deal with this."

*I* needed to deal with it? Not even *we*.

I took a deep breath and heard my dad's voice after his heart attack. When he knew he was dying.

*She's not like us, Livy. She just isn't. Fair or not, you're going to need to be strong enough for two. Can you do that?*

"Is Howard still here?" I called.

"Yes."

"Tell him I'll be down in a minute. We'll—"

The crash of breaking glass cut me off.

I threw open my door. A thump from downstairs. I pushed my mother behind me, shielding her.

"Howard?" I yelled.

"They've broken in," my mother whimpered. "Oh my God, they've broken in."

"They're journalists, Mum, not a lynch mob. No matter how badly they want the story, they won't break in to get it. Just hold tight."

I started for the stairs.

She grabbed my arm. "Don't leave me here."

"Okay, then stay right behind me—" Damn it, that wouldn't work, either. While I was sure we hadn't been invaded by crazed paparazzi, I wasn't taking my mother downstairs until I knew what was going on.

"Howard?" I called from the top of the steps.

He appeared at the bottom. "They broke a pane in the French doors to the patio." His face was calm, but his voice quavered. "I think it was an accident. They were jostling to get a picture and a pane broke."

"Okay, so have you called—?"

A shout from below. So loud and clear that I froze.

"Are they inside?"

"No, no. They're just shouting for you through the broken pane. They want you to make a statement. In my professional opinion, I don't think you should speak to them."

"Good, because I'm not going to. Have you called the police?"

"I don't want to raise a fuss," my mother murmured behind me.

"There are people in our backyard, Mum. I'm raising as big a fuss as I can. Call the police now, Howard. We're going to stay up here until someone comes."

Howard made the call. I heard him speaking into the phone, then his voice got loud. "When you have someone free? Maybe I'm not making myself clear. Mrs. Lena Taylor—who is a generous donor to your force's annual fund-raiser—is under siege, with hooligans breaking her windows."

*Hooligans?* That made it sound like some kid jumped the fence and tossed a rock.

"Wait here," I said to my mother. "I'll handle this."

# CHAPTER SIX

My mother chirped in protest but stayed on the top step as I descended. When I got to the bottom, I saw three faces plastered to the broken patio door, like kids trying to catch a glimpse of an R-rated movie.

A burst of flashes blinded me.

"Ms. Jones?"

"Olivia?"

Shit. Okay, not my brightest move. I retreated out of sight.

"Ms. Jones? Could I ask you a few questions?"

"Olivia? Just a quick statement?"

"Miss Larsen? Hello! Miss Larsen?"

I stiffened.

"Okay," I muttered. "You want a statement—"

A hand grabbed my arm. I looked back to see Howard.

"Do not engage them, Olivia. That's what they want."

"That's why I'm giving it to them, so they'll take their damned statement and get the hell off our property. I don't like them scaring Mum."

I unwrapped his fingers from my arm and, ignoring the flashes, walked close enough to the broken door so they all could hear me.

I held up one hand to quiet them down. "Fine, you want a statement? I just found out tonight that my biological parents are, allegedly, Pamela and Todd Larsen. I will be investigating this claim. In the meantime, I will ask that everyone respect our privacy and—"

A yelp cut me short. Someone was jostling through the crowd toward the patio doors amid shouts of "Hey!" and "Watch it!"

Then, just as suddenly, the crowd went still. The two older journalists in the front lowered their cameras and pens. One leaned over to whisper to a young woman who looked confused. Her eyes widened and she stepped back to give the newcomer room.

It was an old man. Maybe not that old—seventy or so—but tall and stooped, his rheumy eyes blazing at me.

He stuck a gnarled hand through the broken pane, reaching for the lock.

"Whoa!" I stepped forward. "This is private property, sir. You can't come in here."

"I can and I will," he said. "You may have all these people fooled, but I know who you are."

I turned to Howard, then heard a cry of, "Sir, you shouldn't do that" from the crowd.

The old man had flipped the lock. A few journalists continued halfhearted protests, but all of them leaned forward, eyes glittering, cameras raised.

He pushed open the door and marched in.

"Get the police here now!" I said to Howard. Then I turned back to the old man. "You have five seconds to get out."

The man continued toward me. "I don't know how you got here, in this fancy house, but—"

"It's *my home,* and you'll get out of it now."

He stopped right in front of me. I blanched, seeing something in his eyes I'd never seen before. Hate. Pure, unadulterated hate.

"You think you got away with it," he spat. "Think you got yourself a fancy new life. I remember what you did. Every day of my life, I remember."

Howard said, "He's clearly disturbed, Olivia. Go back upstairs."

"Disturbed?" the old man roared. "You're the crazy one, for harboring this she-bitch—"

He hit me with both hands, knocking me to the floor. I landed on the broken glass and felt it bite into my bare arms. As I scrambled up, he grabbed a shard, gripping it so hard blood welled up through his fingers. He swung it at me. I caught his arm. It wasn't hard to stop him—he was an old man. When he snarled, I dug my fingers in until he let out a hiss of pain and dropped the glass.

I glowered at him. "If you think I'm my parents' daughter, then you don't want to do that. You really don't."

Silence. Stunned silence. For a second, I thought, *I've done it. They'll leave now.* Then I saw the shock in the old man's eyes, and knew in that instant that I'd made a very big mistake. That's when the cameras started to flash again. I let the old man go.

"Olivia . . ." My mother's voice from the foot of the stairs.

I wrenched my gaze from the intruders and blinked hard, and when I did, it was like breaking a spell. Suddenly, I was lost in a roar of voices.

"Mr. Gunderson!" someone shouted. "Niles Gunderson!"

"Sir, can we ask about your daughter? About Jan. Does this bring it all back?"

I froze. Gunderson. Jan Gunderson. The Larsens' last victim. I turned back to the old man. "I—"

He slapped my face so hard I reeled back.

"I know you, Pamela Larsen," he snarled as he came after me. "I don't care what you're calling yourself these days or what color you dye your hair. I know you."

My mother screamed. Howard shoved me behind him as he shouted for my mother to get back upstairs.

A stampede of feet clattered across the patio. People were shoving past the journalists—a greasy-haired man with a ragged notebook, a college kid with a video camera. Not real journalists. Just people hoping to sell a picture or a firsthand account. The kind who didn't know that chasing me into my house was against the law. Or the kind who didn't care.

"Miss Larsen?"

"Eden! Look over here!"

"Mrs. Taylor?"

The kid with the video camera rushed past me toward my mother. Mum started up the stairs. The kid reached over the railing and caught her sleeve.

The rip of tearing fabric. A gasp. A thump as she tripped, falling down the steps and landing in a heap at the base.

I shoved past two reporters and scooped her up.

"The car!" I yelled to Howard. "Get your car!"

I half dragged, half carried my mother to the garage. Cameras flashed. Voices shouted. Hands grabbed for us. I kept plowing through, oblivious.

When I got into the garage, Howard was already in his Mercedes, engine running. I pushed Mum forward.

"Get in the car!" I yelled.

She didn't hesitate. Didn't even look back.

Howard hit the button to open the garage door. I shouted to wait until I was in, but the door was rising and I could make out the legs of people outside waiting for it to open. Someone shoved a video camera underneath.

My mother's face was stark with terror. There was a bloody print on her shoulder, from my cut hand. I saw her face and I saw that blood, and I realized I couldn't get into Howard's car. If I did, the reporters would never let it out of the garage.

I had to protect my mother. I'd promised Dad.

I waved at Howard. "Go! Get her out of here."

He didn't need any more prompting. I was probably lucky he didn't throw open the door and shove my mother out in his haste to escape.

He put the car into reverse. My mother just sat in the backseat. I told myself she was in shock, but it looked like simple relief. She'd gotten away. As for me . . . ? Well, I could look after myself.

The Mercedes reversed down the driveway, sending the onlookers scattering like bowling pins. No one tried to stop Howard. Their prey was still in the garage, alone and defenseless.

I ran. No choice really. Well, there was. I could grab the pruning shears and attack anyone who came near me. I considered it. Even wondered whether I could get away with a self-defense plea. I might have done it, too, if I hadn't just discovered who I was and realized that slicing someone up really wouldn't be the way to prove I wasn't truly the Larsens' daughter.

I darted inside my dad's workshop and threw the dead bolt. I took a quick look around at the tools. The heavy tools. The sharp tools. The lethal tools.

A longing look. Then a queasy look, before I raced out the back door. A glance around. No one in sight yet. I followed the line of trees across the property and took off.

# THE PRODUCT OF MONSTERS

The college student huddled behind the tree, listening to the cacophony of voices inside the house. Dear God, had they actually broken in? She rubbed her arms against the night's chill. Her fingers brushed the strap around her neck, and she looked down at the camera, hanging there like an albatross.

It had seemed so simple when he phoned. She hadn't heard from him since school broke for exams. He'd said he'd call, but he hadn't. Then he did.

"Hey," he'd said. "You live in Chicago, right?"

She told herself it wasn't really a question. Of course he remembered where she lived.

She'd said yes, and he'd said, "Good. 'Cause there's this story about to break. I got a heads-up from a buddy of mine. It's leaked on the Internet, but not far, meaning it's still fresh, and it's taking place right there in Chicago. Do you know where Kenilworth is?"

She did. Not that she'd ever been there. People in her neighborhood didn't know those in Kenilworth unless they worked for them.

"Perfect," he'd said. "I need you to snap a couple pictures of a girl who lives there. You can do that, right?"

Of course she could. She was a photographer. That's how they'd met—working for the school paper. While she hadn't liked the idea of sneaking onto private property—especially in Kenilworth—she'd do it for him.

Turned out, trespassing wasn't really an issue, considering she hadn't been the first one there. The others were mainly bloggers and small press, maybe not as concerned about the law as they should be. She thought they might try to run her off, but they just let her hang out with them at the back door.

That's when she'd found out who the girl was.

"Todd and Pam Larsen's kid," one of the older journalists said, his breath reeking of garlic. "Can you believe that? Everyone figured they'd shipped her off for adoption in Australia, and she ends up here. She grew up as the daughter of that department store family."

She'd nodded as he talked, hoping eventually he'd explain who Todd and Pam Larsen were. The names were familiar, and she was sure if he gave her a clue, she'd figure out why, but he'd just kept bathing her in garlic breath until she faked getting a call and backed off the patio.

She'd looked up the Larsens on her phone. When she found out who they were, she knew why she didn't remember them. Because if she'd heard about them before, she'd wiped it from her memory. Would have bleached it out if she could. Now they were stuck there. Imprinted on her brain. The Larsens and what they'd done.

Oh God, what they'd done.

She'd abandoned her post then. Gone to huddle under a tree in the yard and try to keep dinner in her stomach.

The girl inside. The rich girl. The one everyone was waiting for. She was the child of these killers. The product of monsters.

She supposed she should feel sorry for the girl. Olivia Taylor-Jones was apparently only a couple of years older than her. But she couldn't feel sorry for her. Couldn't feel anything but disgust and horror.

If she just found out she was the child of such monsters, she'd take a header off the Sears Tower. You couldn't go on after that. You just couldn't.

She'd been sitting there, thinking of that, when they broke into the house. Now she listened to the commotion inside. Shouts. Crashes. A car starting.

Olivia was getting away. This would be her last chance for a photo. She didn't want the photo. Didn't want to *look* at the Larsens' daughter. But he expected it.

She moved up alongside the house. The car backed out and zoomed down the drive so fast she barely got her camera raised before it was gone.

She leaned against the garage wall and exhaled. She'd tried. She'd tell him that she tried but—

The side door clicked open.

She froze, then pushed back against the wall, crushing vines.

A young woman stepped out. She shut the door and looked around.

It was her. It had to be her. Blond hair. Piercing eyes. Her face hard as she surveyed the yard. She'd been calling Olivia Taylor-Jones "the girl," but there was nothing girlish about her. Nothing soft. Nothing warm.

The product of monsters. A fiend masquerading as a pretty young woman.

Last chance to snap a photo. A perfect shot. Just take it.

But if the flash went, Olivia—or rather, Eden—would see it. She wasn't far enough away to escape . . .

She pressed herself harder against the wall and waited, barely daring to breathe until Eden broke into a jog and disappeared into the night.

Afterward she stood there, shivering and shuddering against the wall, until her legs could hold her and she staggered forward. Her shoe caught on a broken piece of vine and she stumbled, twisting to see the door Eden had come through. To see what she'd left behind.

A bloody handprint.

# CHAPTER SEVEN

If I'd been thinking, I'd have grabbed the keys to one of my dad's vintage cars in the detached garage. I was just lucky I'd had the foresight to snatch up my purse from the front door, with my wallet and cell phone.

There was a convenience store a half mile away. I showed the guy at the counter my cut hand and asked to use the staff restroom to wash up. He'd seen me often enough to know I was a local, and not one of those who sent their driver in and never said hello. So he didn't ask why I was walking around after midnight, bleeding, just let me use the sink and even brought a bandage from his first-aid kit. I wrapped up my hand, then bought a bottle of Dr Pepper I really didn't need.

When I stepped out of the store, something swooped at my head. It was night, but it hadn't looked like a bat. It seemed indeed to be a bird. A crow or something.

*If a bird flies straight at you, prepare for a bad day.*

Yeah, tell me something I didn't know. I shook my head and called a cab. When it arrived, I gave the driver James's address.

James lives with his mother. His parents had divorced when he was in college, and like my mother, his insisted she needed him at home. In her case, it was bullshit. Maura Morgan didn't need anything. Except maybe a muzzle.

She just liked having James close by. That was changing soon. We'd already bought a house, and she wasn't coming along. She hadn't said much about that, but I almost expected her to stumble down the stairs on our wedding day and break her hip, just to thwart this takeover of her only child's affections.

Any hope that James had been spared the media blitz vanished when the cab rounded the corner and I saw cars along the roadside. In this neighborhood, you don't park on the road unless you're lost, and even then, a roaming security guard will send you on your way soon enough. Tonight that guard was nowhere to be seen. Probably realized he was outnumbered and decided it was time to take a very long break.

There were people in the cars, just sitting there, in case James appeared. I could say that was very respectful of them, but the only thing keeping them inside their vehicles was the fact that the Morgans *did* have a big gate, and their beefy driver now stood inside it, playing security guard.

When my cab slowed, he waved us on. I rolled down my window. Recognizing me, he hesitated. I motioned that I'd call the house and he nodded, clearly relieved that he wouldn't be asked to wake the gorgon himself.

I had the driver pull up close enough for me to use the speaker. Sure enough, Maura answered.

"Hey, Maura, it's me," I said. "I'm sorry to come by at this hour. I know you must have had a horrible night, and I feel awful about that. If I could have warned you, I would have, but I only found out myself tonight." I paused. "Is James there, please?"

"No, he is not. He hasn't come home yet."

"Oh? Well, hopefully he's gone out for drinks someplace too

loud for him to hear his cell phone if the press calls. If I can just come inside and wait—"

"You are not coming—"

"Then I'm staying out here. Better yet, I'll perch on your gate and give a press conference."

The latch clicked open.

Maura met me at the door. She wore an elegant bathrobe, cinched tight—and full makeup—which told me she hadn't been in bed at all. She gave me the same look I'd gotten the day James half jokingly told her I was the girl he planned to marry.

Maura raked frosted pink nails through her hair, swept her bathrobe up like a ball gown, and waved me inside. I went into the living room, hoping she'd leave me to wait in peace.

She followed me. "So, Olivia, what do you have to say for yourself?"

"I'm sorry you've been dragged into this mess. My lawyer will sort it out—"

"I'm talking about this . . . news."

What was I was supposed to do? Apologize for my poor choice of DNA? I settled onto the sofa and kicked off my sneakers.

"I didn't know I was adopted." I paused for a moment and decided it was time to construct a lie, for my family's sake. "As for who my parents allegedly are, Mum and Dad didn't know. As philanthropic as my mother is, knowingly adopting the child of serial killers is taking the milk of human kindness a little far. This is news to her, and a huge blow—"

"I'm sure it is. Poor Lena."

*Of course. Poor Lena.* "My mother is shocked by the news, but she's doing fine, thank you."

"Well, of course, your mother is fine. She's locked in a maximum security prison."

I stood. "I'll wait in James's study."

She stepped into my path. "Haven't you put my son through enough?"

"Put James through enough? As far as I can tell, he doesn't even know."

"His reputation, I mean." She studied me, then eased back. "I know he told you his plans, Olivia. About running for senator." Her voice softened. I knew that tone. It was like a cat purring right before it takes a chunk out of your arm. "This is his dream, and if you love him, you'll step away gracefully. Let him mourn you and move on." She paused for effect. "You know it's the right thing to do."

Before I could answer, footsteps sounded on the stairs. I looked through the doorway to see James coming down.

# CHAPTER EIGHT

"**I** thought I heard voices." James kissed my cheek. Then he looked at his mother. "Why didn't you call me?"

"I didn't realize you were home," Maura said.

"Well, I am. Go up to bed. I have this."

Maura hesitated, but James repeated it, firmly, and she left. When she was gone he pulled me into a hug, and I let myself collapse into his arms and stay there, just stay there, fighting not to break down in tears.

"Something—" I said against his shoulder.

"I know. I've been trying to call you for the past half hour. I was just coming down to drive over to your place."

I pulled back so I could see his face. "So you . . . got my message?"

"Yes. And several others. I know everything, Liv."

Everything.

His expression didn't change. No hint of disgust or distaste. I wanted to take that. Just take it. Don't question. Don't probe. Accept.

Only I couldn't.

"About my . . . biological parents," I said carefully, my gaze fixed on his. "You heard—"

"The Larsens. Yes. That's what they're saying."

"It's not just a rumor. There's DNA."

He nodded. "All right."

I looked at him. He looked at me. Patient. Concerned. Just what I needed. What I'd expected. And yet, seeing it, I realized I *had* doubted, deep down. I still doubted.

"You know who they are, right? My parents?"

A faint smile. "Yes, I've met them many times, Liv."

"You know what I—"

"Arthur Jones and Lena Taylor are your parents. They're the ones who raised you. If you mean the Larsens, yes, I know who they are. Convicted murderers. As for what they are to you? Genetic donors. They're responsible for the color of your hair, the shape of your mouth, the length of your fingers. Nothing more."

I kissed him. A quiet thank-you. Only he didn't let it stay quiet. He grabbed me around the waist and pulled me onto his lap in one of his usual oxygen-stealing kisses that left me gasping. Then he put his hands on either side of my face and held it up to his.

"I love you, Liv. You haven't changed. So that hasn't changed. Got it?"

I nodded and eased back, legs still stretched across him as I reclined against the corner of the sofa.

"It's still on, then?" I said. "We're getting married?"

He laughed. "Did you think you could get out of it that easily? You're stuck with me. This is just a bump in the road. It'll go away soon enough."

"It better be very soon," I said. "Only a month until the wedding."

He dipped his chin in something that could be taken as a nod.

"We *are* getting married next month, right?" I said.

"We'll . . ." He stretched his arm around me, gathering me in. "We can talk about that later. For now—"

I shrugged out from under his arm and swung my legs off him. "We *are* getting married next month, right?"

"We're getting married. Absolutely. The timing may need to change, but that's a conversation for tomorrow. Right now, we need to get you out of Chicago."

"Out of Chicago?"

"Of course." He straightened. "This is going to be an absolute media nightmare. Do you remember those reporters hanging out at the dinner tonight? And did you see the ones at the end of the driveway? You need to go someplace safe. Get away from these vultures."

"For my sake? Or yours?"

"For you, of course. To protect you."

"But I can handle it. You *know* I can handle it. The question is: can you?"

He looked away, shaking his head, saying something about how I shouldn't need to handle it. But all I noticed was how fast he'd looked away.

"You're postponing the wedding," I said.

"I've been advised—"

"You've been *what*?" I scrambled to my feet. "You've talked to someone about this *before* me?"

He stood, began to pace. "Neil called when I was trying to get in touch with you. He advised me to postpone the wedding and, honestly, I agree. Can you imagine what kind of circus it would be?"

"You mean what kind of senatorial-dream-killing circus it would be."

His expression hardened. "No, Olivia," he said, barely opening his jaw enough to get the words out. "I'm thinking of you. Of the kind of wedding you deserve—"

"Deserve? Hell, I don't even want a wedding. I'll settle for a justice of the peace. Or Vegas. Let's fly to Vegas and get married."

He hesitated. For a second, I thought he was going to say, *Yes, let's do it*. Then his face went still, eyes clouding and he reached for me, ignoring my struggles as he pulled me into a hug.

"I love you, Olivia. And I wish we could get married right now. Tonight. But your mother—"

"Which mother?"

The flash of anger again. "Don't pull that, Liv. You know what I mean. I'm not going to start our marriage by upsetting your mother and doing something you'll eventually regret. We're going to wait."

"Until when?"

"I don't know. I have to—"

"—talk to Neil?"

"Olivia." His tone was curt now. Losing patience. Damn it, why didn't I understand?

I did understand. I understood that he could pretend nothing had changed. He could kiss me as if nothing had changed. He could say all the right things to convince me nothing had changed.

But *act* as if nothing had changed? No.

I wanted him to say he didn't give a rat's ass what anyone thought. Didn't care if it put his political future in jeopardy. He loved me and he was marrying me now or a month from now, as we planned.

That's what I would do if the situation were reversed. To hell with the road of caution. I'd go my own way.

But he just stood there, frustrated and impatient. Wanting me to meekly accept his reasoning, tell him I understood. I'd go away and hide until this was over. Then I'd wait until he was ready to marry me.

Like hell.

"You want to save your political future? Here, let me help you." I wrenched off the engagement ring and whipped it at him. "You're free. Go find a sweet little wife and get yourself elected."

"Olivia . . ."

I stalked to the door.

"Olivia!"

The cool night air slapped me so hard my eyes stung. I jogged until I reached the end of the garden walk.

The front door creaked open behind me.

"Olivia?"

I raced across the lawn. James's sigh wafted across the quiet yard. Then he padded back into the house, leaving the door open. Getting his shoes. Because the grass might be wet and running after me in stocking feet was foolish.

I wouldn't have stopped for shoes.

I circled back into the shadows beside the house and waited there, hidden. He came out, looked around, then jogged in the direction I'd been heading.

When he disappeared through the hedge, I exhaled and glanced toward the road. My cab was long gone. If I went out there, I'd have to face the reporters.

I really wasn't in the mood to face more reporters.

But I wasn't sticking around here, either.

As I shifted my purse, my keys jangled inside. Keys to my house. Keys to my gym locker. And keys to . . .

I glanced toward James's bedroom window and remembered lying in his bed a month ago, as he handed me a garage key and a car fob. "Yes, I know you love mixing it up with your dad's old cars, but I'd really like to see you in something with air bags, Liv. Take my car out a few times. If you like it, I'll know what to get you for a wedding present."

I'd never actually driven his car. It was a Volvo. Very nice but really not my style. Now, though . . .

I pulled out the keys and sneaked around the house to the garage.

# CHAPTER NINE

I walked into O'Hare airport, stopped in front of the departures board, and thought, *What the hell am I doing?*

Honestly, I had no idea. I'd driven here on automatic and now, looking at the board, I think if I hadn't been too late to *catch* a flight, I might have proceeded on autodrive and boarded one. Done exactly what James wanted. Fled Chicago.

What good would it do to lie low for a few weeks? I couldn't escape this. I shouldn't try. Now that I was alone, my adrenaline had plummeted, and all I could do was stare at the board and think, *Now what?*

I had no idea.

After I checked in to the airport hotel, I called Howard. I wasn't surprised when it went straight to voice mail. I asked him to tell my mother that I needed some time to process all this. Please trust that I'd be fine and I'd call tomorrow.

I was heading to the elevators and saw a sign for the bar. I didn't know if it would be open, but I considered checking. I've never drunk for the sake of getting drunk, but there's a first time for everything. There was just one problem—I didn't know how much alcohol it would take to pass out. That's what I wanted really. Oblivion. For all I knew, I'd have a few drinks and drift off into nightmares.

Instead I went into the gift shop. Not many gifts in it—just lots of overpriced items for travelers, including over-the-counter sleeping pills. I bought a bottle, went up to my room, took a double dose, and prayed for a dreamless night.

I'd lived the first years of my life with Pamela and Todd Larsen. I'd been there at the heart of their killing spree. What living nightmares had been shoved deep into my subconscious, ready now to worm their way out when I surrendered to the deepest sleep?

Or dark desires. Deeply buried lusts and needs and fantasies, coming to the fore when my conscience slumbered. What did I—?

Nothing.

That night, I dreamed of nothing.


Even with the pills, I was up by six. I waited until seven to call my mother. I had my speech all rehearsed.

She didn't answer her cell phone.

I hung up and told myself I'd call back in an hour. I lasted five minutes. I got her voice mail again and spilled my speech onto it instead.

I told her I'd decided to stay away for a while. For her sake. I knew how hard this would be on her and I didn't want to put her through even more by hanging around. I'd stay away until things died down. I didn't know what I'd do or where I'd go, but I'd figure out something.

That last part hadn't been part of the rehearsal. Even as I spoke the words, I felt ashamed of myself. It didn't sound strong. It sounded like a little girl, desperately hoping for Mummy to call back and tell her not to be silly. I belonged at home. With her. We'd handle this together.

Two minutes after I hung up, my phone rang. I hit the answer button so fast, it didn't connect and I had to hit it again.

"Olivia." It was Mum. "Howard says to tell you that you shouldn't be using your cell phone. These tabloid people can get your records. They might even be able to record your calls."

"Right." I swallowed. "Sorry. I wasn't thinking. Do you, um, want me to call back on the hotel line?"

"Yes, and I'm going to give you the number of the new cell phone Howard gave me, in case they're monitoring my usual one as well."

She did. I phoned it.

"I'm sorry," I blurted when she answered. "I'm so sorry about all of this."

I waited for her to insist it wasn't my fault. Instead, she said, "It's out now. There's nothing we can do except deal with it."

I nodded. "That's what I want to do, Mum. Deal with it. Maybe hire a media consultant or a PR firm. We'll figure out how to handle this head on. Get past it."

Silence. Then, "I thought you were going to sit it out. That's what your message said."

"Sure. I could. If that's what you want. But I really think it's best that we face this—"

"I was nearly killed by those reporters last night, Olivia."

I bit my tongue before continuing, "All right. I'll handle it. Tell Howard to phone—"

"Howard thinks you were right. You should go someplace. Wait this out. I agree. That's best for everyone."

Now it was my turn for silence.

Mum didn't seem to notice, pausing only a moment before saying, "I suppose you'll need money."

"*Suppose?*" A white-hot grain of fury ignited behind my eyes.

"My God. You hand cash to street people more graciously than that."

"Then I misspoke." Did I imagine a chill in her voice? "You'll have whatever you need. I'll write you a check today."

"Write me a check? I thought that was *our* money. Family money. No, wait. That doesn't apply now, does it? If I want an allowance, I'll need to visit the Larsens."

"Don't be ridiculous. Of course you're family. This business has no effect on that. Your trust fund is intact. Along with . . . everything else."

Everything else. The store. The estate. I remembered sitting in Howard's office after Dad died, struggling to listen to him read the will. With the exception of my trust fund—which I'd get when I turned twenty-five—everything went to my mother for use during her lifetime. When she passed, it went to me. All of it. At the time, I'd been so numb with grief that the arrangement had only sparked a faint, "Why did he do that?"

Now I knew.

She knew it, too. After Dad had found out who my parents were, he'd made sure my mother couldn't decide part—or all— of the estate was better off going to charity.

"I don't want your money," I said. "I'll have my trust fund in a year. In the meantime, I'll get a job. I'll pay my own way."

"A job?"

"Mmm, yeah. It's that thing people do to make money."

Definite frost in her voice now. "I'm well aware of what a job is, Olivia, but I fail to see how you would get one, under the circumstances."

She had a point. Just yesterday I'd been wondering what sort of career I'd be qualified for with no paid experience. Today, that was the least of my worries. Even if someone didn't mind hiring the daughter of serial killers, they wouldn't want the kind of publicity that might come with having me on staff.

"I won't use my full name. Or my volunteer references."

"Then how on earth do you expect to find a decent position?"

"I don't. I'll take what I can get. Just like everyone else. I'm sure there's a McDonald's hiring somewhere."

"I hope you're joking, Olivia. This is silly. When you decide where you're going, I'll wire you money."

"No."

"I understand you're upset, but if you think I'm going to let a Taylor-Jones—"

"But I'm not a Taylor-Jones, am I? Not really. I think a Larsen would work at McDonald's. Mmm, yes. Pretty sure she would."

My mother started to sputter. I hung up. Then I stood there, holding the phone, resisting the urge to throw it against the wall. Smash it to bits. Better yet, put a hole in that wall, on a bill that would go to my mother. Damage a hotel room so she'd have to pay for it? Was I really that petty?

*Petty? The one time you really need her, she tries to shove money at you. And tells you to go away. Just like James.*

But they were right—I did need to stay away. Only that didn't mean holing up in a French château. That was something Olivia Taylor-Jones might do, but I was no longer Olivia Taylor-Jones. I needed to make choices for me, whoever I was. I'd say I needed to find myself, if that didn't sound like I was heading into the Himalayas, taking only a backpack stuffed with angst and clean underwear.

I was twenty-four. I had a master's from Yale. It was time to do exactly what I would have done if I was not Olivia Taylor-Jones. Get a job. Get an apartment. Live a regular life.

I checked out of the hotel. I'd put it on my credit card and it was only a matter of time before someone traced me there. I should have thought of that.

I went to the hotel ATM and withdrew the maximum on my bank card and the maximum cash advance on my credit card. That gave me two thousand dollars. Enough to pay first month's rent on a small apartment and tide me over until I got a paycheck.

Next I texted James. *Car at O'Hare. Parking garage A. Level 3. Row D. Ticket on dash.*

I stared at the message. Short. Precise. No anger. No hurt. No regret. No trace of all the things I was feeling.

I'd woken thinking of James. I'd reached for him and found a cold bed instead. A cold, unfamiliar bed. The rest had come rushing back, but James stayed there, front and center in my brain.

I could be quick to judge, quick to take offense, quick to get angry. Had I expected too much of him?

Maybe.

Did I expect to wake up to apologetic voice mail and text messages?

Maybe.

There were messages. Brief ones. *Liv, call me. Liv, we need to talk.* Yes, even, *Liv, I'm sorry.* But I didn't want apologies. I wanted . . . I don't know what I wanted. Him, I guess. Here, supporting me through this. But he wasn't and that wasn't his fault. I'd been the one who left, and right now, as much as it hurt, it still felt like the right thing to do. I needed time and distance, to get my head on straight. If that meant I'd lost him—really lost him—then . . .

I took a deep breath and tried not to think about that.

After I sent James the message, I got rid of my phone—removing and destroying the SIM card and resetting it to the factory defaults. Then to the business center, where I put my bank and credit card through the shredder.

And it was done. My ties with the old world were cut. My journey to a new life begun.

# CHAPTER TEN

I watched the floor numbers flit past. Of the five people in the elevator with me, three were staring. All three were male and over forty, and any other time, I'd have chalked it up to the fact that I'm young and female. But today, my heart raced and I struggled to keep breathing.

Had my picture been in the paper? I'd grabbed only the classified section at the hotel. I hadn't checked the rest. I was afraid to check.

Even if my photo was there, I didn't look like it. Not anymore. Before leaving the hotel, I'd chopped my hair off at my shoulders, blow-dried it straight, and pulled the sides back in a severe style I'd never worn before. Also, I was wearing glasses. I've worn contacts since I was twelve, but always carried a pair of glasses in my purse, just in case. Between those, the impromptu haircut, and the Sears-special suit, I was no longer Olivia Taylor-Jones. I was—as my business-center-printed résumés proclaimed—Liv Jones.

So the men in the elevator shouldn't recognize me. But I could feel them staring. It seemed to take forever to reach the twentieth floor.

———

"H-How long?" I asked the man behind the reception desk.

He was young, thin, and impeccably dressed, perched on the edge of his chair, narrow-eyed gaze flicking past me to the others in the waiting area, as if he expected to catch them stuffing the year-old magazines into their briefcases.

I repeated the question. From his look, he'd heard me the first time—he just wasn't rushing to answer. At least not until he'd ensured that the waiting room was safe from larceny.

"At least a month before we have our short list," he said. "Likely six to eight weeks before the position is filled."

I must have looked stunned, because his thin lips pursed.

"The advertisement only went in the *Sun-Times* today," he said. "It takes time to receive and process the résumés. I'm sure you're not finding anything different elsewhere in your job search."

"Um, no. Of course not. A month is fine. Thank you."

I now needed a prepaid cell phone, so I could receive callbacks for interviews. That took 5 percent of my stash. I'd had to buy the outfit and shoes, too, though both were a tenth what I normally paid for clothes. I'd picked up a cheap briefcase, which doubled as a clothing bag, to hold my jeans and shirt from yesterday and a backup dress shirt. It didn't seem like much, but I was down three hundred dollars, and it wasn't even lunchtime.

"You look familiar," said the receptionist.

Receptionist number six of the day. Five minutes later I couldn't have told anyone what she looked like. They'd all blended into a homogeneous mush of dour gatekeepers.

I couldn't have said anything about the reception area, either, except that I was sure it had at least one green plant in the early stages of slow death and a picture of a healthy, flower-bearing one. A desk calendar with a 50 percent chance of displaying the correct month. A bowl of candy. And sporadic voices, maybe even a laugh, from the depths of the offices beyond, teasing me with hints of actual people who could give me an actual job. People I'd never see.

Six receptionists. Six résumés. Six variations on "I'll pass this along" with six expressions that suggested it wouldn't get past the nearest shredder.

And yet, in those first five, not one with the reaction I'd feared. Until now.

"Do you live in Evanston? I grew up there," I lied.

"No, I've seen your picture someplace. Recently. Weren't you in the paper—?" Her mouth formed a perfect O, eyes widening to match. She snatched up my résumé. "Jones? As in Mills & Jones? You're—"

"Sorry to have wasted your time." I retreated as fast as I could.

Six stops. Six rejections. I was not getting a job today. Or this week. At least, not the kind of position I'd envisioned. Like the women I'd helped at the shelter, I didn't have experience. Like them, if I wanted to work, I had to take what I could get.

I'd redo my résumé to highlight my transferable skills, and start a new search tomorrow. In the meantime, I'd find a place to stay.

I stared at the apartment. Two rooms—a bath and a combined kitchen/living/sleeping area. Carpet a half century old, patchy, as if something had been snacking on it. Sofa held up at one corner by a stack of newspapers. The overwhelming stink of cat piss. The smell made me rub my arms, goose bumps rising, anxiety bubbling in my gut.

"I think this is the wrong place," I said to the woman. "I'm looking for the one advertised—"

"In today's paper. This is it. Four hundred a month. Take it or leave it."

I left it. How many times had I helped women find apartments for under five hundred a month? Had I ever seen one of them? Of course not. I just made the arrangements, then someone else took them out to look, and they found one that would do, and I'd ticked another task off my list.

Now, as I tromped through a parade of pest-infested holes, I wondered what kind of place Cathy had ended up in. She'd taken what she could get. It was all she expected from an apartment. All she expected from life.

Finally, I decided I could go as high as six hundred, and found a place that, while tiny and shabby, was in a decent neighborhood, and didn't stink of anything except air freshener.

"I'll take it," I said. "That's six hundred up front, right?"

"Twelve hundred," the portly man said. "First and last's month. Like always."

I quickly calculated. I'd only have a few hundred left, and I had no idea when I'd get a job and—

I could do this. I'd have a place to sleep, and I'd already bought clothing and toiletries. I'd only need food and cab fare. No, *bus* fare. I could figure out how to use public transport.

"Twelve hundred then. Okay. So—"

"There's the damage deposit, too. Another six hundred."

Another six hundred that I didn't have. Another apartment that I didn't get.

The next one on my list was the same price, but also required first and last month's, plus a thousand dollars damage deposit.

"You don't seem like the kind of girl who'd cause a lot of trouble, though," the landlord mused.

"I'm not. Could we do it another way? Take the second month's rent as a damage deposit, then as soon as I can, I'll give you an actual deposit."

"I don't think we need to make it that complicated. You look like a good girl. Pretty, too. I'm sure we could work something out," he said, gaze sliding to my chest.

There was a surreal moment where I reflected that this, too, was something new. I'd always escaped roaming hands at crowded parties, alcohol-fueled invitations from college boys. I suppose something about me said I wasn't the type. But that had changed.

I was vulnerable. And men like this could tell.

"Actually, no," I said. "It's not really right for me. I'm sorry. I'll let myself out."

I would like to say that I walked out, chin up, pace measured. I didn't. I practically bolted from the apartment. I reached the front door and swung out, getting some distance before I stopped under a streetlamp, leaning back, breathing. Just breathing.

When I looked around, I realized how quiet everything was. It shouldn't have been. I was on a busy street, two lanes of late rush-hour traffic making its way to a major thoroughfare. The side-walk was just as busy, commuters cutting across to the nearest L station. But standing on that corner, it was as if someone had shoved plugs into my ears. Everything was unnaturally hushed, muffled. Dimmed, too, as if my glasses had darkened to shades.

The sounds, the sights, the smells were all so much easier for my brain to process—or not process, but skim past, dismissing as unimportant. And I realized it had been like that all day. Maybe I should have thought, *Well, at least one good thing happened to me today*. But, as I looked around, anxiety strummed through me, searching for something to latch onto. I don't know what that meant. Just that I felt as if I was slipping and needed to grab something for traction.

I squeezed my eyes shut.

"Olivia?"

A man's voice. Soft. Concerned.

My eyes flew open. I caught a glimpse of a dark overcoat behind a parked SUV. A man coming my way. Light hair flashed over the roof of the vehicle.

James.

I exhaled, the wave of relief so strong I shuddered.

The man hopped onto the sidewalk and grinned my way, and I just stood there, staring at him, blinking, as if my eyeglass prescription was wrong.

Not James.

A stranger. With a camera. Lifting it. Pointing at me.

My hands flew to my face.

The shutter whirred and every ounce of frustration in me hardened. This was why I was out here, alone and exhausted. It wasn't because I'd discovered I was adopted. It wasn't because I'd discovered my parents were Todd and Pamela Larsen. It was reporters like this son of a bitch, him and all the ghouls at home, slavering for tawdry tidbits.

"People want to hear your story, Olivia," the man said as he continued toward me, camera raised. "They want to know what you're going through."

"What I'm going through?" I snarled, my hands falling away. "They have no goddamned idea what I'm going through. They don't care. They just want a story. A good old-fashioned horror story."

He stepped back and I thought, *There. Just stand firm and they'll back down.* But then I remembered standing in my hallway, telling off Niles Gunderson, just in time to block my face as the reporter's camera started snapping.

"Come on, Olivia," he said. "Show them what you really think of them. This is your chance. Tell them all to go to hell."

I spun and marched down the sidewalk.

"You're news, honey," he called after me. "Get used to it."

# CHAPTER ELEVEN

I wasted five dollars on a three-block cab ride, just to escape that reporter before I completely lost my temper. He hadn't really looked much like James. I suppose that showed just how much I'd been hoping it was him. Hoping for rescue? No. Of course not.

Okay, maybe a little, but perhaps I can be excused for a brief flicker of fantasy.

I wanted to go home and be with my mother. I wanted to do the right thing and stay away. I wanted to see James. I wanted to stick to my guns and not see him. I wanted rescue. I wanted to do this on my own.

Let's face it, at this point, "What would you like for dinner?" would send me into a tizzy of indecision.

When I got out of the cab, the world was still muted, dull, and the nervous twitch of anxiety in my gut had grown to full-blown clenching, complete with sweat trickling down my face.

I looked around, again searching for something to ground myself. I didn't know what it was, just knew that I needed something.

Then I saw a shiny spot of copper on the sidewalk, and heard a woman's singsong voice, deep in my head.

*See a penny and pick it up,*
*And all day you'll have good luck.*
*See a penny, let it lay,*
*And bad luck you'll have all day.*

I picked up the penny. When I did, the world snapped back into focus, like a window being thrown open. Cars screeched and honked. Drivers gestured and swore. Passersby muttered and laughed into cell phones. The scent of exhaust and garbage swirled around me. I closed my eyes and let the smells and sounds wash over me, feeling that familiar prickle that said this was all information and I had to figure it out, make sense of it. Anxiety, yes, but an anxiety I knew.

When I opened my eyes, I saw two women across the road cast glances my way and whisper to each other. That's when I realized why my day had been so quiet. I'd been blocking it all out. Telling myself no one recognized me.

I turned and almost crashed into an elderly woman whose eyes widened when she saw my face. My stomach clenched again, and I stepped aside, ready to flee, but she caught my sleeve.

"Was it a shiny penny?" she asked.

"W-what?"

She smiled. "The penny you picked up. I didn't think young people did that anymore. Was it shiny?"

I opened my hand. The newly minted coin gleamed.

"Then it's extra lucky. That's what my gran always said." She patted my arm. "I'm glad you found it, dear. You look like you could use some luck."

Another smile. Another pat. And she was on her way.

I took a deep breath and glanced over to see the two women again, now pointing out an albino squirrel walking along a fence top.

So they hadn't been talking about me after all. I squeezed the penny, smiled, and headed to the next apartment on my list.

# LUCKY PENNY

The old woman watched the girl pick up her pace, a faint smile on her lips as she clutched her lucky penny. At least she was smiling now, poor thing.

The woman had recognized the girl from the paper. Anyone who'd seen the photos would, despite her clumsy attempts to disguise her identity.

The woman remembered the Larsen case. Her niece had worked at the prison where they'd held Pamela Larsen. Such a nice lady, she'd said. Pretty and quiet and polite. People said he was just as nice, always asking about his wife and his little girl, not caring what happened to him as long as they were safe.

It was a setup, that's what her niece always said. Those murders had the city gripped with fear, so the police needed a scapegoat, and they found a young couple without the money to pay for a proper defense. A travesty of justice. Now their poor daughter was caught up in the mess. Such a shame. Such a tragedy. One that sadly no penny, however bright, could fix.

# CHAPTER TWELVE

When I reached the next apartment, I decided that if the penny held any luck, it was clearly running on a delay. The building was fine—a narrow four-story, yellow-brick structure with huge windows facing the tree-lined street. But the neighborhood . . . let's just say that it proved I didn't know Chicago as well as I thought.

Thirty years ago, this was probably a great place to live. The ancient oaks arching over the street attested to that, as did the wrought-iron fences around each building. But the sidewalks were crumbling, the iron hadn't been painted in a decade, and there was an air of eerily quiet desolation, as if everyone retreated after work and bolted their doors.

The only people on the street were two girls on a bench. They couldn't have been more than sixteen. No homework bags for them, though. They likely hadn't set foot inside a school in years. It wasn't even nine and they were out there in their microskirts and teased hair and layer cake of makeup, not speaking to one another, just staring at the road. Waiting for some middle-aged man, who'd take them to a cheap motel if they were lucky, but more likely the walkway beside the building, where ten minutes later, they'd emerge, twenty bucks in hand, return to their bench, and start all over again.

A few days ago, I'd have been tempted to give them a hundred each and tell them to go home. Now, I couldn't afford it. Besides, even when I'd had the money, I'd have known it wouldn't help. They'd pocket the cash and stay on the bench. Giving them the address of a shelter wouldn't do any good, either. They knew such things existed. If they were interested, they'd go. They weren't.

The best I could do was acknowledge them as I passed, calling out a cheerful, "Good evening." They turned, met my gaze with blank, soul-stifled stares, then returned to their silent watch.

I climbed the steps. As I did, I caught a glimpse of something on the cement landing. Not another penny, but a design of some sort, glittering just as brightly. When I got to the top, though, I saw only gray concrete.

"Drop something, miss?"

The voice was strong, youthful, but the man stepping through the front door couldn't have been under eighty. He was nearly a half foot shorter than me, with a pointed chin and wisps of white hair salting a freckled bald head. In one bony hand, he clutched an empty cloth grocery bag.

"I thought I saw . . ." I shook my head. "Long day."

He gave me a look then. I stepped back, thinking he recognized me, but he only squinted nearsightedly, as if making sure I wasn't a neighbor, then bid me a good evening and continued down the steps.

I pretended to fuss with my purse, as if looking for keys. Once he'd disappeared along the walkway beside the building, I backed down the steps, trying to catch the design I'd seen in the light. Nothing.

As I reached for the front door, a whisper drifted over, and I turned to see the two girls. They were on their feet now, fixing me with stares so blank the hair on my neck rose. One said something to the other, her lip curling as she spoke, teeth bared, almost feral. The other shrugged and hitched up her worn, snakeskin belt. I waited for them to snarl a "Whatchya looking at?" but they just stood there and stared back.

Waiting for me to leave.

I stepped inside, closed the door, then counted to fifteen, and peeked out just in time to catch a glimpse of the girls disappearing down the walkway.

They were following the old man. I shook my head. Unless they had a pocketful of Viagra, they weren't getting any business from that old guy.

I might have felt sorry for those two young prostitutes, but remembering that look in their eyes, I wouldn't be eager to meet them wandering around my apartment building.

And I wouldn't be eager to meet them down a dark walkway. Especially if I was a frail old man.

I glanced toward the landlord's door. Just a day ago, if I'd seen two street girls go into the alley behind an old man, I'd have investigated. Made sure he was safe.

*So why wasn't I already out that door?*

I went out onto the stoop and listened.

*Was I hoping not to hear anything, so I had an excuse to go back inside. Focus on my own problems?*

I shook my head and jogged down the front steps.

The walkway stretched between two apartments and was little more than an alley, but it had been fancied up with an ivy-covered iron arch, a cobblestone path, and a few flowering bushes.

Pleasant enough. Safe enough. And empty enough, with no sign of—

"You aren't supposed to be here." The old man's words drifted from behind a thick lilac. "You know the rules."

"There are no rules," a girl hissed. "You old-timers need to understand that. We go where we want. We take what we want. And what we want is the money you were gonna use to fill that grocery bag."

"I don't have any money. I was heading to the library—"

"Oh, good," I called as I walked down the path. "You're still here. This is your apartment building, right, sir? I'm looking for the landlord and—"

I feigned surprise, stopping short as I saw him backed against the wall, the two girls standing like gunslingers, thumbs hooked in their belts. Matching snakeskin. The height of fashion.

"Oh," I said. "Am I interrupting something?"

The girl nearest me wheeled, snarling, "Mind your own—"

The other one caught her arm. Squeezed. They eyed me, the first still curling her lip, like she wanted to throw down then and there. I'll admit to a prickle of disappointment when the other girl whispered in her ear and talked her out of it. I've never been in a fight in my life, but that roiling ball of pent-up frustration in my gut felt this would have been a fine time to start.

"We were just talking," the second girl said. "Being neighborly."

"That's good to hear," I said. "We don't see enough of that these days." I turned to the old man. He was leaning against the wall looking . . . amused? "About the landlord . . ."

"Here, let me take you." He nodded to the duo. "Happy hunting, girls."

The first bared her teeth, but her friend nudged her and they headed off down the walkway, in the opposite direction.

"You handled that very well," the old man said once the girls were out of earshot.

"I've dealt with their kind before."

"Oh?" He looked surprised.

"Volunteer work with street youth."

"Ah."

"You may want to avoid that walkway this time of evening."

He sighed. "We never used to have to worry about such things." He let me hold open the door as we went inside. "You said you wanted to speak to the super. You aren't looking at that vacant apartment, are you? This isn't the place for you."

"I don't have a lot of choice," I said as I fell in step beside him.

"You always have choices."

I shrugged. "This doesn't seem so bad."

"Well, I'd disagree, but I see you've made up your mind." He waved down the hall. "Last door."

"Thanks."

As I headed down the hall, my footsteps echoed on the old wood floor. The place smelled of pine cleaner, which should have been a good sign, but it somehow added to the air of sterile desolation. Somewhere upstairs, a baby cried, faintly, almost resigned, as if it didn't really expect a response.

As I approached the super's door, strains of salsa music and the smell of chilies warmed the air. The music had been kept at a respectful volume, so I didn't need to knock hard. Or so I thought. After three increasingly louder rounds of rapping, with no reply, I leaned against the door and listened.

Off-key singing to the music told me someone was home. One last round of knocks, nearly a pounding now, then I called on my cell phone. I heard a phone inside ring. And ring. And ring. I hung up. The music and the singing continued. Then it ended.

Footsteps sounded. They didn't seem to be coming my way, so I rapped again. More footsteps. The TV turned on.

"Son of a bitch," I muttered.

A throat-clearing behind me. I wheeled, saw the old man, and flushed.

"Sorry," I said.

"I don't blame you. You made an appointment and she's not there to keep it."

"She *is* there. I heard her."

He shook his head. "That's just the TV. She leaves it on all the time." I was about to say I'd heard footsteps, too, but he continued, "This isn't the place for you. The building's all right. But the neighborhood?" He shook his head. "Not safe these days. Not safe at all."

"You might want to take your own advice."

He smiled and when he did, his teeth were perfect. Not unnaturally perfect, like dentures, but straight and white, like those of a man half his age. "I can take care of myself," he said. "Now, you've helped me, miss, so I owe you one. Have you ever heard of Cainsville?"

I shook my head.

"Little town outside the city. That's where you want to be." He handed me a folded slip of paper.

"I need to stay in Chicago," I said. "The jobs are here."

"Jobs are everywhere, if you're not too picky. Cainsville has its share. And apartments at half the price of this."

He pressed the paper into my hand. "My second cousin Grace owns a walk-up there. She'll set you up. Give her that note, though, or she might try to tell you she doesn't have a room. She's a fickle old bat."

I unfolded the paper. On it was an address and a note. "Give this girl a room." Signed "Jack in Chicago."

"Thank—" I looked up, but he was already back at his apartment door.

"Thank you," I called.

He nodded and went inside.

———

I had no intention of moving to a small town, particularly one I'd never heard of. I appreciated the kind gesture, but I saw no life for me outside Chicago.

I tried a couple more apartments, in even worse neighborhoods, then surrendered to exhaustion and found a hotel. A motel, actually. The kind I'd only ever seen on TV, usually where the bad guys holed up until the cops came busting through the door. Two stories of dirty brick, rusty metal railing along the second floor, neon sign out front promising clean rooms, as if that was a selling point you wouldn't find elsewhere. At thirty-nine dollars a night, it probably was.

I was so tired that when the desk clerk did a double-take, I told myself he didn't actually recognize me. Even when he surreptitiously checked a newspaper under the desk, I stood my ground. This was going to happen, so I'd better just get used to it.

He didn't deny me a room. Just fumbled through the check-in process, not even asking for a credit card deposit when I said I'd be paying cash. He messed up on the room rate, too, charging me twenty-nine. Or maybe, considering who my biological parents were, he thought it best to give me a discount. I didn't care. It was money saved, and I was quickly realizing I'd need every penny, even the lucky one nestled in my pocket.

My room was just big enough to hold a double bed, a tiny table, and a dresser of scuffed particle board. The pink and brown polyester bedspread had a bizarrely intricate design, probably to disguise stains. Matching curtains. As advertised, the room was clean. Or clean enough if you didn't look too carefully.

I made it as far as the bed, dropped onto it, and sat there for at least an hour. I wanted to cry. Sob into the pillow and vent all the day's frustration and loneliness. But I was too tired to manage it. Too empty.

I finally fell back onto a bedspread that stank of spilled beer and sex, and I didn't care. I just lay there and tried not to think about how much I missed home and how upset I was with my mother and how badly I wanted to hear Dad tell me everything would be okay.

I thought of calling James. Just to let him know I was all right.

Instead I called my mother. I blocked my number as I did, telling myself that I had to because otherwise she'd use it to call me later. In truth, I blocked it because it gave me an excuse if she *didn't* use it later.

No one answered the new cell number she'd given me. It didn't even ring to voice mail, suggesting the number had been disconnected. So I phoned Howard. When I announced myself, there was a pause, as if he was wondering whether he could *accidentally* hang up. First thing I was doing when I got things under control again? Firing his ass.

"I'm trying to get in touch with Mum," I said. "I want to let her know I'm okay."

"You told her that this morning, Olivia."

I gritted my teeth. "And I'd like to tell her again. More important, I want to make sure she's okay."

"She is. Her friends have come to her rescue." There was a note of accusation in his voice, as if I'd abandoned her, and I was about to snap back and remind him who advised me to stay away, but he continued, "They've taken her to Europe for a few weeks."

"What?"

"Your mother is taking this very hard, Olivia. She needs a break, and she deserves one. I will pass on messages, though I ask you to keep them to a minimum so as not to disturb her."

Disturb *her*? She hadn't just found out *she* was the daughter of serial killers.

"Olivia, your mother asked me to make sure you have everything you need."

*I need my mother.*

"Like what?" I asked.

"Money, of course. I've been authorized to wire you ten thousand now and another ten thousand next . . ."

He kept talking. I didn't hear him. I just sat there, staring into space, clutching the phone, feeling tears prickle the back of my eyes.

*I don't want money. I don't need money. I need help. Support. A mother. My mother.*

No, I needed my dad. I really, really needed my dad.

I told Howard the money could wait until I was settled. A lie. I would no more take it than I'd accept charity from a stranger on the street. That's what it felt like.

"One more thing," I said. "I hate to make you play messenger, but with every person I contact, there's more chance of the media finding me . . ."

"Yes, there is. Who would you like me to call?"

"James. Tell him I'm fine." I paused. "Tell him I'm fine and . . . tell him I'm sorry."

I hung up before I said more. I sat there for a few minutes, fighting the overwhelming loneliness. Then I ate the sandwich I'd grabbed earlier and crawled into bed, still dressed.

# CHAPTER THIRTEEN

I didn't want to take sleeping pills, but without the knock-out dose, a dream came. Except it wasn't a nightmare. It was a dream I'd had for as long as I could remember. My favorite one, so warm and familiar that if I woke up from it, I'd burrow back under my covers and try to find it again.

I was sitting in a garden, arranging polished white stones on a flat black rock. I'd make one design, then sweep it away and craft another. There was no feeling that I wasn't pleased with the design and needed to try again. Each one was perfect. Each one had meaning.

Somewhere to my left, a woman laughed. A man responded, his voice low, teasing, and she laughed again. I didn't look over. Just smiled and kept laying down rocks, each making a soft, satisfying click.

Tiny tropical birds flitted around me. Living jewels, sometimes landing on the rock, heads tilting as they chirped encouragement.

The heady scent of flowers filled the air. They were everywhere, in as many colors as the birds, rich reds and yellows and purples. Even the greenery was bright emerald, as lush as a rain forest.

Water burbled in front of me, a natural waterfall, tumbling into the rock pool below. As droplets sprayed my sun-bathed face, I licked them from my lips. Sweet, clean water. I'd take a drink in a moment, just as soon as I finished this last design.

I had to work harder at this one, dredging it up from memory. Three stones to the left, four to the . . . Or was it the other way around?

I sat back on my heels. A lock of hair fell over my shoulder and I pushed it back, my fingers brushing the lace. I reached down and adjusted my dress, really just an excuse to touch it. A beautiful, white dress with a long skirt that stretched down to tiny white sandals. My garden dress.

A bird flew past. A big, black one I hadn't seen before. A raven. I rose and stared after it as it swooped into the shadowy darkness beyond the waterfall.

I started going after it. A soft cry sounded behind me, then footsteps.

"Eden!" a voice called.

I turned. A figure stepped from the bushes, smiling as he approached. His face was hidden by the glare of the sun on the water. When he got to me, he leaned down to stroke my hair.

"Stay here, sweetheart. You know you aren't supposed to leave the garden."

I bolted up so fast I tumbled out of bed, legs entwined in the covers. I hung there, hands braced against the carpet, disoriented and panting before I realized where I was and pushed myself back up.

I struggled not to hyperventilate as the dream played back.

Eden. Garden.

Oh God. My dream. My wonderful, beautiful dream. It wasn't a dream at all, but my sleeping brain prodding me with the reminder of another life, another me.

I pressed my palms to my eyes and sat there, struggling not to cry. Of everything to cry over, *this*? Foolish. And yet . . .

I swiped away the first threat of tears, then popped a sleeping pill, swallowed it dry, and lay back down. Sat up and popped another one. Sleep didn't come quickly, but it did come.

I woke again in the dark, groggy now. I'd dreamed . . . No, I hadn't been dreaming. Something else woke me. I lay there in the darkness and listened. Getting up and flicking on the light would be the smart move, but panic buzzed, deep in my skull, telling me to stay where I was.

Lie still. Look. Listen.

There was nothing to see. The room wasn't completely dark—I'd been too tired to close the curtains properly and a strip of moonlight bisected the floor, the end dissolving across the bed. I looked around at the landscape of shadows and saw just a dresser and a bed and a tiny table, with its single chair.

Hadn't there been two chairs before? I was about to lift my head when that buzzing in my skull stopped me.

Lie still. Look. Listen.

The table was barely two feet across. Too small for more than a single person. I was misremembering the second chair. It wasn't as if I'd taken careful inventory.

Nothing to see, then. Nothing to hear, either. No, I could detect sounds. The mumble of a distant television. The screech of a passing car. The clatter and sigh of the water pipes.

In my room, though, I could hear only the soft in-and-out of my breathing. A faint rasp to it, like the first tickle of a cold. Exactly what I needed. Did my throat ache, too?

I moved my hand to touch my throat. Something rubbed my wrist.

No, something rubbed *around* my wrist. I'd taken off my watch. I knew I had, and this wasn't the rub of a gold band. It was softer, smaller. Like a cord—

That buzz of alarm shrieked before I could jerk my arm.

*Don't move.*

There's something around my—

*Don't move!*

A hiss of breath. I froze and I swear my bladder convulsed, with a tingle deep in my groin that had me clenching tight.

I clenched everything tight, going rigid as I strained to listen. Breathing. Quiet breathing, ragged and raspy at the edges.

Not my breathing.

*Where's the second chair?*

I knew without turning my head. There was only one place it could be, the only spot too dark for me to see, the same spot the breathing came from.

The other side of the bed.

I moved my hand, barely an inch, sweat beading as I struggled not to jerk or pull suddenly. There was definitely something around my wrist. Soft, loose. Another inch. It started to tighten.

I closed my eyes and willed my heart to slow. *Don't panic. Oh God, don't panic.*

Don't panic? I'm bound to the goddamn—

*Don't panic!*

I sucked in a breath as deeply as I dared. Then I shifted my legs, as if moving them in sleep, brushing them together as I did.

Okay, there was nothing around my ankles. Nothing around my other wrist either, because if I'd stop freaking out for a second, I'd realize I could see my other hand, on the moonlit bedspread.

Bound to the headboard by one wrist. Bound loosely by a cord. Which would tighten if I jumped up.

*So don't panic.*

If I moved my hand *up*, toward the headboard, I'd give the

cord more slack. Then I could work it off. I'd just slide my hand—

A hitch in the breathing. A squeak of the chair.

I snapped my eyes shut. Then I lay there, blind, every nerve straining, as if I could somehow sense if I was in danger. Only I couldn't. Someone was right beside me, maybe even leaning over me, knife moving to my—

Oh God, oh God.

*Breathe. Just breathe.*

A soft grunt, almost sounding disappointed. Another squeak as the intruder settled back into the chair.

Moving so slowly that my neck ached, I turned my head an inch toward his side of the bed. Then I waited. Counted to ten as sweat trickled down my cheek.

At ten, I waited two more excruciating seconds. Then I cracked open my eyes. It took a moment for my vision to adjust. When it did, I saw a figure sitting beside the bed.

If I opened my eyes just a little more—

*No. Just wait.*

After a moment, the figure began to manifest features. Dark hair cut short. A round face. Wide nose. Clean shaven.

The goddamned desk clerk.

*That bastard. That scrawny, greasy bastard. Did he really think—?*

A faint tug on my left wrist as my hand involuntarily clenched. I quickly released it and inhaled through my mouth.

Okay, anger was far more satisfying than panic, but no less likely to get me in serious trouble. If this guy had me bound to my bed, he'd probably brought either a knife or a gun. I had to relax and get free.

Earlier, I'd thought he recognized me. He hadn't. What he'd seen was the same thing the sleazy landlord had seen. A young woman alone. Uncertain. Exhausted. Vulnerable.

The perfect victim.

I must have forgotten to fasten the chain. He'd used his master key to get into my room and bound my wrist to the bed. Now he was watching me sleep. Waiting for that moment when I'd wake, still sleepy, blissfully ignorant. When I'd stretch and the cord would tighten and I'd realize what had happened. When I realized what *would* happen and became completely, deliciously, helplessly terrified.

If I was only bound by one hand, and I knew about it—and him—that gave me an advantage. Leap up and get free. Rob him of his moment of terror and—

"Are you awake?" His whisper slithered past.

I shut my eyes fast.

The chair squeaked again as he got up. This time I did sense him leaning over me. Heard his raspy breathing getting closer, closer . . .

He was so close that when he moved, his sleeve brushed my bare arm and goose bumps sprang up.

My throat constricted. I had to swallow. No, I couldn't swallow. It would give me away. Just lie perfectly still—

I *had* to swallow. I couldn't breathe. Oh God, I couldn't—

Something brushed my cheek. The touch was so light that it took a moment for my brain to register the feeling. Not warm skin. Not cool fabric. Cold metal.

My bladder convulsed once more.

Oh God, oh God. I had to do something. *Now.* Before—

A metallic click, right over my ear. I leapt up, limbs flailing. He stumbled back. Metal flashed in his hand. I swung at it, with my free fist. I hit his arm and his fingers flew open, the knife falling to the bed.

Not a knife. Scissors. A lock of my hair still jammed between the blades.

I grabbed for it, but he was faster, whacking the scissors with his open palm and sending them sailing onto the floor.

I lunged and the cord around my wrist tightened so fast it wrenched my shoulder. I spun, scrabbling back up the bed and clawing at the cord. But when it tightened, the knot tightened, too, and I couldn't slide it back, couldn't loosen it.

"Don't do that," he said. "You're only going to hurt yourself, Eden."

The hairs on my back rose, like a cat's. A flash of rage, white-hot. It evaporated as fast as it formed, leaving my heart pounding, throat constricting again.

*He did recognize me.*

*That's what this is about. Who I am. Who my parents are. He's going to—*

"Eden?"

I inched up to the headboard, turned and crouched there, my free hand still working at the knot. He stood with the scissors in his hand. When my gaze shot there, he lowered them. The hair was gone now. Fallen free, I thought, then I saw it behind him, on the dresser top, one pale curl carefully laid out.

I looked at him again. Yes, it was the desk clerk, but not the way I'd remembered him when I'd been lying in bed. Not a greasy slimeball. His hair was clean. His face was clean. His clothing was clean. I could say he'd washed up, but I realized this was how he'd looked in the office when he checked me in. I'd just misremembered. Reimagined him the way I'd picture a guy who'd sneak into a woman's hotel room to rape her.

I knew that predators came in every form, but I couldn't help staring at him. He looked too ordinary, too quiet, too well mannered.

A man that a single woman wouldn't mind sitting next to on a crowded train.

A man like Todd Larsen.

"My—my name isn't—"

"Eden Tiffany Larsen. A pretty name for a pretty girl."

"No, my name is—"

"I know what they call you now. Olivia. It doesn't suit you at all. You should go back to using your real name. Your proper one. Eden."

He pulled the chair alongside the bed until it bumped the nightstand. Then he sat and inched it forward, getting closer still. I kept working at the cord. He glanced over, frowning, but said nothing to stop me, just laid the scissors on his lap.

"For twenty years, people have been looking for you. Some said they'd hidden you too well. But the believers never gave up hope."

"I don't have anything to do with Pamela and Todd Larsen. They're my birth parents. That's it. I don't remember them. I'm sure they barely remember me. If you're going to use me for revenge—"

"Revenge?" He laughed. "We don't want revenge. We want to honor them."

"Honor?"

"What your parents did . . ." He shuddered. It wasn't the kind of shudder most people would give thinking about what the Larsens did. It wasn't the kind of shudder *anyone* should give thinking about it.

"They made a statement," he said. "An incredible statement."

Statement? The Larsens killed people. Brutally murdered them. No politics involved. Nothing but death.

"Angels of death," he said, as if reading my thoughts. "They took what they wanted without a thought for anyone but themselves. And you, of course. That's all that mattered to them. Their family. Nothing else. They understood what it meant to take a life."

No, I was pretty sure they didn't. No one could destroy other human beings that way and fully comprehend what they were doing. Unless they just didn't care.

"You look like her, you know." He rose from his chair. "Except for the hair. Hers is dark. Maybe if you dyed it . . ."

The tip of his tongue slid between his teeth, rapturous. I glanced down at the scissors that dangled by his side and inched my fingers along the sheet.

"No," he said, straightening. "That wouldn't be right. It's Todd's color. A tribute to both of them. As it should be." He rested a knee on the edge of the bed. "You *are* beautiful, Eden. A perfect blend of your parents."

I resisted the urge to inch back. *Keep still. Let him think he can come closer.*

But he just stayed there. My gaze dropped to the scissors to measure the distance. He followed it and lifted them, casually, no menace, but I pretended to flinch.

"I'm not going to hurt you, Eden. I just brought these to get that." He pointed to the curl on the dresser. "I'd never hurt you."

"Then put them down."

His lips twitched in a knowing smile. "Um, no. That wouldn't be wise, would it?"

"You said you aren't going to hurt me—"

"I'm not. But that doesn't mean you won't hurt me, does it? First chance you get. I know that. I'll keep these. To defend myself and"—that smile again—"to keep you from getting your pretty hands on them and making a pretty mess of me with them."

"I wouldn't do that. You're a"—I struggled for a word. Hated the one that came to mind—"*fan* of my parents."

"Which wouldn't keep them from gouging out my eyes with these if they caught me in your motel room. And won't keep you from doing the same to get away."

"I'm not like them. I've never hurt anyone."

"But you could. You just need the right circumstances. And I'd rather not provide them." He twisted, lowering himself to the edge of the bed, scissors resting on his thigh. "I'm supposed to help you, Eden. You walked into my motel, and I knew it was a sign." His gaze met mine. "Do you believe in signs?"

"Only the ones that give me directions."

He laughed. Loud and long, the sound raking along my spine. "Oh, signs all give directions. Mine told me that you needed help. They kicked you out, didn't they? Those people who stole you from Todd and Pam. They kicked you out, and now you're all alone. That's why you had to come to a cheap motel like this. You don't have any money. I do." He pulled a thick wad from his pocket.

"I don't need—"

"I know you do. I bet you need information, too. About them. Your parents. I know all about them and their lives and what they did. I'll give you that, and I'll give you money. I just want one thing."

He rose, gaze fixed on me, eyes glittering. I inched away.

"No, not that," he said. "I respect your parents too much for that. I just want to touch you. That's all."

He moved closer, hands on the bed, scissors loose under one. His breath came harsh, pupils dilated.

"You can leave your panties on. I won't touch you anywhere you don't want me to. I just want to touch—"

I grabbed the scissors before he could get a firm grip on them. He lunged across me. I swung the scissors with everything I had and buried the blades in his side. He howled. I yanked them out and stabbed him again. Blood sprayed across the white sheets, across him, across me.

I wrenched the scissors free and cut the cord. He lurched for me again. I stabbed him in the thigh. He let out a wail and dropped to the bed, clutching his leg, scissors still embedded in it. I leapt out of bed, grabbed my glasses, purse, and briefcase.

He was stretched across the bed, yowling and holding his thigh. Blood streamed between his fingers. I hesitated. Then I ran to the phone and yanked it over onto the bed, within reach.

I started for the door again. Stopped again. Looked at the wad of money fanning across the carpet. Reached down, scooped it up, and raced out the door.

# MISSION ACCOMPLISHED

He listened to her footsteps pound down the hallway. Then he rose, wincing as pain shot through his leg. He grimaced as he looked down at the damage. His favorite jeans, too. Shit.

Another wince as he pulled the scissors from his thigh. Fresh blood gushed and he grabbed a pillow to staunch the flow. Then he looked over to where the money had fallen.

It was gone.

He lifted the bedspread and looked under it. No, she'd definitely taken the money. He smiled. Good. Now he could just hope this little scare would send her exactly where she belonged: Cainsville.

Fate could be as capricious as a drunken *piskie*, and she certainly seemed to have been amusing herself with Eden Larsen. But occasionally the fickle wench settled down, straightened the road, and posted the appropriate signs. As for what would happen when Eden arrived in Cainsville, that wasn't his concern. He'd played his role. Now he'd bow off the stage and return to its shadowy wings.

He pulled the pillow from his thigh. The blood flow had stopped. When he stretched back the ripped denim, he could see the edges of the wound, already knitting together. If only it was as easy to fix his jeans. He sighed, collected the bloodied pillow and scissors, and left the room.

# CHAPTER FOURTEEN

I ran from the motel. Kept running until I reached the street, where I slowed to a jog. Two blocks away, I went into an all-night drugstore, where I bought a bottle of Dr Pepper and a Snickers bar. I still had fourteen hundred dollars stashed away, some in my bag and some in my purse, but I didn't use that. I pulled out a twenty from my pocket—the money I'd stolen—and slapped it onto the counter. Then I went out front, under the store lights, guzzled the Dr Pepper, and wolfed down the candy bar.

Blood still flecked my shirt, hidden under the jacket I'd pulled on before going in the store. I should have been emptying my stomach, not filling it. I should be shivering in an alley as I retched onto the gravel. But I didn't feel sick. I felt hungry. Starving. The syrupy soda and cheap chocolate tasted better than any gourmet meal.

My whole body still trembled. But there was no fear there. No voice screaming that it was four in the morning, and I was alone in the street and had to get somewhere safe.

No, I *was* safe. That trembling in my arms and legs wasn't fear. It was victory.

Did I feel bad about stabbing him? No. I'd left the phone. He'd be fine. Same went for taking the money. No guilt. For all

I knew, it was his life savings. Too bad. I needed it, and he deserved to lose it.

As the pop and the candy bar settled into my stomach, the adrenaline ebbed and I sobered. Okay, I'd won a round. Good for me. But I might not be so lucky next time. Apparently, I had more to worry about than bloodthirsty reporters and the grief-crazed relatives of the Larsens' victims. There were some serious nut jobs out there, and the next one might want more than a lock of hair.

I opened my purse and pulled out the folded note the old man had given me. Cainsville. If it was outside Chicago, people might be less likely to recognize me. After what just happened, that had become my main priority.

Still . . . moving to a town I'd never heard of? There had to be another way.

As I stood there thinking, a truck pulled up to refill the newspaper box out front. The *Chicago Tribune*. It was day two—any story would have moved off the front page by now. I'd try the *Tribune*'s classifieds today, and with any luck, find different ads for apartments and jobs.

I waited until the truck pulled away. Then I walked over to the box, bent to put in my money, and saw the headline, just above the fold.

"A Mother's Desperate Jailhouse Plea."

Then the subhead: "Pamela Larsen Collapses at News of Long-Lost Daughter."

I straightened and walked back into the drugstore.

Cainsville, Illinois, here I come.

An hour later, I was in a coffee shop restroom. I wore a fresh shirt, the blood-spattered one deep in my bag. I should probably have thrown it out, but that motel clerk wouldn't dare call the cops, and I couldn't afford new clothes.

On the counter was a box of hair dye. Red. Or, as the box proclaimed, dark copper. Strands of my hair snaked toward the drain. More filled the trash. I'd dyed it, then I'd cut it more. As it got shorter, the light curl became more pronounced. When I got it down to a few inches and added some gel, I ended up with a tousled, coppery mop. The new cut even made my glasses look different, the dark green frames funky and playful. In other words, I didn't look like me at all.

Perfect.

It was barely six. So I hung out in the coffee shop, feasting on caffeine and sugar—as if I hadn't had enough of both already. I spent a few dollars on cell phone calls, searching for a method of public transportation to Cainsville.

Greyhound had never heard of the place. Neither had Amtrak. I was starting to wonder if it existed outside the old man's imagination when a clerk at a regional bus line said she knew it.

"I grew up a few towns over," she said. "But you're not going to find a bus heading out that way, hon. Too far from the interstate." She laughed. "Too far from anywhere anyone wants to be, if you ask me."

Which made it exactly where *I* wanted to be.


Is there such a thing as an adrenaline hangover? I certainly had one on the trip from Chicago to Cainsville. Maybe a better analogy would be laughing gas wearing off after a dental visit. I'd felt fine—better than fine—until I sat down on the cab's cracked vinyl upholstery, and then what I'd just done hit with the force of a sledgehammer.

I'd attacked a man. Stabbed him. More than once. I'd left him there, bleeding, and I'd stolen his money before I went. Yes, I could argue that I'd been defending myself and maybe three blows weren't warranted, but I couldn't risk the guy coming after me. Still . . . taking his money?

It wasn't just what I'd done that bothered me. It was how easily I'd done it. There'd been no hesitation. I'd reacted on instinct.

And where did that instinct come from? That was the real question, wasn't it?

# AHEAD OF SCHEDULE

Ida and Walter Clark left their house that morning at nine, as they did every day. Or roughly thereabouts. Ida had risen early to do the laundry. Then Walter hung it out to dry, which meant they actually left at 9:10. Still plenty of time to make it to the school for morning recess, which was the objective.

They didn't lock their door. No one in Cainsville did.

"Do I have time to get a cup of tea?" Ida asked as she looped her arm through her husband's.

"From the coffee shop. Not from Larry's."

She sighed.

"We should support the coffee shop, too," Walter said. "They're good people. Even if they don't know how to make a proper cup of tea. But those coffee drinks are good." He smiled at her. "I know you like the vanilla ones."

True. The concept of putting so much milk in your coffee still struck her as foreign. Italian, wasn't it? But it was delicious, and her bones could use the extra calcium. They'd pick up a bag of the almond cookies, too, for the others who'd be at the school.

Watching the children at recess was a ritual for the elders of Cainsville. There were even benches along the fence, like bleachers at a sports field. There was joy to be found in watching the young, so carefree and happy. It reminded them what this town stood for, the way of life they worked so hard to protect.

There weren't nearly as many children as the elders would like, but they had no one to blame except themselves. The town was a mere hour from Chicago. These days, that was considered a reasonable commuting distance, and Cainsville could easily become a sprawling bedroom community, with hundreds of children, even a high school of its own, and a real sports field, where they could cheer on their home teams.

It was a pleasant dream, but like so many dreams, it masked an uglier reality. To get those children, the town would need to grow significantly. There would be new housing developments along every border. Strangers moving in. Strangers who didn't understand what it meant to live in Cainsville.

The town's location had been chosen specifically because the geography forbade expansion. Nestled in the fork of a river, with marshy, inhospitable ground on the only open side. That meant it was protected.

It also meant there was no room to grow. The city council wouldn't permit bridges over the river forks. They hadn't even allowed an exit to be built off the highway—to reach Cainsville, you had to take one miles away, and it fed onto a narrow county road.

The few children who lived here were happy, treasured, and coddled. Once they reached adolescence, that coddling could become suffocating. The elders understood that. Teenagers didn't want everyone knowing their name, watching over them, however indulgently. They didn't want to live in a town you could walk across in a half hour. They graduated from high school, left, and stayed gone . . . until they married and had children of their own. Then they looked around at the world and looked at their children and decided it was time to go home. Back to Cainsville.

Not everyone returned, of course. So the town stayed roughly the same size as it had always been. Which was for the best, all things considered.

It wasn't that they didn't welcome newcomers. Look at the people who owned the coffee shop. Been here about a year and everyone tried really hard to make them feel welcome, even if they didn't know how to fix a proper cuppa. They were the right sort of folks. That's what mattered here. In that case, new blood was welcome. Or old blood, as the case may be.

Ida and Walter had just walked onto Rowan Street when a taxi pulled to the roadside. An odd sight in Cainsville.

A young woman got out. Hair as bright as a copper penny, worn in loose, short curls. Glasses that seemed designed to mask a pretty face, and were doing a poor job of it, judging by the look Walter was giving her.

"Is that the Larsen girl?" he asked.

Ida looked closer. "Hmm. It just might be."

As they approached, the young woman shut the taxi's door and the car sped off, spitting up gravel, making the girl step quickly back.

"Rude driver," Ida sniffed.

"City folk."

She nodded. As they passed the girl, Ida offered her a smile and a good morning, which her husband echoed, and the girl returned.

"Yes, it's definitely the Larsen girl," Ida said after they'd passed. "She's ahead of schedule."

"That's not a bad thing."

"True. We should tell the others."

"We will. After we get you your coffee drink."

She smiled, took his arm, and they continued on.

# CHAPTER FIFTEEN

The taxi had barely gone thirty miles past Chicago before it turned off the highway. I expected the town to be right there, but it was at least another twenty-minute drive until we passed the sign welcoming us to Cainsville. Actually, "welcoming" might be an exaggeration. The sign was so small I had to squint to see it. It didn't even say Welcome. Just Cainsville, Pop. 1,600, as if state law decreed there be one or they would have left the population sign off altogether.

It looked welcoming enough, though. Classic mid- to late-nineteenth-century architecture—heavy on brick and stone and flourishes. A pretty town, in better shape than most. The main street—called Main Street, naturally—was heavily Renaissance Revival, red brick with the occasional yellow brick facade thrown in for variety. Arched windows topped by simple keystones. Elaborate cornices of tin or painted wood. Trees lined the road, and there were flowering pots and raised beds everywhere.

Almost every shop on Main Street was occupied, and from the looks of the signs—J. Brown and Sons Grocers, the Corner Diner, Loomis Bros. Fine Fashions—they'd been there for decades. That was a huge accomplishment these days, where many town cores were filled with For Rent signs, dollar stores, and pawnshops.

A flicker of movement near a roof caught my eye and I looked up to see a bluebird alighting on the long nose of a gargoyle. A spring bluebird. That was a good sign.

As the cab paused at the crosswalk, I took a better look at the gargoyle. It was a real one, the mouth opening in a spout for water draining off the roof. It was far from the only gargoyle, too. Now that I looked, I saw them everywhere—on rooftops, on gateposts, over doorways.

"A town filled with gargoyles," I said. "Must be well protected."

The cabbie looked up and muttered something in a language I didn't recognize. Then, as the light changed, he said, "This is Cainsville. I let you out here."

"I have an address," I said. "Five Rowan Street."

"I do not know where that is." He pulled to the side. "You get out here."

"No, I have an address." I put the window down and called to a young woman pushing a stroller. "Excuse me, do you know where I'd find Rowan Street?"

She gave me directions, friendly as could be. Even warned us that there was no parking on the east side of the road.

Rowan adjoined Main Street, making it an easy drive. The cabbie turned onto it but didn't park. He barely stopped. Just took my fare and left me on the side of the road. I didn't tip him, either. A first for me, and I thought I'd feel guilty. I didn't. Instead, I was happy for the excuse to keep the money.

An elderly couple tut-tutted as the cabbie sped off, then gave me smiles and good mornings, which I returned before they carried on.

I stood on the curb for a moment, waiting for that sensory

overload after the cocooning quiet of the car. It didn't come. I smelled lilacs and freshly mown grass. I heard the wind and the distant *ding-ding* of a bicycle bell. But that was it.

I relaxed and looked around. The apartment building was across the road. When I saw it, I had to double-check the address. The building was gorgeous. Three stories of Renaissance Revival beauty. Smooth, yellow-gray stone walls forming a rectangle. A recessed, arched front entrance topped by a triangular gable. Red-clay tiled hipped roof. Deep eaves with huge, decorative brackets. Balconies under every window, most too narrow to use.

On closer inspection, I could see the signs that the building had not been kept in the shape befitting such a grand old dame. Disrepair is harder to spot with a place like this—the stonework will survive anything short of a bomb blast. No factories in the area meant the stone had stayed reasonably clean. But there were little signs—the crumbling edge of a window rail, the slight sag in the roof—that it was only good bone structure that left her looking so fine in her old age. Even the plain ivory curtains in the windows seemed as if they hadn't been replaced in decades.

Speaking of curtains . . . as I walked down Rowan I noticed another pretty place, this one a fraction of the size. A dollhouse of a two-story Victorian, narrow and shallow, its height making it seem bigger than it was. Weathered boards cried out for a fresh coat of paint. Ivy covered every surface. The yard was well kept, though. Exceedingly well kept, with a golf-course-perfect lawn and gardens so lush they seemed to have time-warped into midsummer. It was jarring, that juxtaposition. Like something out of a fairy tale, the perfect yard enticing the unwary into the witch's abode.

The witch herself seemed to be in residence, peering out from that open curtain. Below her, in the first-floor window, a sign read "Tarot, palmistry, and astrology. By appt. only." A fortune teller? Seriously? I squinted to get a better look at the woman. The curtain fell.

As I crossed the road, I noticed the apartment building had gargoyles, too. Under the eaves and tucked into the corners of the fake window balconies, stone gargoyles standing watch. I marveled at them, then climbed the steps and reached for the doorknob. There, above my head, was yet another Gothic touch, this one far more subtle and definitely unintended. A massive spiderweb, dew-dappled and glistening in the morning sun. The spider was there, too, big and black, waiting in the middle of its web.

*If you wish to live and thrive,*
*Let the spider stay alive.*

That was a new one. Just what I needed. More superstitious crap filling my brain.

I shook my head and pulled open the door.

# CARDS DON'T LIE

Rose ducked back behind the gauzy curtain as the girl squinted her way. The red hair had thrown her, but only for a moment. She'd known the girl was coming. The cards never lied. So Rose had been watching. Now she was here.

Eden Larsen. Olivia Taylor-Jones. As for what her arrival in Cainsville portended . . . The cards were, as usual, long on declarations and short on interpretations.

The girl had stopped on the stoop of Grace's building. She was staring up into the corner of the front doorway.

What was she gaping at? Whatever it was, it held her attention for at least a minute before she opened the door and walked through.

Rose picked up her binoculars from the table and peered out. She looked where the girl had been staring. Nothing. She adjusted the lenses and looked again. It didn't help. She was looking right at the spot.

There was nothing there.

# CHAPTER SIXTEEN

The front door opened into a vestibule with stairs going up and a perpendicular hall for the apartments. No locked door to pass through. No panels of buzzers to alert the residents to company. Not even names on the mailbox slots.

The hall was paneled plaster with a wooden floor. My knowledge of architecture was confined to the external, so I didn't know how historically accurate this was. It looked right, though. It was definitely nicer than any of the apartments I'd visited so far. Yes, the floorboards were worn, unvarnished paths showing the main routes, and the walls could use fresh paint. But it had a comfortable, lived-in look. Benign neglect.

I looked down the main hallway. Two doors on each side, four apartments on each floor. Twelve overall, then. Small, but it certainly didn't feel full. The long corridor was dimly lit and cool, like a cave. Smelled a lot better than any cave I'd explored. I picked up teasing traces of sandalwood. The sounds were as muted as the smells. Hushed. Not so much a cave, then, as a church after hours, dark and cool and peaceful.

I knocked on 1D, the number on the note. It took three tries for the landlord to answer, and when she did, the look she gave me said I should have taken the hint after the first two.

She was at least as old as her cousin in Chicago. Steel gray hair pulled back in a severe bun. Sharp nose. Sharp chin. Even sharper gaze.

"What?"

"Are you Grace?" I handed her the note without waiting for a reply. "Your cousin Jack in Chicago—"

An abrupt wave, silencing me as she snatched the paper. As she read it, her frown deepened, until she wouldn't have been out of place perched on top of her building.

"Got one apartment," she said. "Three hundred a month."

"Could I see—?"

"No. Wasn't expecting to be showing apartments today."

"Is it one bedroom?"

"You need more? Too bad. It's one."

"One is fine. Separate kitchen and living area?"

"It's five hundred square feet, girl. You won't be doing much *living* in there. But if you're asking if it's all one room, like one of those bachelor pads, no, it's a proper apartment. Kitchen, living room, bedroom, bath."

"Furnished?"

"If you call a fridge, stove, twin bed, and sofa 'furnished.' Might not be up to your standards, though. Got them at a yard sale." A pause. "Twenty years ago."

"Could I replace them if I wanted?"

"Can do anything you want. Replace the furniture, paint, carpet. Hell, you can even clean the place. Might need it. Haven't opened the door since the tenant moved out last year."

*Lovely . . .*

"Okay, so three hundred a month," I said. "First and last's makes that six—"

"Did I say you could stay two months? You pay one. Then I decide if you can have it for another."

Renting a place unseen was ridiculous. But three hundred was a steal, especially with no second month's rent or damage deposit.

I took another look down the hall. I wouldn't even want to think what I'd pay in a place like this in Chicago.

"I'll take it."

A grunt that might have been "good" but probably wasn't. She held out her hand, and it took me a second to realize she wanted her money. Now. I peeled three hundred from my wad and handed them over.

She took a key ring from inside her doorway, then strode along the hall so fast I had to scamper to keep up. No arthritic knees or hips here, despite her age. As we walked, she didn't say a word, just worked on getting a key off the ring.

We went up the stairs to the top floor. She walked to one of the front apartments and swung the door open. Left unoccupied *and* unlocked for a year?

The stink of must hit me as soon as the door opened. Nothing worse, though. A few hours—okay, a few days—with the windows open, and it would be fine.

As I followed her in, I realized she wasn't kidding about the cleaning. There were newspapers and empty boxes littering a floor so thick with dust that I kicked up clouds with every step.

Still, as with the rest of the building, the apartment was in good shape. Pretty even, with worn wood floors and plenty of decorative flourishes. It just needed a thorough scrubbing. The mauve painted walls would have to go before they gave me a headache.

Grace handed me the key. Then, without a word, she walked out.

If it hadn't been for the smell, I think I'd have collapsed on the bed and called it a day. But that stink got me out—with the windows left open.

Grace was on the front stoop, in a ratty lawn chair, surveying the street as if expecting an invasion of Mongols. I offered a cheery "Have a good morning!" as I started down the steps.

"Where you off to already?" she said.

"Job hunting."

"You just got here."

"I need a job."

"Well, you won't get one here. Not this fast."

I walked back up the stairs. "The town doesn't look like it's hurting too badly. There must be jobs for someone willing to take what she can get, which I am."

"Oh, there are jobs. But folks don't know you yet. Not going to hire you until they do. Only ones who'll take you so fast are other new people." A dismissive wave at a young woman herding two preschoolers toward Main Street. "They'll hire you to clean their houses and look after their brats."

"Then that's what I'll do."

She snorted and shook her head as I went back down the steps.

"Waste of time," she called after me. "But if you insist on going out, might as well stop by the diner."

I turned. "Do they have an opening?"

"No. I want a scone. One of those cranberry orange ones. If Larry says he's out, you tell him Grace says he's full of shit and he'd better find one."

# CHAPTER SEVENTEEN

G race was right. I hit every shop on Main Street. Some people said they weren't hiring. Others peered at me and asked me who my folks were.

My parents, they meant. I definitely wasn't answering that. But what they were really asking was whether I was local, maybe gone off to college and come back and they didn't recognize me. When I told them I was new in Cainsville, they said they didn't have any openings, but I should come back in a week or two. In other words, once people around here got to know me.

I'd just left the last store when I passed a sign for the library. It was in the community center, which was an amazing building. It looked like a small version of Altgeld's castles, the Gothic Revival halls built at five Illinois universities. When Altgeld was governor in the late nineteenth century, he'd expressed concern about the ugliness of public buildings and suggested a style that would be both functional and attractive. The result was those five buildings.

The Cainsville community center was clearly modeled after them. It was a long, gray stone building, complete with turrets, battlements, a front tower, and of course, gargoyles. It should have looked horribly out of place, but it fit right in.

I walked through the front doors. There were lots of postings on the community board for local activities, everything from book clubs to karate lessons. None for jobs. Oddly, none for commuting partners, either—I'd considered whether I could carpool to a job in Chicago. Before I left, I popped into the library to check out the computers. They had a row of them, all with free Internet. It might look like a sleepy town, but the computers were relatively new. Very nice.

I considered sending a message to James. I could create a new e-mail account—that would be safe, wouldn't it?

Um, no. The guy owned a tech company, and I was seriously thinking he didn't have someone on staff who could track the e-mail's originating IP address? And after he tracked it to the library, how long would it take to find someone who would tell him that, yes, there was a new young woman in town.

Did I want him to find me? Or did I want to test him, see if he'd bother? Or test him another way, see if he'd respect my privacy and my ability to take care of myself?

If I truly intended to make it on my own, I had to send him a message the next time I was in Chicago, not from here.

I finished my job hunt in the Corner Diner, which looked like someone had transported it from the fifties. Red vinyl seats. Gleaming chrome. The smell of fresh coffee and apple pie. A cool air-conditioned breeze, just enough to lift the heat from the midday sun streaming through the windows.

There were plenty of windows. As the name proclaimed, the diner was on the corner, so glass wrapped around both sides, giving a street-side view to as many patrons as possible.

The worn linoleum floor squeaked under my shoes, and people glanced up at me. A few curious looks. A few smiles, not overly friendly but warm enough.

There were a couple of people eating a late lunch, but most seemed to be on a coffee break. Three tables of postretirement couples. Two of construction workers. Two more of shopkeepers, all of whom I'd met earlier in the day, and all of whom greeted me with a nod and a smile. And, finally, one table occupied by the obligatory "guy working on his novel."

As I crossed the diner, the would-be novelist looked up from his laptop. He was in his early twenties, with a lean face, dark eyes, and darker hair tumbling over those eyes. I'd have thought he was seriously cute if I were five years younger. And if I went for the tortured artistic types. As it was, I smiled and continued to the counter.

"Margie?" called a rich tenor voice behind me. "I need a refill."

I glanced back to see the novelist holding out his mug. The server—a wide-hipped woman in her early thirties—picked up the coffeepot . . . and headed for a patron on the other side of the restaurant. I walked to the counter, where a beefy man with prison tats frowned as he watched the server.

"Excuse me," I said. "Is the manager in?"

"That'd be me." He extended a thick hand. "Larry Knight. Owner, proprietor, and chief cook."

"*Only* cook," said a reedy male voice behind me.

"Which is just the way we like it," a woman chimed in. "Best in the state."

As Larry blushed, I turned to see the elderly couple that'd greeted me this morning when I'd gotten out of the taxi. We exchanged smiles.

I asked Larry if he was hiring.

"Mmm, no," he said with what sounded like genuine regret. "This is a small operation, miss. Me at the grill, Margie and two other ladies sharing serving duty. Have you tried the—?"

One of the construction workers started coughing, his face screwed up as he spat on the floor. He lifted his coffee mug, peered in, and let out a roar.

"Margie! The cream's turned. That's the second time this week."

"Count yourself lucky," one of the shop owners said. "Three times for me, plus once with salt in the sugar container."

Larry scrambled from behind the counter, cream carton in one hand, fresh coffee mug in the other, sputtering apologies.

"Not your fault, Larry," the construction worker said. "We all know who's responsible for condiments around here." A glare at Margie, who squawked that she checked the creamers every day and those ones weren't due for another week.

"Then you'd better check the fridge," Larry said. "Make sure it's working right."

"Any chance on that refill?" called the writer. "I don't even take cream."

Larry apologized some more, took the pot from Margie, and hurried over. The old folks nearest me watched Margie disappear into the back, then one murmured, "Larry really has to let that gal go."

"He's too softhearted," the other replied.

They both nodded, half approvingly, half not, then checked their tea before sipping it.

"Sorry 'bout that," Larry said to me as he returned to his place behind the counter. "And sorry about the hiring situation. Can I get you something to eat? On the house? My way of saying welcome to Cainsville."

I took him up on the freebie, but ordered the cheapest thing on the menu—a grilled cheese sandwich. "And I need to buy a cranberry orange scone for Grace over on Rowan, please."

"We're all out of—"

"Don't even try it, Larry," one of the old ladies cackled. "Not with Grace. You should know better by now."

Larry sighed. "I'll bake up a batch from the freezer."

When he went into the kitchen, the elderly couple waved me over to squeeze into the booth with them. They introduced themselves as Ida and Walter. As I waited for my lunch, they gave me—unprompted—Larry's life story, at least as it pertained to Cainsville. To them, that was the only part that mattered, despite the fact that he'd only been here a few years. Before that, all they'd say was that he'd spent some time traveling the wrong road, which I could have guessed by the prison tats.

"Got mixed up with a bad crowd," Walter said.

"He's too trusting. People take advantage. Like her." A poisonous glower in Margie's direction as she took an order.

My sandwich arrived, and as I ate Ida and Walter filled me in on the town's inhabitants, an endless litany of names I'd never remember. When I finished, I got Grace's scone from Larry. As I was heading out, the would-be writer was trying to get another refill from Margie and, again, being ignored. He glanced at me as I passed the coffee station, then lifted his mug and eyebrows simultaneously.

I looked at Margie. She was on her cell phone. Well, as long as I was trying to make a good impression . . .

I took the coffeepot over and refilled his mug. He thanked me and said, "Now I bet you expect a tip."

"Um, no. I was just—"

"Being nice?" The smile that tweaked his lips was mischievous, but with a twist that was more devilish than boyish. "Didn't your momma ever tell you never to give something unless you can get something in return?"

"That wasn't how I was raised."

"Then you were raised wrong. As for that tip . . ." He

lowered his voice. "If you want to work here, I'd suggest you come back for breakfast tomorrow. Then maybe for coffee in the afternoon. Repeat as needed. I have a feeling that opportunity will knock." A pointed look at Margie. "Sooner rather than later."

"Thanks."

"No need to thank me." He lifted his full mug. "It was a fair exchange of services."

He gave me that same unsettling smile, and I had to check my pace so I didn't hurry away.

When I stepped out of the diner, I noticed a black cat grooming itself on the diner windowsill. As I watched it, a voice whispered in my ear. *Black cat, black cat, bring me some luck.*

I spun. There was no one there. I rubbed my ear and made a face. Another forgotten ditty, resurfacing from my subconscious. I guess it was a testament to my mental state. I could act like I was motoring forward, doing fine, but something inside me had fractured, and this was what came bubbling up.

"Superstitious nonsense," I muttered.

The cat gave me a baleful look, then rubbed its paw over its head, flattening both ears with one swipe.

"Storm's coming," I whispered.

"Is it?" said a voice behind me.

I turned to see Ida and Walter exiting the diner. Ida peered up at the sky.

"Figures," she muttered. "Just when I decide it's safe to put the laundry out."

"No, I didn't mean—"

"Move those old legs," she said to her husband. "Or you'll have wet drawers waiting at home." She smiled over at me. "Thank you, dear."

I tried again to protest that I'd only been mumbling to myself. The sky was bright and clear. Rain wasn't coming anytime soon. But neither seemed to hear me, and only hurried off to get their laundry in before the skies opened.

# CHAPTER EIGHTEEN

All these years of hiding my superstitious side, and suddenly I was blurting weather omens to strangers. A cat washing its ears meant rain? I'd never heard of that before, no more than I remembered hearing that killing spiders was bad luck or that a black cat was good luck. Even people without a superstitious bone in their body knew that black cats were supposed to be *bad* luck.

Was this the first sign of a breakdown? Where other people would begin triple-checking locks and refusing to leave the house, I started babbling omens?

My apartment was only about a quarter mile from the diner. I'd seen a tiny park behind the bank that seemed like it could be a shorter route. It was on a half acre of land, cut by cobbled paths that ran between the surrounding houses and buildings, providing direct access to each street—including Rowan.

The park was beyond adorable, bounded by a gated wrought iron fence. Every third post was a thick stone pillar topped with a chimera—fantastical hounds and birds and mythical mixtures. Many of them were shiny with wear, as if local children had each adopted their own, rubbing it for luck when they came to play.

Inside there were benches and a tiny burbling fountain, the fountainhead another chimera. The water came not out of its mouth, but from both ears, which made me smile. The park wasn't big enough for a full-blown playground, but there were swings, two for older kids and one basket type for little ones. The basket swayed gently, as if recently vacated, and I imagined a child in it, shrieking with delight, chubby arms and legs pumping.

*"High, Daddy. Go high!"*

A man's laugh. *"I think that's high enough."*

*"High! Go high!"*

*"Okay. But hold on tight. If I bring you home with skinned knees again, Mommy will kill me. Are you holding on, Eden?"*

I tore my gaze from the swing and hurried across the park to the rear gate. My fingers trembled as I unlatched it. It swung open with a squeal loud enough to make me jump. I turned to close it properly. As I did, I noticed patterns of stones in the garden. I bent over one. White stones arranged against black soil.

I jerked up, blinking. A deep breath, then I looked down again. It didn't look anything like the patterns from my dream. Just a child at play, arranging stones in the dirt.

I gave one last look at the swing, still twisting slightly in the breeze. I clutched the bag with Grace's scone, still warm, the comforting smell wafting out. I turned from the park and headed down the pathway toward Rowan.

As I hurried along, the sky grayed so fast I looked up in alarm. Rain? I shook my head. Wishful thinking, as if having my weather omen come true would somehow prove I was perfectly sane. Because "storm-prediction-by-cat" *was* sane.

Yet when the sun disappeared, it seemed to suck the spring warmth from the air. I shivered and pulled my jacket tighter. As I did, I caught sight of a shadow on the wall beside me. I looked over sharply. No shadow.

How could there be a shadow when the sun was gone? Damn, I really was losing it.

Yet I couldn't shake that sense of something creeping along behind me. Finally I spun. There was something there—a black shape crouched on the fence of the now-distant park. A chill crept up my spine and I squinted. The shape lengthened, stretching until it became the black cat, languidly arching its back, then settling in on the fence post to watch me.

The urge to run tingled down my legs. Instead, I forced myself back toward the cat. It just sat there, watching me.

"If you're looking for handouts, this"—I waggled Grace's bag—"is not kitty food."

The cat yawned and stretched again before settling back on its perch. Something passed overhead and the cat sprang up so fast I stumbled back. It gave me a scornful glare, then looked up into the sky. I followed its gaze to see what looked like a crow, soaring high overhead.

"A little out of your reach," I said to the cat.

It ignored me, tail puffed, yellow eyes following the distant bird.

*Crow, crow, get out of my sight*
*Or else I'll eat thy liver and lights*

"Great," I muttered. "Just great." I shook my finger at the cat. "You guys really *are* bad luck."

The clouds overhead shifted, sunlight coming through again. As I headed back to the pathway, I glanced over my shoulder once, but the cat hadn't moved. It just kept staring at that crow, as if hoping it would come lower. If it did, the cat would be in for a surprise. The bird was probably as big as it was.

When I was about halfway down the path, I could make out the Victorian house across the road, the one with the psychic in residence. Again, I saw a face in a window. And two black circles. Binoculars. They pulled back and I smiled to myself. Psychic, my ass. In a town this small, all you needed to pull off that gig was the gift of nosiness.

A cloud moved across the sun again and I looked up. Maybe it would rain after all. That might establish *me* as a psychic. Look out, lady—

A throat-clearing. And as my gaze dropped from the sky, I realized it wasn't a cloud blocking the sun at all. There was a man barely a yard away.

"Ms. Taylor-Jones?"

The first thing I saw was his suit. It was a good one. Excellent, in fact. Worth more than some of the cars parked along the road behind him. I thought, *James has hired someone to find me.*

There was a reason the guy seemed to block the sun. He had to be at least six foot four with shoulders so wide I had to bump up my estimate of the suit's worth. Nothing off the rack would fit him.

Whoever sprang for a fancy suit, hoping to make him look less intimidating, had wasted his money. One look and you knew exactly what he was—a high-class thug. Property of a very wealthy man. This wasn't the sort of person James would send. Not unless he wanted me running the other way.

My gaze went to his eyes. Instinct, honed by my dad. *Look strangers in the eyes right away, Livy. That's the only way to get a good read on them.* Usually a good rule. Except when the stranger was wearing shades so dark I couldn't see through them.

The man took a long step backward and the corners of his mouth twitched.

"Is that better?" he said, his voice deep, tone amused. "You look ready to scamper back down the path. Not what I'd expect from the daughter of Pamela Larsen." Before I could react he pulled a card from his inside pocket and presented it with a mock flourish. I glanced at it, noting only his name—Gabriel Walsh—a Chicago address and the words "Law Firm."

Not a thug, then. An investigator . . . probably with a little thug thrown in, for getting information people didn't care to give.

"You work for a lawyer," I said. When one brow arched, I continued, "Whatever your boss—"

"I don't have a boss, Ms. Jones."

He reached out, and I struggled against the urge to move back. He tapped the card with one huge but perfectly manicured fingernail.

I read it again. Gabriel Walsh. Attorney-at-law.

"Oh," I said.

"A common mistake. I represented your mother. The biological one."

I glanced up sharply. "You were—?"

"Not her original lawyer, of course." He wasn't old enough for that. "I represented Pamela Larsen in her most recent appeal attempt. Lost, unfortunately."

"I wouldn't say that's unfortunate at all."

His only response was an oddly elegant shrug.

"I suppose she sent you," I said. "That heartrending jailhouse plea to see her only child? You can tell her—"

"I said I represented her, past tense. She fired me when our request for an appeal was denied."

"And now you want to get her back."

"No, I was fired only because she didn't give me time to quit."

"I really do need to be going," I said as I hefted my paper bag. "If you'll excuse—"

"I've come with a business proposition." He turned toward Rowan Street. "There's a coffee shop down the road. The food isn't as good as the diner's, but it's quieter."

He knew Cainsville? I checked the card again. The office address was definitely Chicago.

"How did you find me?" I said.

"I had a tip." He waved toward the psychic's house. "Now, about that coffee . . . ?"

I shook my head, said, "Not interested." I stepped to the side, to go around him. He hesitated, and I thought he was going to block me. My heart picked up speed, brain calculating the distance back to the park. He let me pass, but followed, still talking.

"You may be aware that your mother wrote a book. You may not be aware that it continues to sell quite well. The proceeds, naturally, do not go to Pamela. In the absence of an heir, her royalties are donated to charity. However, now that her heir has been found . . ."

"You'll help me gain control of those assets," I said, still walking. "For a price."

"Fifty percent." He said it without hesitation. I should have been appalled, but all I could think was, *At least he's honest.*

"Those proceeds are going to the victims, aren't they?"

"Their families." He clarified this as if it made them less worthy of compensation. A pause for dramatic effect, then he lowered his voice, "The only living victim here is you, Ms. Jones."

I laughed. I couldn't help it. He only dipped his chin, as if granting me a point in a game, which I supposed this was. For him, at least.

"I can see that your standard of living has dropped significantly as the result of this revelation. Your adopted mother has apparently disowned you—"

"No, I'm just taking some time away."

"Oh?" He looked around. "So this is where you usually come on vacation?"

I kept walking. He followed in silence until we reached the sidewalk, where a sleek Jaguar had taken the last spot on Rowan—the one in front of the fire hydrant.

"May I suggest that poverty is not the grand adventure you expect, Ms. Jones?"

"I know what poverty is."

"Do you? My mistake then."

I glanced back. His lips were slightly curved, this time not in a smile but in disdain. Bastard. I climbed the apartment steps. Grace was still there on her battered lawn chair, pulled back into the shadows. She nodded. But it wasn't me she was looking at.

"Gabriel."

"Grace. I brought you a scone." He lifted a small brown bag, which looked remarkably like the one . . . I looked down at my empty hand.

How the hell had he done that?

"Fresh from the oven," he said. "Still warm."

Grace took it with a queenly nod, then glowered my way. I started to claim the scone, but realized it would sound like whining. If he got it from me, that was my own fault. Bastard.

"You two know each other?" I said.

"We're acquainted." Gabriel turned to me. "I've made my offer, Ms. Jones, and I hope you'll take some time to reconsider it."

"I don't need to."

"I think you might."

He nodded to Grace, then walked down the steps and headed for the Jag. Got in, peeled from the curb. I watched him go, then turned to Grace.

"You know who I am," I said.

"Maybe." She peered into the bag and pulled out the scone. "Don't expect me to feel sorry for you."

I stood there as she took a bite, gray eyes closing in rapture.

"He said *she* called him." I waved toward the fortune-teller's house. "Tipped him off about me."

She opened one eye, then the other, piqued at the interruption. "If you think it was me, say so. Don't beat around the bush. Makes you look weak."

"Okay. So you called him."

"I wouldn't call Gabriel Walsh if I was on fire." She pursed her lips. "No, I might. To sue everyone responsible—from the person who lit the match to those who made my clothes. But I'd wait until the fire was out. Otherwise, he'd just stand there until I was burned enough for a sizable settlement."

"So he's an ambulance chaser."

"He's a money chaser, doesn't matter where it comes from. Young as he is, he runs his own practice. Makes him look like some kind of prodigy, but the truth is with his reputation, even the sleaziest firm in Chicago wouldn't hire him. He is honest, though, in his own way. If he said Rose called him, I'm sure she did, because she called me about you, too. The part Gabriel left out? That old gossip is his great-aunt."

"Oh."

"Yes, *oh*. Gabriel Walsh comes from a long line of hustlers. He's just the first one to go to law school and get a license for it."

So the last lawyer to represent Pamela Larsen had an aunt who just happened to live across from my new apartment? Seems my luck in finding Cainsville came with a price. I supposed I should have expected as much. Fate is capricious. Nothing comes free. And Gabriel Walsh was an irritation I could deal with.

Grace took another bite of her scone and sighed with pleasure. "Damn. You must have made a good impression on Larry if you got him to bake me up a fresh batch."

"You knew . . . ?"

"That you brought me this? Course I did."

"But you thanked—"

"He got it from you. You let him. You need to pay more attention, girl. Especially around that one."

"In other words, keep my distance."

"Never said that. Men like Gabriel have their uses. You just need to keep your eyes open and your hand on your wallet."

Thunder cracked. Lightning split the sky. When I looked up, the clouds had rolled in again.

"Huh, looks like we're getting a storm," she said.

She stood and walked to the door, then waved impatiently at her chair. I folded it and carried it inside just as the downpour started.

# CHAPTER NINETEEN

I returned to my apartment only to realize there was nothing for me there. No food, no drink, and most urgently, no cleaning products. So I waited for a break in the rain, then jogged to the grocery store a block over. I spent an hour there. Ten minutes to grab basic foodstuffs. Fifty minutes reading every freaking label in the cleaning supply section to figure out what I needed.

After three hours of scrubbing, I collapsed onto the bed . . . only to realize I'd left sheets off my shopping list. I managed to struggle to my feet, considered the likelihood that any shop in town was still open, and fell back onto the bare mattress.

I woke on a rocky plain. Bitter wind whipped my hair into my eyes. A salty mist sprinkled my face, but I couldn't see or hear the ocean, just looked out over an endless dark field of fog and rock and gnarled trees.

I shivered and wrapped my arms around myself. I was barefoot and dressed only in a thin shift, the wind cutting through it as if it was nothing.

Someone raced past me and I caught a glimpse of a girl with long blond hair before she disappeared into the swirling mist. I took a few tentative steps across the ice-cold rock and damp moss, and I saw her there, still shadowy against the darkness but turned now, watching me. She didn't speak or smile, just waited until I drew close, then ran into the fog again, only to stop and wait until I got closer.

"Where are we going?" I asked.

My voice echoed. She lifted a finger to her lips, then scampered off.

At last I stepped through the fog to see her crouched in the middle of a mist-shrouded circle of misshapen dead trees.

I looked around. Did I know this place?

Familiar yet unfamiliar.

Same with the girl.

I walked over. She was throwing something onto the ground, like jacks. The mist curled around her face, shrouding it.

When she saw me, she nodded solemnly and moved back, as if to give me room. I walked over and bent down. She picked up what looked like a stubby piece of wood and held it out.

"I don't know how to play," I said.

"Yes, you do."

"No, I'm sorry, I—"

"Shhh. Don't wake them."

"Who?"

When she said nothing, I looked around, but saw only the gnarled, fog-misted trees. I started to rise. She caught my hand and tried to tug me down.

"They're resting," she said.

"Who's resting?"

The croak of a raven answered. I looked over my shoulder to see one perched on a branch, pecking at the pale bark. The girl leapt to her feet and waved her arms.

"Shoo! You aren't supposed to be here."

The raven fixed her with one beady eye and croaked in protest, but took flight, soaring off over our heads.

The girl sat again and threw her sticks, and I saw that the sticks were bones. Polished white finger bones.

White bones against black rock.

Black rock on the edge of a pit filled with murky water, stinking like a swamp. More rocks piled above it. A waterfall. A *dry* waterfall.

My garden.

The raven swooped past. The girl waved her fist at it. *"Ewch i ffwrdd, bran!"*

She turned to me. "The *bran* know better," she said. "They aren't to disturb the dead. It's disrespectful."

"The dead?"

She waved at the tree and the mist began to clear, as if swept away, and I saw that the gnarled trunk wasn't a trunk at all. It was a corpse. Bound to a dead tree, arms spread, naked and bald, empty eye sockets, skin an oddly marbled red and white.

Then the last of the mist cleared and I saw the marble surface wasn't skin. There was no skin.

I stumbled back and wheeled to see that every tree was the crucifix for a flayed corpse. That's when I started to scream.

I woke up still screaming. I clapped my hands over my mouth and huddled there, heart pounding as I strained for any sign that I'd woken up the whole building. But all stayed silent.

When I closed my eyes, I saw the corpses again. I saw those horrible, flayed bodies and a half-remembered rumor about the Larsens surfaced.

I vaulted from bed and made it as far as the bathroom door before hurling my last meal onto the freshly scrubbed tiles.

I returned to bed but couldn't get back to sleep. Each time I closed my eyes, I saw that raw muscle and sinew and—

I couldn't get back to sleep.

I called James. I couldn't help myself. But I did manage, halfway through dialing his number, to stop, think, and punch in his work number instead. He wouldn't be there. That was the point. I listened to his voice message, hung up, called back, and listened again, feeling my heart rate slow, the dream fading into wisps that floated away as he asked me again to leave a message. That time I did. Just a brief, "Hey, wanted to let you know I'm okay. Hope you got the car."

*Hope you got the car.* I'd broken off our engagement. I'd thrown the ring at him and stolen his car and run into the night . . . and that was the best I could come up with? Yes, it was.

While hearing James's recorded voice helped, I still couldn't sleep. Finally I broke down and took a pill. That only made things worse. Now I dozed in twilight sleep, dreams and hallucinations rolling into an endless drama. I'd see those bodies in my room, hanging from the walls, lying on the bed, sitting up and talking to me.

Then I'd see the Larsens. But I wasn't seeing them with the corpses. It might have been better if I did. Instead I dreamed of them, laughing and teasing and singing, scooping me up and holding me tight and making me feel . . . wonderful. In Pamela Larsen's arms, I felt something I never felt in my own mother's awkward embraces. I felt adored.

It was those images that sent me back to the bathroom, over and over, until I gave up on going back to bed and just huddled on the floor, the cool tile against my cheek. Lying there, I tried to force the two images together—my birth parents and the flayed corpses. I tried to imagine them in that grove, as if the image would freeze and shatter those warm memories. But no matter how hard I tried, my brain refused to insert the Larsens into that scene.

When dawn's light finally flooded through the glazed window, the nightmare dreams fluttered away and instead I saw that newspaper headline: *"A Mother's Desperate Jailhouse Plea."* I saw that and I knew I had to see her.

No, I had to *face* her.

She'd helped my father murder eight young men and women. My brain knew it. My gut refused to agree.

I now realized I'd locked away memories of a happy childhood, but I wasn't sure if they were real memories or the inventions of a miserable, abused child. I had to face my past, which meant facing my biological parents. Or at least the one who'd reached out.

First, though, I needed to know exactly what they'd done. No more nightmares based on half-remembered stories. I needed facts. I got ready, then realized the library wouldn't be open yet. I couldn't stomach the thought of breakfast, so I just lay on the bed for another hour, haunted by my dreams, worried about my future.

When I opened my apartment door, I halted. Then I tried to figure out what had stopped me. A sound? A smell? A flicker of movement?

I looked down the hall. Three closed apartment doors, plus the stairwell. I inhaled. Just the faint smell of pine cleaner. I listened. Nothing. Really nothing—that church hush I'd noticed yesterday still enveloped the corridor. It was strange, actually, the silence and the peace, when I was so accustomed to the usual assault on my senses. While I still noticed smells and sounds, they didn't seem to have the same effect on me here in Cainsville. I could say it was like the other day in Chicago, when I'd been too shocked to notice anything, but this felt different. Like stepping off a busy street into a library. Maybe it was just the difference of small town life.

But something *had* caught my attention out here. I stood there, feet on the lintel, unable to step into the hall.

I looked down. There was something on the floor, just outside my doorway. Some kind of dark gray powder, almost hidden on the hardwood. I bent. Scattered powder.

No, not scattered. It seemed to form lines. A pattern?

I rubbed the back of my neck. Then, after a glance down the hall, to be sure no one was watching, I hunkered down with my face almost to the floor, trying to get a better look. It might be lines. It might even be a pattern. Or I might be an idiot, prostrate on the floor, staring at dropped cigarette ash.

The more I stared, the more certain I became that it was ash. I could even detect a faint smoky smell.

I shook my head, went back into the apartment, and grabbed my brand-new dustpan and broom. I swept up the ash, dumped it, and headed off to the library.


The Internet confirmed that the Larsens had killed four couples. One was dating, two were engaged, one married. All were in their early twenties.

The Larsens themselves were only twenty-six when they'd been arrested. They'd been born on the same date, in the same Chicago hospital, delivered by the same obstetrician. The media had made much of that coincidence. I don't know why. It only meant that their mothers had met in the maternity ward and become friends, so Pamela and Todd grew up together. To hear the tabloids tell it, though, you'd think some nurse had injected them with Serial Killer Serum in their cribs. Or practiced satanic rites on them while their mothers slept.

Speaking of satanic rites . . .

Normally, when couples kill, it's about sex. Brady and Hindley, the Gallegos, the Bernardos . . . Torture and rape and murder as a cure for the common sex life. But none of the Larsens' victims had been sexually assaulted. All the indignities committed on the bodies had occurred postmortem. Eventually, the experts came to realize these weren't sex murders. They were ritual sacrifices. What kind of ritual? Well, that had been a little less clear. It still was.

There were five elements of the murders identified as ritualistic. An unknown symbol carved into each thigh. Another symbol painted on the stomach with woad, a plant-based blue dye. A twig of mistletoe piercing the symbol on the women's stomachs. A stone in the mouths. And a section of skin removed from each back—which was the part I'd vaguely remembered hearing about and had mentally exaggerated into the flayed corpses of my nightmares.

There. I had the facts. Cold facts. My parents had brutally murdered eight people. And now, knowing that, I was going to see them.

I couldn't face the Larsens. Not wouldn't. *Couldn't.* There was, apparently, no way to get near either of them. Not right now.

At the library, I'd researched the prisons where they were being held according to old articles. Then I looked up the phone numbers, returned to the apartment, made the calls, and got the news. Three months ago, Todd Larsen had been transferred to an undisclosed prison for an undisclosed security reason. I told the officials I was his daughter. The bored clerk on the other end replied that I was welcome to fill out the required forms to establish that, and if approved, they'd tell me where he was being held. Then I'd need to contact that prison, fill out more forms, complete a background check, wait another month or two, and maybe, just maybe, be allowed to see him. When the clerk asked where to send the forms, I told her not to bother.

Then I called the facility holding Pamela Larsen to ask about visiting her and discovered that her visitation privileges had been revoked temporarily. When I asked how long that would last, I couldn't get a straight answer. The only contact she was allowed was with her lawyer—and apparently she hadn't hired one since firing Gabriel Walsh.

I decided to make breakfast. Then I realized I'd bought coffee and bread, but had no coffeemaker and nothing to put on toast. Back to the diner to eat, then.

When I reached the first floor, Grace was in the hall, lawn chair on her arm. Without a word, she handed it to me and marched ahead. Outside, I handed it back. She sniffed, clearly put out that I wasn't going to set it up for her. I softened the blow by saying, "I'm heading to the diner. Can I grab you a scone?"

"You ever go to the diner and don't get me one, you'll be looking for lodgings elsewhere, girl. I want a coffee, too. Cream and sugar. Bring the cream on the side or it'll make the coffee cold."

"The scone is my treat. The coffee I'm willing to get but not on my dime."

She muttered and rooted around in her pocket, then dropped coins into my palm.

# MICK AND MARGIE

Margie was not having a good morning. Margie had not had a good morning—or a good day—since 1993. That was the year she graduated from elementary school and left Cainsville. It'd been only temporary, hopping onto the bus for high school each morning and returning before dinner, but it had been enough.

At the time, she'd have said she changed for the better. Last week, she'd come across a stack of old yearbooks in her mother's attic, and she'd cringed as she leafed through the pages, seeing her thin face and sunken eyes. Worse was her expression. A defiant smirk. And the messages her "friends" wrote? None that she'd want her young nieces and nephews to read.

Margie—rechristened Mick in high school—had been voted most likely to end up dead. Her best friend, Nathalie—rechristened Nate—was "most likely to end up in jail." Their schoolmates got the prophecies right; they'd just mixed them up. By twenty, Nathalie was dead of an overdose. A year later, Margie was in jail.

She got fifteen years for knifing the girl who'd sold Nathalie the drugs. It sounded good—avenging a friend. Eventually that helped her get parole from a sympathetic board. The truth, one she only admitted to herself, was that she hadn't knifed the bitch for Nathalie. She'd just wanted free dope.

She'd been out for two years now. Clean for nine. But life hadn't rewarded her turnaround. She supposed she still hadn't earned it. After eighteen months of trying to make it in Chicago, she'd come home to Cainsville at the insistence of her family. A new guy owned the diner. An ex-con. He would cut her some slack and give her a job. And she'd be home.

Home.

This may have been home once. In prison, she used to lie in her cot and dream of Cainsville the way others dreamed of Hawaii and Acapulco. Paradise.

Only she'd soiled her paradise years ago. Shit on it every chance she'd gotten, and people here had long memories. When she came back, they didn't see the new Margie. They only saw the kid who'd broken into their homes, threatened little kids in their park, stolen cars from their driveways.

It'd been the dope—she'd needed money for more and had been too stoned to care what she did to get it. That didn't matter. She'd made them lock their doors. She'd made them call their children in before dark.

They'd get past it, her mother said. Margie just had to hang in there.

She could. She would.

If only the universe would see fit to recognize her efforts and give her a break.

Being a waitress had seemed easy enough. There was a learning curve, and she expected that. What she didn't expect was that she seemed incapable of getting around that curve. No matter how hard she tried, things were always going wrong. Plates dropped when she was sure she had them balanced. Cream curdled weeks before the sell-by date. Salt turned up in

the sugar dispensers even when she'd taste-tested it before
putting them out.

Then there was the nurse. After her mother's hip replacement
last month, they'd hired someone to come in while Margie was
at work—it cost almost as much as Margie made, but it kept her
job safe. The damned woman phoned her several times a shift.
Margie had complained to the agency, but they had no one else
within commuting distance. So she was trying to keep the calls
as short as possible.

And speaking of unwanted interruptions . . .

"Margie," Patrick called as she came out from behind the
counter, weighted down with plates. He lifted his empty mug.

She pretended not to see him. Damned parasite. Took up one
of the best tables for hours every day. And what did he buy in
return? A single cup of coffee. She wasn't even sure he paid for
it. She'd tried to give him a check her first day on the job, and
Larry came roaring out of the kitchen so fast you'd have thought
his shorts were on fire. He'd snatched it from her and said
Patrick paid monthly for his coffee.

Like hell.

Patrick had something over Larry, something that made the
poor guy break into a sweat when Margie suggested they kick
him out if he didn't buy food.

Larry didn't deserve that, and she wasn't putting up with it.
She wouldn't jump to refill his coffee every time he raised his
mug. If they were lucky, Patrick would get the hint and take his
damned novel to the coffee shop. Isn't that where writers were
supposed to work?

Until then, she'd just keep ignoring him and otherwise do her
best. Because she couldn't afford to lose this job, not when she
was so close to turning her life around.

# CHAPTER TWENTY

As I walked into the diner, the first people I saw were the elderly couple from the day before. Ida and Walter.

"Thank you for yesterday," Ida said, giving my arm a pat. "I had my silk blouse outside. The rain would have ruined it."

"Any more predictions?" Walter asked. "I'm taking the boat out tomorrow. Hate to drive all the way to the lake and have the weather turn on me."

He smiled when he said it, but the look in his eyes was dead serious. Across the aisle, two old ladies leaned closer, listening.

"No predictions today," I said. "I don't even know why I said that yesterday. Just a hunch, I guess."

"Hunch?" one of the women called over, loud enough to make me wince. "That's no hunch. You read the signs. Some people can."

Ida nodded. "There are always signs, dear. You just need to pay attention." She moved over in the booth. "Come sit with us. Don't worry. We won't pester you for any more predictions."

As I was sitting, the would-be novelist caught my eye and lifted his coffee cup. I hesitated. There was no sign of the server, but he was closer to the coffee station than I was. He could damned well get his own refill. And yet . . . Well, he gave me this feeling that said ignoring him would be . . . unwise. I wouldn't mind a job here, so showing my willingness to work wasn't a bad thing.

I got the pot and filled his cup.

"Looking for a tip today?" he said.

"Sure."

He leaned over, voice lowering. "Larry's in a foul mood. Breakfast isn't even over and Margie's already dropped two plates, including the one for Peter Marks, which landed on his lap, right before he took off for a big meeting in Chicago. Marks is the landlord—gives Larry a good deal on the place. Larry said if she screws up again, she's gone. And he just might mean it this time."

"Thanks."

He lifted his mug. "Quid pro quo."

I filled a cup for myself and took it back to Ida and Walter's table. I looked around for Margie—I was starving—but there was still no sign of her.

"I hear you met Gabriel Walsh," Walter said as I sat.

I nodded and took a wild guess. "Someone said he's a local? Or he used to be."

"Oh, yes," Ida said. "But Gabriel himself never lived here. His momma did. Moved out when she was just a young one herself."

I'd heard of towns where you were considered local if you were born there, but this seemed a little extreme. As I poured creamer into my coffee, I could hear Larry tearing a strip off someone in the kitchen. Margie, I presumed. The novelist was right.

I unwrapped my napkin-wrapped cutlery for a spoon to stir my coffee. Only a fork and a knife fell out. I lifted the knife.

*Stir with a knife,*
*Stir up strife.*

I hesitated. I glanced at Ida and Walter, but they were engrossed in their conversation. I glanced at the kitchen doors and started to put the knife down.

No, that was silly.

And even if it wasn't, I shouldn't . . .

I lifted the knife again and gave my coffee a quick stir. As I laid it down, I noticed the novelist watching me, his eyes dancing. I turned back to Ida and Walter, and I was about to say something when a construction worker rose, a twenty in his hand.

"Where's that girl?" He peered toward the kitchen. "Margie!"

She came out bearing a tray of steaming plates. A couple across the diner looked up expectantly. She nodded and moved a little faster. As she rounded the corner to our aisle, Ida's cane fell. It didn't drop with a clatter, just silently slid to the floor.

Margie didn't notice. No one seemed to notice. Margie was heading straight for it. I looked around. The writer caught my gaze. He looked at the cane, then back at me, smiling slightly, as if in challenge.

I glanced at Margie. Her expression was determined, but her nostrils were flared, her eyes a little too wide. Anxious. Exhausted, too, if the circles under her eyes were any indication.

I took another swig of coffee and lifted the menu. I thought I heard the writer chuckle. I didn't, of course—he was too far away and the clatter of plates and murmur of voices would have drowned him out.

Margie tripped over the cane. Not just a stumble, but a full-out sprawl that sent the plates crashing to the floor, oatmeal splattering everywhere, including on the two diners who'd been awaiting their breakfasts.

Larry ran from the back, apologizing as he handed the customers damp towels and promised to cover dry cleaning. Margie picked herself up, babbling about the cane. I quietly slid from the booth and cleared away the broken bowls and plates.

"You're fired," Larry said, spinning on Margie. "Go on. Get your things. I'll send over your last check."

"It wasn't my fault," she protested.

"It never is. Get out."

She started to say something else, but a glare from Larry shut her up, and she slunk away. Larry bent to help me with the broken dishes. "You still looking for a job, miss?"

Larry needed me to start right away. Fortunately, it was only until lunch, when the other server—Susie—could take over. I say "fortunately" because, while I may have been able to draft funding proposals and counsel abused women and prepare keynote speeches, when it came to taking orders and serving tables I was about as competent as your average five-year-old. Maybe less.

I took it slow and steady, not carrying too much, and writing down every order—complete with a numbered map of tables and descriptions of the diners—so I wouldn't screw up. Luckily the breakfast rush was over before I began. Otherwise I might have been on the street competing with Margie for employment.

I took Grace back an extra-large steaming coffee and two scones. I returned her money, because I'd been late, but she still grumbled.

What she didn't mention—and I'm sure she knew—was that I'd had a visitor. I opened my door to find a business card slipped under it. On the back, in thick strokes, someone had written: "In case you misplaced the last one."

I turned it over. Gabriel Walsh. I tossed the card into the trash with the first and headed into the apartment. I sat at the dinette and took out the notes I'd made at the library—the list of things I needed to compile to apply for permission to learn where the prison system had stashed Todd Larsen.

It was not a short list.

I thought of spending months waiting for the forms and background checks. Months of nightmares, bureaucratic and otherwise. And what if, after all that, Todd Larsen refused to see me?

Pamela was an hour away, and she did want to see me. There had to be a way.

I glanced down the hall at the wastepaper basket, walked over, and took out Gabriel Walsh's card.

A suitably sultry voice answered his office phone. I gave my name, and she checked to see if Mr. Walsh was in. Given that Grace said he was the only lawyer at his firm, one wouldn't think she'd need to check, but she came back to tell me he was out. She would relay the message.

Twenty minutes later he returned my call. His timing was perfect—long enough so he didn't seem too eager, not so long that I might change my mind about speaking to him.

"I'd like to reconsider your offer," I said. "I'm still not convinced it's something I'm prepared to do but . . . I'll hear you out."

"How about dinner?"

"Actually, before we talk, there's something I'd like you to do for me."

He didn't hesitate, as if reciprocity was to be expected. "What might that be?"

"I want to see my mother."

It couldn't have been easy to get permission, because two hours passed before I heard from him again. I suppose I should have felt guilty—making him do all this when I had no intention of reconsidering his offer. But as Grace said, men like Gabriel could be useful. And I was sure he wouldn't hesitate to use me, too.

# CHAPTER TWENTY-ONE

Gabriel had offered to pick me up, but while I could ill afford a taxi, I wasn't spending an hour alone in a car with him. My cab was coming at three. I quickly showered and changed.

Before I stepped into the hall, I checked for powder at my door. I don't know why I bothered. It wasn't as if the stuff was going to mess up my dark pumps. But something compelled me to check, so I did.

Nothing. Still, I stepped over the spot. As I did, I heard a girl's voice, raised in a singsong rhyme.

I looked down the hall. No kids. I hadn't seen any in the building. In fact, I hadn't seen much of anyone. Just a glimpse of a neighbor or two, ducking in or out, usually too quick for more than a "good day."

Children, though, were rarely so quiet, meaning I was pretty sure there weren't any living here. Something told me Grace wouldn't allow it. The girl must be outside then. As I started down the stairwell, though, I could hear a child skipping along a hallway below, the irregular *tap-tap* of little shoes as she sang.

> *Monday's child is fair of face,*
> *Tuesday's child is full of grace,*

"Wednesday's child is full of woe," I whispered, then stopped myself.

Well, at least it wasn't superstitious doggerel. Not really. As her voice faded, I struggled to remember the rest of the poem. Which one was Friday? That was my day. Loving and giving, wasn't it? Proof that it really was just a poem, considering what I'd done to Margie that morning.

When I reached the second floor, I could hear the tapping of the girl's shoes clearly as she skipped back my way.

I opened the hall door to pop my head in and say hello. The *tap-tap* came closer, her voice high and clear.

*Saturday's child works hard—*

The hall was empty.

I blinked and looked both ways. No girl. No singing. No skipping.

I backed into the stairwell again. Everything stayed quiet. I let the door close.

*And the child that is born on the Sabbath day*
*Is bonny and blithe, and good and gay.*

I yanked open the door just as the last word faded. I stepped into the hall and looked around. It was just like my corridor—a short one with two doors on each side, all four shut tight. I strained to pick up the sound of singing from any of the rooms, or coming through a window, but that churchlike hush blanketed everything.

I turned to go.

*"What's Thursday's child, Mommy?"*

I spun, the words still seeming to hang in the air. An empty hall stretched out in both directions.

*"Thursday's child has far to go,"* a woman's voice answered.

*"That's me!"* the girl giggled. *"I have far to go."*

The woman laughed. *"You do indeed, my Eden. You do indeed."*

I hurried into the stairwell.

I made it to the front door, grabbed the handle and was about to push it open when I was yanked by . . .

Gabriel Walsh. He was opening the door, one hand on the knob, the other on his sunglasses. Seeing me, he left his glasses on and stepped back to wave me out.

I took a moment to regain my composure before looking up at him. "I told you I didn't need a ride."

"No, you said you didn't want one. Considering the cost of a fare and the fact that you're apparently working as a waitress"—did I imagine it or did his lips twitch?—"I decided you do need it."

"I have a cab coming." The only vehicle in sight was his Jag, purring in front of the building.

"I told him you wouldn't be needing his services." He closed the door behind me. "Our appointment is at four. That's the latest I could make it."

In other words, ride with him or don't go at all. Damn him.

I looked up. He hadn't gotten any smaller. I'm not usually intimidated by men of any size, but those sunglasses made me anxious. Silly, I know, but unsettling all the same. As was the hint of a smile on the visible part of his face. Amused? Mocking? Insolent? I couldn't tell without having his eyes to complete the picture.

He reached into his suit pocket, took out his cell phone, and handed it to me.

"You can put 911 on speed dial."

Okay, definitely mocking.

He steered me toward the car. "If it makes you feel better, you can call the CPD and ask about me. You won't hear anything flattering, but they'll admit I've never been accused of assaulting anyone." A pause as he opened the passenger door for me. "Well, not any clients."

I slid into the cool interior. The sharp smell of new leather and strains of Bach swirled around me. As Gabriel got in, I braced myself for the sales pitch, but he only turned up the stereo and roared from the curb.

He didn't say a word for the first half of the trip, which was good because, considering how fast he drove, I really preferred he kept his attention on the road. When he whipped past a cruiser, I glanced in the rearview mirror.

"We're fine," he said. "I drive this route regularly. They used to pull me over, but it got tedious. Now I offer a generous contribution to their annual fund-raiser, and we call it even."

"Nice."

"Efficient."

We fell back into silence.

Zooming along the highway, I managed to close my eyes and soon realized I was enjoying the rumble of the road beneath me, the sensual perfection of Bach coming from the car's stereo, the rich smell of fine leather. I also realized I felt safe for the first time in four days. Cocooned in a world I knew.

"Safe" probably wasn't the right word to use with a man like Gabriel in the driver's seat, but even he seemed to add to the ambience, like a tacit chauffeur who could play bodyguard in a pinch.

He didn't speak until we were within sight of the prison gates. Then he pulled onto the shoulder and sat there, hands on the wheel, gaze forward, car idling.

Now it was coming. The sales pitch, delivered before we passed those gates. Damn. I'd gotten so close, too.

After a moment, he said, "What do you know about Pamela Larsen, Ms. Jones?"

"Olivia, please."

He glanced over then. Even if I couldn't see his eyes, I knew the look—telling me he wasn't falling for that. This was all business, and if I was being friendly, I had an ulterior motive.

"Olivia, then," he said. "What do you remember of your mother?"

"A week ago, I'd have said nothing. But I've been remembering things. I'm not sure if they're real."

"And you want to see if she's what you remember?"

"I want to face her."

"Face her." He rolled the words out, considering them. "Yes, I suppose so."

"You think I shouldn't?"

"That wouldn't be in my best interests." He swung the car back onto the road. "And clearly you are resolved on the matter."

Gabriel said nothing as he parked. Nor as we got out of the car. He just silently steered me in the right direction.

Having him beside me was a comfort as I approached the looming jail. Again, I knew that was silly. I was hardly in danger of being jumped by rioting prisoners. But right or wrong, as I listened to the distant clang and imagined a cell opening, imagined Pamela Larsen coming out to meet me, having a silent monolith at my side did make me feel better.

As we approached the doors, I said, "You asked what I know about her. Is there something you want to tell me?"

He said nothing. I thought he was considering, but we went through two doors and he didn't say another word.

"If there's something I should know about her, I'd like to hear it."

He made a noise in his throat, as if he preferred to keep silent on the subject but couldn't quite bring himself to say there was nothing I should know. I glanced over, in the vain hope of seeing an actual expression. Instead, I forgot what I'd been asking.

He must have taken off his sunglasses when we'd come in. To say he had blue eyes sounds so innocuous that I'm reluctant even to name the color. They were ice. Not cool in that sexy way that sends delicious shivers down your spine. I mean cold. Completely and utterly cold.

The irises were such an unnaturally pale blue that for a second I thought they weren't real. Couldn't be real. They must be colored contacts meant to throw a prosecutor or reluctant witness off balance. But this wasn't the kind of color you could get from contacts.

The edges of the irises were dark. Blue, I suppose, but I didn't look close enough to be sure. The impression I got was of black rings around pale irises. Black lashes, too, so thick and long that they should have been gorgeous frames to a pair of remarkable eyes. They weren't. The contrast between the dark pupils, the dark lashes, and those odd dark rings set against the pale irises and whites was too unsettling.

Dear God, was I crazy? This might be the most terrifying thing I'd ever done in my life, and the only person I had for support was this man? This complete stranger I couldn't even look in the eyes?

"Yes?" he said.

"Nothing."

I let him take the lead.

# CHAPTER TWENTY-TWO

Getting inside took a while. Finally they escorted us to a room with a table and three chairs.

I paused inside the doorway. "So she'll just . . . come in here?"

"Is that a problem?" Gabriel asked as he headed for a chair.

"No, I just thought there'd be a barrier."

He turned those cold eyes on me. I must have flinched. I saw it on his face, and I was sure what would come next. A look of amusement for a reaction he must get all the time. But his brows drew together in a frown, as if he didn't understand why I'd pulled back. Then he turned away and sat before he said, "Would you *like* a barrier?"

"No. I just . . ."

"Expected more security for a woman convicted of horrifically murdering eight people? If it was your father, yes, you'd never get so close to him. But in situations like this, the woman is seen as the lesser threat."

"Bullied and pushed by the real killer. She's the weak partner."

"Weak . . ." He rolled the word out, tasting it.

"I don't mean—"

"No, I understand. You're correct. The woman is always seen as the follower."

"And is—?" I began.

When I didn't finish, he looked over. "Hmm?"

"Never mind."

He waved me to a chair. "They do still take precautions. She'll be cuffed and allowed no physical contact."

"Good."

I took my seat. Then we waited. He kept looking over at me, and it wasn't in any way a woman likes to be looked at by a man. His gaze was impersonal, yet all too personal, too probing, too intense. I told myself he was just concerned that I'd break down and, God forbid, he might have to deal with it. But it felt as if my every twitch was being studied and evaluated.

It didn't help that there wasn't even a poster I could pretend to read. Just a stark, white room that smelled of chemicals and body odor. Overhead, a fan turned, catching on each revolution. I'm sure I jumped with every click. I'm equally sure Gabriel noticed. I wanted to leap up and shout, "Yes, I'm nervous. In fact, I'm about five seconds away from hurling my lunch onto the floor, so stop looking at me like that or if I do hurl it, I'll aim for your lap."

That made me smile. He noticed and arched his dark brows. I met his gaze. It wasn't easy, but it gave me something to do. Look him straight in those cold eyes and don't back down until—

The door opened. I jumped. Gabriel stood, partly blocking my view.

A guard entered first. Then a woman. No, not just a woman. Pamela Larsen. My *mother*.

After hearing how much I looked like her, I was braced to see a face that would ensure I wasn't going to regain my comfort with a mirror anytime soon. She was shorter than me by a couple of inches. Heavier, too, almost plump. Dark, gray-laced hair to her shoulders. Eyes of an indeterminate blue-green shade. Maybe there was a resemblance, but I didn't see a carbon copy of myself.

What did I see?

My mother.

I recognized her. I felt a leap in my gut, the burst of joy that a two-year-old might feel. I felt it, and I disowned it. Looked away and shut down that part of myself, hard and fast.

She hadn't noticed me yet as her gaze fixed on Gabriel. That made it easier.

"Gabriel," she said. "I should have known." She stepped closer. "Are you trying to get your money again? You scammed me, you bastard. You stole my appeal, and you expect me to pay you? The fact I didn't gouge out your eyes with your gold pen should prove I'm innocent."

She turned to the guard. "Take me back. We're done here."

"Oh, I don't think you want to do that, Pamela," Gabriel said. "I brought someone to see you."

"I don't care who—"

Gabriel stepped aside. She stopped. Her cuffed hands flew to her mouth.

"Oh." She inhaled. She rushed toward me, but the second guard yanked her back.

She spun on the woman. "That's my daughter, you heartless bitch. My little girl."

"You know the rules, Pamela."

She pulled away from the guard's grip, but made no move to come closer.

"Eden," she breathed.

"It's Olivia."

She flinched. "Yes, of course. I'm sorry. Olivia. Look at you. So beautiful."

That voice. Dear God, that voice.

*Thursday's child has far to go.*

Was the rest of it from her, too? All the rhymes and superstition I couldn't pry from my brain? Not from some long forgotten nanny. From Pamela Larsen.

And what else? Forget the silly rhymes. What else had she taught me? How much more of *me* came from her? How much of *me* was a lie? Even something as simple as my birthday was obviously false.

*Thursday's child has far to go.*

Pamela had turned to Gabriel.

"I'd like to speak to my daughter alone."

"You know that isn't possible," he said.

"I don't know how you tricked her into coming here, but if you made her pay you a dime—"

"She didn't even contribute gas money. She asked to see you, and I thought it might be a good opportunity to remind you of my outstanding bill."

She turned back to me. "You asked to see me?"

Did I imagine it or did Gabriel wince? I opened my mouth to say it wasn't exactly like that, but her face glowed and a little girl inside me basked in the radiance, and wouldn't—couldn't— do anything to bring back the shadows.

Damn. It wasn't supposed to be like this.

I took a deep breath and straightened. "We'll be fine, Mr. Walsh. Thank you."

He nodded and went to stand by the door. Pamela shot him a look, but he only glanced at me, brows arching to ask "Is this okay?" I nodded.

"You are so beautiful, E—Olivia," Pamela said. "Your father would—" Her hands flew to her mouth again, head dropping, eyes squeezed shut. "I wish he could see you. He'd be so happy. So proud."

She took a moment to compose herself as the guards ushered us to the table. I could feel Gabriel's gaze on me, but didn't look over.

"The Joneses have treated you well?" she said after a moment.

"My parents have been great."

She flinched at "parents" and I felt a pang of sympathy, as hard as I tried to fight it.

"Tell me about yourself," she said. "Your life."

I managed to give her a brief biographical sketch, the kind I'd provide a stranger. When I finished, she leaned forward, her cuffed hands reaching across the table.

A throat-clearing from the guard stopped her short, but she stayed bent forward as she lowered her voice and said, "I know this is a huge shock for you. They—they tell me you didn't even realize you were adopted."

"That's right."

"So you don't . . . remember us?"

"No."

The grief on her face cut through me and I wanted to say I did remember her, snatches of memories, good memories. I clamped my mouth shut and struggled to keep my face as expressionless as possible.

She leaned toward me a little more. "We didn't murder those young couples, Olivia. If you remember anything about us, you know we didn't."

I glanced at Gabriel. I didn't mean to. His face gave nothing away, but I knew what he was thinking. My parents had been convicted by a jury of their peers. They'd lost their first appeal and several subsequent attempts. Was I desperate enough—foolish enough—to entertain even the slightest doubt of their guilt?

"I'm sorry," I said. "I didn't come here to . . ."

I couldn't finish that. What would I say? *I came here because I already know you're a monster and I needed to see you so I could believe that in my heart, too. Except now . . .*

It wasn't supposed to be like this.

I looked at her and the temperature in the tiny room seemed to jump twenty degrees. A bead of sweat trickled down my cheek and I had to struggle for breath.

I got to my feet. "I need . . . I have to step outside."

Pamela leapt up. "No, please, E—Olivia. I didn't mean—"

"I'll be back."

# CHAPTER TWENTY-THREE

Gabriel held open the door and I hurried out over Pamela's protests. Once I heard that door close behind me, I stopped, facing the corridor wall, breathing in and out.

I was smarter than this. I knew she was guilty. I wanted to come here and feel that, and instead the doubt had crept from my heart to my head.

"Oh God."

My hands flew up. I had a mental flash of Pamela's hands going to her mouth and yanked mine away.

I'd lived with her for the first few years of my life. When I'd seen her, there'd been no doubt how I'd once felt about Pamela Larsen. How much of her had I absorbed? How much did I still unknowingly emulate?

"Stop. Just stop," I muttered, then wheeled and found Gabriel right behind me.

"Oh," I said.

He didn't speak. Just stood there, as if patiently waiting for me to finish my breakdown.

After a moment of silence, he said, "Would you like to . . . ?" and waved to a chair down the hall.

"No, I'm okay."

"Take a moment then."

"Really, I'm fine. She's just not . . ."

"What you expected."

"Not what I wanted."

"Ah." Another nod.

We stood there for a minute, then I said, "She thinks you ruined her appeal chances on purpose, doesn't she?"

"Yes."

"Did you?"

"That wouldn't be in my best interests."

"So why does she think it?"

He shrugged. "I didn't win."

"But you gave it your best shot."

I expected another brow arch, to say of course he had, but he just stood there, cold eyes betraying nothing.

*So what should I do?* I wanted to ask. The impulse shamed me. Yet I suddenly felt very young and very lost and very confused. And Gabriel Walsh happened to be the only person here.

"Yes?" he said.

I shook my head. "I should get back in there."

"If you like."

He didn't move, as if to say the choice was mine. We could still leave, despite my promise to return. I could run. Hide. Refuse to hear anything else she had to say.

I took a deep breath and said, "I'm ready."


"I'd like you to do me a favor, Olivia," Pamela said after I sat down again.

I tensed.

"I have a list of names. People who might be interested in fighting for a new appeal for your father and me."

"Lawyers."

She shot a pointed look at Gabriel. "We're done with lawyers. We need help from someone less opportunistic. It's a list of journalists and organizations who might be willing to take up our cause."

"Nonprofit organizations?" I said carefully. "Like the Innocence Project?"

"Not them specifically. They only deal with wrongful convictions based on DNA. But nonprofit, yes. Specifically, the Center on Wrongful Convictions out of Northwestern, but I've listed some national organizations as well. I'd never ask you to spend a penny on us, Olivia. You've already lost too much by being our daughter. I'm not even asking you to plead our case with these people. Just to pass along the information."

"Is there something specific you need them to look at? That's how it works, isn't it? There needs to be a specific problem with the conviction."

Another glance at Gabriel. "It seems my daughter knows more about law than some who've passed the bar." She turned back to me. "Yes, I have something specific for them. The murder of Peter Evans and Jan Gunderson."

Niles Gunderson's daughter. An image of the old man flashed in my memory, his eyes wild with crazed grief.

She continued, "There's a reason we couldn't have done it, which was overruled because of the other evidence that tied the cases together. It goes both ways, though. Prove us innocent of this crime and the other evidence will be called into question. A house of cards. Pull out one and the rest topples." She leaned forward. "Can you do that for me, Olivia? Just pass on the case to these people? I've tried, but it's so difficult contacting anyone from in here."

I had to hold every muscle tight to keep from glancing at Gabriel for his opinion. I didn't want to do anything for her. I shouldn't. And yet, if these people could prove her innocent . . .

If she could *be* innocent. Yet I shouldn't think that. Shouldn't dare to hope that.

For at least two minutes, I couldn't answer, mired in doubt and fear. But then I realized it wasn't about hoping she was innocent. It was about doing whatever it took to be sure that the jury had made the right decision, beyond doubt—reasonable or otherwise.

"Yes," I said.

I wrote down the names of the organizations she wanted me to contact. Then our visiting time ended.

Before Pamela was taken back to her cell, she told Gabriel she'd transfer five thousand to his account, in partial payment of her bill. Each time he brought me to visit—of my own free will—she'd add another five thousand.

I could tell he didn't like that. It was money owed to him, not payment for playing escort. But he agreed.

"Now I'd like a moment alone with my daughter," she said.

The guard cleared her throat.

"You don't count. I was talking to him. Out of the room this time."

Gabriel adjusted his cuffs and leaned back in his chair.

"I'd like you to leave, Gabriel."

"Yes, I'm sure you would. And I will next time. If the five thousand has found its way into my account."

She glowered at him. Then she looked at me. I got to my feet. He stood then, too, and waited, expressionless.

Before I could step away, she rose. Her fingers brushed my wrist. I jumped. Gabriel moved forward so smoothly I didn't notice until he was between us, his hand at my back, barely touching the fabric as he steered me toward the door, murmuring, "We should go."

"You won't keep me from her, Gabriel Walsh," Pamela said.

Her voice was low. I didn't turn to see her expression. I wasn't sure I wanted to.

"I don't intend to," Gabriel said. "But, sadly, our time is done today. I'll leave my account number at the front, so you can transfer the money."

"I have it."

"I'll leave it anyway. To ensure there's no mistake."

I said good-bye then and he ushered me out the door.

Before we'd gone into the prison, I'd told myself I'd call a cab for the ride home. No matter what the cost, I wasn't riding with Gabriel. But by the time we did leave . . . ?

I didn't call the cab.

Gabriel Walsh was a manipulative bastard who would screw me over if he saw profit in it. But he was also, as Grace said, useful.

In the car, I said, "You're certain she's guilty, aren't you?"

"I have no opinion on the matter either way."

"Bullshit."

He looked over.

"You were her lawyer. You must have an opinion."

He pushed the ignition button. "The fact that I defended her explains exactly why I have no opinion. You want me to say I'm certain she's guilty so you can forget about her. I won't do that. Nor will I say I believe she's innocent and raise false hopes. Whatever you decide, Olivia, I'm not taking any responsibility for it."

My cheeks warmed. I cleared my throat. "About your offer, the book deal . . ."

He pulled out of the parking space. "You have no intention of entertaining my offer. You never did. You simply needed a way into that prison."

"I—"

"Don't deny it. Worse, don't apologize. I was the only way in, and I wanted something from you, so you used that."

"So why did you agree?"

"For the same reason I'd take a reluctant client to dinner. Laying the groundwork. In the meantime, five thousand dollars was an acceptable fee for my afternoon."

"Even if it's already your money?"

"Money that I'm unlikely to see otherwise."

When we reached the highway, I said, "There's something else I'd like. Access to your files on my mother's case. Not just the official record of the appeal, but your complete file."

"A lawyer is not permitted—"

"I'll pay."

He glanced at me.

"You heard Pamela. She wants me to pass her case on. Reasonably then, one could presume she meant for me to see the file."

"I doubt that."

"But it was open to interpretation, and the guard overheard her ask me, so an innocent mistake could be made."

He'd put his shades back on, but I could feel the weight of his stare.

I continued, "I'll pay you for your time to discuss the file with me. Or for a consultation, during which you could be called out on business and inadvertently leave it on the table."

"As amused as I am by option two, the first is preferable. Now let's discuss my fee."

# CHAPTER TWENTY-FOUR

Gabriel's price was reasonable. He knew I could get most of the information from the court documents, and I would, if necessary, but I was willing to pay for expediency and the opportunity to discuss it with him . . . which gave him another chance to woo me as a reluctant prospective client. He would return at ten the next morning, despite the fact it was a Saturday.

I needed to work at the diner that night. The regular shifts were seven to three and three to eleven, starting thirty minutes before the seven-thirty opening, then cleaning up for an hour after the diner closed at ten. The other weekday server, Susie, had a second job so Margie and Susie had arranged their schedules to accommodate it, meaning I could expect to be on an ever-changing mix of days and evenings and even split shifts, opening and closing. Today, because Susie had been called in early, I was due back at seven.

When I stepped out of the apartment building, I found Grace in her spot, glowering at the black cat, now perched on the gate pillar. The feline wasn't lowering itself to glaring back but simply sat there, yellow eyes fixed on her. I walked over to pet it.

"Don't encourage him," Grace snapped.

"But he's good luck."

I expected her to say no, a black cat was bad luck, but she only snorted. "Only good luck is his, if he cons you into letting him stay."

As I walked away, the cat followed, running along the top of the wrought-iron fence. It didn't meow or try to get my attention, just kept pace with me.

I took the shortcut through the park. When I was close enough to see the fountain, a long shadow slid over the cobblestones. I glanced up. It looked like a crow, but the shadow it cast was huge. A trick of the mind, I supposed. We don't have ravens in Illinois. But seeing it made me think of the dream with the flayed corpses and huge black birds.

I picked up my pace and the crow's shadow crossed me twice more. I squinted up, hand shielding my eyes against the sun. The bird was circling erratically. It seemed to be dodging something. Another bird, I presumed, until I realized it was darting away every time it flew too close to the bank's gargoyles.

I smiled. Nothing terribly sinister about a bird so stupid it couldn't tell real predators from stone ones.

"Kitty!"

I glanced over at the park. An elderly woman was putting fresh paint on the fence as a mother tried to convince her toddler that it was time to leave. The little girl had found a new excuse to linger—the cat. She was straining in her mother's grip, both arms reaching for the cat, which had zoomed onto a low branch and crouched there, watching the girl as if considering the potential mauling-to-affection ratio.

I was reaching to give the cat a reassuring pat when the girl screamed. The old woman gasped, and I turned as the raven swooped straight at me. My hands shot up. I saw two black blurs—the bird dropping and the cat leaping for it. The cat managed to claw the raven, but as it fell back to the ground, the bird swooped down and grabbed the cat in its talons. The cat's scream joined the child's. I ran and kicked the bird as hard as I could.

It dropped the cat, which started to run, but the bird flew after it. I went after the bird. It was huge, twice the size of the cat. When it dropped low enough, I kicked it again. The old woman shouted, and a rain of stones hit the bird.

It croaked and turned on me. I stood my ground. When it spread its black wings, I got ready to kick it yet again, but the old woman was at my side now. She pitched another handful of pebbles at the bird, shouting, "Go away!"

The bird stopped and eyed us both. Then with a croak, it spread its wings. As it launched into flight, it listed to one side.

"I think I hurt it," I said.

"Good." The old woman scowled after the bird. "Nasty things."

"That was a raven, wasn't it? It sure looked like it."

"They aren't supposed to be here," she said.

I hesitated. For a moment, I didn't see a tiny white-haired lady. I saw the girl from my raven dream. Heard her saying to the birds, "Shoo! You aren't supposed to be here."

"They used to come around when I was little. Nasty things." She shook her fist at the raven, still climbing. "You're not supposed to be here."

A soft sob interrupted her words, and I noticed the little girl, crying and shaking in her mother's arms. I glanced around for the cat and spotted its tail peeking from under the bench. I opened the gate, went inside, and bent down. It stared out at me from the darkness. When I reached in, it rubbed against my hand but would come no farther.

"Can't say I blame you," I murmured.

I turned to the little girl. "He's okay. Just scared. Come see." She did, and the cat craned its neck out far enough to be petted. "I need to run," I said. "I'm late for work, but he seems fine." They agreed, and I took off.

# MATAGOT

The old woman scowled up at the sky. The raven was long gone. Were there more? There'd better not be. She would tell the others, though. They should know there had been a raven in Cainsville.

She walked over to where the cat was hiding. It was still there, staring balefully.

"Leaping at ravens, *matagot*?" she murmured. "Trying to protect the girl? Or merely getting her attention?"

The cat only lifted a black paw and began cleaning itself.

The old woman straightened. The Larsen girl had scared the bird off nicely. The others should know about that, too. They were worried about the girl. It was difficult for some, having a Bowen in town again. It had been so many years, and things had gone so badly the last time. Yet most of the elders, like Veronica herself, were excited, too. The girl gave them another chance.

Born outside Cainsville, her mother had been lost from the start. Usually the children did not stray far enough to warrant attention. With Pamela Bowen however . . . They had all under-estimated the danger. The chance she'd get to know Todd Larsen. That would not happen again.

Veronica went to the child and helped her mother comfort and reassure her until she stopped crying. A terrible thing for a child to see. That shouldn't happen in Cainsville.

When mother and child left, the old woman returned to her painting. Before taking the first stroke, she glanced up at the sky. After a look around, she took a plump cloth bag from her pocket, untied it, and shook a little extra powder into the paint. Then she swirled it in and resumed her work.

# CHAPTER TWENTY-FIVE

In a town where half the population seemed old enough to collect Social Security, the diner wasn't exactly booming after dinner hour. By eight, even Patrick had gone home. After that, we had one middle-aged couple that worked in the city and got home late, and one family—the Pattersons—with two pre-adolescent children who'd apparently rebelled against Meatloaf Night. Otherwise, it was a slow stream of seniors coming by for a cup of tea and slice of pie.

Another problem with an elderly population? Call me ageist, but after seventy, they all start to look alike. If I wanted decent tips, I needed to be able to put names to faces . . . and remember "the usual" for each. I made notes like "Bob Masters: bad dentures, black coffee, blueberry pie" and "Sue Masters: hairy moles, Earl Grey with milk, tea biscuit with honey." I kept the notes in my deepest pocket and prayed I never dropped them.

I wasn't a good server. I wasn't even an adequate one. But I tried my damnedest, and I did get tips, though I suspect they were more like doggy biscuits for the obedience class dropout—gentle encouragement that would lead to better performance in the future.

———

On my way back to the apartment for the night I turned onto the walkway to the park and heard a *whoosh-whoosh* ahead. I stopped. The sound came again. The beating of large wings. I hurried around a bush and saw a huge bird ripping apart something on the ground.

I ran and realized it was *two* huge birds. They dropped their prey and soared away, as silent as wraiths. When I saw the black bundle on the ground, my gut twisted. The cat.

I hurried forward, then slowed. The bloody mess of red and black looked . . . wrong. The fur was . . . Not fur. Feathers.

It was the raven. Dead. Ripped apart so badly it was only a bloody mess of feathers and entrails.

I glanced up just as a massive brown form alighted on a gatepost. The owl stared at me, unblinking. Then it settled in, talons gripping the stone, leaving bloody claw marks.

The second owl landed on the opposite gatepost.

Two huge owls perched like live gargoyles. Waiting for me to go away. To leave their prey.

I took a step back. One started unfolding its wings and then stopped. I moved back again as they watched. The other one spread its wings and hopped from the post, sailing down gracefully, grabbing the raven in both claws. With a flap of its wings, it took off.

The second owl stayed for another moment, round eyes fixed on mine. Then it followed the other in silent flight.

"Mrrow?"

I spun. The black cat leapt onto the gatepost vacated by the owl. It arched up, purring. I petted it and checked its back. I saw dried blood, but the punctures had already sealed and weren't tender enough for it to complain when I prodded.

I stepped back to get a better look at the cat. It leapt to the ground, strolled over to the bloody spot on the cobblestones, and began licking it.

"Getting rid of the evidence," I murmured. "Good idea."

I returned to the diner, hoping Larry was still there so I could grab a bucket of water and clean the bloody stones before any kids came to play the next day. When I got back with the bucket, the cat was gone. I cleaned up the blood as best I could.

I opened my apartment door to see yet another business card waiting for me.

ROSALYN Z. RAZVAN, AAP
Professional Prognostication

By Appointment Only
Take Charge of Your Future

The address was for the house across the road.

I flipped over the card. In precise handwriting, she'd written: *We must speak. You need my help.*

"For a hundred bucks a session, I'm sure." I tossed it into the trash, the same place I'd thrown her nephew's card two days ago. This one would stay put. I needed his services; I certainly didn't need hers.

The next morning, I made my daily call to Howard before heading out for a much-needed walk. His voice mail picked up right way, and I wondered if he was just hitting ignore when he saw my new number. No matter. I'd keep making these calls and he'd keep passing on the messages to James and my mother. My family paid him too much not to.

On my way past the library, I popped in to check the bulletin board. If I planned to stay in Cainsville for a while, I should get more involved. I could join the knitting circle. Or the book club.

Or, if I waited a few weeks, lawn bowling season would start.

I skimmed to karate lessons. *Join anytime. Weekly at the community center. Five dollars per session.*

That I could afford and self-defense lessons wouldn't be a bad idea. I jotted down the particulars.

It wasn't yet ten when I got back to my apartment, but Gabriel's Jag was already out front, and the man himself was on the stoop, talking to Grace.

"Let me grab my notebook," I said, by way of greeting.

"I brought the file." He lifted it.

"Which is good, considering that's what I'm paying you for." I started to walk past him.

"I meant that we don't need to go anywhere," he said. "If you're uncomfortable having me in your apartment, we can leave the door open."

"Um, no, I know how to scream. And I'm sure Grace would call the cops for me. Otherwise she'd lose the rental."

Grace nodded, not the least offended.

"I'm suggesting we don't do this inside because my apartment stinks," I said. "Despite hours of cleaning."

"Buy an air freshener," Grace said.

"I did. A lovely peach-scented one. Now my apartment smells like rotten peaches. I'm going to paint the place next week."

"Wash the walls first," Gabriel said.

I looked up at him.

"You need to use a bleach solution on the walls, or you'll only temporarily cover the stench."

Obviously someone who had experience with cheap apartments. I struggled to picture it—the guy looked like he wouldn't be caught dead outside the penthouse.

"And buy good paint," Grace said.

"Will that help?"

"No, but if you buy cheap-ass crap and it peels, I'll—"

I cut her off with a wave and headed inside. Gabriel followed.

When I opened my apartment door, he took one sniff and said, "You're right."

"Checking my alibi, counselor?" I said. "If I wasn't comfort-able being alone with you, I'd say so."

As I grabbed my notebook and pen, he stepped in. His gaze went to the wastepaper basket and I remembered the card in there.

"Not yours," I said. "Seems pushing business cards under doors runs in your family. Your aunt wants a consultation. Or, I suspect, she wants me to buy one from her."

"I presume you aren't interested."

"You presume correctly."

"Good. I'll speak to her. She won't bother you again."

So he didn't want me talking to his aunt? Interesting.

I fished the card out of the trash. "Maybe I shouldn't be so hasty."

He plucked the card from my fingers. "My aunt sells supersti-tion, Olivia. While you may be at a point in your life where you wouldn't mind some guidance, I'd suggest you spend your money on decent paint instead. It will brighten your future far more than any psychic reading."

Was he worried his aunt might warn me against him? Or was he merely pretending he didn't want me to visit her, because I'd already shown signs that I was a contrary bitch?

Damn.

I let him keep the card and locked the door behind us.

As we walked out of the building, Gabriel began listing places we could talk—the library, the coffee shop. I vetoed them all and instead steered him down the alley to the park.

We arrived just as the only occupants—a woman with two preschoolers—were heading home. I held the gate for her. As we walked through, Gabriel rubbed the head of a chimera griffin.

"For luck?" I said.

"No. For . . ." He paused. "Protection."

"Protection? Against what?"

"Bogeymen and goblins and fairies and everything else that might threaten the life of an innocent child."

I studied his face. "You're serious."

"Serious in the sense that it's what I was told, growing up. As for whether they still tell children that . . . ?" He shrugged. "My aunt is far from the only superstitious soul in this town."

"And those?" I pointed at the gargoyles on the bank. "Protection against flying monkeys?"

"Plague."

I shot another look his way.

"That's what I heard. When the plague struck Chicago, the townspeople here erected the gargoyles, and nary a soul was lost to the Black Death."

"The bubonic plague predates Chicago by about five hundred years."

He lowered himself to the bench. "I know. I was very disappointed when I found out. Almost as bad as when I learned there were no fairies. The world is much more interesting with goblins and plagues."

"Unless you *catch* the plague."

"It's a risk. But imagine the market for quack cures. One could make a fortune." He gazed up at the gargoyles. "I suppose there's a more prosaic explanation. Someone puts up a gargoyle. His neighbor puts up two. Before you know"—he swept a hand across the vista—"monsters everywhere."

"Speaking of monsters . . ." I pointed at the file.

"That's an awkward segue," he said. "You can do better."

"Lawyers bill in fifteen-minute increments. Stop stalling and give me the damn file."

He handed it over.

# OLD BLOOD

Patrick closed his laptop and waved to Susie that he was leaving it behind. She didn't meet his eyes as she nodded. She hadn't met his gaze since the day he'd gone for a walk and come back to find she'd moved his laptop behind the counter. Patrick hadn't complained. He'd simply mentioned it to Larry, and said he'd appreciate it if that didn't happen again.

He had no idea what Larry told the girl. Patrick had never been anything but respectful and friendly to him. But like most *boinne-fala* with a hint of old blood, Larry had an innate sense that Patrick was not someone to be trifled with.

The new girl recognized it, too, yet her respect wasn't mingled with fear. She was cautious but curious. A different type of old blood; a different type of reaction. He preferred hers. While there was a sweetness to fear, it was a closed door. Curiosity cracked that door open.

As he turned toward the park, he saw it was already occupied. Not with children, thankfully. He wasn't fond of children. They were too easily manipulated. It lacked challenge.

No, it was the new girl. Olivia. She was sitting with . . .

He smiled. Olivia was sitting with Gabriel. Well, now, *that* was interesting.

Footsteps sounded behind him.

"Whatever you're thinking, bòcan, you can stop right now. This doesn't concern you. *They* don't concern you."

He turned. Ida and Walter. Of course.

"Gabriel always concerns me."

"He's not yours," Ida said.

Patrick tilted his head. "Technically, yes. He is."

"No. You know the rules. You have no claim to him. You will not interfere with him."

"Or with her," Walter added.

"Mmm." Patrick eyed Olivia. "I'm surprised you let her stay. I hear the ravens have already come."

"That's no concern of yours, bòcan," Walter said.

Ida fixed her faded eyes on his. "If you wish to be concerned, I'd suggest you take a more active role in the community, instead of wasting your days tapping away on your computer."

"The only way I'm going to another town meeting is if I start suffering from insomnia."

"Then that is your choice. Remember it. And don't interfere."

Which was, they all realized, like asking the sun not to rise. But he had been warned, and they seemed satisfied, hobbling off to rest their old bones in the diner.

# CHAPTER TWENTY-SIX

n that file were all the details of how the Larsens killed four couples. I know my phrasing would not please Pamela. I should say it contained the evidence used to convict the Larsens of killing four couples. I might be her last hope, and even my language choices refused to give her the benefit of the doubt.

The police had only found the Larsens because they were tipped off by an anonymous source—which formed the basis of every "wrongly accused" conspiracy theory to follow. They'd received the tip after the third set of murders. But they'd taken one look at the Larsens—the quiet carpenter husband, the sweet former-teacher wife, the adorable toddler daughter—and tossed the lead aside.

Then, after Jan Gunderson and Peter Evans were killed, some-one running through the files had found an eyewitness account of a young couple seen hurrying from the vicinity of the first crime scene. A man and a woman. Midtwenties. Handsome couple. He had shaggy blond hair. She had long dark hair. Wait a minute . . . Didn't that sound like the couple they'd received the tip about?

The year was 1990. A newfangled piece of crime scene tech-nology was just starting to be used. Something called DNA analysis. The crime scenes had been almost pristine—generic footprints, no hair, no fibers, no fingerprints. The fact that the bodies were left outdoors made the technicians' work even more difficult. But there had been a few drops of blood found on a rock by the second set of victims. The police speculated that the killer had nicked himself. He'd pulled back his hand in surprise. The first drops spattered on the rock. He bound the hand and didn't realize he'd left something of himself behind.

Only it wasn't a *him*. The DNA matched Pamela Larsen's.

The eyewitness from the first scene picked the couple out of a lineup. A local sporting goods store clerk ID'd Todd Larsen as a man who'd liked hunting knives. He'd bought four, all in the year of the killings. Three of the four murders had taken place on Fridays. That was the Larsens' "date night" when they left little Eden at Grandma's house.

Then there was the witchcraft.

Investigators had discovered a cache of occult material in the Larsen home. A locked cedar chest filled with candles and dried herbs, a silver dagger and chalice.

That box sealed the Larsens' fate.

"That was the evidence I used to argue for an appeal," Gabriel said. "The box of witchcraft supplies. Pamela Larsen had admitted to being a practicing Wiccan and everything in the box supported her claim. Simple paganism. Burning incense and making herbal teas, not sacrificing cats in the basement. The jury had failed to understand the distinction. I hoped things would have changed."

"They hadn't?"

He paused. Stretched his legs. Considered the question. "Yes, they had," he said, as if reluctantly admitting to a failure. "The overall distinction was recognized by the appellate court. The average Wiccan is extremely unlikely to commit ritual human sacrifice. However, the key words there are *average* and *unlikely*. Just because the tenets of a religion prohibit something does not mean none of its adherents ever break that prohibition. It didn't help that Pamela was a solo practitioner, with no coven to support her claim to be a Wiccan."

"What rituals did they think were being performed with the murders?"

"No two experts could agree. In the end, they decided they were chasing a classification where none existed. If you read the accounts of so-called occult murders, you'll find that in most cases, the killers were following no recognized branch of anything. They pulled in aspects from old books and modern movies and everything in between."

"In other words, they made it up."

"Exactly."

"So that was the basis of your appeal attempt? That a jury of that time was likely to be prejudiced against Wiccans? That's flimsy."

"Thank you."

"I don't need to be a lawyer to know it was flimsy. Pamela didn't like it, either. She thought there were better grounds."

"She did."

"What were they?"

"You can't tell? Clearly she expected the answer to leap from the file."

I flipped through it again. "She said it was about the fourth pair of murders—Jan Gunderson and Peter Evans—that there was a reason Pamela and Todd couldn't have committed them. There's no alibi, which would be the obvious answer. All of the elements of the fourth pair were found in at least one of the previous ones."

"So what *is* different?"

"Only the day of the week. This couple wasn't murdered on a Friday."

"Exactly."

He settled back.

"Um, okay . . . It's a minor deviation, sure, but hardly grounds for an appeal."

"I said the same thing. If you asked Pamela, she would be shocked—appalled even—that you didn't immediately see the problem. Why did the prosecution believe the others were committed on Fridays?"

"Because it was their date night. Their daughter—" I stopped. Cleared my throat. "Me, I mean. Obviously."

*Obviously.*

Except it hadn't been so obvious. While I knew I was the child in the file, I'd disconnected from that.

The adorable toddler the police met when they first questioned the Larsens? That was me. The child who'd stayed overnight at her grandmother's while Mommy and Daddy butchered eight people? That was me. The girl described during the arrest, screaming for her mother, biting the social worker, howling and sobbing uncontrollably for hours?

That was me.

"I was at their—I mean, my grandmother's that night." I paused. "Is she—?" I shook my head. "Never mind."

"Your grandmother passed away years ago."

"Right. Okay." I wanted to ask about other family, but Gabriel wasn't the person to answer that.

"Take a moment."

As at the prison, he said it with a veneer of empathy, yet he couldn't mask a note of impatience.

"I'm fine," I said. "So where was Eden—I mean, where was *I* on the night of the last murders?"

"No one knows. That is the crux of Pamela's argument."

A shadow passed overhead. I looked up. Just a sparrow.

"I don't understand," I said.

"Your grandmother was the only person your parents entrusted with your care, and she was out of town. Therefore, your parents could not have killed anyone that night."

"No, they just left me in bed. Or in the back of the car."

Sleeping in the car. While they murdered two people.

I continued, "At that point, the Larsens had already been questioned about the murders. It makes logical sense to shake things up."

"Yes, but as Pamela points out, they weren't actually questioned as suspects. The police spoke to them under the pretext of investigating a neighborhood break-in. Pamela's argument is that they would never have left you alone, either in the house or in the car. And they certainly wouldn't take you along to a murder. That would be irresponsible parenting."

I sputtered a laugh, then looked at his expression. "You're serious?"

"She is. To her, the fact you were not with a sitter proves they couldn't have committed the murders. Oddly, she has trouble finding a judge—or a lawyer—to agree with her."

"And it's not grounds for appeal anyway. So you based yours on prejudice against Wiccans?"

"No, I *attempted* to base it on this." He took folded papers from his breast pocket. "Your mother refused. We settled on my backup—the Wiccan business. Which I expected to use in conjunction with this." He waved the folded sheets. "On its own, the Wiccan defense was, as you say, flimsy."

"So what's that?" I pointed at the sheets.

He unfolded them. The papers were part of a police report. Withheld until he could present it with the proper degree of drama.

I read the sheets. Then I put them into the folder and set it on my other side—away from Gabriel.

"The answer is no," I said.

He feigned confusion. "I believe I missed the question."

"You held back those pages because they offer the strongest proof that the Larsens may not have been the killers. You also know if I go to these innocence groups, they might not take me seriously—I'm just a spoiled rich kid who wants someone to make all this nastiness go away. So you're going to offer to investigate for me. I just need to stop this silly charade and go back home to my family ATM so I can hire you." I glanced over. "Close?"

He considered the question. "No. I suspect you have no intention of going home until you've found your place in the world. Or until you see a pair of Jimmy Choos you can't live without. Your current lack of funds, though, will make it difficult to hire me. But I have a solution."

"Of course you do."

"I will accept promissory notes due one month after your twenty-fifth birthday, when you receive the trust fund set up by your adoptive father. The extra month should allow you ample time to access the funds."

"Done your research, I see."

"Of course."

"Why do you want this case?" I asked. "Yes, you can probably soak me for some serious cash, but your firm isn't struggling for business. I've done my research, too. You're successful enough that you don't need to shill for clients."

He opened his mouth.

I lifted my hand. "No, let me guess. Anything I can deduce is infinitely more trustworthy than anything you're going to tell me."

"Careful, Ms. Jones, you might offend me."

"I owe you one for the Jimmy Choo jab. By the way, I'm a Louboutin girl, and their new line isn't out until fall, so I won't be going home for money until then."

The faintest quirk of a smile. "I stand corrected."

"As for why you'd do this? If you freed Pamela Larsen, your professional star would ascend into the stratosphere. That's why you took her appeal. Except she didn't like your strategy, so you lost your chance. This evidence isn't good enough to pursue without a paying client. I can be that client."

"You could be."

"No, Mr. Walsh. I'm not that gullible. Or that desperate. Bill me for this morning, as per our original agreement."

So what was in those pages Gabriel had removed from the file? That most valuable and elusive prize for any defense lawyer: a plausible alternate suspect. Jan Gunderson's older brother, Christian.

On paper, Christian Gunderson was ideal. Midtwenties. A loner. Socially awkward. Anger-management issues that had led to three arrests for assault. Two charges had been dropped, probably because they'd been against family members—his father and his sister, Jan.

The police had zeroed in on Christian as soon as Jan and her fiancé were killed. Shortly before the deaths, Christian apparently had a huge fight with his sister, and Peter had interceded, where-upon neighbors swore they heard Christian threatening him.

But that didn't explain the first three pairs of murders. You could suggest Christian had killed only Jan and Peter and then made it look like the other deaths, but the pattern fit too well, including details never released to the press. There was no evidence that Christian had access to those details.

Then investigators found a link. Christian and the first female victim, Amanda Mays, had both attended City College. The police theory was that pretty, vivacious Amanda rebuffed an advance from Christian. Maybe she said she was engaged, which she was. Maybe he'd stalked her, watched them together. Then he snapped and killed them both and tried to make it look like an occult murder.

Police found a more tenuous link to victim number two, Lisa Tyson. She'd worked within two miles of Christian's job. Police postulated he'd seen her. Maybe he asked her out. Or maybe after his experience with Amanda, he just stalked her. Then he killed Lisa and her husband, Marty.

There was no obvious connection to couple number three, but police didn't care by then. He'd killed four people and decided he liked it.

Then came his fight with his own sister, and he decided to make it four. After all, he'd gotten away with it so far. It was like being his own copycat killer.

So why wasn't Christian Gunderson arrested? Because within hours of the police questioning him in his sister's death, he hanged himself. The family—the parents and their remaining daughter—closed ranks after that. They could not recall why Christian and Jan argued and the neighbor who heard the threat was angry with the Gundersons for refusing to contribute to a new fence. Amanda Mays? Never heard of her. Not Lisa Tyson, either. And besides, Christian had been home every time a couple was murdered. Friday was family movie night. Check with the corner video store—Mrs. Gunderson rented a movie every Friday.

The police kept trying but found no solid evidence to link Christian to the crimes. Then they processed the blood that linked the second murder to Pamela Larsen and left the Gundersons to their grief.

The evidence against the Larsens still held. Of course they'd explained it away. The blood? The Larsens did a lot of hiking with little Eden. They'd been to that patch of woods before the murders, and Pamela vaguely recalled cutting her hand on a fruit salad lid. The knives? Again, they were outdoorsy. Todd fished. He also had a bad habit of leaving his knife uncleaned in the tackle box, until Pamela found it and swore the smell would never come off, so she made him buy new ones. The eyewitness? Everyone knew eyewitnesses were notoriously unreliable.

The jury didn't buy it.

The Larsens were tried and convicted. The public had their monsters locked up where they belonged.

# CHAPTER TWENTY-SEVEN

'd lied to Gabriel. I couldn't just drop this. Not yet. I needed to know more. I was sure I could get more. My dad used to give me every problem-solving task that could arise in a department store, from shoplifting to public relations. That did not give me the skills to investigate murder, but if I had more details, maybe I *could* interest one of those innocence projects, which—unlike Gabriel Walsh—wouldn't charge me for its efforts. I still wanted these answers, needed these answers. Which meant I had to do what it took to get them.

After leaving Gabriel, I stopped back at the apartment to grab my memo pad and headed to the library.

My research did not go well. The only mentions I found of Christian Gunderson were newspaper accounts dramatically labeling him another victim of the killers. Unable to cope with the horrific death of his sister, the sensitive soul took his own life. If that was his epitaph, no one was going to appreciate me suggesting he may have been her killer.

The articles had mentioned a younger sister, Anna. I could speak to her . . . if I could find current contact information. I couldn't. I did find something on Christian's mother, though. An obituary. She'd died three years ago. The only address I found for a living, close relative was for Niles Gunderson—the mentally unstable father who'd mistaken me for Pamela and attacked me.

Definitely not.

Sunday morning I was in a cab, taking the first step in my investigation. Ida and Walter had offered me the use of their car anytime I needed to make a trip "to the city," but I didn't feel comfortable taking them up on that offer. Not yet.

So I was footing the big bill for a cab to Chicago. And where was I going? To pay a visit to Niles Gunderson.

Madness, of course. But it was the only avenue of investigation I could see. He must have been off his meds when he came to the house. By now he'd be back home, on his regime and lucid. With my new look, a little role-playing, a few shadows, and a lot of luck, I might be able to convince him that I was an old friend of Anna's looking for her phone number. I'd tried calling of course but he wouldn't answer. Maybe because he didn't recognize the number.

When I reached the apartment, I knew the "few shadows" part of the equation would be easy. A week ago, I'd have said Gunderson's building was little more than tenement housing. Now, having seen actual tenements, I knew better.

It was just a tired building on a tired street, filled with people who looked equally tired, trudging along without even a glance my way. Inside, the building was quieter than I might have expected. Darker, too. Hence the shadows. It was like walking into a tunnel, gray and gloomy and empty, with dark walls and irregular lighting.

As I made my way up to Gunderson's fifth-floor apartment, I began to think that maybe this desolate place wasn't exactly where I wanted to meet a man who'd tried to kill me.

This was crazy. Bat-shit crazy. With every step, I thought of new and more colorful descriptions of my decision to visit Niles Gunderson. But I kept walking.

His door was at the far end of the hall. I gathered my courage and knocked. As I did, I noticed something on the floor. A splash of red.

Blood.

It took only an eye-blink to tell me it was just a plastic poppy, the kind you wear at Remembrance Day, though we were about as far in the calendar as you could get from November 11.

I made a face and rubbed my nose. The building smelled of garbage and cooked food, but I'd just caught a whiff of something worse.

I knocked again, louder now. Still nothing.

My gaze tripped back to the poppy and stayed there, as if glued to the sight.

*It's a damn poppy. So what?*

But even when I looked away, I could feel the poppy niggling at me. A clue? I snorted. If a dropped poppy could tell me anything, I'd need to be Holmes himself to figure it out.

I rapped again, but by now didn't expect an answer.

There wasn't a dead-bolt keyhole. I looked down the hall. All clear. Couldn't hurt to try. As I reached for the knob, my gaze caught on that damned poppy again. I stopped and pulled my sleeve over my hand. Then I turned the knob, testing the door before I . . .

It opened.

I glanced around. Then I pushed open the door and slipped inside. As I did, the smell hit me.

Death.

It smelled like death.

I chastised myself for being overly dramatic. No matter how

sheltered one was, it was hard to reach the age of twenty-four and not know the smell of decay, if only a dead mouse in the basement. Judging by the state of Niles's apartment, a rotting mouse or two would probably go unnoticed for a while.

Yet I knew the smell didn't come from dirty dishes. Or even dead mice.

When I walked into the kitchen and saw Niles Gunderson—slumped back in his chair, mouth open, eyes closed, two flies feasting on an open sore on his chin—I didn't think, *Oh my God, the poor man is dead.* I thought, *Shit, there goes my only source.*

After the shock passed, I *did* think of how pitiful he looked, how old and how broken. Twenty-two years ago, he'd been living the American dream. Son of immigrants. College educated. White-collar job. Wife. Three kids. House in the suburbs. Then Death paid a visit and decided to stick around. One child savagely murdered. Another dead by his own hand. Finally, Death claimed even his wife—the only person keeping him from the final descent into . . . I looked around. Into this. Dead in a filthy apartment. No one to notice. No one to care.

I suppose my next move should have been to call the police. Or flee the scene. But if no one had found Niles yet, they weren't likely to in the next few minutes. Besides, there was no sign of trauma, other than that wound on his face, which seemed like a shaving nick that the flies had taken advantage of.

This all sounds remarkably calm of me. Yet I was not calm. Something was wrong here. Seriously wrong.

It was like that discarded poppy niggling at me. A steady whisper snaked past. *Pay attention.*

I rubbed goose bumps from my arms and found a phone in the living room. I didn't use it to call 911. I just wanted Niles's phone book, which I found beside the phone.

I used my sleeves again when opening it, even if logically I knew there was no way they'd be dusting a phone book for prints after a natural death. The book was falling apart, many of the numbers faded, people who'd passed out of the Gundersons' lives years ago. The only recent entries were for health care workers and pharmacies and delivery services. Except one. A recently changed address and phone number for "Anna." His daughter.

I made a note of the number and then flipped through the book. Nothing grabbed my attention, possibly because that niggling feeling kept drawing me back to the kitchen. Finally, I closed the book and pocketed my note. One last look. Then I was leaving.

I rounded the corner. Niles Gunderson was upright in his chair, staring at me. Flies covered his chin. Maggots crawled from his mouth. And his eyes—he had no eyes, just empty sockets staring—

My hands flew to my own eyes, palms pressing against them, brain stuttering, some part of me screaming, "See! I told you something was wrong!"

I took a deep breath and let my hands fall away, and when they did, I saw Niles as he'd been before—slumped back in his chair, dead. His eyes were closed. No maggots. Not even any flies.

Something moved to my left. I jumped so fast my feet tangled, and I grabbed the counter. A dark shape stretched across the kitchen floor until it covered Niles, and I turned to see a shadow coming through the open balcony curtains. There, perched on the railing, was a raven. It flapped its wings, and the shadow retracted to normal size.

I slowly walked to the balcony doors. The bird sat there, watching me. It cocked its head.

"Shoo," I whispered. "You aren't supposed to be here."

As I said the words, I saw the little girl from my dream, shaking her fist at the raven as it perched on a flayed, eyeless corpse.

*The bran know better. They aren't supposed to disturb the dead. It's disrespectful.*

The raven opened its beak and croaked. Then it spread its wings and swooped at the window, talons out. It hit the glass, claws scraping, and let out a raucous caw.

*"Ewch i ffwrdd, bran!"*

I heard the words the little girl had spoken, and it took a second to realize they came from me, shouted so loud my throat hurt. The bird let out a noise, almost like a hiss. Then it pushed back from the window, twisting in midair before flying off.

I stood there, staring after it. When I swallowed, my throat ached, and I remembered saying the words. Shouting them. Standing in the kitchen of a dead man, shouting.

I got out of there as fast as I could.

# CHAPTER TWENTY-EIGHT

I f the Romans could have fortified their cities the way the human brain fortifies itself, we'd still be wearing togas. The mind is an amazing piece of biomachinery, really. A serious threat presents itself at the gate and up fly the walls, standing firm in the face of earth-shaking revelations, ideological bullets, and plain old logic.

I retreated from Niles's apartment, still in a daze. I wandered until I found a coffee shop. Then I holed up in the corner, slurping caffeine until I found the strength to make sense of what I'd just experienced.

By the time I finished my drink, I'd decided the hallucination of Zombie Niles and the raven weren't important. What mattered was that I'd broken into an apartment and found the body of a man who'd publicly threatened me. I had screwed up. I'd thought I was capable of handling this on my own, and I so clearly was not.

When I left my apartment for my Monday shift, I noticed curtains move across the street. Rosalyn Razvan, watching me. They closed when I glanced up, but I stayed there, looking at the house, considering . . .

Gabriel Walsh should be at the bottom of my list of potential investigative partners. But under the right conditions and with an insane amount of caution, he might be exactly what I needed. Except I'd already rejected his offer.

While neither my dad nor James had Gabriel's shark instinct, they'd introduced me to men who did, and I'd learned a few things. If I wanted to work with Gabriel, I had to let him win me over. I couldn't crawl back or the balance would be forever skewed.

After my shift, as I walked to the psychic's door, a black blur shot from behind a parked car. The cat. I hadn't seen it since the night of the raven attack, and I was relieved that it was obviously fine.

"Warning me not to venture into the witch's lair?" I said as it raced past me.

The cat leapt onto a porch rocking chair. It stretched on the gingham cushion, purring as it got comfortable.

"Okay, not a warning. Unless you're her familiar lulling me into a false sense of security."

I swore the cat rolled its eyes.

I laughed. "Fine, I'll willfully interpret your reappearance as a sign of good fortune, meaning I am indeed making the right choice."

I gave the cat a pat and rang the bell. The harsh buzz was oddly out of tone with the Victorian surroundings. The tinny voice that followed was even more jarring.

"Hello?"

I looked around and found a speaker hidden in the ivy.

"Hello?" the woman's voice said again.

"Rosalyn Razvan?"

"Yes."

"It's—" I started to say Liv Taylor, then remembered that she knew who I was. "Olivia Taylor-Jones. You wanted to speak to me?"

"Six o'clock."

"What?"

A metallic whoosh, like a sigh. "I'll speak to you at six o'clock. It's by appointment only."

"I'm not looking to buy a reading. Your card just said you wanted to speak—"

"Six o'clock. No charge."

The speaker clicked off. I looked at the cat.

"Any more advice?"

The cat started cleaning itself, leaving me to retreat across the road.

Seeing the cat made me decide to take a step I'd been avoiding. I went to the library and I researched "black cats and luck," as well as every other odd thing that had happened.

I'd wanted to forget these so-called omens. Brush them off and tell myself they meant nothing. Except they did mean something. All my gut-level interpretations of the omens matched the folklore.

In America, we see a black cat and think its bad luck. In other places, particularly Britain, they're considered *good* luck. Kill a spider? Bad luck. Stir with a knife? Causes trouble. See a cat wash its ears? A sure sign of rain.

Which only proved that someone *had* indoctrinated me with this folklore at an early age, and now it was popping back up because I was remembering my past life with Pamela Larsen, the woman who'd put all that nonsense there in the first place.

What bothered me most was the poppy. It turned out they were a death omen. I'd seen a poppy outside the door of a dead man . . . before I knew he was dead. Maybe there'd been no poppy. Maybe I'd smelled death and manufactured the illusion.

Next I looked up the word "bran." It was Welsh for raven. So

I was guessing that whatever the little girl in my dream said—
the line I'd regurgitated at Gunderson's apartment—was Welsh.
I had no idea what it meant. I typed a few variations into online
dictionaries, but got nothing. I'm sure my phonetic guesses were
nowhere close to the real spellings.

Why was I dreaming of a girl speaking Welsh and how had
my dreaming brain known that *bran* meant raven? Back to
Pamela Larsen. Her maiden name was Bowen. Plugging that
into a search told me my maternal grandmother's name was
Daere Bowen. That was Welsh, and from the unusual first name,
I was guessing she was a recent immigrant. So Pamela may have
spoken some Welsh and taught me. Young children were amaz-
ingly quick to pick up language.

I did come across something else in my searches. I accidentally typed Walsh instead of Welsh. Not surprising—Gabriel was
still on my brain. Turned out the similar spelling wasn't coincidental. Walsh was a very old Irish name meaning "foreigner."
Quite literally, a Welshman. It meant nothing, of course, but
after hours of researching omens and portents, I couldn't help
but see this as a sign that I was on the right path, considering
him for the role of investigative partner. Or I was just desperate
to believe it.

# CHAPTER TWENTY-NINE

When I rang Rosalyn's bell at six there was a car parked in front of her house. A little old lady opened the door, and I extended my hand to introduce myself, but she walked right past me, her gaze distant, lips moving, as if talking to herself. She carried on down the walk and climbed into the passenger seat of the old Buick. After a moment, she got out and went around to the driver's door.

"Okay," I murmured. "*That's* not a good sign."

A grumble sounded behind me. "I tell her not to drive right after hypnosis. If she keeps that up, it won't be the cigarettes that kill her."

I turned and thought, *Snow White's mother*. I don't mean the one from the modern telling of the fairy tale, the kindly queen who pricks her finger and wishes for a daughter, only to die and be replaced by the evil stepmother. My memories are of the real Grimm's fairy tales and others where Cinderella's stepmother cuts off her daughter's toes to fit in the glass slipper and the Little Mermaid kills herself after her prince chooses someone else. Even when I learned the modern ones, I preferred the brutal and macabre old versions. I always wondered why. Now, knowing who my real parents were, I suppose that was another question answered.

In the original telling, the jealous witch who persecuted Snow White was her real mother. When I looked at Rosalyn Razvan, that's who I saw. She had black hair, cut in a bob, with a perfect frosting of white. Elegantly tweezed black brows. Bone-china skin. Ruby red lips.

I knew she was Gabriel's great-aunt, but she only looked in her late fifties. He'd inherited his height from her side of the family. She was a few inches taller than me. Military posture. Sturdily built with wide hips and ship-prow breasts.

She had blue eyes, like Gabriel, but hers had more color. I'd say more warmth, too, but warm wasn't a word to describe Rosalyn Razvan.

"Your mother owes my nephew money," she said.

"It's a pleasure to meet you, too."

"He worked for her in good faith, and she hasn't paid her bills."

"That's what he says, and she doesn't deny it, so I guess it's true."

"And you take no responsibility for your mother's debts?"

"Considering that I didn't know Pamela Larsen *was* my mother until after she incurred those debts, the answer is no."

"If you pay him—and I know your adoptive family can afford to do so—then Pamela Larsen will repay you. Gabriel says she's eager to renew a relationship with you. She won't want to start by mooching off her daughter."

"If Gabriel put you up to this—"

"My nephew puts me up to nothing. He is owed money. I would like to see him get it."

I reached for the door handle to leave.

"It's an easy matter to resolve, Ms. Jones. Ask Lena Taylor for the money. Or allow my nephew to make your claim on the proceeds of Pamela's book. It will cost you nothing, and it will free you from the shadow of this debt."

I laughed and turned back to face her. "What shadow? My mother hired Gabriel because she's in jail for murdering eight people. That has nothing to do with me."

"Are you sure?"

"What? I was two years old at the time. I—"

I stopped myself. *Don't feed the crazy lady, Liv.* What did I expect from a fortune-teller? I grasped the door handle again.

"He'll be very persistent, Ms. Jones."

"Yes, I'm sure he will, but the guy drives a hundred-thousand-dollar car. If he's in hock, he should sell it and live within his means."

"My nephew lives within his means." There was genuine annoyance in her voice now. "He's a Walsh. We pay as we go. We owe no one."

"And neither do I. Which is why I wouldn't ask my adoptive mother for the money. As for the book, I consider that stealing a debt owed to the victims."

She eyed me with the same intense appraisal I'd gotten from her grandnephew.

"He's right," she said finally. "You have a backbone."

"You didn't believe him?"

She shrugged and put her hand on a pedestal table, letting her posture relax. "You're an attractive young woman. Gabriel isn't usually blinded by such things, but it is possible, combined with the equally blinding attractions of a healthy bank account and an intriguing back story."

"So you were . . . what? Seeing if you could bully the money out of me?"

"It was worth a try. He worked for that money, and he deserves it. I understand why you don't want to go to your adoptive family for it, but I think you're a fool for rejecting the book income. Pamela Larsen is your mother. You've been damaged by that. You will be damaged more. I don't need the second sight to foresee that. Maybe you'll change your mind. In the meantime . . ." She waved toward an open doorway. "A reading."

"I'm not—"

"It's on the house."

"Right. Let me guess. My future will be so much brighter if I paid my mother's bills."

A harsh croak of a laugh. "That would be insultingly obvious."

She headed into the side room. I followed. Once I crossed the threshold, I stopped to stare. To the layperson's eye it might look like a cheesy fortune-teller's room, but to anyone who knew something about the history of spiritualism, it was like stepping into a museum exhibit.

I stopped in front of a very old reproduction of a photograph, showing what looked like tiny, gauzy-winged people in the grass.

"The Cottingley Fairies," I murmured.

Five photographs taken in 1917, probably the most famous "evidence" of fairies. Four were of two girls playing with little winged people. This was the fifth, without the girls. The photos were a huge sensation at the time and were taken as proof of the existence of the little people. It wasn't until the eighties that the girls admitted they'd faked the first four photographs using cutouts of fairies from a book. On this fifth one, though, they disagreed, one claiming it was another fake and the other insisting it was real.

How did I know this? Because the best-known article written on the Cottingley fairies was by Sir Arthur Conan Doyle, published in a Christmas edition of the *Strand*. He'd been convinced they were real. That had been the actual subject of my master's thesis—a reanalysis of his ultralogical famous detective in light of Conan Doyle's interest in the otherworldly.

"It looks real, doesn't it?" Rosalyn said.

"It's a double-negative. That's the theory anyway. The girls shot a photo of the cardboard fairies and got a double-negative of the images."

Another croaked laugh. "You have a very firm opinion on the subject, don't you?"

"I do. I could tell you my opinion of fortune-telling, too." I turned. "I'll warn you, prognostication is wasted on me. I had my palm read once, on a lark with friends. The psychic told me I'd marry a handsome, rich man."

"Which you were going to, were you not?"

"Past tense. Meaning it was wrong, though I'm sure if I pointed that out, she'd say there's still time. Even if I married two ugly, poor men in a row, she could tell me there was still time."

"It was a reasonable guess, though. She could tell you come from money. Even today, you may think you're hiding behind department store attire, but you're wearing a Cartier watch. Besides, a trained ear can pick up the softened midwestern accent that suggests private school. If you come from those circles, it is likely your husband will be wealthy."

"And handsome?"

"Beautiful women sometimes choose unattractive men to move up on the social ladder. Again, you don't need that. So it is a reasonable guess you will marry a man who is both wealthy and handsome."

"She also said I'll have two children."

Rosalyn settled into a chair at the table and motioned for me to do the same. "There she was wrong. Or relying on out-dated information. The current national average is less than two. Higher socioeconomic status often results in fewer children. Based on that alone, I'd have said one. However, in your case, I'd say none."

"Because I won't want to pass on my tainted serial-killer genes?"

"No, because you don't like children."

When I started to protest, she continued, "Perhaps that's too harsh. You don't dislike them. But to you, they are like parrots. Pretty to look at, fun to play with, but you wouldn't want to be saddled with that responsibility for the rest of your life."

"That's a big leap to make for someone you just met."

"Not really. I don't know who broke the engagement, you or James Morgan. The papers say he did. I suspect it was you. Pride, most likely. Either way, had you been eager to start a family, you would have tried to work it out. Also, you don't strike me as being particularly maternal. So I would have said no children is most likely, though I would hedge my bets by adding that there is the possibility of one later in life. What else did your fortune-teller say?"

I shrugged. "More of the same. Things she thought I wanted to hear or things she could guess. A mix of fantasy and truth."

"For psychics like that, it's a con job. Anyone willing to learn to read the signs can do it."

"Not exactly a good promotion of your services, Ms. Razvan."

"It's Walsh. Rose Walsh. Rosalyn Razvan is my professional name. In this business, people want a gypsy, not a fourth-generation Irish immigrant. You can call me Rose. As for admitting to chicanery, I was referring to psychics like the one you visited. I have the sight. I can see the futures."

"Futures? Plural?"

"Of course. That's the problem with most theories of prognostication. They presume a single future. You will marry a handsome, rich man and have two children. Is life so predetermined from birth to death, like a car on a fixed track, no room for detours, no allowance for free will? There are *futures*, Olivia.

Possible outcomes based on choices. My gift is not the ability to predict you will marry a handsome, rich man, but to say, if you marry this particular handsome, rich man you will live a comfortable but constrained life. If you do not, your life will be fuller, but you will look back with regret. The choice, then, is yours."

"More life coach than fortune-teller."

"Yes, and I will pretend I didn't notice the sarcasm in your tone." She took a deck of well-worn tarot cards and fanned them before me.

"Choose."

I slid one out, still upside down.

"Now turn it over."

I did. It was a gorgeously rendered Victorian-era card showing a circus clown balancing on a ball, surrounded by dogs with tiny hats.

"The fool," I murmured. "I'm afraid to ask what that means."

"That's not how this works. I don't interpret the card. You do. When you first saw it, your reaction was dismay."

"I didn't mean—"

"You're afraid of being played for a fool. Take another."

I shook my head.

"Too revealing?" she said. "You're uncomfortable sharing emotional reactions."

"No, I just—"

"You are." She scooped up the cards. "Now take another."

I did.

A half hour later, Rose said, "I believe our time is almost up." She pulled a cell phone from her pocket and checked it. "Yes, my next appointment will be here soon."

"So where's my reading? Oh, wait. I have to *pay* for that, right?"

"I already did the reading. I read *you*. Now you need to ask me a question."

"I don't have any."

She met my gaze. "Really? I doubt that, under the circumstances."

"If you expect me to ask whether Pamela and Todd Larsen are really serial killers, I'm not going to."

"Good, because I have no idea. Even if I did, my answer would mean nothing to you. First, you don't believe I have the sight anyway. Second, you would presume, whatever I say, that I have an ulterior motive. In this you need to find your own answer. I can simply help you with the smaller questions. When you have one, come back." She stood. "My first answer will be at no cost. After that the price will escalate as I prove my worth. In the meantime, let me offer some free advice. You need protection."

I thought of Gabriel in the park, rubbing the griffin's head. "Against plague?" I hooked my thumb at the Cottingley photo. "Or fairies?"

That had her cracking a smile. "You never know when a plague may strike, Olivia. They say it'll be any day now. And plagues come in many forms. As do fairies. I could offer you an amulet or crystal or other protective talisman. But you'd only stick it in a drawer. For now, I'll focus on the more prosaic dangers and strongly suggest you buy a gun."

"A gun?"

"Yes, a gun. Now—"

The doorbell buzzed.

"Well, it seems my next appointment is early. Would you mind letting him in when you go?"

She left the room before I could answer. I headed for the front door. Aside from that earlier bullying about Gabriel, the visit hadn't been nearly as bad as I'd feared. Now, I could only hope she'd let him know I'd visited and that would provide just the excuse he needed to take another run at me.

I opened the front door . . . and there stood the man himself.

# CHAPTER THIRTY

"**M**s. Razvan will be with you in a moment, sir," I said. "Please take a seat in the parlor."

I made a move to slip past him. Useless, of course. If Gabriel Walsh wanted to block a doorway, he just needed to stand there.

I looked over my shoulder.

"Yes," he said. "My aunt let me know you were coming. I'd like to speak to you."

"Fine. I charge in fifteen-minute increments. Hundred bucks each."

"That would be *my* profession. For yours . . ." He dug loose change from his pocket.

"Is that suppose to be a tip? Don't expect more than five minutes of my time, and I'll forget half your order and spill coffee on your sleeve."

A twitch of a smile. He pulled out a twenty. When I took it, he looked surprised.

I shoved the bill into my pocket. "You have fifteen minutes. Walk and talk. I need the exercise."

As I'd expected, he was still hell-bent on selling me his services. While most lawyers hire private investigators, Gabriel's methods were irregular—in other words, not always legal or ethical—so he undertook the fieldwork himself.

Next came the list of credentials. His success rate was excellent, which may be a little disconcerting, considering he specialized in cases others wouldn't touch. As my research had already revealed, he was best known as the lawyer for Satan's Saints, a Chicago biker gang with a record so clean it was the envy of Illinois' homegrown Outlaws.

If the hard sell didn't convince me he really wanted the job, he sealed it by offering to negotiate a reduced rate. He claimed it was only fair, as success would benefit him as well.

"Yes," I said as we walked toward the empty school yard. "But I don't *need* to solve this. I won't spend a day in jail or owe a dollar in fines if I don't hire a lawyer. It's pure curiosity and self-interest, and I won't blow my trust fund on that. For starters, I want a sliding scale."

"A—?"

"Sliding scale. Your aunt offered me one for her services."

"My aunt and I are hardly in the same line of—"

"A matter of opinion. I want one day of your time for free. Then the rate will increase on a predetermined schedule, as you prove your worth."

His brows shot up. "Prove my—?"

"Yes. You won't use your usual scale of billable hours, either. I'm not paying fifteen minutes for a two-minute phone call or thirty for an e-mail."

"That's standard practice—"

"—in a law firm where the partners are breathing down your neck, making sure you put in eighty billable hours a week. You're your own boss. You can set your own rates. I want real-time charges, and I don't want you doing anything that I could do myself—phone calls, e-mails, letters, library research—unless we've agreed to it in advance."

"I believe you're overestimating my interest in this case, Ms. Jones."

I met his gaze. Hard to do when he was still wearing his shades, but I approximated. "No, I don't think I am."

His lips pressed together. Annoyed with himself for tipping his hand.

When I'd looked up Gabriel online, his work record suggested he was no more than thirty. In other words, he might act like a seasoned professional, but he wasn't really. More of a quick study, passing the bar, then attacking his job with a single-minded ferocity that earned him a reputation fast. Young enough that he could screw up and act rashly.

"Those are my terms," I said. "I'll give you a minute to consider them."

I wandered over to the fence, gripped the cool metal mesh, and peered into the school yard. Picture-book quaint, like most of Cainsville. A small enclosure with a bright colored play structure, freshly mown grass, and asphalt decorated with a chalk hopscotch court. I didn't think anyone played hopscotch anymore.

A sprinkler turned on. It was dry here, the warm spring having sucked up any moisture from the other day's storm. Yet right under the fence a line of darker colored soil looked damp.

I bent and touched the line. No, it was dry. Just darker. I rubbed my fingers together. Brownish-red. Odd.

"Thinking of taking up gardening?"

I stood as Gabriel walked over. "Maybe. Depends on if I get my murder investigation or not."

"And that depends on what you're willing to pay for it." He waved to a bench outside the fence. "Let's discuss that."

———

I suspect that my terms cost me any "discount" he'd originally been willing to give. I tried to dicker, of course. He stood firm, and the set of his jaw told me he wasn't budging. It was, admittedly, a fair price for his services.

So I agreed.

"Good." He tucked his shades into his suit-coat pocket. "We'll begin tomorrow. I have an idea where we can start. I'll call you in the morning."

He started to stand.

"One more thing . . ." I said.

His shoulders tightened.

"I want a gun," I said.

He turned slowly and looked down at me. "A gun?"

"It was your aunt's idea."

A faint sigh.

"Hey, you wanted me to talk to her."

"No, I believe I said—"

"*Don't* talk to her, which you knew would make me talk to her, so in the event that I didn't take you up on your offer, you'd have a second crack at me."

"You give me too much credit, Olivia."

"No, I don't think I do. Anyway, she's right. I'm the daughter of two very unpopular people. I should have a gun."

"And you think I can provide it?"

"Ask your biker gang buddies."

"They prefer the term 'motorcycle club.'"

"I'm sure they do."

He leaned farther into the bench, lips pursed. "While I'm not against such a thing in theory, I'd need to provide lessons, too. Otherwise, I'm liable to lose my client to a fatal gun cleaning incident before she ever sees her trust fund."

"How much will you charge for those lessons?"

He considered. "A hundred dollars each. Discounted because it's in my best interest to keep you from shooting yourself."

"Fine. I want a gun I can put in my purse. Small, reliable, and cheap."

"I'll see what I can do."

Gabriel called at eight thirty the next morning, as I was in the clothing store looking for jogging sweats.

"I've arranged our first appointment," he said.

I flipped through a stack of pink T-shirts. Were they *all* pink?

"Who is it?"

"Jan Gunderson's sister."

"Anna?" Damn it. My one lead and he already had her contact information. And I was sure he hadn't needed to break into an apartment with a dead body to get it. Figures.

He continued, "You'll pose as my intern. Dress—"

"Businesslike. I know. Unless we're interviewing hookers or bikers, that'll be my default. If we do interview hookers and bikers, warn me in advance, because I have nothing to wear." I looked around the shop. Fifty percent polyester. Fifty percent loungewear. "And I won't find it in Cainsville."

"Jeans and a T-shirt would suffice for such situations."

I'd been joking. Was he? I honestly couldn't tell.

He continued, "Business wear for this one, but dowdy."

"Dowdy?"

"Frumpy. Plain. No makeup. Tie your hair back if you can."

"What is she, Amish?" I found a navy and white sweat suit in my size and pulled it out.

"Just do it, Olivia. I'm in court this morning. The interview is at noon. I'll—"

"I work at three. I'll need to be back by then."

A pause. "So you intend to keep playing server, even though you have something else to occupy your time?"

I gripped the phone tighter. "I'm not *playing* anything. It's my job."

"You have an Ivy League education, and you're working in a diner."

"That's not your concern."

"It is if it interferes with this investigation. I have a job, too, Ms. Jones. You cannot expect me to work around your schedule when with one call to your adoptive mother, you could solve your insolvency."

"No." I took the sweat suit into the change room. "You're right about the scheduling, though. We'll work it out."

"We'll see. Be ready at eleven." Before I could argue, he said, "I can dictate to my secretary on the drive there, so it isn't lost time. I'll bill you a hundred dollars flat fee each way."

Which meant it was roughly the same cost as a cab. And the cab would not be a luxury sports car.

I agreed, hung up, and went to try on the sweat suit.

I was sitting on the front steps when Gabriel pulled up to the curb. He put down the passenger window and lowered his shades to look at me. I tried to open the door. It was still locked.

"I thought we talked about your appearance," he said.

"I have one business suit. This is it. My hair is too short to pin up."

"Makeup?"

"Not wearing any," I said. "I'm twenty-four. I don't need to trowel it on."

He nudged his shades up and opened the car door. I got in.

As he peeled from the curb, he said, "Your hair color is washing out."

"Yes, apparently, I bought temporary dye by accident. I'll get the proper stuff."

"Don't bother. It isn't helping."

I glanced over.

"The cut, the color, and the glasses are useless. To anyone who has seen the photographs, you are obviously Eden Larsen in hiding." He turned onto Main Street. "Do you want to look like Eden Larsen in hiding?"

"No."

"Then I'd suggest you don't bother with the rest. Your features are too strong to disguise yourself with anything short of plastic surgery. And as long as you insist on playing poor, you can't afford plastic surgery."

I wasn't touching that. "Is that why you insisted on the dowdy disguise today? In hopes Jan Gunderson's sister won't recognize me?"

"Partly. I'm hoping that the families of victims will avoid the articles." He paused. "The exception, of course, being Niles Gunderson. I hear you've already encountered him."

I tried not to react. I must have given something away, though, because he glanced over.

"Yes, I'm sure that was unpleasant. Being attacked in your home. But the man is mentally unstable. Everyone knows that, including the journalist—or more likely Internet blogger—who alerted him that night. He clearly did it hoping for exactly the kind of scene he got."

I cleared my throat. "Maybe there's another reason he" I stopped myself before referring to Niles in the past tense —"*is* unstable. The family closed ranks after Christian killed himself. Presumably because they thought he'd been innocent. What if Niles knew he wasn't?"

"And was driven mad by guilt?"

"Maybe. I know what it's like to have a serial killer in your gene pool. But at least I can say I'm not responsible for what the Larsens did. If it's your child who is the killer? Not only could it be in your genes, but you might have done something to make him commit murder."

Gabriel murmured something that could be agreement.

I reclined my seat and closed my eyes, and he turned up the stereo—Haydn this time—and accelerated onto the highway.

Anna Gunderson lived in an older suburb of North Chicago, a once-separate town, swallowed by urban sprawl. According to Gabriel, she'd moved there with her daughter after a recent divorce. She had a small bungalow with frilly curtains in every window. On the door hung a handcrafted welcome sign adorned with red flowers. There were more flowers in every garden. Lawn cutting service truck out front, young guy unloading a mower. He stared at the Jag as Gabriel pulled in.

"Sweet ride," he said as we got out. "What's she got under the hood?"

"I have no idea," Gabriel replied, his tone freezing out further comment.

"Bullshit," I whispered as I rounded the car. "You drive like that, you know what's under the hood."

"No, I do not. When I hit the accelerator, it speeds up. When I turn the wheel, it corners. When I hit the brakes, it stops. If it does all that to my satisfaction, then the particulars are unimportant."

"It'll be a five-liter V8. At least four hundred horses. Maybe five. Which, as the boy said, is very sweet. Yes, I know cars. It was my dad's hobby."

"And you left yours behind when you made your vow of poverty?" he said.

"I didn't have my own. With my dad's garage to choose from, that would be like Hugh Hefner sticking to one girlfriend. I also like being chauffeured. Which, may I say, you do very nicely."

He shook his head and ushered me to the door.

# CHAPTER THIRTY-ONE

'd seen photos of Jan Gunderson. She had looked as if she'd time-warped from the seventies, with long blond hair, a fresh complexion, and a penchant for peasant blouses and long skirts. Had she lived, I suspected she'd now look a lot like her sister, Anna. Blond hair cut to her shoulders, pin-straight. Dark eyes behind retro glasses. Loose khaki pants and an even looser blouse.

I think Anna's house was meant to be welcoming and cozy, but for me, it was anything but. The busy geometric wallpaper seemed at odds with the landscape art. The intermingled scents of candles and air fresheners made my temples throb as my brain tried to sort out the scents. Too many noises as well—the *tick-tock* of an antique grandfather clock, the tinkle of wind chimes through an open window, an NPR host chattering in the kitchen.

I actually appreciated the mental distraction, though. It kept me from feeling guilty. Anna was clearly not in mourning, which meant her father's body hadn't been discovered. When she found out, I bet she'd spend the rest of her life thinking of him there dead, alone and forgotten.

Anna took Gabriel's jacket, asked how the drive had been,

offered him tea or coffee or a cold drink—and completely ignored me.

"Coffee please," he said.

As she ushered him into the living room, she was so busy staring at him that she practically tripped over an ottoman.

"It's black, isn't it?" she said, as if she hadn't stumbled, but merely stopped to ask. "No cream, no sugar."

Which would, I think, be the definition of black coffee, but Gabriel only smiled—yes, smiled, and somehow managed *not* to look like he was about to devour anyone—and said, "Yes, please. If it's not too much trouble."

"None at all. I have cookies, too. Lemon."

"That would be wonderful. Thank you very much."

His voice had changed. Less growl. More purr. Anna went bright red and almost tripped over the ottoman again as she scampered off to fetch his coffee.

Once she was gone, he turned to me and murmured, "No coffee for you."

"Apparently. No cookies, either."

I didn't get a smile, but his lips did twitch. As he checked his phone, I tried to see what had Anna Gunderson tripping over herself. He was good looking enough. Not to my tastes. He had a hard face. Harsh even, asymmetrical and rough. Some women go for big, overtly masculine guys. I don't. And those eyes . . . I'd get used to them, but it would take a while, and from what Gabriel said, he'd only met Anna once. Why didn't they bother her?

When she came in with his coffee and cookies, he asked about her daughter as if he was genuinely interested. As he talked, I thought, "Maybe I'm wrong about the guy." Put him with someone like Anna Gunderson, a nice woman who has suffered a great tragedy, and his empathetic side came out.

And then I realized he was faking it.

He knew Anna had the hots for him, and he knew how to act so she'd relax and open up. Warm and friendly and attentive, even a little flirtatious.

There was only one thing missing from the performance. He couldn't make physical contact.

It was a natural extension of the act. Give her your full attention, and when the chance arises, make contact. Brush her hand when she gives you the cookie plate. Touch her arm when she admits that her father has not been well.

He knew all the right moves. Except he couldn't quite pull them off. There was a hesitation. An awkwardness. A faint setting of the jaw, as if forcing himself to breach that barrier of personal space. Anna didn't notice. She just seemed grateful for the attention.

I noticed, and I was fascinated. I took notes. Actual notes, since I now understood why I had to be invisible. Scribbling on a legal pad cemented my position as the dull, studious intern. I watched Gabriel take this woman—the victim of a tragedy she'd rather forget—and within fifteen minutes have her ready, eager even, to revisit it with him. I was impressed. This was an extension of my acting skills that was well worth learning.

Once the small talk was done and the ice broken, he eased into the interview. "As I said over the phone, I've heard rumors that Pamela Larsen is mounting a new appeal based on some recently discovered evidence. Now, I have contacted the prison and they know nothing about her hiring a new lawyer, so this may be mere gossip, but as the rumored evidence and direction of the appeal involves your brother, I thought you should know."

"I appreciate that." She met his gaze. "I really do, Mr. Walsh."

"Gabriel, please."

He leaned forward, elbows on his knees, his expression so sincere it mesmerized me.

He went on. "As I'm sure you deduced from my visit at the time, I had also considered using Christian in my strategy. I apologize for that. As a defense lawyer, I must look to my client's interests first. Even when the client has done something as reprehensible as murder, she is entitled to a complete defense. The fact that Pamela Larsen is still in prison only confirms that the system works. I do my part in ensuring it *continues* to work by taking on such cases."

"I understand."

"When I realized your brother seemed a very unlikely suspect, I focused my attention elsewhere. Now, I don't know what this alleged new evidence may be, but I stand by my original conviction that Christian could not have been responsible for the murder of your sister and even to suggest that—" His lips tightened. "Your family has been through enough."

Anna's eyes welled, and she couldn't respond.

Gabriel continued, "If there are any problems, I will offer you my services to deal with the defense team. Your father doesn't need the aggravation, given his health problems. Of course we're hoping it *doesn't* come to that, but if it does, I want to be prepared. The best defense is a quick defense. Today I'm gathering information, at no cost to you. If Pamela does hire a lawyer who contacts you or your father, give them my name. With any luck, they'll see we are prepared to defend Christian's reputation and will rethink their strategy."

He straightened, just a little, still leaning toward her. It was more of a flex really, his shoulders bunching, his jaw set, resolute. A physical reminder of his size. The big, strong man prepared to leap into battle to defend her family's honor. I glanced around for the nearest bowl of potpourri, in case she swooned.

"Thank you, Gabriel."

"You're very welcome."

Hot damn, he was good. I had wondered how he was going to pull this off. He might make Anna Gunderson's heart—and other body parts—flutter, but he was still the guy who'd tried to get her sister's killer acquitted. Pretending he needed the truth to *defend* Christian's memory, though? While framing the new appeal as a rumor that could never be proven either way? Genius really.

"I'm not sure how much help I can be," Anna said. "I'll try. I know it's important and I'm the only one who *can* help. Dad isn't in any shape for this."

"I'm not going to bring him in. In fact, it would be best if we kept this from him until there's a reason to broach the subject."

She nodded. "I'm not going to tell anyone right now."

Gabriel agreed that was wise.

Anna continued, "The problem is that Jan and Christian were so much older than me. Jan was—" She paused, eyes filling with tears.

He leaned forward, voice lowered. "Take a moment."

A wan smile. "Thanks. I was just thinking that Jan was only five years older and how little that would mean now. But when we were young, it was a huge gap. We got along, Jan and I, but I was always the little sister. I didn't know her as well as I would have liked."

She got along well with *Jan*. No mention of her brother.

"They were close," she continued. "Jan and Christian. Only fifteen months apart. Inseparable."

Gabriel flicked through his notes. I doubted he was actually reading them, just looking as if he had to refer back. He pulled one page to the front.

"According to this, they weren't that close when she died. Friends said they spent very little time together."

"Oh, that's just Jan's friends. Mom said they liked talking to the police officers, because some of them were young and cute. They exaggerated things to get attention. Jan and Chris were close."

Gabriel shuffled the papers, his gaze down. He looked troubled. After a moment, he gripped the file and looked up, jaw set, as if determined to speak, however much he'd rather not.

"Anna . . ."

A nervous flutter of her hands as she quailed under that intense stare. "Yes?"

"Do you want me to defend your brother's memory?"

"Y-yes. I really appreciate—"

"Then you need to be honest with me. It says here that multiple acquaintances reported that Jan and Christian were *not* close at the time of her death. Even your mother said they'd . . ." He consulted the file for effect. "Grown apart."

"Yes. Right. I'd . . . forgotten that. They were so close when they were young. I remember how much I envied that. As they got older, they drifted apart a bit. That's natural."

"Did it seem mutual?"

Anna shifted. Sipped her coffee. Even nibbled on a cookie before blurting, "You're right. I should be honest, and this is just the kind of thing a lawyer could use against Christian, so we need to be prepared. It was Jan who drifted. She was the popular one. Christian was . . . not popular. Her friends decided he wasn't cool enough for them. Jan was young. She made mistakes."

Jan had been a year younger than me when she died. From Anna's perspective, that now seemed very young, but from mine, it was past the age where you could blame peer pressure for making you avoid your geeky brother.

"And how did Christian feel about the estrangement?" Gabriel asked.

"It hurt him. A lot. For years he tried to get their old relationship back. I always thought that's why he killed himself. Because he'd lost her for good."

Gabriel nodded and gave her time to relax before he said, "You know I need to ask about the fight."

Anna didn't flinch. Instead, she let out an audible sigh of relief and relaxed back into her seat. "I never understood why Mom and Dad made such a fuss about that. By refusing to tell the police what happened, they made it sound important, and it wasn't."

Gabriel waited, his gaze on her until she continued.

"It was about Pete."

"Peter Evans? Jan's fiancé?"

"I don't know if this was in the file," she said. "The police probably didn't consider it important. Jan had been engaged to another man before Pete."

Tim Marlotte. He did have a page in the file, because an estranged fiancé made a good suspect when the victims were his ex and her new boyfriend. Marlotte hadn't been a serious suspect. Too much time had passed between the breakup and the murders. The cops investigated, though, and found Marlotte had a rock-solid alibi—he'd been at a family dinner, where a dozen people could vouch for him, including his new girlfriend.

"Tim was Christian's best friend," Anna said. "The three of them had hung out together since they were kids, and Tim and Jan dated all through college. Then she met Pete. That was tough enough for the family—everyone liked Tim—but combined with the other issue, it made for some serious family drama."

"Other issue?"

"The age difference."

"He was younger than Jan," Gabriel said.

Anna nodded. "Three years. Pete was barely nineteen when they started going out. My parents were embarrassed. His parents weren't happy. Tim was confused. Christian was upset. No one was pleased."

"Except Jan and Pete, I presume."

She wrapped her hands around her mug. "Yes. They were very happy. I look back now and I feel bad for everything we put them through when they were obviously in love. Even I wasn't nice about it. I think I was jealous. Pete was only two years older than me and he was such a great guy. Tim was nice and sweet, and I'd known him forever, but he and Jan . . . there weren't sparks, you know? Maybe it was because they knew each other so long. It was like a comfortable marriage before they even got engaged. They genuinely liked each other but *like* isn't enough for a relationship. Jan realized that when she met Pete. She loved him and he loved her back, and I wish we'd all seen that and left them alone."

"So the fight was about Jan and Pete?"

"Yes. Tim had started seeing a new girl. Christian had still been hoping Jan and Tim would reunite. He found out that Jan had called Tim to say she was happy for him. Christian exploded. He told Jan it was rude and cruel to congratulate Tim on finding a replacement for her. They fought. Christian stormed out. He came back that night after Jan was in bed. They didn't speak the next day and then . . ."

And then Jan and Pete were dead.

"So it was nothing," Anna said. "A family fight. Hardly anything that would make Christian . . ." She shook her head. "I can't even say the words."

After a few more questions, Gabriel wrapped it up. He asked if Anna had any contact with Tim Marlotte. Turned out they still exchanged Christmas cards. She had his number and was happy to ask him to speak to us.

As we left, Gabriel was closing the door and I noticed the welcome sign. Earlier I'd seen only red flowers on it. Now I saw what they were and tried not to stiffen.

"Poppies," I murmured. "An odd choice for decoration."

"Why?"

"Do you know what they signify?"

"Opium?"

I shook my head and started down the steps. "Death. Appropriate, I suppose, given all she's been through." I tried not to think of her father, of what she'd go through then. "God, I don't think I said one word in there."

"You did very well." He reached into his pocket. "Have a cookie."

I took it. "I didn't even see you swipe that," I said as I circled the front of the car.

"Just like you didn't see me take Grace's scone the other day. You need to pay more attention, Olivia. You're very good at listening. But paying attention is about more than listening."

"Yes, sir."

We got into the car.

As he backed out, he checked his watch. "Not yet one o'clock. We can talk on the way back to Cainsville or we can go to lunch."

"Lunch, please. Keep it under fifty bucks and you can even put it on my tab."


Gabriel took me to a deli near our highway exit. We ordered at the counter, then took numbers to a table to await our food.

"So now I know why you wanted me to look frumpy," I said as we sat. "You could have just told me."

"Could I? Let's see. I'd say, 'You need to dress down for the interview today because Anna Gunderson finds me irresistible,' and you'd say . . ."

I sputtered a laugh.

He turned a look on me.

"Sorry," I said. "It was . . . the way you worded it."

"I'm sure it was."

I pulled the paper from my straw. "I was impressed by how you handled it. You knew what she wanted to see, and you pulled it off so well even I was almost convinced."

"Almost? What gave me away?"

I hesitated.

"Something gave me away. I'd like to know what it is so I can correct the oversight. What was it?"

"Physical contact."

A lift of his brows.

The server arrived with our sandwiches. I waited until she was gone and said, "When you brushed her hand or touched her arm, it was awkward. That was the only time I could tell it was an act. My advice? Work with it. Start to reach out and then stop yourself. It'll look like you *want* to touch her even more than if you actually did."

He considered. "That might work. Thank you."

"You're welcome."

I took a bite of my sandwich. Then I opened my notebook.

"Okay, we have Anna's story. So what's your take on it?"

# GETTING THE STORY

The journalist spooned through his soup, looking for more meatballs, annoyed by the shortage but really, if he admitted it, annoyed with himself for blowing a story. It'd been an easy assignment. Everyone knew the councillor was a huge fan of the Cubs—or, at least, a huge fan of the player her husband had hired for his car dealership ads. The problem? No one could prove it.

Then the *Post* got an anonymous tip. The Cub boy toy had checked into a motel and the tipster saw the councillor slip into his room. The journalist got there and staked out the place. Two hours later, he'd heard the roar of the ballplayer's Porsche peeling from the parking lot, which meant the fifty-year-old councillor must have climbed out the motel window. Hey, she was banging a twenty-six-year-old, so she wasn't exactly an arthritic old lady. But his editor wasn't going to buy that. He was in deep shit.

And that's when he saw Gabriel Walsh.

He knew Walsh on sight. Everyone at the *Post* did. Their readers loved him. Or loved to hate him. Same thing, really. At thirty, the man was already a legend. Graduated first in his class. Grew up on the streets. Had a juvie record for picking pockets. Paid for law school with an illegal betting ring where he'd played the triple role of bookie, loan shark, and collection agency. Or that was the legend. The truth, as anyone who'd done his research knew, was a little different. Walsh had graduated in the top quarter of his class but hardly first. The betting? Street life? Juvie record? All unproven. Even his age varied from story to story.

Yet the fact that the rumors were unproven and not *disproven* meant they were still in play. Oh sure, they could just be mean-spirited gossip invented by envious colleagues. Maybe despite his reputation, Gabriel Walsh was a very nice guy.

The journalist laughed, nearly choking on his Coke. While some girls at the office were certain Walsh only played the role of a cold son of a bitch, it was generally accepted he was *not* a nice guy. Or even a reasonably decent guy. There were too many stories.

If the journalist could prove one of those uglier rumors was fact, he'd have a real article. Others in his esteemed profession had tried. A couple from lesser publications had written stories rife with innuendo and anonymous sources. One resulted in a lawsuit that forced the closure of the weekly rag and the reporter's decision, at thirty-two, to take early retirement in Mexico. In the other case, the magazine survived the lawsuit, but the reporter had ended up where he'd hoped to put Walsh—in jail. Apparently it wasn't a good idea to go after a guy like Walsh when you have a coke problem so serious you're dealing on the side to pay for it. Of course, there were those who said the dealing started *after* the article came out, at the prompting of the journalist's supplier, who had some tenuous connection to the Satan's Saints. But that was just rumor.

All things considered, though, it was probably best if he forgot about digging up a story on Walsh and settled for enjoying the very nice legs on his female companion. When he'd noticed her notebook and pen, he thought maybe she was a reporter, some cute young thing who'd managed to snag an interview. But no, others had tried that gambit. Walsh allowed his clients to do interviews but never gave them himself.

Was she his date, then? She was attractive enough, with the kind of face you noticed and thought was beautiful, then on closer inspection realized wasn't really—nose and jaw a little too strong—but you kept looking anyway. Her glasses were flattering, but why the hell would she wear them when she had such a striking face? And her hair . . . That was the worst. A horrible red dye job that was already fading. Underneath, her hair looked blond. That was as much a crime as the glasses. Why would you dye your hair when—

The young woman turned, her gaze following a woman's bag adorned with poppies. She frowned slightly and when she did, at that angle . . .

Holy shit.

It couldn't be. He never got that lucky.

He yanked out his phone and ran a quick Internet image search. The tiny screen filled with results. He clicked on one and looked at the photo, then at the young woman, now listening to something Walsh was saying.

Olivia Taylor-Jones.

Eden Larsen.

The society-brat-turned-serial-killers'-daughter was having lunch with the man who'd once represented her mother.

Now he had a story.

# CHAPTER THIRTY-TWO

As we walked to the car, Gabriel gave me research assignments. "Summarize your findings and e-mail them to me. I'm in court most of tomorrow, but if you have it to me tonight, I can give it a read and suggest new research directions."

"I can't do it tonight. I work until eleven and the library closes at six."

"Library? Why . . . ?" He sighed. Deeply.

"Yes, I need a computer. I'm saving up for one."

He waved for me to cut through a parking lot. "I imagine that's a new experience for you."

"It is. I'm catching up on everything I missed not being raised by the Larsens. Counting my pennies. Saving up for a new bike, a Ouija board, a hunting knife to teach a lesson to all the mean girls . . ." I put my notebook away. "Speaking of which, how's the gun situation coming along?"

"I'm reconsidering the wisdom of that right now." He waved me to the left. "It's coming. As for the computer . . ."

"I need better Internet access, I know. Larry has a computer at the diner. He'd probably let me use it—"

"Mr. Walsh!" a man's voice called behind us.

As Gabriel turned, he pulled me behind him, the move so

smooth I didn't even realize what he was doing until I was confronted by the wall of his back.

"Yes?" Gabriel said.

The patter of jogging footsteps. "Colin Hale. *Chicago
Post*. I—"

"Turn around, Mr. Hale, and go back the way you came."

"I just want—"

"I don't speak to reporters, Mr. Hale. Turn around now."

"It's actually your client I'd like to talk to." A nervous laugh.
"Or maybe *client* is the wrong word. I imagine Miss Larsen is
looking for information on her mother. Right? Family history,
so to speak."

Hale tried to sidestep, but Gabriel blocked him. I stayed
where I was. As much as I might like to stand up for myself, I
didn't need another "serial-killer junior" photo in the paper.
And Gabriel did make a very good wall.

"I'm going to ask you one more time, Mr. Hale. Turn around
now."

Hale tried to dodge around him again and Gabriel's arm
swung. I heard the crack of fist hitting bone. I saw Hale fly off
his feet, blood spraying from his mouth.

Hale hit the pavement, and Gabriel strode over. He reached
down and patted the man's jacket pockets. When Hale's hands
flew up to ward him off, Gabriel just swatted them away, his
face expressionless. He found what he was looking for—the
reporter's cell phone—and took it, then walked back and nudged
me to resume our journey to the car.

Gabriel stayed behind me. When I glanced back, he was doing
something on the phone, nonchalantly, as if unconcerned about
turning his back on a man he'd just decked. At the scrabble of
gravel, he tensed. He didn't look back or even stop walking, but
he was clearly listening.

He glanced up from the phone and gave me a "keep going" wave. A moment later, he murmured, "Good."

I looked back to see him pitch the phone in Hale's direction. "No photos?" I said.

"Just a poor one of us in the diner. I erased it and checked his e-mail in case he'd sent it. He hadn't."

We continued to the car. I waited until we were on the road, then said, "You aren't worried you'll get in trouble for hitting him?"

"No, I do it all the time."

He was joking. I think.

Gabriel turned onto the road leading to the highway. "He can't write about it without witnesses, which he doesn't have. He could report the assault, but he wouldn't get far. A reporter tried that back when I started my practice. He approached me for an interview. When he wouldn't leave, I responded in what could be called a threatening manner. He reported that I assaulted him. I had not. That was proven beyond any doubt. Shortly after that a photographer tried something similar with the same results. Clearly I was being stereotyped by my size and my choice of clientele and being persecuted by the media for my refusal to grant them unrestricted access to my clients."

"So now, if you do hit a reporter and he wants you charged with assault, the cops ignore it. Lucky break for you, then, getting two false accusations right off the bat."

"There's no such thing as luck, Olivia."

I laughed. When I did, he glanced over and studied my expression before turning back to the road.

I suppose if he was saying that he'd engineered the false accusations, I should be appalled. I thought of what happened in the parking lot. The way he'd hit Hale. The casualness of it. Punching the man hard enough to knock him off his feet. Maybe even hard enough to loosen teeth.

I remembered Gabriel's expression. No anger. Not even annoyance. He'd warned Hale. When the man tried to get past, he hit him. A reasonable response to a threat.

I glanced over at him.

"Yes?" he said, gaze still on the road.

"You have blood on your cuff."

He stretched his arm out over the steering wheel, suit jacket sleeve shooting back, his right cuff speckled with Hale's blood. A murmured curse of annoyance, and he adjusted the cuff so it wouldn't show.

"I think what happened proves my earlier point, Olivia. You are recognizable in that 'disguise.' While Hale didn't get a photograph, he may still write a piece saying he saw you with me. He may include a description of your attempts to disguise yourself. You need to give this some serious thought."

"How? He'll print that or he won't. I . . ." I paused. "Shit. I need to warn my mother." I took out my cell. The battery was dead. I swore again.

"Can I use yours?" I said. "I'll block the number. It's a local call. I'm just passing a message through the family lawyer."

"For your mother?" Gabriel glanced over. "She's not speaking to you?"

"She's in Europe avoiding the media mess. Which doesn't mean she won't hear of this if it's printed, unfortunately."

"Europe?" His brows lifted. He said nothing, but his expression spoke for him. Part of me wanted to make excuses for her. And part of me saw his reaction and felt relief, vindication even. If someone as objective as Gabriel Walsh found my mother's behavior odd, I wasn't wrong to be annoyed with her.

"If you're speaking to *her* lawyer, perhaps *yours* should speak to him," he said. "I can convey your message."

And in doing so, he'd convey a real message to my mother—

that I had delegated the responsibility of communicating to her to someone else. It was tempting, but I wasn't ready to go that far.

"I'll handle it," I said. "I need to warn James, too."

"Morgan? I thought the engagement had ended." He paused. "Or are you keeping him informed in hopes of changing his mind?"

"He's not the one—" I bit off the sentence. "I'm keeping him informed because it's the right thing to do."

"Ah." He turned the corner. "Back to my earlier point. I suggest you may want to stop hiding altogether. Speak to a reputable journalist and deal with the problem straight on. Journalists are like hounds, Olivia. The more you run, the more they chase and the more excited they get. I have some contacts—"

"No. If they find me, so be it. I'm not inviting that. Not yet."

He tapped his fingers against the wheel, gaze on the road. I waited for him to say something. When he didn't, I took out my notebook and went back to organizing my thoughts on the case.

I was an hour into the next day's breakfast rush when my phone started vibrating. I headed into the back with empty dishes, then checked.

Gabriel.

He didn't leave a message. I texted him back, saying no, I hadn't gotten a chance to use Larry's computer last night—which I'd said already, when I texted him eight hours ago.

I hadn't even sent the message before my phone started vibrating again. I glanced up to see Larry watching. I sent the text and left my phone in the back as I grabbed the next order.

Ten minutes later, as I was doing rounds with the coffee, Larry came out with my phone.

"Someone's really trying to get hold of you, Liv." He motioned me back to the kitchen. "Go ahead."

I answered my ringing phone with a snapped, "Yes?"

"Have you read the paper, Olivia?"

I went quiet. "Shit. Hale. He wrote that he saw me having lunch with you. Which paper? Wait, he said the *Post,* right?"

"There is no article about you, Olivia. It's something else." He paused. "I need to keep this brief. I'm on my way into the courthouse."

As he said that, I noticed the background noise. The screech and roar of rush-hour traffic. Someone talking too loudly on a cell. The faint click of heels on the sidewalk. Then a *whoosh,* as if he'd opened a door.

"Mr. Walsh?" a woman's voice said. "Can I get a comment, Mr. Walsh?"

"That's not about me, is it?" I said.

"No, my client. He's on trial for killing his business partner and dissolving him in quicklime. Which is ridiculous."

"Uh-huh."

"It is. Anyone in my client's line of work knows that quick-lime is a very poor solvent. Chemical hydrolysis is the method of choice these days."

"Did I apologize yet for snapping at you?"

A rumble that might have been a chuckle. In the background a man called his name.

"I apologize for the abruptness of this, Olivia, but I thought you should know. Pamela Larsen was attacked last night. There was a mention of it in the morning paper."

"Wh-what?"

*Poppies. Yesterday, I saw poppies.* I squeezed my eyes shut.

"Is she . . . dead?"

"No, but she's in critical condition. She asked to see you. They called me."

I stood there, struggling to think of something to say. The little girl inside me screamed, "My mother could die!"

"I . . . should see her then." I almost added, "Shouldn't I?" but angrily shook off the question. Not his place to answer. I took a deep breath. "Right. I'll go see her. I'm sure I can get Susie to cover. I'll take a cab to the prison. Or is she in a hospital?"

"A hospital. However, the doctors have assured me she's stable. I would advise against rushing to see her, given that she asked for you."

I paused, working through what he was saying. "You think she did this to herself? You said she was attacked."

"She was. Part of an ongoing dispute. The woman jumped her in the shower with a homemade knife."

"Okay, so unless she walked *into* the knife, she didn't do this intentionally."

"I never said she did. I'm merely suggesting that running to her bedside might not be the move you want to make. Wait and I'll take you."

I shifted the phone to my other hand. My right one was sweaty, cramping, as if I'd been holding it for hours.

"Olivia?"

"You're right. When?"

"Court ends at two. Your shift finishes at three, I presume?"

"Yes."

"I'll be at your apartment at three thirty."

# CHAPTER THIRTY-THREE

At 3:05, as I was walking back from the diner, Gabriel called. "Good, I caught you," he said. "Are you going back to your apartment to get ready?"

"If you mean changing out of my uniform, yes."

"You'll want to do more than that."

"Are you going to tell me what to wear again?" I asked. "Once was fine, but twice gets a little creepy."

"I'm merely going to suggest—strongly—that you take extra care and consider the image you want to present. There's a possibility we may encounter media at the hospital."

Of course. I should have thought about that.

"The question you need to ask yourself, Olivia, is are you still hiding? And if so, how much longer do you intend to do so? It's understandable that you didn't wish to face the media right away. You had to process the news about your parents. But as I said yesterday, journalists are like hounds. If you don't run, they lose interest in the chase."

"Great. But I just spent the last week setting up some semblance of a life here. Are you suggesting I just throw that away? Let photographers besiege my apartment until Grace evicts me? Let journalists hang out at the diner until Larry fires me?"

"Would that be so bad?" Gabriel said.

I gritted my teeth to keep from snapping. "I know you think I'm being silly living here and working in a diner. You've made that abundantly clear. However, I did not hire you to give your opinion on my life choices."

A pause. "All right."

"That includes not only advice but snarky and sarcastic side commentary."

A longer pause, and when he said, "All right" again, his voice was as bitingly cold as vodka straight from the freezer. Yes, I'm sure angry clients told him off all the time, but they didn't really mean it, because they were all too aware that he held their freedom in his hands. I'd grown up with lawyers, though, and in my world, they were employees. Valued and respected, but employees nonetheless.

After a moment, he said, "I'm not suggesting you reveal all aspects of your current situation, Olivia. Even if by some chance they tracked you to Cainsville, the town values its privacy. Anyone who asked for you would be told they'd made a mistake—you aren't there."

"That seems a little too good to hope for."

"As I'm sure you've noticed, it's a very insular community. My aunt tells me you've become quite popular with some of the older residents. In Cainsville, town elders still hold power. They'll protect you."

That sounded like something out of another century. But it was comforting, too, and when I glanced up at the omnipresent gargoyles, I *felt* comforted, as if their fierce scowls would ward off all the plagues that lurked beyond the town borders—including reporters.

"You will need to face the media eventually, Olivia. Do you want a surprise shot, like the ones they've taken so far? Or do you want one that presents the image you wish to convey?"

I paused, considering. Then I said, "Tell me what you have in mind."

His basic advice was simple: set the stage for a photograph, and that "stage" was me. How did I want to look in those photos? Like Olivia Taylor-Jones. Polished, poised, and prepared.

He gave me until four. It was enough time to do the best with what I had, which wasn't much, and as I sat on the front step waiting for him, I began reconsidering the wisdom of the entire plan.

When a shadow passed over me, I started and looked up to see Gabriel at the foot of the steps.

"Ready?" he said.

I nodded and followed him to the car.

"There's more than one way into the hospital, isn't there?" I asked as we drove from town. "I'm guessing any reporters will be parked at the main entrance."

"Most, yes, so I'll take you in the back. I'm sure we'll encounter a more enterprising journalist on that route. Preferably only one. That will allow us to control the situation."

"Actually, I . . . I'd rather control it by avoiding it altogether."

A faint smile. "I'm sure you would."

I looked over at him. "I'm serious." I lifted a hand against his protest. "Yes, you're right that I should dictate when and how I let myself be photographed. But I look like a twelve-year-old who tried to cut and streak her own hair. I can't afford my usual brand of makeup, and I picked the wrong shades. This is the best clothing I have—the jeans and shirt I wore when I left home. Not exactly haute couture."

"Not exactly Walmart, either. The cost of your sneakers could feed a family for a week."

"Which is the problem. With the crappy haircut and bad makeup, I look as if I'm trying to pretend I'm just a regular girl, yet I'm wearing three-hundred-dollar blue jeans. *Not* the image I want to project."

"I think you're overreacting."

"Really? I've spent a lifetime being taught how to project an image. I want to show the world I'm still Olivia Taylor-Jones. This"—I swept a hand over myself—"is not Olivia Taylor-Jones."

"Should it be?"

"If you're going to give me some existential bullshit about whether or not I still am Olivia Taylor-Jones, you can save it. What's important here is the *image*. Give me a week and I'll have enough tips saved to get myself a real haircut, decent makeup, and an outfit. The laptop can wait. Not the way I'd like to structure my priorities, but if I'm going to get myself in the paper again, I need to think of what my mother and James would want, too."

"Do you?"

"Yes." I reclined my seat, ending the discussion. "I do."

Gabriel bustled me into a side door. His gaze traveled along the corridor and darted into each open doorway we passed. He might not have been thrilled with my decision to postpone my media reveal, but having agreed to respect it, he apparently wasn't going to betray that by letting me "accidentally" bump into a reporter. I appreciated that.

I also appreciated the brisk pace. Nobody loves hospitals, but just one whiff of that smell—antiseptic and overcooked food— and my chest seizes up. Soon I'm gulping air, praying I don't hyperventilate. I've been told it's a panic attack. Which would make perfect sense . . . if I wasn't so damned healthy that I'd never spent a day in a hospital. I'd only been to the emergency room once, when I was fourteen and broke my arm playing rugby at school and my parents weren't home. Otherwise, my family doctor came to us; my deep phobia of medical care extended even to office visits.

That day, I had enough else on my mind that I didn't go into a full-blown panic attack. I still had to breathe deeply, and I caught a few concerned glances from people walking past, but Gabriel was thankfully too intent on vulture-watch to notice.

We were near Pamela's hospital room before I saw any sign of added security, and even then, it was only a young officer posted outside her door. He was reading a newspaper, as if his job was more to keep curiosity seekers out than to keep a notorious serial killer in.

When I commented on that, Gabriel said, "True. There will be another one or two inside, though. And they'll be eager to get her back to prison as soon as the doctors say she can be moved. But that's not because they're worried she'll escape. They're ensuring her condition doesn't worsen at the hands of someone who thinks the world would be better off if Pamela Larsen suffered a fatal relapse."

"Oh."

My mother had to be guarded against being murdered . . . by a complete stranger who might decide the justice system was better served if she left this hospital in a body bag.

As Gabriel spoke to the guard, I caught the murmur of Pamela's voice, and my shock froze into a moment of perfect clarity. I heard the squeak of a bed being pushed down the hall and caught the faint smell of urine and tasted something cold and harsh and metallic. And pain. I felt pain, a sudden wave of it and Pamela's voice, saying . . .

Nothing.

Pamela's voice was a mere undertone, nearly drowned out by the squeak of wheels.

I turned to see a nurse pushing a bed with a woman on it, so thin she seemed like a skin-covered skeleton. The woman opened her eyes. They were empty sockets, blood weeping from the holes, spilling over her sunken cheeks.

I wheeled and plowed into Gabriel. He caught me and murmured, "Olivia?" I blinked and turned. The nurse was still there, pushing the bed, frowning at me. The old woman lay on the bed, but her eyes were closed. She wore a white nightgown covered with red flowers.

Poppies. She wore poppies.

"Olivia?"

I struggled to snap out of it, but the halls seemed to sway, everything slightly gauzy, every sound garbled.

I forced my mind back to what I'd been thinking before I saw the old woman and the poppies. Hospitals and Pamela Larsen.

I said I'd never stayed in a hospital, but there were two years of my life I knew nothing about. I must have spent time in a hospital.

I should have felt relieved. All those times I'd chastised myself for such a groundless fear, and it might not be groundless at all. But I didn't feel relieved. I felt angry. Angry with my mother and my dad, who'd known damned well that I must have had an early bad experience before I came to them, but they hadn't told me, fearing it could spark memories of the life they wanted me to forget.

"Olivia?" Gabriel said.

"Sorry," I said. "Are we ready to go in?"

He peered at me, then waved me to one side. "Take a moment."

I stepped away from the guard and motioned for Gabriel to follow. When he did, I lowered my voice and said, "Do me a favor? Erase those words from your vocabulary. At least with me."

A frown. "Which words?"

"Take a moment."

The frown deepened. "I was giving you—"

"—a moment to collect myself. I'm sure you need to do that with your clients. They get angry, emotional, distraught . . . But remember yesterday when I advised you not to make physical contact? Same principle here. You can't pull it off."

"Pull what off?"

"Expressing genuine concern. I'm upset, and you see that as weakness, which you make very clear, however inadvertently. You say, 'Take a moment,' but what I hear is, 'Good God, not this again.'" I turned to the hospital room door. "Now let's get this over with."

# CHAPTER THIRTY-FOUR

Pamela Larsen lay flat on her back, her skin so pale she was lost against the white sheets. Even her lips looked white. The only signs of color were a yellowing bruise on her cheek and purple half-moons under her eyes.

*She's dying.*

*That's why I'm seeing poppies.*

*My mother is dying.*

I started to turn to Gabriel for reassurance, then stopped myself and looked over at the doctor by the foot of the bed, jotting notes on her chart.

"How is she?" I whispered.

The woman's gaze lifted to mine. I saw nothing in it. No reaction. No clues.

"Eden . . ." Pamela whispered.

I turned. She lay there, eyes still closed, lips barely parted. One hand clutched the sheets, grip tightening.

"Eden . . ."

I walked over and laid my hand on hers. Her eyes fluttered open. Then she blinked, lips forming an "oh" of surprise.

"Eden?"

I bit back the urge to correct her and nodded.

She smiled and took my hand in a squeeze so weak I barely felt it.

I asked the doctor again, "How is she?"

She told me what had happened. Where the knife went in. What damage it had done. All the coldly clinical medical terms that I didn't give a damn about, and I stood there, nodding, sifting through her words to find the ones I really wanted. When they didn't come, I said, "Can we step outside, please?"

"If you want to know the prognosis, barring any unforeseen complications, she'll be fine."

Emotion finally tinged the doctor's voice. Regret. *She'll be fine*. This was a doctor. Sworn to heal, not to judge. But judge she did, in the twist of her lips and the chill of her tone.

"Thank you," I said. "That will be all."

A faint widening of her eyes. "I beg your pardon?"

"You're dismissed."

She met my gaze, indignation flashing.

Gabriel stepped forward. "Ms. Taylor-Jones would like a few moments with her mother. As it appears you have completed your visit, we'd ask that you grant her that courtesy."

The doctor's mouth tightened. She said nothing, though. Didn't even look my way. Just returned the clipboard to its place and walked out.

"I want another doctor assigned to her," I said to Gabriel. "Can you do that?"

His chin dipped.

"Thank you."

As I turned back to Pamela, I noticed the two guards assigned to her room. The older woman stood as still as a statue, giving no sign that she'd witnessed anything. The younger man shot a smile my way, then ruined it by checking me out.

"Thank you for coming," Pamela said, her voice a papery whisper.

"How are you?"

A wan smile. "Feeling foolish. I've been in prison too long to be caught off-guard like that. My own fault. I've been distracted."

Distracted by the return of her long-lost daughter. I slid my hand from hers and pulled over a chair.

As I sat, she said, "You don't want to be here."

I shook my head. "I'm fine. Just . . . hospitals in general." I hesitated, then plowed forward. "Did I ever stay in one? I can't remember."

"You did. For a fever when you were two. Nothing serious, but you were dehydrated, so they kept you overnight."

"Not a happy childhood experience, I take it."

Her lips pursed, as if in remembered anger. "You'd never been away from us. Your father wanted to spend the night in a chair by your bed. They wouldn't allow it. We stayed in the waiting room. At two in the morning, we heard you screaming because you'd woken in a strange place. Your father was furious. Tore a strip off the nurse."

The younger guard snickered. "I hear he's good at that."

Pamela turned to him. She said nothing, just met his gaze with a level look. He drew back and muttered something under his breath.

How many other early childhood experiences with the Larsens had formed my character? All the things about myself I would have understood, if only my parents had said, *You were adopted.*

"I'm sure this is very difficult for you, Ed—Olivia," Pamela said. "This isn't how it was supposed to be. We wanted your grandmother to take you, but she'd had . . . problems. In the past. It didn't matter. She was deemed unfit."

"And there wasn't anyone else?"

Pamela shook her head. "Your father's parents had passed. We were both only children. So we were told adoption was the only recourse. The children's services people tried to persuade us to let you grow up not knowing about us, but your father wouldn't listen. That was the one thing he really fought for. Keeping access to you. And they promised it. We would get updates and annual visits for as long as you wanted to see us."

"So what happened?"

"Money. The Taylor-Jones had it and they wanted a little girl on their terms. Which did not include a second set of parents. Particularly ones in prison."

I shook my head. "They didn't know who you were until a couple of years ago."

Her voice came stronger now, anger seeping in again. "Then that's because they didn't want to know. They had custody of you weeks after we were arrested. I swear the adoption went through the same *hour* we were convicted. That's not normal. They paid someone off. Then there's a so-called bureaucratic mix-up, and suddenly our daughter was lost in the system."

"That's not possible."

"It is if you have money. Especially if the birth parents are serving consecutive life sentences for murder. We hired private investigators, but they took our money and did nothing."

"I'm sorry."

She studied my expression. "But you'd rather I found something else to talk about. Something that doesn't insult your adoptive parents."

"Yes."

Her gaze dropped and her voice lowered. "I'm sorry, Olivia. Obviously, this upsets me a great deal. But it has nothing to do with you, and from everything I can see and everything I've heard, the Taylor-Joneses did a . . ." She seemed to struggle before saying, "Very good job of raising you." Another pause. Another struggle. "They gave you everything you could have wanted, and if we couldn't be there, that's what we would have wanted, too."

She shifted in her bed. When she spoke again, her voice was calmer, the strain of speaking well of my parents past. "On the inside, you meet young women who were adopted, even more with foster parents. You hear stories. Horrible stories. I kept reassuring myself that you were fine, but I still had nightmares. So as upset as I am with the situation, I'm glad that wasn't an issue. Your father will be, too." She looked up. "You haven't been to see him yet, have you?"

I shook my head. "I need to apply for permission."

"Then do that. Please. Nothing would make him happier." A wistful smile. "We both loved you so much, but you were always Daddy's girl. Do you remember anything about him?"

"I . . ." I wanted to pretend that I didn't. But her expression was so hopeful that I found myself saying, "I remember him pushing me on a swing. I wanted to go higher but he was afraid I'd fall and skin my knees again."

She laughed. "Yes, that would be your dad. You loved swinging and swirling. I used to worry he'd make you sick twirling you around. Or scramble your brains." Another laugh. "Silly first-time-parent worries, I suppose." A wistful look. "We were so young."

I barely heard her. I was still back on what she'd said about twirling. I could still picture that in my memory except I didn't see Todd Larsen; I saw my dad—Arthur Jones—picking me up and swirling me around.

Had Dad done that, too? Or was I really remembering . . .

My stomach clenched.

Pamela looked over at Gabriel, the first time she'd acknowledged his presence. "You'll handle the paperwork for her."

"Will I?" he said.

"For another five thousand you will."

I swear his icy gaze dropped another ten degrees, but he only said, "If Olivia wishes it."

The door opened and a nurse looked in. "Five more minutes."

When the nurse left, I said, "About your case. You'd asked me to take a look at it."

Her eyes widened. "N-no." Her gaze shot to Gabriel. "You didn't let her see—"

"She was hardly going to turn it over to these innocence organizations without knowing what she was being asked to do. And since I have your file . . ."

"You *bastard.*"

"I didn't show her anything that was privileged information, Pamela."

"No, just the details of those horrible crimes." Tears sprang to her eyes. She reached out and took my hand. "I'm sorry, Olivia. That's not what I meant you to do at all. What you must have read—" She sucked in air and blinked back tears. Then she met and held my gaze. "We did not do that. None of it. It was horrible. Sick. Disgusting. To even think a sane person could . . ."

Her hand started to shake. She lifted her other one and wiped away the tears. "We didn't do it, which is why I want you to help us by taking our case to those organizations."

"I will. First, I—"

The door opened again.

"Time's up," the nurse trilled, a little too cheerfully.

Gabriel met my gaze with a faint shake of his head, warning

me not to tell Pamela we were investigating ourselves. She was too weak to answer questions anyway.

"I am going to pass on your case to someone," I said. "I'm just compiling what they'll need."

She nodded. Was she disappointed that I wasn't moving faster? I couldn't tell. She only assured me she could answer any questions that arose and would love the excuse to see me again, and then the nurse hustled us out.

We'd barely gotten ten steps down the hall before Gabriel asked me to wait, and he returned to speak to the officer guarding Pamela's room.

Gabriel spoke to the man, then shook his hand. It seemed an odd gesture . . . until I caught a flash of green, the officer being a little less proficient at accepting a bribe than Gabriel was at giving one.

When Gabriel returned, he waved me in the other direction.

"Taking the stairs?" I said.

"Service elevators. The officer said two reporters are waiting at the front door, and he believes there's an intern by the stairwell." He paused before pushing the elevator button. "This is your last chance, Olivia. If you'd like, I can go down, see who's there and discreetly arrange a meeting around back."

"Thanks, but no. Not yet."

"As you wish."

He pushed the button.

"About doing that paperwork to visit Todd Larsen," I said.

"Yes?"

"Dealing with one long-lost serial-killer parent is enough for now. But if it's worthwhile for you to make the arrangements . . ."

"My secretary can handle it. So, yes, it's worthwhile. Thank you." He held open the elevator door and ushered me out. "I don't know if you're feeling up to it, but I did manage to contact Tim Marlotte—Jan Gunderson's ex-fiancé. He could meet with us this evening."

"Good." I checked my watch. "If you'd drop me off at a library, I can—"

"Ms. Jones?" a voice called.

# CHAPTER THIRTY-FIVE

froze. The voice had come from my left. I wheeled the other way and—

And do what? Run for the nearest exit?

I adjusted my shirt, fixed on a pleasant look, and turned—to nearly smack into Gabriel's wide back.

"I'm sorry," he said as he blocked me. "Ms. Jones isn't giving interviews right now, but if I can take your card, we'll be sure to consider you."

"I just want five minutes of her time, Mr. Walsh. Please. My name is—"

"I know who you are."

"Then you know I've covered several of your cases. Satisfactorily, I believe. I'd have heard from you otherwise."

Gabriel paused.

"Five minutes," the man repeated. "You're free to advise your client against answering any of my questions. I'd like a picture, but it will be posed. I'm not going to sneak a shot of Ms. Jones racing from her mother's bedside."

Gabriel glanced back at me, then turned to the reporter. "May we have a moment?"

He took me aside without waiting for a response.

"I know, I know," I muttered before he could say anything. "I should do this. It's one guy. A few questions. Posed photos. You can vouch for his rep. I just wish . . ." I exhaled. "Do I look all right?"

"Yes, but if it'll make you feel better, I can buy you a few minutes in the restroom. As long as you promise not to crawl out the window."

"Tempting . . ." I glanced around Gabriel at the reporter. A small guy with a potbelly. Well groomed. Unassuming. He met my gaze with a polite smile.

"Two minutes with a mirror," I said. "Then I'll do it."

I didn't ace the interview. My mind was still with Pamela—worrying about her and getting annoyed with myself for worrying. On a scale of one to ten, I'd rate my performance a six. Still, it was a lot better than my earlier encounters.

Naturally he wanted to know my thoughts on my biological parents. An interview without that was useless. So I said I was still processing the news, still in shock, blah blah. Not the most exciting answer but an honest one. My others were less honest. I didn't lie outright, but I hinted—strongly—that I was living in Chicago and looking for work. The only questions I refused were about James. That was one topic I wasn't ready to speak on.

There was a question that I kicked myself for not expecting. What was I doing with my mother's former lawyer? Luckily, Gabriel smoothly covered for me, saying that he was facilitating contact with Pamela Larsen, ensuring that I got everything I needed from my biological mother—medical information and so on. When we finished, the journalist—a freelancer named Martin Lores—exchanged cards with Gabriel and promised to call with publication details.

———

We were in the car before Gabriel spoke.

"You handled yourself very well, Olivia."

I gazed out the window. "I did adequately."

I vaguely heard him say something as he backed the car out, but I didn't quite catch it.

"Olivia?" he prodded.

"Sorry. Just . . ." I rubbed the back of my neck. "This whole media thing has me feeling . . . helpless. I was looking forward to taking control of the situation, and I didn't get the chance."

A pause. "I see." Awkward. Damn it. I'd overshared.

I settled into my seat. "Go ahead, set the appointment for seven and dump me at the nearest library."

"Skip the research. It's not critical. We'll get dinner and I'll distract you with tales of my day in court."

"The guy who dissolved his victim with quicklime? Or was it chemical hydrolysis?"

"Chemical hydrolysis. Or that's what he *would* have used, had he killed the man, which he most certainly did not."

"Of course." I smiled. "Okay, take me to dinner and distract me."


We'd been inside Tim Marlotte's condo for less than five minutes before we knew exactly what had gone wrong between him and Jan, and why he hadn't been terribly distraught over their breakup. It wasn't the tasteful decor that gave it away. This was Wicker Park, a trendy neighborhood filled with wannabe artistic types. According to Anna Gunderson, Marlotte had recently given up a bank job to pursue dreams of being a sculptor. So I wasn't jumping to any conclusions . . . until a guy my age slipped into the foyer and gave Marlotte a kiss before leaving the apartment.

As we settled into the living room, I said, "As I'm sure Mr. Walsh explained, we're here to talk about your breakup with Jan Gunderson. I'm guessing that"—I hooked a finger toward the foyer—"is the reason."

Gabriel cleared his throat. "What Ms. Jones means is—"

"Yes, I'm not being subtle." I looked at Marlotte. "But that kiss wasn't subtle, either. Did you know you were gay when you were engaged to Jan?"

Marlotte scratched his neat beard. Then his ear. I kept waiting for Gabriel to jump in and say something soothing, take the edge off my bluntness, but he stayed silent. After a moment, his gaze flicked my way. Prodding me.

"I take it that's a yes," I said. "You knew, but at the time you had no intention of coming out. So you dated the sister of a good friend. You'd known her for years, liked her, could imagine a life with her, if you had to, and you thought you had to. Then she meets Pete Evens and discovers what was missing in your relationship. She breaks it off. You realize you're relieved. You let her go gracefully."

"I wasn't . . ." His fingers drummed the arm on his chair. "When I was engaged to Jan, I wasn't using her. I *did* care for her. I loved her. Just not . . . not that way."

"Did Christian know? He was your best friend."

"My *straight* best friend. That makes a difference, Ms. Jones. If a gay man confesses to his male best friend that he prefers men, he may very well find himself looking for a new friend."

"So Christian never suspected anything."

"I never confirmed anything."

I glanced at Gabriel. He motioned for me to keep pressing. Apparently, I was playing bad cop tonight.

"That's not what I asked, Mr. Marlotte. Did Christian *suspect* you were gay?"

He wriggled in his chair, pretending to just be shifting for comfort, but from his expression, wishing he could disappear into the deep cushions.

Finally he said, "I don't see what this has to do with—"

"It is important, I'm afraid," Gabriel said, his voice spiced with apology and regret. "You are aware, I know, that Christian was viewed as a potential suspect in his sister's death. We have heard that he was very upset about your breakup. Angry with her, which would be very unlikely if he knew you were gay."

"I . . . he . . . I confessed one night, just after I got engaged to Jan. We went out drinking, and I had too much."

"Before the breakup?" I said.

He nodded.

"And what did he say?"

"That it didn't matter."

"What?"

"He said it didn't matter." Marlotte spit the words now, old anger and resentment bubbling up. "Jan loved me, and as long as I treated her well, it didn't matter." He turned sharply to face me. "I wasn't really drunk. I pretended to be so I could confess. No one wants his sister marrying a guy who's gay, right? Maybe Chris wouldn't talk to me again. Maybe he'd beat the shit out of me. But whatever happened, I'd be free from the lies and maybe, just maybe, it would be the kick in the ass I needed to come out."

"Only that's not what happened."

"No, it's not." Bitterness etched lines around Marlotte's mouth. "I confessed to my best friend, and he told me to keep lying. Keep hiding. Which I did. For nearly twenty years. All because of Christian."

# CHAPTER THIRTY-SIX

As we were leaving Marlotte's place, Gabriel checked his e-mail. One so engrossed him that he walked right past the car.

"Everything okay?" I called.

"Hmm."

I figured that was all I was getting. Not surprising. I'd only asked to be polite. When we got into the car, though, he started it up and said, "You won't need to worry about Niles Gunderson anymore."

My heart thudded, and I said nothing. Then he looked over, frowning slightly, and I realized some response was required.

"Been locked up in the psych ward again, has he?" I said, as casually as I could.

Gabriel's head tilted. A barely perceptible movement, but I noticed it, and I knew what it meant—that behind those dark shades, his eyes were studying mine. I had to force myself not to turn away. After a moment, I said, "Gabriel?"

He put the car into reverse and backed from the spot.

"After the incident at your house, I was concerned that Mr. Gunderson might be a problem for you. I put out a request to various contacts, asking to be alerted if he spoke to the media or issued a threat of any sort."

Again, silence. Again, a split second too late I realized a response was required.

"Thank you," I said.

He glanced over at me. Was my tone too casual? As if I'd known that Niles Gunderson wasn't a threat—and why.

"You are my client," he said. "As such, I will look after your interests. It seems, though, that it was unnecessary. Niles Gunderson was found dead in his apartment this morning."

"What?"

Gabriel paused. I was sure I'd sounded shocked enough. Too shocked? Damn it. I should tell him.

Why? To clear my conscience? Leaving Niles dead in his kitchen was wrong, but if I admitted that, I'd only be burdening— and entrusting—Gabriel with my secret.

"He's been dead a few days, it seems," Gabriel continued. "Natural causes. It doesn't affect our investigation, but we will need to temporarily avoid contacting his daughter."

"Okay," I said, and lapsed into silence for the rest of the trip.

My phone rang while I was still sound asleep, and I leapt up, thinking I was late for work. I was so paranoid that I had two alarms for my 7 a.m. shifts—a bedside clock and the one on my phone. In my old life, the only time I woke before eight was when I had an early flight. My biological clock wasn't liking the new world order.

When I glanced at the clock, though, I saw that it was just past five thirty. I fumbled for my phone and peered at the screen.

Gabriel.

Why would—? Oh, shit. The article. I'd been sure it wouldn't run today. Lores still had to write it and sell it.

I answered. "The article ran, didn't it?"

"Good morning to you, too. Yes, it did."

"How bad?"

"Not bad at all. I think you'll be pleased. My apologies for calling so early, but I have court today and I know you're on the day shift. I've e-mailed you the article. I thought you'd want to take a look as soon as possible."

"Thanks."

"Also, you'll be getting a delivery at my aunt's. You can pick it up there after work."

"Files?"

"No, a laptop. I recently replaced mine, and I still had the old one."

"I appreciate that, but I don't want—"

"—charity. I know. And if I'm not inclined to give it to a homeless man on the corner, I'm certainly not giving it to someone with a multimillion-dollar trust fund. Twenty-five dollars a week seems a reasonable rental fee for a used laptop. Is that acceptable?"

"Yes, but I'll still need to find Internet—"

"My aunt has wireless. I'm sure I can persuade her to part with the password if you promise not to download movies."

"I don't have time to *watch* movies. Thank you. That will make research much easier."

"Which is the point, so gratitude is not required. I despise online research, and I'm happy to delegate all of it to you."

"So happy that you'll reduce the rental to twenty bucks?"

"No, but I'll persuade my aunt not to charge you for the Internet."

The article was fine. There was nothing to link me to Cainsville. No speculation over what I was doing visiting Pamela Larsen. It was all in my words—or an edited version of them that I was satisfied with. As for the photo, because it was black and white, you couldn't see the leftover red in my hair or that my makeup wasn't the right shade for my skin tone. Martin Lores had treated me fairly and gotten his scoop—the first words from the long-lost daughter of Illinois' most notorious killers. I was old news now. At last.

After work, I went over to Rose's to collect my laptop. I'd intended to just grab it and go, but walking into her appointment room was like stepping into a candy store.

"I'll make tea," she said.

"No." I yanked my gaze from a spirit photograph. "I mean, thanks, but that's not necessary."

"I'm making tea." She waved to the room. "Poke around."

When she came back, I was leafing through an old book.

"Which one is that?" she asked as she set down the tea service.

I showed her the cover.

"*A Magician Among the Spiritualists*. Do you know what it is?"

"Harry Houdini's accounts of his attempts to debunk spiritualists." I waved the book. "This cost him his friendship with Conan Doyle."

She smiled. "It did. Have you read it?"

I shook my head. "I've read *The Edge of the Unknown*, Conan Doyle's response. Wisely published *after* Houdini's death."

"Indeed. Borrow that if you like. It's interesting reading."

I hesitated, then nodded. As I approached the table, I saw the flower arrangement in the middle and stutter-stepped.

"Hawthorn blossoms?" I said.

"Yes. I stole them from Grace's tree."

"No, but . . . It's May." When I saw her expression, I gave an embarrassed laugh. "Sorry. Old wives' tale. Bringing hawthorn into the house in May is bad luck."

"Is it?" She stood and pulled the flowers from the vase, water droplets spraying.

"No, I didn't mean— It's just a superstition."

She walked to the window, opened it, and tossed them out. "Yes, and while I'm sure Houdini would be appalled, I prefer to hedge my bets." She came back to the table. "I also keep a sprig in the rafters to ward off bogarts. I wonder if that's allowed in May?"

"Bogarts?"

"Brownies gone bad."

"You keep hawthorn in your attic so your cakes don't go stale? Freezing them would be much easier."

She gave me a look. "I mean brownies of the wee folk variety. Bogarts are a particularly nasty form. Troublemakers. Not to be confused with bogan, which are just as troublesome but less maliciously so."

"Bogan . . . ?"

"Bogan, hobgoblin, bòcan, whatever you wish to call them."

"Goblins, I know. They're like trolls."

Her brows shot up, in a look very much like her nephew's. "My dear girl, you may know your superstitions, and you may know your fake fairy photography, but your knowledge of the wee folk is woefully inadequate. Hobgoblins are not trolls."

"Troll-like creatures?"

A slow, sad shake of her head. "I take it you've seen *A Midsummer Night's Dream*?"

"Sure. At the Shakespeare Theater out on Navy Pier."

"Do you recall the character of Puck?"

I nodded.

"He's a hobgoblin."

I frowned. "Are you sure?"

An exasperated sigh. She tapped my laptop. "Look it up when you get home." She poured the tea. "Now, about Houdini and Conan Doyle. What do you know?"

We fell into a long, nicely distracting chat about spiritualism.

As I finished my third cup of tea, I said, "Before I go, I have a question for you."

"Ah." A smug smile. "I knew you would eventually."

"Not that kind of question. It's about Gabriel."

Her smile evaporated as she said, carefully, "Yes . . ."

I leaned forward and lowered my voice. "Is he seeing anyone? 'Cause I think he's totally hot."

"Can't even finish that one with a straight face, can you?"

I choked back my laughter. "Sorry. But the way you were looking at me, that's what you were expecting, and I hate to disappoint."

"Actually, no, it wasn't. I've just learned to dread any sentence that contains the phrase 'question about Gabriel.'"

"Well, don't worry. It's strictly business. Yesterday he suggested I do a media interview. I refused, because I wasn't ready. We got ambushed by a reporter and he helped me through it. I want to say thank you."

"I see."

"While I'm sure what he'd really like is a big check, my budget is limited these days. But he did me a favor, and I'd like to acknowledge it."

"That's very thoughtful of you. And I believe I know just the thing."

She warmed my tea with another half cup and gave me her suggestion.

When I returned to my apartment, I had a visitor waiting at my door. The black cat.

"Sorry, but unless you like toast with peanut butter, there's nothing in there."

It just waited, the tip of its tail flicking, gaze fixed on my door. I opened it. The cat zoomed inside.

As I set up my new laptop, I heard a squeak. Then a crunch. The cat trotted over to me, dead mouse hanging from its mouth.

"Oh, so it wasn't about me at all. Your dinner squeezed under my door."

I walked back to the entry hall and opened the door. The cat didn't follow. I returned to see it crouching in the middle of my kitchen floor, ripping into the mouse, tiny bones crunching.

"Lovely. You'll let me know when you want to leave?"

The cat continued to ignore its host as it chowed down. I shook my head and started working.

# OLIVIA AND EDEN

Rose watched the cat cleaning itself in the girl's apartment window. She'd seen it around before, sneaking and slinking and killing, as cats were wont to do. So the girl had taken it in? Surprising. She didn't seem the type. No more than Rose herself. Maybe the girl was lonely. She'd noticed that earlier, when she'd offer more tea and the girl would hesitate before sheepishly accepting. Staving off the return to her empty apartment. Rose knew what that was like.

*The girl.* She shouldn't call her that. She had a name. Two, in fact, which was the problem. Olivia was too haughty. Pretentious. It suited the daughter of the man who owned the Mills & Jones department stores. And it suited the coolly beautiful girl Rose had seen in society page photographs. But it did not suit the young woman who'd been in her house an hour ago. Cool, yes. Self-possessed, yes. But not haughty, not pretentious enough to be an Olivia. An Olivia was all surface, an empty shell of sophistication. With this girl, the shell was a veneer. One that was slowly beginning to crack.

Eden suited her better. It wasn't perfect. A little too cute, conjuring up images of idealistic young parents searching naming books to find just the right one for their little treasure. Still better than calling her "the girl." As long as she remembered not to say it aloud. She couldn't afford to alienate Eden. Not now.

Speaking of alienating . . .

Rose looked over at her cell phone and stifled the overwhelming urge to call Gabriel and deliver a verbal smack upside the head. That was the price of having her grandnephew in her life. She must not meddle. A lesson she'd learned when he was fifteen, after his mother left.

A deplorable situation. Her niece had the parenting skills of a . . . Rose didn't even know how to finish that sentence. Any creature in nature so incapable of caring for its young would have died out centuries ago.

Rose pushed the phone aside, then swept the last hawthorn petals from the desk. A test for Eden. There were others, but this was the one she'd noticed. The power to innately detect and decipher omens was a strange skill, one that most psychics would deny even existed. And yet Rose had seen it once before— an old woman who could read omens. She'd been accepted and even quite celebrated in the community; Cainsville was an odd sort of place that way.

Rose had been only a child at the time, the woman merely a vague memory now, and she knew no more about her and her power. But when she'd seen signs in Eden, she'd set out the tests and Eden had detected one. Only one, though, meaning it was an ability as yet undeveloped. Rose could help with that, and she would, because it was in her best interests. For a Walsh, that's what it came down to. Eden Larsen or Olivia Taylor-Jones or whomever the girl was becoming would be useful, and it behooved Rose to take advantage of that.

# CHAPTER THIRTY-SEVEN

The cat never did leave. When he finished his mouse, he started meowing at me. I opened the door. He ignored it. I quickly laid out newspaper. He kept meowing. I got a towel—one of only two I owned—and reluctantly surrendered it. He curled up on it and went to sleep.

My Internet access wasn't smoking hot, but it was decent enough if I set up close to the front window. I spent the evening scouring the web for anything on Jan Gunderson, Christian Gunderson, Tim Marlotte—anyone and anything that might help me make a case against Christian. Or proved he was innocent and the Larsens had been rightfully convicted. I found nothing.

I woke up, let the cat out, and went to work. Or something like that. I attempted to let the cat out. But he had apparently stuffed half the dead mouse behind my stove, and when I tried to kick him out, he recovered his breakfast and set about eating it. Then he jumped into my sink and meowed until I got him a bowl of water. At least he didn't expect cream.

When I was ready to leave for work, I opened the door again, and even prodded him in that direction. He pretended not to notice. So I scooped him up and carried him out.

I reached the front doors just as Grace, dressed in a housecoat and a scowl, was retrieving her morning paper.

She glowered at the cat. "No pets allowed."

"Tell that to whoever let him *in*." I shifted the cat under my arm. "Also, you have mice."

She squawked as I left. Once I reached the sidewalk, I put the cat down. He gave me a baleful look, then tore back into the front yard, leapt onto the porch, and crouched behind a stone urn, gaze fixed on the door, waiting for it to open.

"So that's how you do it," I said. "Just don't let Grace catch you or you'll end up baked in a pie."

As my shift ended, Gabriel called to say we had evening interviews with one of Jan's old friends and a former teacher of Christian's whom the police had questioned about his association with the first female victim, Amanda Mays. It seemed like retreading well-trodden ground, but nothing else was popping up. Should I really expect it to? How many professionals had taken a crack at this case? I sure as hell wasn't going to prove the Larsens were innocent by questioning two people.

Gabriel knocked at my door at ten to six. When I let him in, he sniffed the air, frowning slightly. Then he noticed my guest.

"You have a cat."

"Not by choice." I shut down my laptop. "He came in last night chasing a mouse and apparently he likes it here. I kicked him out in the morning and found him at my door when I got back. I left him in the hall, but he started caterwauling. Grace came. She tried taking him outside. He scratched her arms, so she threw him in here and told me I have a cat."

"I see. Does he have a name?"

"That would imply I'm keeping him." I scowled at the cat, who simply tucked his paws under himself and continued ignoring me. "He gets a towel, some kitty litter, and that empty tin can for a water dish."

"From the looks of him, he'll settle for that. And maybe a flea collar."

On cue, the cat scratched behind his ear.

"Great," I muttered. I started for the door, then I handed Gabriel a box from the counter. "My thanks for getting me through the interview."

He took the box gingerly and stood there looking down at it.

"What? Is it ticking?" I reached over and pulled off the lid. "Cookies. That's what you smelled earlier—I hope. My first batch ever. Well, actually, my second. There was a test run. I'll feed them to Grace."

He looked down at the cookies.

"I asked your aunt what I could do to thank you," I said. "She gave me the recipe. Said they were your favorites."

"Ah. Yes. Well . . . this . . . wasn't necessary."

"Shit," I said, leaning back against the counter. "Too personal, isn't it? I told her that, but she insisted you wouldn't take it the wrong way."

"I'm not. It's . . . very thoughtful."

"Guess I should have just gone for a card." I slapped the lid onto the box. "You can throw them out when you get home, but they are edible. I ate two."

"They smell good."

"Whatever." I waved him out the door.


Gabriel drove into a largely residential neighborhood near Garfield Park. He pulled in between two beautifully restored greystones. The lane was clearly marked "Private parking. Violators will be towed."

As we got out, I noticed a video camera aimed at the spot where he'd parked.

"Um, Gabriel?" I gestured to the camera.

He nodded and ushered me along the lane. We came out between the greystones. In New York, they'd be brownstones. Same concept, different colored brick.

Gabriel led me up the wide front steps to the front door. As he opened it, I saw a small bronze plaque affixed to the stonework: Gabriel Walsh, Attorney-at-Law.

"This is your office?" I said.

Obviously it was. When I'd pictured his office, though, I'd imagined something unrelentingly modern. A sterile chrome and marble suite on the fortieth floor of some skyscraper.

He hesitated on the stoop, frowning at me slightly. Then he nodded. "Ah, I neglected to mention the pit stop, didn't I? I need to sign some papers before my secretary arrives in the morning." He hesitated. "I suppose you could have just waited in the car."

He glanced back toward the road. He looked faintly confused, as he had when I'd asked about his office. No, not confused. Distracted. He had my cookie box in his hand and was holding it out awkwardly, as if it might leak and stain his jacket.

I was about to say I'd go in with him. Seeing the outside of his office made me curious about the rest. Then, before I could speak, I caught a movement down the road—someone getting out of a car—and suddenly I was the one forgetting what I was doing as I stood there, gaping. Luckily, Gabriel was still too distracted to notice, and I recovered before he did.

"Maybe I'll walk around a bit out here," I said. "Stretch my legs after the car ride." As he reached for the doorknob, I said, "Take your time. I'll probably go around a block or two."

He nodded absently. "I should make a couple of calls."

I waited until he'd gone in. Then I hurried down the steps. I paused at the bottom. The car I'd seen was only about fifty feet away. The man who'd gotten out was even closer, coming toward me. There was no doubt who it was, yet I paused there, sure I was mistaken, as I had been once before.

He'd been smiling when I first came down the steps. As I paused, worry flickered over his face, as if I might dart into the office instead.

When I continued toward him, the smile returned, blazing bright now.

"Liv."

James covered the last few paces with his arms out, hesitating just before he reached me. I walked into his arms and hugged him back.

"You look good," he said into my hair.

"No," I said, backing up to look at him. "I look like shit. But thank you anyway."

A sputtered laugh as he hugged me again.

"I saw the article," he whispered as we separated. "I came by to speak to Mr. Walsh, hoping he was working late. I was just about to leave when you drove up."

"Howard did warn you about the article, didn't he?"

"Yes, I got his message. I got yours, too, from last Thursday night." His hands rested on my hips. "I've been forwarding my line to my cell ever since, in case you called again."

"I—"

"I didn't really expect you to. I made a mess of things. I know that." He took my hands, holding them and looking down at me. Then he glanced over my shoulder. "Can we go someplace? Talk?"

I wanted to say yes. Absolutely yes. Then I imagined telling Gabriel I was bailing on the interviews he'd arranged so I could spend some quality time with my ex.

"I can't," I said, then quickly added, "I will. We will. But . . ." I gestured back at Gabriel's office. "He's on the clock. He's helping me sort things out with the Larsens."

A faint tightening of James's lips. "Yes, I read that. You need to be careful of men like that, Liv. I'm sure he told a good story when he tracked you down, but he's only after your money. You really should have checked him out before hiring him. Or at least spoken to Howard. Walsh has a reputation—"

"For getting the job done," I said. "For being a helluva good lawyer."

I hadn't meant to defend Gabriel, but this was about me. My ability to exercise common sense and good judgment.

"I'm sorry," he said, moving forward again to take my hands. "I just thought that, under the circumstances, you might not be . . . yourself."

A brief hug. I didn't fall into it as I had before. He noticed and let me go awkwardly.

"So can we get together later? For a drink? A coffee?" A faint smile. "I promise not to question your choice of legal counsel."

His smile was genuine, but his tone rankled. I told myself to relax. I was on edge, surprised to see him, happy to see him, but nervous and anxious, too.

"I can't do it tonight," I said. "I have to work early."

"You got a job?"

I told myself that what I heard in his voice was surprise not shock. His smile seemed to confirm it as he said, "I should have known you wouldn't be sitting around feeling sorry for yourself. Charge into action. That's my Liv."

There was nothing wrong with his words. Or the sentiment. So why did I feel that old prickle at the base of my neck, like a starched tag left in my shirt?

"It's manual labor," I said. "But it pays the bills."

"Like I said, you always do what it takes. I'm proud of you. But I suspect that if you do come out with me tonight, you won't need to go to work tomorrow." He met my gaze. "We can work this out. Just meet me after you're done with Walsh and . . ." He pulled his hand from his pocket and opened it. In his palm was my engagement ring. "Give me an hour, and all this will be over. You can come home."

"I *can* come home?" I stepped back. "I was the one who left. No one—"

"That came out wrong. I'm . . ." A twist of a smile. "I'm a little nervous here, Liv. There's a reason I have you write all my speeches, remember? I just meant that you don't have to do this anymore. You don't need to stay away. Come back, and I'll take care of you."

That scratching again at my collar. "I don't need—"

He lifted his hands. "I know, I know. You can take care of yourself. I'm just saying you don't need to."

"What if I want to?"

His forehead furrowed. "Why?"

"Because I think I need to. I'm figuring out who I am, and that's important right now."

He stared at me as if I was speaking gibberish. Finally, he shook his head. "You're still hurt and confused. There's no need to punish yourself—"

"Punish myself?"

"Whatever the Larsens did has nothing to do with you."

"Of course it doesn't," I snapped. "I was a toddler. I'm not punishing myself. Like I said, I'm figuring things out and I need time—"

"You're still angry." He sighed. "Are you punishing *me* because I didn't—"

"No," I said, my voice ringing along the empty road. "It is

not about you. It's about me. Just me. I—" I stopped. Took a deep breath. "I'm going to walk away now. I think you need to keep that ring."

"Olivia . . ." There was a warning note in his voice that made my hackles rise. I resisted the urge to turn and kept going.

"*Olivia*." Sharper now, as if speaking to a sulking child. "I came after you once. I'm not doing it again."

*No, James. You didn't come after me. Not really. You let me run, and you followed a week later, not to talk, but to scoop me up and take me home. Give me time to learn my lesson and realize I want to go home.*

I didn't say that. I feared if I tried, I'd end up snarling it, and I didn't feel like snarling. I felt like . . . Not crying, though there was a bit of that. I heard his words and his tone, and I just wanted to walk away. Go someplace quiet and grieve, because after a week of telling myself it wasn't really over, I realized now that it was.

I turned slowly. "I'm sorry. I know you don't understand this, and I don't think I can explain it. I just need time to figure things out, on my own, and if you can't give me that—"

"You can't expect me to, Liv."

I swallowed a small surge of anger. "You're right," I said, my voice soft. "I can't. I don't. I never did."

I turned and walked away. He let me go.

The exterior door to Gabriel's building opened into a short hall with stairs to one side and a polished wood door to the other. There was a second nameplate, beside the door, confirming the door let to Gabriel's office. I stood there, catching my breath as if I'd been running.

The door opened. Gabriel walked out and stopped short.

"Ah, good timing," he said. "How was the walk?"

"Fine."

Whatever had been distracting him earlier had passed—unfortunately. He noticed my tone was a little less than perfect, and I got his hawkish stare. I ignored it and headed out.

# CHAPTER THIRTY-EIGHT

The interviews did little to improve my mood. With Marlotte, Gabriel had begun introducing me as "Ms. Jones." I never did figure out whether Marlotte understood who I really was. I suspect he didn't care. Same went for the teacher we interviewed that night. Jan's friend, though, knew exactly who I was, though I told myself that she only herded her teenage daughters away because she didn't want them hearing any gruesome details.

The teacher barely remembered who Christian Gunderson was. Jan's friend recalled more, but it quickly became apparent that Anna was right—Jan's friends had elbowed their way into the investigation because the cops were cute, not because they knew anything.

I struggled to hide my frustration, acutely aware of Gabriel's time clock ticking. It didn't help that I was worried about Pamela and how she was recuperating. I didn't want to. Yet the more I saw her, and the more I remembered of our past, the harder it was to see Pamela Larsen as a serial killer, not as the mother I'd once adored.

I stayed in my funk until Gabriel drove me to a shooting range and announced he had my gun. Had anyone ever told me I'd one day be cheered up by getting a handgun, I'd have laughed. The old Olivia might have wanted one, as a purely practical matter, given some of the places she went for her volunteer work, but she'd never have suggested it or she'd have been told simply *not* to go to those places.

Chances were I'd never fire this gun outside a range, but I liked having it. Gabriel seemed less happy. He clearly didn't like being the one to put a lethal weapon into the hands of a former debutante—or the child of serial killers. If something went wrong, he might feel responsible, and I got the feeling Gabriel Walsh preferred a life where he felt as little responsibility for others as possible.

So as we checked into the range, he turned into a walking, talking safety poster. Treat every gun as a loaded gun. Never point it at anything except your target. Keep your fingers away from the trigger unless you plan to pull it. When you are not carrying the gun, store it in a safe place.

"I was thinking of keeping it under my pillow. Is that okay?"

The look on his face made me wish I was faster with my cell phone camera.

"Fine," I said. "I'll keep it in my bedside drawer, in case I'm woken in the middle of the night and mistake the cat for an intruder. An honest accident."

"You're not shooting the cat. It would leave a mess."

"True. Also, the killing of small animals is the entrance ramp onto the serial killer superhighway." I paused. "Damn. I bet the cat knows that. He picked me because I can't hurt him, or I'd be fulfilling my biological destiny. So I'm screwed. The cat stays. Unless you'll kill him . . ." I glanced at him. "How does fifty bucks sound?"

He shook his head and ushered me to a spot on the range. "So where on the target do I aim?" I said after enduring another lecture on gun safety and a demonstration on weapon loading. "They don't have any arms or legs, so I can't just wing him."

"Which you wouldn't do anyway. If you're shooting someone, you're in honest fear for your life, meaning you need to take him down. Aim for the main body mass."

"How about the head?"

"Your chances of hitting the target at all are slight enough. Don't push it."

"Will you give me twenty bucks if I hit the head?"

"I'll give you ten if you just shut up and shoot."

I lined up the target and fired three rounds. Gabriel leaned across the barrier, as if to reassure himself that he wasn't imagining the trio of holes.

"It would have been much more impressive if I'd shot out my initials." I motioned him back, aimed again, and fired three more. "Hmm. You're right. Best not to aim for the head. Only two out of three that time."

"You've used a gun before."

"No, I'm just naturally good at killing things. You should see me with a knife." I reloaded. "My dad kept a gun at home for security. When I was a teenager he decided I should have access to it, and Mum insisted on lessons. Dad and I made an annual trip to the range. Father–daughter quality time."

"And you didn't see fit to tell me this?"

I shrugged. "You would have thought I fired a gun once and was exaggerating to avoid paying for lessons." I pulled the target forward. "Also, having never used this particular caliber or model, I really should practice. So if it's okay with you, that's what I'll do for the rest of my hour." I unhooked the target, then handed it to him. "But since I'm still paying, you can change the targets."

He wadded it up and tossed it into the trash.

"Don't grumble," I said. "Or I'll bake you more cookies."

On Saturday, Gabriel took me to see Pamela. It was a brief visit, barely ten minutes before they kicked me out. She was doing fine. I'd known that—Gabriel had been keeping me updated on her condition. She wasn't ready to go back to jail yet, though. She'd been spiking a fever. Nothing serious, but enough to keep her in the hospital.

With such a short visit, there wasn't time for much more than greetings and good-byes. She did ask how I was coming along on turning over her case. Gabriel covered for me there, lying and saying he was setting up the appointments. No way she could call us on it. That's one advantage to dealing with someone in jail.

After the visit, Gabriel and I went for lunch. We talked. Nothing earth-shattering there, either. Just talk really. About the case and not about the case. I enjoyed his company. There was, I admitted, the possibility I enjoyed it a little too much. I could say I was just lonely, but there were times over that weekend when I was keenly aware that Gabriel Walsh was not an unattractive man.

At Anna Gunderson's place, I'd acknowledged a physical appeal of a very masculine man, but said I didn't see it myself. I lied. Or maybe I'd changed my opinion. It could be because Gabriel was so different from James, and I wanted to distance myself from my ex-fiancé. Oh, hell, let's be perfectly honest. It was probably just hormonal. I like sex. A lot. Two weeks of chastity wasn't exactly torture, but after all I'd gone through emotionally, I really could have used the distraction. Put a good-looking, virile man in prolonged close contact with me and even if I'd never thought of him as my type, a primitive part of me still occasionally shouted, "Hell, yeah!"

With Gabriel, the attraction only blazed in blessedly brief flares, usually when he came close enough for me to be physically aware of him. Then that would pass, and he'd revert to being simply a guy I found fascinating. Yes, I found him fascinating—his world, his thoughts, his opinions, his entire way of looking at life.

However I felt, though, I knew better than to take that fascination or that attraction beyond a business relationship, even if he had been interested, which he gave absolutely no sign of being. And I was glad of that. As much as I enjoyed sex, I've never been able to manage it without emotional involvement. Gabriel didn't do emotional involvement.

I'm sure there were many women who'd made the mistake of thinking they'd be the one to break through that ice and make a connection. I wasn't ever going to join them in their delusion.

# DAMNED COOKIES

Gabriel Walsh leaned back in his office chair, fingers drumming the arm while he scowled at his laptop, as if its failure to automatically write briefs was inexcusable. It was Monday, and his murder trial had just wound up. The jury had retired to decide on a verdict and it looked like a long wait. His client didn't need hand-holding, so Gabriel had come back to the office to get some work done. Or that was the plan. He had yet to actually accomplish anything.

It wasn't that he was anxiously awaiting a verdict. He knew what it would be. Guilty. And that didn't bother him, because his success could be measured by the very fact that the jury needed time to deliberate at all. When the case hit the papers, it was presumed his client would plead guilty. Anything else would be a waste of taxpayers' money since the outcome was inevitable.

It was the idiot's own fault. Dissolving a corpse in quicklime? Any fool with a basic knowledge of chemistry knew quicklime was a preservative, and it could only be used to destroy a body if done with extreme care. His client had not taken extreme care. The result was a corpse that was only superficially burned. His client was guilty and would go to jail, but Gabriel had given him a hell of a defense, one that would bolster his own reputation better than any easy victory.

So what was keeping him from his work? That box of cookies.

Damn Rose. She swore she wouldn't meddle, but she always found a way. If he confronted her, she'd snap back, "I told the girl you like cookies. Is that a state secret?" It wasn't, of course. It had been a very thoughtful thing for Olivia to do. But under the circumstances, such a show of appreciation was a direct jab at his conscience.

He had nothing to feel guilty about. If he knew one thing about life, it was this: look out for yourself. No one else would do it for you. If you were cheated or tricked, it was your own fault, and a lesson best learned before the world devoured you. So he had done nothing wrong. And yet . . .

He eyed the box. He should just throw the damned thing into the trash. But he couldn't, because it would suggest he felt that prickle of conscience. So he should eat them. But if he did, and he couldn't get them down, that, too, would suggest guilt.

Or it might suggest inedible cookies. Olivia had said it was the first time she'd baked. She'd seemed so pleased with herself, too. Perhaps that was what really bothered him. The smug joy she'd taken in doing a task that was for many a chore.

His efforts to mask his annoyance with Olivia's "life choices" had been less successful than he'd like. That irked him. His clients routinely made decisions he found repugnant. Olivia's choice was, in contrast, a minor thing, but he found himself unable to hide his response.

He suspected that Olivia's particular life choice hit a little too close to home. Olivia "giving up" her life of privilege reminded him of his mother and Lent. They'd never set foot in a church—he didn't even know if they were Catholic—but every Lent, she gave up something, just for fun. While one could argue there were many things Seanna Walsh could give up that would improve her life—and her son's—it was never any of those, but something frivolous, like chocolate. A meaningless sacrifice. She'd made him do it, too. He'd cheated, sneaking candy bars into his room, but those stolen snacks had been as bitter as a guilty conscience, made all the more stomach-churning by the conviction that he had nothing to feel guilty for.

Olivia giving up her life of privilege was just as meaningless. She should accept her advantages and be grateful for them. But no, she'd voluntarily walked away, taken a smelly apartment and a menial job, and it was, for her, a grand adventure. Like a suburbanite roughing it in a cabin without electricity or running water. If it got too rough? Pack it in and go home.

Real poverty was not a choice. If you knew what that was like, then you would look at Olivia Taylor-Jones and you wouldn't be impressed. She had everything she wanted. Turning her back on that was the foolish act of an immature, spoiled child.

Except that Olivia was not particularly immature or spoiled. Which, he could argue, only made her decision all the more repugnant.

Still, it wouldn't last much longer. One of these days, she would wake up, go to ring the bell for her cappuccino and crois-sants, remember that she'd voluntarily chosen a life without cappuccino and croissants and maids, say "What the hell was I thinking?" and hightail it home to Mommy.

When she did, he would convince her that she still wanted the Larsen case investigated. Then there would be no waiting for her trust fund—he'd be paid up front. While she hadn't proved as incompetent as he feared, he worked better alone. For Olivia, the allure of playing detective would wear off soon, taking her enthusiasm and commitment with it.

The intercom buzzed. "Mr. Walsh?"

"Yes?"

"There's a Mr. Morgan here to speak to you."

He hesitated. No, it was a common enough name.

"Morgan?" he repeated.

"James Morgan," his secretary, Lydia, said. "Olivia—"

"Yes, I know who he is. Tell him I'll be out in a minute."

Olivia's ex-fiancé. Coming to see him. What the hell for?

His gaze shifted to the pile of newspapers on his desk.

The article. Morgan had seen Gabriel's name, looked him up, and asked around. Now he was riding to Olivia's rescue, to free her from Gabriel's clutches—and cut Gabriel loose from her employ.

Damn. This could be inconvenient.

He crossed the office and hit the button on the camera that fed into the reception area. Sometimes it was advantageous to watch waiting clients, judge their mood, decide exactly how long they could or should be kept waiting.

With one glance at James Morgan, Gabriel knew that ignoring him was not an option. The man hadn't even taken a seat. He was important, damn it, and he would not be kept waiting. The white knight, on his feet and prepared for battle.

Very inconvenient.

Gabriel sized up the man. He had doubtless seen photographs of Morgan before, but when he'd learned whom Olivia had been engaged to, he'd been unable to pull up a mental image. Now he knew why. Because there was absolutely nothing memorable about him. Oh, he cut a dashing enough figure. Handsome, trim and fit, well groomed, custom suit. But walk down the Loop and you'd see a dozen men like him. Corporate Ken dolls with just as much personality as the plastic version.

Before Gabriel had met Olivia, he'd have doubtless thought James Morgan was a good match for her—Corporate Ken and

Debutante Barbie. But now he looked at Morgan and thought, *What the hell does she see in him?*

The answer came quickly. An easy life. That's what Olivia would see in a man like James Morgan. Good genetics. Deep pockets. Political aspirations. And dull enough that she could wrap him around her finger or pin him beneath her heel, depending on which served her purpose. Olivia might like to think she was a decent, well-bred young woman, but there was a streak of ruthless survivalism there, and Morgan was further proof of it.

Interesting.

Gabriel opened his door and walked into the reception area.

"Mr. Morgan?"

Morgan turned. Relief flickered across his face, as if he hadn't expected Gabriel to see him.

"Gabriel Walsh," Gabriel said, extending his hand.

As Morgan shook it, he gave Gabriel his own sizing up. He doubtless hadn't been thrilled to hear that his beautiful ex-fiancé was being spotted around town with an unattached, successful young lawyer. But James's satisfied nod said that once-over was all he needed to reassure himself that the relationship with Olivia was simply business.

Asshole.

"You wanted to speak to me?" Gabriel said.

"I did. Do you have a few minutes?"

"Certainly." Gabriel waved him toward his office and motioned for Lydia to hold his calls.

# CHAPTER THIRTY-NINE

When I walked away from my family home, I left a lot of things behind. There were times when I did miss those advantages. Like when it was dinner hour and my stomach was grumbling, and I hadn't thought of what to make, much less started cooking. Tonight that was covered. Gabriel had texted me to say he was coming to discuss the case and would be bringing takeout for both of us. Very nice, even if I suspected he'd add it to my bill.

So I was working at home, drinking cold coffee from the diner, and munching on slightly burned cookie rejects. The cat was on his towel. I'd broken down and bought him some food. Also, a flea collar. I'd seriously contemplated a real collar—a sparkly green one—if only because I was sure it would offend his dignity.

At 5:50 my phone rang.

"It's Gabriel," he said, as he always did, as if I might not recognize his number. Or his voice. "I just had a very interesting visitor."

He paused. I played along, asking, "Who?"

"William Evans."

"Who?" I barely got the question out before the name clicked. "The father of Peter Evans. Jan Gunderson's boyfriend."

"Correct."

"He stopped in to speak to you?"

"Not quite. He came right after I left for an appointment. I suspect that was not a coincidence. When I represented Pamela, Mr. Evans made it very clear he wanted nothing to do with me. Refused all my requests for interviews. Now it seems he wants to speak to you."

"Me? Why? To threaten me like . . ." I trailed off as I thought of Niles Gunderson.

"Mr. Gunderson was mentally unstable. William Evans is not. While he is nearing seventy, he still works as a clinical psychologist."

"He's a shrink? That's not much better." I sighed. "Are you saying I should call him?"

"Yes. We can do that tonight if you'd like me to coach you through it."

"I can handle it."

"All right, then. I'll give you his number."

I Googled William Evans before I called. I had to add "Chicago" and "psychologist" to narrow it down, but once I did, he popped up. A well-known guy it seemed. Lots of awards and accolades for his work. Several charity affiliations, particularly Peter's Angels, an organization he'd founded to offer free grief counseling for the victims of violent crime.

I dialed his number.

"Oh God, do I smell miso soup?" I said as I let Gabriel in.

"Small-town life has its limitations, doesn't it? Not much hope for Japanese in Cainsville, which lacks even the requisite Chinese takeout."

"Having eaten from small-town Chinese takeouts, I'm not missing anything. Though if those old urban legends about them are true, it might solve my cat problem."

The cat glanced up from his spot by the stove and fixed me with a baleful stare.

"Don't give me that look," I told the cat. "You've caught one mouse since you've been here. And what do you get in return? Food, shelter, and a human servant to clean up your shit. You didn't even warn me when someone was at the door."

"Because his sixth sense tells him I can be trusted."

"Then his sixth sense is broken."

I took the soup to warm in the microwave.

"Did you call Evans?" Gabriel asked as he emptied the take-out bag.

"Yes. He'd like to see to me. Seems that friend of Jan's called to warn him I was investigating Peter's murder. He wants to help."

"Help?"

I shrugged as I brought the soup to the table. "He says he has information that the police weren't interested in at the time. About Christian."

I had to smile at how fast Gabriel whipped around, nearly dropping a box of sushi.

"And he didn't see fit to give it to me when I was representing Pamela?"

"He doesn't like you," I said. "You're . . . how did he put it? Pathologically ambitious. Me? In my own way, I'm as much a victim as the families who lost loved ones in this tragedy."

Gabriel snorted as he took his soup and sat.

"I seem to recall you saying almost the exact same thing once," I said.

"That was before I knew you."

I sat down and took a salmon roll. "Anyway, Evans obviously likes taking care of victims, so I'll play one for him tomorrow."

Gabriel frowned. "You've arranged an appointment? I'm

waiting for a verdict on the Rivers case, Olivia. I cannot—"

"You're busy, I know. I'm not. It's my day off. So I'll handle this. He doesn't want you there anyway."

"I would prefer to be there."

"And I'd prefer to have you there. But it ain't happening. Either I go in alone or we don't get this interview."

"I'll drive you. We'll reschedule if necessary."

"I'm perfectly capable of—"

"You were already attacked by the father of one victim. You're my client. I can't have you getting yourself killed."

"Getting *myself* killed?" I shook my head. "No wonder you're a defense lawyer. We'll discuss transportation later. Let's eat."

After Gabriel left, I couldn't relax, much less consider winding down for the night. I kept thinking about William Evans and what he might have to say to me.

Finally, I gave up trying to relax and went out for a walk. By ten, Cainsville had shut down for the night. Main Street was a movie set of a picture-perfect town, the road empty, the sidewalk bathed in soft lamp glow, the wind whispering past. I suppose that could be eerie, too, postapocalyptic even, but I knew where all the people were—at home, snug in their beds, dreaming.

Even the gargoyles weren't sinister at night. They loomed from rooftops like grumpy old men on a small-town porch, ready to yell at any kid who dropped a candy wrapper, but making sure they stayed safe, too. When one gargoyle seemed to move, I only glanced up. I think if it had spread its wings and flown off, it wouldn't have fazed me. It was just that kind of night. It was a cluster of bats, though, launching from their stonework perches, to pirouette and swoop across the sky.

When the bats were gone, I continued on. The breeze

changed direction, bringing with it the smell of moonflowers from a storefront garden. Planting moonflowers for a place that never stayed open past dark? It seemed a touch of whimsical defiance.

I could smell honeysuckle from the lamppost pots, too, along with the rich scent of damp earth, as if they'd just been watered. One was still dripping. It made no sound, which seemed odd until I realized there were strategically placed sidewalk-level pots under each hanging one. I put out my hand, letting a few drops fall on it. In the glow of the streetlamp, my fingers seemed red and I lifted them for a better look in the light. Then I caught a few more drops. Yes, definitely a red tinge, like the water on the school yard.

If I was being macabre, I could imagine it as blood. But I wasn't in that kind of mood. It was iron or runoff from clay or red bark or red stone. I wiped my fingers on my jeans and turned to see a face staring at me. A gargoyle face embedded in one of the stone medallions carved around the bank's thick doors. I must have walked this way a dozen times and had never noticed it. I even ran my fingers across the bulbous nose and hooked chin and curved horns, in case I was seeing wrong.

"I see you found one of our hidden gargoyles."

I jumped and turned to see Veronica—the old woman who'd helped fight off the raven. She was coming around the corner, tugging a contraption that looked like a mobile watering can with a sprayer hose. It wheeled along silently on rubber tires.

"I hadn't seen this one before," I said, touching the gargoyle.

"That's because it's a night gargoyle. It only comes out after dark." She waved to the garden across the road. "Like the moonflowers."

"Ah." I smiled. "Well, it was definitely well hidden. Are there any more?"

"Lots. I could tell you how many, but that would be cheating. Only a few select elders know the total number of gargoyles in Cainsville and where to find them. Otherwise it would spoil the May Day contest."

"May Day contest?"

"Every year, at the festival, the children can submit a list of all the gargoyles they've found so far. There are prizes for those who get more than half of them, more than sixty percent, and so on." She smiled. "It's quite a competition. The kids jealously guard their lists year after year, and they are forbidden to pass along hints to their own children later."

"What happens if someone finds them all?"

"We add another gargoyle . . . modeled after the child. Of course, the last time that happened was almost twenty years ago. To the youngest winner ever. He was ten." She looked at me. "Care to guess who?"

I thought of all the locals who would be about the right age, then shook my head.

"Gabriel Walsh," she said.

I tried to picture Gabriel as a boy, visiting his aunt, racing through the streets, laughing as he hunted for gargoyles. I couldn't. But as I peered out, I imagined another little boy, a serious dark-haired child, notepad in hand, searching with a single-minded drive, determined not just to win but to set a new record. Yes, that would be Gabriel.

"So where's his gargoyle?" I asked.

Veronica's eyes danced. "You need to find it." She rubbed her lower back and grimaced.

"Are you okay?"

"Old bones. A sit-down is next on my to-do list." She waved at a bench near the diner. "I'd love company if you care to chat, but I know you're a busy young woman."

"I have time. I want to hear about May Day."

I knew a bit about the tradition. It was pre-Christian, marking the celebration of Beltane on the first of May, heralding spring. People put on their spring suits and dresses, danced around the maypoles, crowned a May queen, and feasted. As Veronica explained, the town of Cainsville stuck close to the old traditions.

"We have four major festivals every year," she said. "May Day is the spring one, and always includes a wedding or two, for the young people who come back, set on getting married in Cainsville."

"You mean if they don't want to get married in church?"

She stared at me a moment before bursting out laughing. "For a girl who notices so much, sometimes you notice very little. Where are these churches in Cainsville?"

"Where are . . . ?" I thought. "You know, I haven't seen any . . . Wait. There aren't any."

"Correct. So you did notice. You just didn't process the information. Cainsville has no churches."

"Why? I mean, it's big enough, isn't it?"

"It is. But the gargoyles kept them out."

"Uh-huh."

"It's true. The gargoyles protected us from organized religion. And as an old pagan, I'm perfectly happy with that." She gave a sly smile as she stretched her legs, getting comfortable. "Cainsville was settled by immigrants from the British Isles. Hence, May Day. There were a few Anglicans, a few Presbyterians, a few Catholics, a few pagans . . . In other words, the religious background wasn't cohesive enough to choose a representative church. So everyone worshipped in their own way. As the town grew, people of other faiths joined and that continued. If you wanted services, you'd drive to a neighboring town. A perfectly suitable arrangement that recognized freedom of religion. All very American . . .

"But one of the churches didn't think so," she continued. "They sent a letter to the town council saying they wished to build here. The council politely demurred. The church insisted and there was pressure from neighboring towns, who've always thought we were a little odd. So the council relented. The church sent a representative. He took one look at the gargoyles and hightailed it from town. Declared we were all terrible heathens. The church demanded we remove some so they could feel comfortable building here. We refused. So we have no churches. Thanks to the gargoyles."

"Notre Dame is famous for its gargoyles. Plenty of old churches have them."

"Do you know why?"

"I know their original purpose is architectural. They divert water from the building itself. That's why they lean out—to let water fall away from walls so they aren't damaged by runoff."

"Correct. But churches also used them for two other functions. Some thought they would scare people into churches—remind them of the hell and damnation that awaited if they skipped service. Others viewed them as guardians, keeping the worshippers safe. There developed, however, a third view. That they were demonic themselves or, at the very least, idolatrous. That's why they kept churches out of Cainsville." She rose, rubbing her back. "I should get back to work. Anytime you want to chat, though, I'm around. But if you're interested in more, you can also speak to Rose Walsh. She's quite the expert on folklore."

"I have talked to her a couple of times. We had a, uh, session."

"I'd be more pleased about that if your tone told me you took it seriously. You don't believe in the sight, child?" She shook her head. "I bet you don't believe in the protective powers of gargoyles, either." A smile and a wink, and she trundled off with her cart.

# CHAPTER FORTY

Gabriel insisted on taking me to the interview with Evans. I suppose it fell under the same category as teaching me to use a gun—a dead client would look very bad on his résumé.

I made him drop me off a block away. Having William Evans glance out to see me stepping from Gabriel's Jag would not be a good way to start the interview.

Evans lived with his wife in River Forest, an affluent suburb west of Chicago. Their house was in an older part, where the houses weren't obscenely large and you actually had some green space between you and your neighbors. My original plan was to have Gabriel drop me at the nearest bus stop. But this wasn't the kind of neighborhood where anyone took the bus.

When I reached the Evans home, a middle-aged housekeeper was on the front porch, speaking to a young gardener. She showed me into the study, where William Evans waited.

Evans sat at his desk. He was a thick-set man with an iron-gray, military-short buzz cut, dressed in a golf shirt that showed off biceps that would be the envy of men half his age. Not what I'd expected, given the soft-spoken voice on the phone.

"Ms. Jones," he said when the housekeeper ushered me in.

He strode around the desk to take my hand. "Do you go by Jones? Or Taylor-Jones?"

"Jones. Keeps things simple. But Olivia is even better."

"Excellent. Please call me Will." He looked over at the housekeeper. "I'm sorry, Maria. I know you were just leaving, and I completely forgot to mention Ms. Jones's appointment. Is there any chance you could . . . ?"

She smiled. "I'll bring coffee."

He thanked her and waved me to a seat as he took his. We talked about the weather until the coffee arrived. Then he said, "So you're investigating my son's murder."

"I'm not a detective. I'm just . . ." I pretended to be debating how honest I should be, though I'd worked out a game plan already. "Pamela Larsen wants me to take her case to the Center on Wrongful Convictions. She would like them to focus on irregularities in the murders of your son and Jan Gunderson. I don't want to do that until I've checked a few things myself. Otherwise . . ." I shrugged. "It gives the wrong impression."

"That of a naive, socially advantaged young woman who believes her parents cannot be guilty simply because she doesn't want them to be."

I could feel the weight of his stare on me as he studied my reaction. I struggled not to squirm. I don't like shrinks. They're always assessing you, and even if their assessment seems wrong, you can't help but wonder because, after all, they're pros. Skilled scuba divers into the murky waters of the unconscious.

"Yes," I said. "I want to know what I'm giving them and to agree that there is some modicum of doubt."

"There is."

When I glanced at him sharply, he said, "I believe there *is* some doubt. I believe you are correct to look closer at Christian

Gunderson. I believe I know a reason why Christian may have murdered his sister."

As determined as I'd been to play my cards close, his chuckle said I'd failed miserably.

"Did you expect mind games?" He shook his head. "I'm too old for that. If we're being honest, I was always too old for that. Too impatient. I believe it is possible Christian Gunderson killed my son. Only possible. Perhaps not even likely. But that possibility has haunted me for twenty-two years."

I met his gaze. "But it wasn't haunting you a year ago? When Gabriel Walsh told you he was working on Pamela Larsen's appeal?"

His smile didn't falter. "Touché. The truth is that I don't like defense lawyers, Olivia. I particularly do not like Gabriel Walsh. More than one family with Peter's Angels has had to deal with the man, and it was a very unpleasant experience. Some lawyers defend criminals because they believe in the system and trust that it will convict the guilty. Others do it because the rewards assuage those jabs of conscience. A few, though, do it because they have no pricks of conscience. They see it as a game."

"So you withheld the information because you dislike Gabriel Walsh."

"No. I was quite willing to give it—if he pushed. I wanted to feel confident that he'd use it. When I rebuffed him, though, he lost interest, which suggested he didn't really see Christian as a viable suspect. I feared that if I gave him what I had, he'd misuse it."

"And you trust me to use it properly?" I said.

"I've done my research on you, Olivia. When I spoke to a mutual acquaintance, she couldn't sing your praises highly enough. You weren't merely a debutante taking a monthly shift in the soup kitchen. You worked hard. You care about people. I wondered what you were doing with Gabriel Walsh. I believe I see it now, though. He is beneficial to you, is he not? To your investigation?"

"He is."

"Good. Make use of him, then, but please, be careful. He is not a man to be trusted. Also, I would ask that anything we discuss here not get back to him."

I agreed. Quickly, easily, and—if his reaction was any indicator—believably. Which proved that my acting skills were improving. Once he'd secured my agreement, he began to talk.

In all my research on Jan Gunderson and Peter Evans, I'd never learned how they met. It seemed inconsequential. It wasn't. Jan had been Dr. Evans's patient. She'd been coming to his house for treatment, which is where she'd met his son. That was why the Evanses had objected to the relationship. Not because of the age difference but because of the circumstances.

"Eventually, we got past that," Evans said. "Jan was a wonderful girl, and she was in love with our son. He was in love with her."

"Were you still seeing her professionally?"

"No. As soon as she started dating Peter, she knew she should no longer see me as her therapist. That was correct and shows, I think, what a mature and levelheaded young woman she was. That decision was, however, part of the reason I was against the relationship. Jan and I were making headway. She had a serious issue to work through. I had to choose between seeing her achieve happiness by a breakthrough or by my son."

"And you thought a therapeutic breakthrough was better."

"Young love is fickle. Peter . . . liked to date. He rarely had one girlfriend at a time. I thought his relationship with Jan was simply a new phase."

"Test-driving fidelity. Which wouldn't last."

"Yes. But it did. Which is when I came to realize that this was indeed what Jan needed, psychologically."

"So she didn't transfer to a new therapist."

"She was going to. I made a couple of appointments for her. She found excuses to cancel, and I realized she needed a break. I didn't push. Maybe I should have."

"What was she seeing you for? Or is that still covered under client–patient confidentiality?"

"There's the rub. Does confidentiality extend beyond death? Opinions vary. If Jan said to me, 'I think my brother is going to kill me,' then clearly I have an obligation to turn her files over. But if those files only suggested a possible motive? Not as clear. I decided that if the authorities requested her files, I'd hand them over. They did not. Nor did the Larsens' lawyers."

"Did the police know Jan had been your patient?"

"Yes. But because the professional relationship ended almost a year before her death, they didn't see any causal link to her murder. They didn't subpoena my files or ask me anything about our sessions."

Which was a serious oversight when they'd been investigating her brother as a potential suspect. Maybe they'd trusted that Evans would volunteer anything that could help them catch his son's killer.

He took a file folder from his desk and handed it to me. "Take this with you. I've redacted information that I feel is an unnecessary invasion of Jan's privacy, but in those remaining pages, I believe you'll find a motive."

I took the file as he again warned me against sharing it with Gabriel. Again, I lied and said I wouldn't.

Before I could leave, he said, "Are you seeing anyone, Olivia?" he asked. "A therapist, I mean. Since you discovered the Larsens are your parents?"

I stiffened.

"I can tell from that reaction that the answer is no and that you don't appreciate the question. I'm sorry, but I had to ask. I'd be a poor psychologist if I wasn't concerned about the effects of such a revelation."

"I'm coping."

"So I see. When I heard you were investigating the murders, I'll admit I was concerned you might be in denial. That doesn't seem to be the case, though. Still, if you'd like to talk to someone . . . free of charge, of course. You're doing me a favor, setting my mind at ease about Christian."

"I appreciate the offer. I know talking helps a lot of people, but it really doesn't do it for me. I just need to work through this on my own. No offense."

"None taken. You're right that you don't seem an ideal candidate for traditional therapy. I was going to suggest more of an information session. After my son's death, I became something of an expert on serial killers. I'm sure you have questions. About them. About yourself."

I had to struggle to keep my expression blank. I thanked him again and promised to call with any questions on the file.

# CHAPTER FORTY-ONE

Giving me Jan's file seemed like a breach in doctor–client confidentiality, but when I told Gabriel what Evans had done, he said that according to Illinois law, psychologists weren't bound after a client's death. Evans could refuse to turn it over, but it had been his idea, and he'd redacted information, so he was acting ethically.

As I read the file, Gabriel drove to Starbucks. River Forest wasn't the kind of place where you were likely to find a nice little generic coffee shop. Which was fine, because I was craving a mocha and espresso brownie about as much as I'd been craving sushi.

We ate outside. It wasn't perfect weather for it—a little windy, which in Chicago-speak means gusts that will snatch your newspaper but not your breath. It was overcast though, so we had the patio to ourselves.

I told Gabriel what Evans had said about him. He only snorted as he ripped a chunk from his muffin.

"Seems he did a background check on you when you first started sniffing around," I said. "Allegations of drug dealing. Assault with intent. Murder."

"I didn't go *sniffing around*."

"That's the only accusation that bothers you?" I shook my head. "Anyway, yes, he doesn't trust you, so I can't share this." I waved the file.

"Judging by the noises you made while reading it, I presume there's something useful in there."

That breeze gusting past seemed to turn to an icy blast. I shivered.

"Is it that bad?" Gabriel's voice dropped.

"Do you have siblings?"

"No."

"Me neither, but I still can't imagine . . ." I trailed off and yanked my gaze from the folder.

He waved at my drink and snack. "Chocolate therapy?"

"Yes. A cliché, I know. But it works for me." I pushed the folder over to Gabriel. "There's no way you can help me on this investigation without reading that. So enjoy." I paused. "Or not."

According to that file, Christian Gunderson may have broken the oldest taboo. If he hadn't, it wasn't for lack of trying.

It started when Christian was thirteen and Jan was twelve. They'd been goofing around—Jan swiped something of his and when he caught her, they started play-wrestling and . . . well, it may not be a good idea to play-wrestle with your thirteen-year-old brother. From what I recall of that age, guys can get "stimulated" by rubbing against pretty much anything. Not their fault. It's just hormones, and I'm sure it's embarrassing as hell, especially when it's your sister you're rubbing against.

I'd think the natural reaction to that would be shame and humiliation. You'd feel like a pervert, even if it was a purely physiological response and didn't mean you thought of her "that way." Except that wasn't what happened. Not according to Jan. Christian had his "reaction" and freaked out a little, but she pretended not to notice what happened. A mature response. When Jan feigned innocence, though, Christian seemed to think it meant she was okay with it. Evans didn't speculate on Christian's thought process. Jan was his patient and all he cared about was her reaction, her emotional fallout.

Was Jan ever a willing participant? She never said. How far did it go? Evans didn't push. All he knew was that at fifteen, she'd gone to spend the summer with her grandmother and ended up staying with her for almost a year. When she came back, she'd told Christian to keep his hands off her or else.

That should have ended it. Instead, his physical advances turned to protestations of love. He loved her and, yes, it was wrong, but he couldn't help himself. That continued until she left for college. When she returned, things seemed to have changed. Now Christian was actively trying to set her up with Tim Marlotte. Jan agreed to date him and soon they were engaged and all was fine . . . until she dumped Marlotte for Peter Evans.

I'd wondered why Christian would push his sister on a friend he might have always suspected was gay. Now I knew. Because Marlotte was safe. Christian was sharing her without really sharing her and someday Jan would come to him, frustrated—emotionally and sexually—and he'd be there for her.

Gabriel read the file in silence.

I suspect Gabriel Walsh could read murder files all day and not bat an eye. He didn't bat one now, but his hands tightened around the folder and his lips tightened, too, and when he set the file down he opened his mouth . . . and nothing came out.

"Yep, pretty much my reaction, too," I said, then told him my theory about Jan, Christian, and Tim Marlotte.

"It explains why Christian would be furious when Jan broke it off with Marlotte," I said. "Especially when she took up with Pete Evans, an attractive younger guy who seemed to be crazy about her. Christian reaches a boiling point, they argue, and he accidentally kills Jan in a rage. Then he kills Pete and stages it to look like the recent killings of young couples. Or Pete's his target, Jan catches him, and they fight. He kills her and stages it."

"Plausible, but don't get too wrapped up in specifics, Olivia. If you're convinced you know who did it and why, you'll ignore other possibilities."

"Right. Thanks. So we should . . . ?"

"Make notes of the theories, then speak to Dr. Evans again. He seems to expect that."

"He does."

"Good."

Gabriel checked his e-mail while walking to the car. He did that a lot, as if the mere act of locomotion wasn't sufficient use of his time. Sometimes he tapped out a quick reply; sometimes he called Lydia; sometimes he simply seemed to skim his inbox. Only once had I seen him react to his messages—when he'd learned Niles Gunderson was dead. Now, as he slowed to read something, my gut clenched.

"Niles Gunderson was murdered," Gabriel said before he opened the car door.

"What?"

My surprise was absolutely genuine, but I still felt him studying me over the roof of the car. He even raised his shades, those pale eyes pinning me.

"What?" I said again.

He motioned me into the car. When the doors were closed, he made no move to start the engine, just turned to me, glasses off now.

"Is there something you'd like to tell me, Olivia? About this?"

I blinked. "What would—? You think I killed—"

"No." The word came quick and firm. Then he paused. "You wouldn't murder anyone in cold blood. An accidental killing in self-defense? I could see that. Yet if that were the case, I would have realized it when I first told you he was dead. You're a decent actor, but we need to work on your instinct-ive reactions."

He was right, of course. Just this morning, I'd given myself away to Evans once, caught off guard.

"Niles Gunderson was murdered by his neighbor," Gabriel said. "Poisoned, it seems, over a disputed poker game. The man confessed. Senselessly, considering that the coroner had already ruled it a natural death. In light of the confession, they delayed the funeral, tested Gunderson's body, and confirmed the story. The man will spend the remainder of his natural life in prison. But at least he'll have a clear conscience."

Sarcasm and contempt twisted through that last sentence and, without thinking, I found myself nodding.

"On the subject of Niles Gunderson and confession, though, is there something you'd like to tell me, Olivia?"

"Relieve *my* guilty conscience?"

"No. Whatever it is, you don't seem to feel guilty. But you are troubled."

Damn it. The man might claim to have inherited none of his aunt's second sight, but he had an eerie ability to read people.

I shook my head. "It's nothing I'd burden you with."

"Burden?" He said the word as if he wasn't familiar with it. "I'm your lawyer, Olivia. You could tell me that you murdered Niles Gunderson, and I would only offer to handle your defense should you be charged."

"And it wouldn't bother you? If I killed an old man because . . . I don't know, because he attacked me at home and I wanted revenge?"

I expected him to say that I was his client and what I did was of no personal concern to him. Instead, he spent a couple of minutes considering the matter.

"Yes," he said finally. "If that was your rationale, it would concern me."

"Because you'd be working with a psychopath?"

He seemed to think on that, too. "I suppose that could be a problem."

"Just maybe, huh?"

"If you displayed murderous intentions, I'm sure I could take care of myself. The point, however, is moot, because you did not kill Niles Gunderson. Nor, I believe, would you have unless it was a matter of necessity. Yet when I told you the other day that he was dead, you didn't seem surprised."

I took a deep breath. "Because I wasn't. I went to his apartment last Sunday. I was going to pretend to know Anna, in hopes of getting her contact information. I found Niles there. Dead."

"I see."

"The door was unlocked," I said. "I thought . . . well, I thought maybe he was out and I could slip in and find Anna's information."

His nod was almost impatient, as if breaking into someone's home was such a natural response to the situation that it didn't warrant comment.

"I left him there," I said. "I found him and I didn't do anything about it."

"You think you should have?"

Now it was my turn to pause and consider. "I think I should have felt worse about not doing anything. I think it shouldn't have been so easy to just leave him there."

"Had you called me, I would have advised you to do exactly as you did. Witnesses saw him confront you only days before.

You broke into his apartment. Even if his death appeared natural, there would have been questions. You instinctively made the right move, and I'm pleased to see it."

Which was not particularly comforting. I didn't say that, of course. Just nodded and waited until he'd pulled from the parking spot before I asked, "About the murder, though. Does it seem weird to you? Poisoning someone over a poker game?"

"Yes," he said. And nothing more.

# CHAPTER FORTY-TWO

When I stepped into my apartment, I knew something was wrong. It was like . . . I'm not sure how to describe it. Like the hairs on my neck rose.

I walked into the kitchen. There was no sign of the cat. Normally, when he wasn't curled up on his towel, he was making the arduous five-foot trek to his water bowl or litter box. I'd tried several times to send him outside to play, but he seemed to think I was trying to kick him out. Which maybe I was.

When I heard a low growl, I followed it to my bedroom. Two yellow eyes appeared under my bed. The cat came out and rubbed against my hand.

"Big bad mice scare you?"

He slunk to the doorway and peered out. Then he craned his neck to look back at me, as if to say, "Is it safe?"

I walked out ahead, and he followed. Then, with a satisfied *mrrow*, he plunked down on his bed.

I looked around. Something had spooked him. I knew the weather could upset animals, but I'd seen no sign of a storm or high winds. I wandered through the few rooms. No sign of a break-in. The front door had been locked, and nothing had been moved. It didn't appear as if . . .

Wait.

I headed down to Grace's apartment and found her setting up on the front porch.

"You bringing my scone?" she asked as I stepped out.

"It's my day off."

Her look said that was no excuse.

"Were you in my apartment doing maintenance?" I asked.

"I don't do maintenance."

"Was *anyone* in my apartment?"

"Not on my say-so. I don't hand over my keys to anyone, and I don't waltz in whenever I feel like it. I know what's right. You'll get twenty-four-hours' notice if I need to come in."

"Thank you. It just looked like someone had been in there."

"Probably that damned cat of yours knocking stuff over. They do that if you keep them cooped up. You should let him out. At least open a window so he can leave."

"I'm on the third floor."

She shrugged. Before I could walk away, she said, "I want a scone." She held out two dollar bills.

"I really wasn't going to the diner." I paused. "I *could* use a coffee, but I'm low on cash."

She glowered and exchanged the bills for a five.

"Thank you. I'll leave in a minute."

She squawked as I went back inside.

Once again, when I stepped into my apartment, the hairs on the back of my neck rose. I looked down at the cat.

"Someone was here, right?"

He stared at me.

"Come on," I said. "Give me a hint."

More staring at the crazy lady. I sighed and looked around. Nothing seemed out of place. If someone did break in, what would they be—

I checked where I hid my laptop. It was still there, untouched.
"What then?" I muttered.

I slowly circled the kitchen and living room. When I walked into the bedroom, I felt a twinge, as if a sixth sense was telling me I was getting warm.

I walked to the dresser. *Cold* . . . To the closet . . . *Cold.* To the nightstand . . . *Warmer.* I turned to the bed, and felt that now-familiar prickle.

Bingo.

One of the pillowcase openings faced inward. I always make sure mine face out. I could say it's because it looks neater, but the truth is that it's another superstition—if the pillowcase opening isn't facing out, bad dreams will get trapped and disturb your sleep. Crazy, but I knew damned well I hadn't left it like this.

I yanked off the bedsheets and looked under the bed. Nothing. I grabbed the mattress with both hands and heaved it up. A line of dark powder formed a semicircle on the box spring. No, not a circle. Some kind of symbol. The sight of it made the back of my head ache.

*Get rid of it.*

*Get rid of it now.*

I shook off the impulse, retrieved my cell phone, and took pictures. Then I scooped some powder onto a piece of paper and folded it up. I put that aside and examined the remaining powder. It looked like ashes, and smelled . . . like wood, I think, but not quite. Maybe something mixed with wood.

*Just get rid of it.*

I did. Then washed my box spring, replaced the mattress, and remade my bed.

*Had* someone really broken into my apartment? What if the symbol had been there when I moved in? A good luck charm placed under the mattress by the former tenant. I knew Grace hadn't cleaned between occupants.

It took only about twenty minutes for me to convince myself that the symbol had already been there. I didn't delete the photos, though. Or throw out the powder carefully folded in paper. I just pushed it aside for now. Moved on to something more concrete and less unsettling. Something mundane and distracting. Like getting Grace's scone and a coffee.

When I returned with my coffee, my brain was still buzzing, so I decided to tackle another dull task—sending a thank-you note to the reporter who'd interviewed me.

Lores's card only bore a phone number and e-mail address. My mother had taught me that a proper thank-you card went through the mail. Gabriel might know Lores's mailing address.

As I went to grab my cell phone, I noticed my shoes in the middle of the floor. They were upside-down. I detoured to fix them. Upside-down shoes were bad luck, and I was usually careful not to just drop them like that, but I'd kicked them off when I'd come back, still distracted by that symbol.

I got the phone and returned to the main room. I started dialing Gabriel's number, then stopped, my gaze slipping toward the hall, thinking about the shoes.

*A bad omen is a warning. A sign to stop and reconsider. Proceed with caution.*

Oh, hell. I'd been doing so well since embarrassing myself over the hawthorn.

I looked down at the phone.

*Stop and reconsider.*

Reconsider what? Calling Gabriel? Was he going to answer the phone while on the Chicago Skyway, knock over his coffee, scorching himself, then lose control and go through the guardrail?

And yet that pause did make me reconsider. Not the safety of making the call, but the need for it. Shouldn't I take two minutes to see if I could find Lores's address online instead of running to Gabriel for help?

One search and the screen filled with results. News articles with Lores's byline. I scrolled down past the search engine results. As I was zipping past, a familiar name jumped out. Gabriel Walsh. I scrolled back to it. Not my interview but one with another client of Gabriel's. Lores had said he'd done pieces on Gabriel's clients before.

I started scrolling again, then stopped.

No, Lores said he'd covered Gabriel's *cases* before.

Close enough.

And yet . . .

I opened the article. It was an exclusive interview with a woman accused of disfiguring her daughter's beauty pageant rival. A case so newsworthy that even I remembered it.

I checked the date. Recent enough that Gabriel should certainly remember granting the man an exclusive. Yet Lores had had to prod his memory.

I ran a new search now. Cross-referencing Lores's articles with Gabriel's name. I got eight hits. Eight over almost three years. Again, not unusual, given that Lores seemed to cover crime. Except that of those eight, five were exclusive interviews with Gabriel's clients.

Son of a bitch.

I called the number on Lores's card. He picked up on the third ring.

"Mr. Lores? It's Olivia Taylor-Jones."

A heartbeat of hesitation. "Yes. How are you, Ms. Jones?"

"Better after that article." I let out a sheepish laugh. "I wanted to apologize for being such a difficult subject. I'd had a few bad encounters, and I fear I was less than polite with you. But I was very pleased with the results, so I wanted to thank you."

"Oh. Well, you're quite welcome. You were very easy to interview."

"Good. Because . . ." I cleared my throat. "I have another reason for calling. You were so kind to me and so fair in your interview, and it's made it much easier for me to go out in public. I'm old news. But I fear that will change, and I think it might be wise for us to establish a working relationship. To avoid other media interest."

"Of course. I'd be flattered."

"About that . . ." More throat clearing. "This is so embarrassing."

"What is it, Ms. Jones?"

"I . . . You may know that I'm estranged from my adoptive mother right now. Which means my income is practically nonexistent. I know about your arrangement with Gabriel, and I'm wondering if . . ." A deep breath. "If it would stand with me, as well."

"You mean . . ." Wary now, letting the words drag.

"Payment," I blurted, then hurried on. "Not as much as you'd pay him, of course. And I can guarantee you newsworthy interviews. Exclusives on my visits with Pamela Larsen. My memories of life with her and Todd. You'd only pay if you could use it."

"I see." A pause.

I waited, holding my breath.

"I'm sure we could arrange something," he said finally. "Would Gabriel be part of this arrangement?"

Now it was my turn to pause, pretending to think. "He doesn't know I'm calling but, yes, he should know. And probably get a finder's fee. He'd expect that."

A dry chuckle. "Yes, he would. When would you be ready to speak to me again, Ms. Jones?"

"Mmm, no rush really. I just wanted to confirm a few things."

He let out a curse as I hit the button to end the call. Then I speed-dialed Gabriel.

# DEATH PENALTY

G abriel pitched an empty water bottle across the room, doing a rim shot off the trash can. Lydia had given up on the recycling bin after a six-month battle of wills. She now settled for muttering loudly as she separated his trash every week.

He'd shut down his computer for the day. It was still early, but the advantage of owning your own firm was getting to take off early now and then. It wasn't as if he'd leave empty-handed. His briefcase was already stuffed with files, and he'd synced his documents to his laptop account.

Today he had earned an early departure. He'd barely made it back to the office before being summoned to the courthouse. The jury had returned with its verdict. His client would be going to jail for twenty years. Which, Gabriel supposed, did not make it a good day for Nelson Rivers, who'd left the courtroom cursing Gabriel. He hadn't put much venom into the curses, though. Rivers was a smart man. He might not like going to jail, but he'd known he didn't have a hope in hell of an acquittal.

Gabriel's day had started equally well, with Olivia's meeting with William Evans. He'd been anxious about that, unconvinced Olivia could get anything useful on her own. But she had. And what she'd gotten could be the key to proving the

Larsens' innocence. Or at least to raising enough of a doubt to give him another shot at a career-making case.

He was equally pleased by how quickly she'd handed over that file, despite Evans's warnings. She seemed to trust him in a professional capacity, which would make their partnership much easier.

To his surprise, it was indeed becoming a partnership. There was a reason he ran his own law firm. All right, there were several. But one of them was the simple fact he didn't play well with others. They brought too much baggage to the table, petty annoyances like morals and ethics.

While Olivia certainly had those, she'd demonstrated a capacity to nudge them aside when the situation demanded it. He'd seen a glimmer of ruthlessness there, which cemented his own growing sense that he could actually work—and work well— with Olivia Taylor-Jones.

He checked his watch. Enough of that or he wouldn't get out early after all. He popped open his briefcase and dropped in a last file.

When his cell phone rang, he considered letting voice mail pick up. But years of jumping every time his phone rang, praying for work, had conditioned him well. He'd check caller display and if it wasn't urgent . . .

Olivia.

Almost certainly not urgent, but he still found himself answering.

"Hey, is this a bad time?" she asked.

He clicked his briefcase shut. "Not at all."

"Did you get your verdict?"

"I did."

"And?"

"Guilty. He's off to jail for twenty years."

"Hey, at least he didn't get the death sentence. Illinois still has that, as my research into the Larsens taught me. I thought we'd gotten rid of it."

"Probably because there was a moratorium on it for the last decade. And, actually, it is now illegal. It was abolished last year."

"Ah, well, at least your client didn't get life, then. So how'd he take it?"

Gabriel paused. Olivia didn't make small talk, which may be one of the reasons he found working with her less than painful. That meant she was expressing an interest in his work because she wanted something.

And yet . . . He didn't mind telling her about the case. She'd seemed genuinely interested in it earlier, in a purely intellectual way, divorced from any actual feelings about a man who'd murdered his longtime business partner and tried to dissolve the body. That was refreshing.

And it wasn't as if he was rushing off *to* anything. He did have plans for the evening. Dinner with a potential client at seven. Then a game of one-on-one with an assistant DA who seemed to think Gabriel needed friends, and that by filling the void, he might earn insight into Gabriel's cases and win a promotion. To get that information, though, the young lawyer realized he ought to give some in return, which was making it a very profitable relationship for Gabriel.

He sat back in his desk chair, and told Olivia how the case had ended. As they talked, his phone beeped, telling him he had another call coming in. He checked the display. Martin Lores. He ignored it.

At last he said, "I should probably let you go. I was just leaving." And waited.

"Right. Actually, um, sorry about this, but could you do something for me first?"

He felt his lips twitch in a small smile. She was good at this. "Yes?" he said.

"You mentioned you have research notes on the ritualistic aspects of the Larsen killings. Expert opinions."

"I do."

"Could I get those? I've been doing some research here and I . . . might have found something."

He let the chair snap upright. "What?"

A laugh. Almost teasing. She was obviously in a good mood, and when she was, that side of her came out—warm and quick-witted.

"I'd . . . rather not say just yet."

He imagined her eyes flashing as she said it. Definitely teasing. "If you don't say, then you don't get the files."

"Oh, come on. Give me the chance to look exceedingly clever. And to avoid making a complete fool of myself by telling you, then reading the files and discovering I'm completely off-base."

"Hmm."

"I could let *you* do the research instead," she offered.

"No, thank you."

She laughed. "Didn't think so. So, can I have them? Please?"

Now he really did smile. When Olivia wanted something from a man—whether it was information or extra whipped cream on her mocha—her contralto voice took on a husky note. She didn't even seem to be aware she was doing it. A fascinating bit of learned behavior.

Not that it worked on him. A lawyer couldn't afford to be susceptible to female clients, so he'd developed an immunity early on. Which was useful, working with Olivia, who was undeniably attractive, in an intriguing variety of ways.

Still, there was no reason not to give her the files. He turned his computer back on.

"I'm e-mailing them now," he said. "With any luck, they'll be more useful to you then they were to me."

"Got 'em," she said after a moment. "So I'll talk to you— Oh, wait. You said you'd arranged interviews for later this week. Who was it again? I should do some research on them, too."

He chuckled. "You can do all the research you like. I'll e-mail you the names now." He did that, too.

"Damn, you're good. Okay, then. Thanks and have a good night."

She hung up. He was just about to put the phone into his pocket when it rang again. Lores. What the hell did he want? Gabriel checked his watch, hesitated, and answered.

He'd barely gotten a hello out before Lores spilled his story, peppered with so many anxious apologies that it took Gabriel a few moments to realize what he was saying. When he did, he knew why Olivia had called for those files.

Damn.

# CHAPTER FORTY-THREE

It had been three when I called Gabriel. That meant he would probably knock on my apartment door by about four fifteen. Unless Lores didn't tell Gabriel he'd screwed up. But Lores seemed smart enough to realize his mistake wouldn't go undetected for long. He'd confess before Gabriel found out so he could smooth things over.

Gabriel would realize this was too serious for a phone call. He'd come in person to tell me it was all a misunderstanding and, really, I was making too big a deal out of it.

Four fifteen, then.

I checked my watch. Four twenty-five. I dug into my meat loaf as Gordon Webster—who owned the hardware store—stopped by my table to say hello. *How was the meat loaf? Was I working tonight? He thought it was my night off.* It was a little creepy that people were following my schedule, but Gordon was this side of forty, recently divorced, and Ida claimed he'd been coming to the diner a whole lot more since I started. That was fine. He was a nice enough guy, and he tipped well.

I said yes, I was on as soon as I finished eating. Larry had said that if I ever wanted extra hours, I could come by any dinner hour that Trudy worked. She'd been with the diner since before

Larry bought it. Since before the previous owner bought it, too. She was proud of her ability—at seventy—to still take on weekend dinner rushes single-handedly, but was quite willing to share the load.

As Gordon left, he murmured an apology for almost mowing down someone coming in the door. I heard a dry response in a voice I knew well. I checked my watch. Four thirty. Right on time.

I'd sat with my back to the door. Gabriel stopped at my shoulder, as if waiting for me to sense him there and turn. I took another bite of meat loaf.

He finally stepped around. As he pulled out the other chair, Veronica called, "Gabriel Walsh."

He greeted her, staying politely on his feet.

"It's good to see you, Gabriel," she said. "I've noticed that car of yours in town more often these days. Which is not as welcome a sight when it's flying so fast I can barely see it."

I bit my cheek to keep from smiling. Gabriel exceeded the speed limit in Cainsville by remarkably little, never dropping the pedal until he was past the town limits.

"Yes, well, perhaps I should pay more attention—" he began.

"You should," she said. "We have children here, Gabriel. We didn't allow that sort of behavior when you were a little tyke, visiting your auntie. You should be more careful. And more respectful."

He murmured, "Yes, I should. My apologies," and even sounded like he meant it.

Veronica softened the rebuke with a smile. "It *is* good to see you around more."

He nodded and lowered himself into the seat across from me. Before he could speak, Trudy approached.

"Can I get—?" she began.

Gabriel waved her away without looking.

"I think she was talking to me," I said. "I would love a slice of apple pie if you get a sec, Trudy. Thanks."

When I said her name, he looked up sharply. "Trudy. Sorry. I—"

"Yes, you're only rude to people you think you don't know. Which is a very poor way to treat anyone, Gabriel Walsh."

"Yes, well, perhaps I will have a coffee and—"

"You know where it is," she said and tromped off, orthopedic shoes clomping.

After a moment, Gabriel said, "Could we step out—?"

"I have pie coming. What do you want, Gabriel?"

"I know you spoke to Martin Lores. I believe—"

"—that I may have misinterpreted what he said? That you didn't set up that interview with him? Or that you weren't paid for it? If either of those lies comes out of your mouth, I will get you that coffee . . . and dump it over your head."

He eyed me, as if trying to figure out whether I was serious. He considered long enough for Trudy to return with my pie. Then he cleared his throat.

"Were you pleased with the outcome of that interview, Olivia?"

"You know damn well I was. I made you cookies."

Did he flinch? Just a little?

"You were pleased," he said. "You admitted it was the right thing to do. So I don't see the problem."

"You don't?"

"No."

His gaze met mine. His shades were off, as they had been so many times in the last week that I'd gotten used to those frozen blue eyes. Every now and then, I'd even thought I'd seen a flicker of something in them. Something human. But now they were empty again. I dropped my gaze to my pie and dug in.

After I swallowed a mouthful, I said, "Then we have nothing to talk about. You're fired, Gabriel. As I'm sure you figured out when you realized why I asked for those files."

His fingers drummed the table. "This is ridiculous, Olivia. I did you a favor."

"Bullshit. You did yourself a favor. It just happened to work out in my interests, too, so you're assuaging whatever nub of a conscience you have by pretending you did it for me. I told you I wasn't ready for that interview. When we bumped into Lores, I was terrified. Genuinely terrified. You saw that. You didn't care."

"You were overreacting."

"How much did he pay you?" I said.

"I don't see how that's—"

"It can't be much for a single interview. Does it cover a week's gas for your car? Pay for a new shirt? You didn't need the money. I don't even think it's about the money. That's just an excuse to cover up the real reason you do shit like that." I looked him in the eye again. "Because you can. You get off on manipulating people."

I thought that might make him flinch for real. But his gaze seemed to go even colder, that chill seeping into his voice.

"I helped you, Olivia."

"Inadvertently. If you really gave a shit about helping me, you would have admitted you'd already called Lores and offered to coach me through it. I don't *expect* you to help me, Gabriel. Not unless it helps you, too. But I do expect to be treated with respect. That wasn't just cruel. It was disrespectful. That's why I'm firing you."

He leaned back in his chair. Studied me, then said, "So you're giving up on Pamela Larsen's case?"

"No, and you know that. I've got your files."

"So you plan to continue alone?"

"I do."

He smiled. A week of working together and I've never seen the bastard do more than twitch his lips. This made him smile. If my coffee wasn't so hot, I'd have thrown it at him. I was still tempted.

"How far do you think you'll get with that, Olivia?" he said. "You're a liberal arts grad who's never held any job other than"—he looked around pointedly—"here. You are in no position to investigate a string of twenty-two-year-old murders. Really, I didn't think you were that naive."

"Good-bye, Gabriel."

He got to his feet. "You have twenty-four hours to reconsider. If you attempt to retain my services after that, you will find my fee has risen. Significantly."

I wanted to tell him to go to hell. Instead I looked him in the eye and said, "Good-bye, Mr. Walsh."

He hesitated a split second, then buttoned his jacket, pulled his shades from his pocket, and strode out.

After my shift, I went home—yes, the apartment was finally becoming home—and read the ritual research files, making notes and looking things up on the Internet until my eyes hurt. Would firing Gabriel mean I'd lose my free Internet access? Would he send a repo man to take back the laptop? Fifty-fifty on both, I figured. Rose seemed to like me, so she might not listen if Gabriel asked her to change her Internet password. Would he be petty enough to ask? Hard to say. Better to do what I could quickly.

# CHAPTER FORTY-FOUR

I was up early the next morning. Stressed about firing Gabriel, if I was being honest with myself. I worked it off with a 6 a.m. jog. I was rounding the corner by the community center when I saw a new gargoyle. It was on an ivy-covered stone post, and I wouldn't have noticed it at all if the breaking light hadn't hit the post at just the right angle, making the gargoyle's green stone eyes glitter.

"Clever," I murmured as I cleared away the ivy for a better look. "Another one for my list."

I started to smile, then stopped myself. Thinking of gargoyle lists only brought my mind back to a place I'd been trying to leave—Gabriel. I shook it off and started to run again, but I kept thinking about the gargoyles, and when I passed the bank, my gaze instinctively went to the place where I'd seen one the other night, with Veronica.

It wasn't there.

I walked over to the stonework. The door was framed with rosettes. The other night, though, one of those carvings had been a gargoyle face. And now? All I saw were rosettes.

I looked from several angles. Even ran my fingers across the one that I was sure had been the gargoyle. Nothing.

"A night gargoyle," I murmured.

I looked back down the road at the post by the community center. That "hidden" one made sense—you just didn't notice it if the sun didn't hit it right. But this . . . ?

I ran my fingers over the rosette again, then gave my head a sharp shake and continued on.

I spent my shift thinking about ritual murder. It wasn't as common as Hollywood and the tabloids might lead one to believe. There's no human sacrificial tradition in Wicca, satanism, voodoo, or any of the faiths we associate with modern American occultism. According to the experts Gabriel had hired, if you find corpses with evidence of ritual sacrifice, you're probably dealing with fringe nut jobs.

There were no indications that Pamela and Todd Larsen were fringe nut jobs. She'd admitted to being a practicing Wiccan, but everything the police found in that chest was evidence of the benign, Earth-mother-worshipping form embraced by college students everywhere.

The experts Gabriel hired hadn't been able to identify most of the ritualistic elements in the murders. There were no pentacles drawn in blood. No black candles. No dead animals. In the end, both experts decided the Larsens had made up their own ceremony. One was convinced they were secret occultists who believed their self-made ritual would grant them some boon. The other thought they'd simply invented it to throw the police off the trail.

I liked theory two. Two sociopaths want to kill people and get away with it. One has some minor experience with occultism. They decide to add fake ritual aspects to their murders to mislead the authorities.

And yet I couldn't help thinking there was more to it. Maybe I was looking for patterns where none existed. I've often thought that's where my obsession with omens and superstitions comes from—trying to find order and meaning in a chaotic world. In trying to make sense of these ritual elements, maybe I was just falling into the same trap as the other investigators.

When my shift ended at three, I offered to come back to help Trudy again. Since the dinner rush in Cainsville starts at five, I'd eat an early meal there and work quietly at a corner table.

That was the plan, anyway. The reading and note-taking wasn't so easy when Ida and Walter stopped by for tea and wanted to talk about whatever I was working on so hard. I shut my folders quickly and said, "Just some research."

In my haste to scoop up the pages, one fell and Walter got to it before I could.

"That's just—" I began.

"About your parents," he said, glancing at the page before he handed it back. "The Larsens. You're investigating their crimes."

Ida nodded, looking as concerned as if I was researching new appliances for my apartment. At the next table, Veronica perked up and inched her chair closer.

"I, uh . . ."

"You're curious," Ida said as she sat across from me. Walter took the extra chair at Veronica's table and swung it over. "That's natural. It must have been a huge shock for you. You need to understand it."

When Lores's interview came out and no one in Cainsville mentioned it, I'd told myself no one had noticed. That had seemed odd, but they'd said many times that they weren't interested in city news. Now I realized they'd known who I was for a while. Maybe even before the article came out. They just hadn't brought it up.

"I'm just checking a few things," I said. "Are you staying for dinner? The special is roast ham—it wasn't ready for me to snatch some early, but it smells amazing."

"Is that what you were doing with Gabriel?" Walter said. "Investigating the murders?"

"He's not working for me anymore. Did I mention there's strawberry and rhubarb pie? Trudy brought fruit in from her garden, and Larry made it this morning."

Ida reached out and patted my hand. "You don't need to hide things from us, dear. We know you're investigating the crimes and we think it's a lovely idea."

*Lovely?*

"What are you working on now?" Veronica asked. She'd moved her chair up beside Walter and was peering at the folder.

"Um, just, uh . . ." Oh, hell. They weren't about to be brushed off. Might as well get it over with. "There were ritualistic aspects to the murders. I'm trying to understand them."

"Witchcraft, wasn't it?" Ida said.

Walter shook his head. "They're called Wiccan now, dear."

"No, Wicca is a different thing altogether. Mavis's granddaughter became a Wiccan when she went away to college, and she certainly never killed anyone. That's witchcraft. Or a satanic cult." She looked at me. "What did they think it was with the Larsens?"

"They didn't know. That's what I'm looking into. What they did to . . ." I cleared my throat. "The ritualistic aspects don't fit any known occult branch. I'm trying to make sense of it myself."

"Oh, that sounds interesting." Ida reached out for the folder. "May I take a look?"

*Hell, no.* I lowered the folder onto my lap. "I can't. Sorry. They're official files."

"Perhaps you can give us an overview," Ida said. "I do love mysteries."

"I really don't think—"

"She's trying, very politely, to say, 'not a chance in hell,'" said a voice behind me.

Patrick strolled over. As he met my eyes, he rolled his.

"Those weren't polite little Agatha Christie murders," he said to the others. "Liv's not going to share it with folks whose idea of horror is Bela Lugosi in face paint."

"I didn't say—" I began.

"Why give the old folks nightmares when they sure as hell aren't going to know anything useful about the occult."

It wasn't the first time I'd heard Patrick talk to the town elders like that. They might rebuke Gabriel, but they only glowered and muttered at Patrick. Odd, considering how young he was.

"Shoo," he said, waving his fingers at them. "You can't help here. I, on the other hand, am well versed in the black arts."

I don't know what kind of look I gave him, but he burst out laughing.

"No, I don't mutilate cats in my basement. I'm a writer, remember? This is my specialty."

"Horror?"

He shrugged. "Something like that."

"He's playing with you, my dear," Ida said. "He can't help you."

"Oh, yes, I can," Patrick said. "Not in here, though. Too many nosy senior citizens. How about we take a walk to the park, and you can test my knowledge of arcane occult trivia. See how helpful I can be."

"I need to be back by five," I said as I rose. I could feel Ida's and Walter's chilly displeasure, but with Gabriel gone, I couldn't afford to turn down help.

I murmured a good-bye to the others, and let Patrick lead me from the diner.

# COEXISTENCE

Patrick glanced back at the old folks as he shuttled Olivia out the door. Their scowls deepened, just in case he was unaware of how much they disapproved. He knew, of course—he lived under a perpetual cloud of their disapproval.

It had been like this since they'd settled Cainsville. He'd been the sole dissenting voice when they'd devised their silly rules for coexisting with the *boinne-fala*. They had presumed he would come around, and eventually do things their way. He had not. He never would. Which annoyed them to no end. They could simply have asked him to leave. That, however, would be . . . unwise.

Yet it was his very flouting of the rules that allowed him to waltz off with their prize today. He had to laugh at their clumsy attempts to discover Olivia's progress. She looked at them and saw old people, beyond the ability to help, particularly with something so disturbing. It might stop their aged hearts.

They were curious, of course. Concerned, too. Would Olivia find anything? Was there anything to find? The problem was that none of them knew. When Pamela Bowen and Todd Larsen were arrested for killing those four couples, the elders of Cainsville heard only rumors of what had happened, from those who lived outside the town. They helped when they could, like the *brùnaidh* who gave Grace's address to Olivia or the *spriggan* who scared her out of Chicago. Both had been quick to contact the elders, like eager puppies expecting a scratch behind the ears. They might not live here, but they knew it was wise to ingratiate themselves with the residents of Cainsville.

Now Olivia was investigating her parents' crimes. Gabriel was helping . . . Or he had been. Their apparent estrangement concerned Patrick, which was terribly annoying. He hated to be concerned. It wasn't in his nature. He had a soft spot for Gabriel, though, more than he usually did for his *epil*. If Olivia was to discover anything of interest, it would behoove Gabriel to be there, at her side, to reap the benefits.

Patrick hoped the situation between them would resolve itself. He was sure it would. But if it didn't, he might give it a little push.

# CHAPTER FORTY-FIVE

"So you write horror?" I said as we walked to the park.

"No. Paranormal romance."

I glanced over.

A mock-offended look. "You think I'm kidding?"

"I'm not sure, because I have no idea what that is."

"Exactly what it sounds like. Vampires, demons, witches, and the like. With romance. It's a hot market."

"So you're trying to break in by writing it?"

"Break in? I have six books out already. How do you think I can afford to sit in a diner typing all day?"

"Sorry. You just seem young to be published."

"I'm older than I look."

We turned onto the path to the park.

"Do you publish under a pseudonym?" I asked.

"Have to, being a guy writing romance. Shall I tell you my pen name, so you can pretend you'll get one from the library? Let things become horribly awkward when you don't and I ask how you liked it?"

"So you won't tell me your pseudonym?"

"I'll do one better. I'll bring a copy of my latest to the diner. Just to make it even more awkward, because you won't have any excuse for not reading it."

He opened the gate on the empty park and ushered me to the bench inside. "In paranormal romance, you need three elements to stand out in a crowded market. One? Sex. I'm very good at it." He sat down. "I'm not bad at writing it, either."

I rolled my eyes. He only smiled.

"And the other two?" I asked.

"Originality and attention to detail, both of which require extensive research. While most writers focus on the Hollywood tropes—vampires, werewolves, and such—I dig deeper. Which means I know a lot about the occult and everything currently labeled as the occult by Western Christian society, more correctly known as folklore and pagan religions."

He leaned over and lowered his voice, fake-conspiratorial. "So, do I qualify to hear the juicy heretofore unrevealed details?"

I mentally ran through the various elements and picked the least sensational. "Mistletoe."

His brows lifted in an expression that for a split-second reminded me of Gabriel. Proving that my former lawyer was playing on my thoughts a little more than I liked.

"Mistletoe?"

"There was a sprig of it left near the bodies."

"Ah, that is indeed a tricky one. Very arcane lore. You see, there's an obscure cult in Malta that worships Saint Nicolas, and every December twenty-fifth, they hang mistletoe from trees and engage in debauched kissing orgies."

I gave him a look.

He laughed. "Well, at least you don't believe me. Some people might. As for the real answer, either you're just testing me or the prosecution hired some very dim-witted investigators. Mistletoe is traditionally associated with the Druids. The first known reference was by Pliny the Elder. While it's not nearly as common as bloody pentacles, it wouldn't be completely unexpected if one considers these potential sacrificial murders."

"Because the Druids practiced human sacrifice."

"Possibly. The jury's still out on that. The problem is that we have no records from the Druids themselves. Unless you count neo-Druids, and I don't. They're as close to real Druids as Tinker Bell is to fairies."

"*Real* fairies."

Another flash of a grin, and his voice dropped into a perfect brogue. "Aye, ye dinna believe in the wee folk, lass? That's trouble. The pixies will sour your milk."

"I thought it was hobgoblins who soured milk."

"A dirty lie. Spread by the pixies, no doubt. Nasty buggers. I'll amend my analogy. Neo-Druids are as close to real ones as Tinker Bell is to the traditional fae of folklore. We have no writings from the Druids because they lacked a writing system. What we have comes from something even worse than pixies. Romans."

"When the Romans discovered Britain."

"Discovered? Like Columbus *discovered* America? The Romans were bloody invaders, worse than the Vikings. Spreading their culture on the tips of their lances. They thought the natives were barbarians, led by bloodthirsty Druids."

"So the accounts we have of human sacrifice all come from the Romans, which means it may have been a public relations smear? Convince everyone back home that all Brits are murderers who need to be annihilated."

"Or it may have been true."

I looked over at Patrick.

He shrugged. "I have no love for the Romans, but I'm not convinced the Druids *didn't* practice human sacrifice. The problem comes in the interpretation. Or the misinterpretation.

The Romans saw it as a fundamental disrespect for human life. It wasn't. Romans understood the core concept—like the Celts, they practiced animal sacrifice. But when you really want—or need—to get the attention of the gods, you offer them your best. Something you value more than the life of an animal."

"The life of a human."

"Exactly. So, too, would the Druids, if they did indeed practice human sacrifice. Are you really telling me no one interpreted that mistletoe as Druidic?"

"It was mentioned, but none of the other elements seemed to be Druidic, so it lent credence to the theory that the Larsens were incorporating disparate elements to fake ritual sacrifice."

"The Larsens. Is that how you think of them?"

"Yes."

He made a noise in his throat. Not really disapproval. Just a noise.

"I know they're my biological parents," I said. "But I don't think of them as Mom and Dad. I already have those."

"Fair enough. So what did the Larsens do with the mistletoe? I suspect it wasn't just lying beside the bodies."

"It pierced a symbol on the women's stomachs."

He frowned. "What kind of symbol?"

I hesitated, then pulled out a drawing of it.

"Pictish v-rod," he said. Then he shook his head. "Did Gabriel hire these researchers? I'll have to speak to him. He should demand a refund if they couldn't identify this one."

"By Pictish you mean the Picts, right? Iron Age tribe? Northern Scotland?"

"Late Iron Age, early medieval."

"Any connection to the Druids?"

He nodded. "Before they converted—or were forced to convert—to Christianity."

"And the v-rod means?"

"No one knows. Again, no records. No reliable ones anyway. It's believed to have something to do with death. As for piercing it with mistletoe?" He shrugged. "I've never heard of that."

A mishmash of symbols. Someone randomly linking them in a made-up ritual.

I showed him the symbol carved onto the thighs next, but he didn't recognize it. Nor did he know what a stone in the mouth might signify, further supporting my theory.

As we walked back to the diner, he offered to look into the other symbols. No charge. He liked a challenge, and as long as I kept his coffee cup filled, we could call it even.

After my shift, I did a little more research on my laptop. I was popping over to read an old article on the *Sun-Times* website when a name on the home page caught my attention. James Morgan. There was another name there, too. One I knew well. Eva Talbot.

James always joked about how long it took to catch me. But he left out a few pertinent details that made the story a little less romantic.

At a Christmas party the year before last, James had overheard me make an offhand reference to Chicago history. He'd minored in history in college, so we'd talked about it later, probably the first private conversation we'd ever had.

A few days into the New Year, James had called. His firm wanted to run a white-ribbon campaign and the shelter where I worked seemed a good recipient for donations. That led to long talks on the phone, then over coffee, then over lunch . . .

James was trying to gauge whether his interest was mutual before he asked me out because . . . well, there was an obstacle. Eva, a socialite he'd been dating for two years.

In retrospect, I suppose this should have told me that James was never, ever going to chase me out that door when I broke off our engagement. Never going to suggest we fly to Vegas and get married. Never going to say, "To hell with everything—this is what I want." He had to be sure that the ground was firm before he stepped on it.

When I hadn't given him the signs he was hoping for—I don't flirt with unavailable guys—he'd finally asked point-blank. If Eva wasn't in the picture, would I go to Paris with him?

I should have said, "Get her out of the picture and then ask." Force him to take a chance. But at the time, the question spoke to me of honesty, not a lack of spontaneity. So I said yes, and Eva Talbot got the breakup talk.

Now I was reading a piece about a charity dinner last night where James and Eva had been spotted together. Complete with a photo of them at the table, James leaning over to whisper something, Eva gazing at him adoringly. Sources confirmed the two were seeing each other again, Eva consoling him. There was even a quote from her, after the dinner, about poor James and all he'd been through.

Bitch.

That was the most vitriol I could work up for Eva, though. Only a little more for James. I stared at that picture and I thought of us, at our last dinner together, how happy we'd been.

I'd given that up. Willfully given it up. And he'd already moved on.

# CHAPTER FORTY-SIX

With Gabriel gone, my reluctance to impose on Ida and Walter Clark faded fast. As long as I refilled the gas tank and paid with returned favors, I could justify borrowing their car for my Thursday morning meeting with Dr. Evans.

When I arrived at the house, Mrs. Evans was on the front porch, waiting to be picked up by a friend for brunch.

We chatted before she left. She knew who I was, obviously, but she gave no indication that my parents' purported actions reflected on me. The tragedy of her son was past.

She told me to go on inside. Her husband was in his office, and he had a tendency to ignore the doorbell, presuming someone else would answer it.

When I walked in, Evans was deep in a client file, scribbling notes. I waited until he was finished writing before clearing my throat.

"Olivia," he said, smiling as he stood. He checked the clock. "It is that time, isn't it? My apologies."

He waved me to the client seat and poured coffee. He didn't ask what I took, but made it with cream, the way I'd had it the last time.

"I think Gabriel Walsh may have taken a couple of pages from the file," I began—to explain how Gabriel would know about the file, if he did an end run around me to get to Evans. "I had to stop by his office after our interview. I kept the file in my sights, so I don't know how he could have gotten it."

"Oh, I have a good idea," Evans said as he dropped sugar cubes into his coffee. "Gabriel Walsh's mother made her living with her light fingers, and I don't mean she was a pianist."

"A pickpocket."

He nodded. "There's much that's said about Mr. Walsh, most of it unsubstantiated. That is not. His mother had a record of arrests. None of it stuck. She was very good at her vocation. Her son apparently learned the trade. His juvenile records were sealed, but I have it on good authority that he was charged with pickpocketing himself. Just the once. Which likely only means that he was even more skilled than his mother."

I remembered the scone the first time we met. Apparently, he still had the touch.

"Well, I am sorry," I said. "I don't know what he saw, but I'm going to presume he knows what is in the file. He won't be able to do anything with it, though. He doesn't have an excuse to investigate now."

"You've fired him?"

I nodded. "Your warnings already had me concerned. Taking those pages was the last straw." I sipped my coffee and looked thoughtful, maybe even a little despondent. "I know it was the right move, but I'm not sure how I'll proceed without him. I don't think anyone connected to the crimes is going to speak to the Larsens' daughter."

He smiled. "I think I can persuade the other families that helping you is the right thing to do."

"Oh? I'd really appreciate that."

"And I'm sure you have questions about that file," Evans said. "Why don't we start by discussing that."

There wasn't much more Evans could tell me. He explained a few things about brother–sister incest. More than I cared to know on the subject.

Evans warned me not to get hung up on the incest angle. I needed to see it as any obsessive relationship. Killing the object of your desire might seem crazy, but it was, sadly, not that unusual with truly obsessed stalkers.

As the meeting seemed to be winding down, I said, "You said I could ask you questions. About the Larsens. About serial killers. Do you have time for that now?"

"Of course." He leaned back. "From the phrasing of that question, I presume that you haven't ruled out the possibility your parents did commit murder."

"I can't. If Christian—or someone else—killed Jan and Peter, that still means the Larsens could have killed the others. I have to prepare myself in case I really am the daughter of sociopaths. Or psychopaths. Or whatever you'd call them."

"First, Olivia, I wouldn't get too tangled in terminology. Even within the field, we can't agree on it. When we zero in on so-called sociopaths or psychopaths, we're generally referring to people who seem unable to tell right from wrong."

"Can't *tell* right from wrong? Or don't care? Because from what I know, people like that are very good at fitting in, playing a role, which suggests they know the difference, and they can pretend to abide by the rules when it suits them."

"That would be the mark of a high-functioning individual with antisocial personality disorder. They know the difference, but they see no reason to follow the rules if it doesn't suit their needs. Sound familiar?"

Did he mean me? I tried not to react.

"Your former lawyer?" he prompted when I didn't answer. "Gabriel?"

Did I think Gabriel was a sociopath? No. As furious as I was with him, I didn't think that.

"I don't know him that well," I said. "But I understand what you're saying."

"Good, then you'll see why he concerns me. Now back to the topic. If your parents did kill these couples, it is highly likely they have some form of antisocial personality disorder. What does that mean for you? First, bear it in mind when you speak to your mother. She may appear to be a loving and kind parent . . . for a reason."

"Because it's what I want to see. Because it will get me on her side, helping her appeal."

He nodded. "Or she might truly be innocent. You see the conundrum? Just be aware and be wary. More important, though, I think you're wondering what it means for you. If both your parents did have some form of disorder. Is it hereditary?" He leaned forward. "I wish I could answer that, Olivia. But psychiatry is such an imprecise science. We aren't diagnosing cancer. Personality is a combination of genetics and learned behavior, and we have no idea how much of each explains why people do what they do."

"Nature versus nurture."

"The great debate. I can tell you this, though. There is no evidence of a genetic basis for serial killing." He eased back. "Now, you wanted to know more about serial killers in general. I think it might help to talk a bit about couples who kill. It's rare, but your parents' case is even rarer."

"Because there were no sexual aspects."

He smiled. "You've done your homework. Yes, in every case I've studied—and I'm happy to share my notes on them—couple killings included sexual violation of the victims. These did not."

"Because they were ritualistic. *That* was the purpose."

"Perhaps. But I would argue that the killings did *not* deviate entirely from the established pattern for serial killing couples. Just because the Larsens didn't violate the victims doesn't mean there wasn't a sexual motivation. It was just less overt. Less direct."

I thought about that, then said, "You think they used the violence as a stimulant. Sadistic foreplay."

"Yes, and I think that explains the ritual aspect. They were acting out a fantasy." He paused. "Of course, that only applies if the Larsens were actually the killers."

I nodded.

"I do think you need to pursue Christian, Olivia. There's a chance he killed Peter and Jan. There might even be a chance he committed all the murders. But if you want to consider motivations for the Larsens, I'd strongly suggest you take a look at that one. I'll give you my notes. You can draw your own conclusions."

What did I think of Evans's theory? I had no idea. Figuring out why my parents might have killed eight people wasn't my priority right now. I needed to focus on the last two and whether Christian Gunderson could be responsible.

# CHAPTER FORTY-SEVEN

I had the day shift on Friday and took a five-minute break to call Tim Marlotte. He had little interest in seeing me again . . . until I told him I'd learned a few things about Jan and Christian's relationship, and he decided he could find time for me after all. We set up a meeting at his condo.

Our interview was not pretty. I lied, I bullied, and I charmed with an eerie deftness, and in the end he actually thanked me for persuading him to unburden himself.

I don't believe Marlotte had known that Christian had the hots for his sister, but he did suspect their relationship was a little too close. As the years went by, I think he'd understood more, looked back, and wondered if, subconsciously, he'd known exactly what was going on and had joined Christian in manipulating Jan because it benefited him. Now he knew that deception may have played a role in her death and the death of Peter Evans. Heavy stuff.

To redeem himself, Marlotte was willing to share every vaguely sinister detail he knew about his former best friend's life. I didn't even need to prompt him with the "potential serial killer" checklist Evans had provided. The guy already knew the early signs from a college psychology project. Coincidence? Maybe not.

From sleepovers, Marlotte knew that Christian had been a bed-wetter until he seemed to overcome the issue around twelve. He'd never been known to kill small animals, but Marlotte did have a cat go missing once, and he seemed to recall that it happened shortly after the animal scratched Christian's eye, a minor but extremely painful injury. While he couldn't recall Christian committing arson, he'd been very keen on camping bonfires and always insisted on tending them. Though he'd only attended community college, he had an above-normal IQ—he just couldn't seem to achieve the grades to match. As for his family, there were none of the obvious markers—no absent father, no domineering mother, no alcoholic parent, no unstable family life, much less time spent in institutions. His father obviously had a few loose wires, though.

All this meant Christian hit some markers on the checklist. Or grazed them. I suspect many people would. As for occult connections, Marlotte remembered that Christian enjoyed Halloween. He'd liked horror novels as a teen. He'd owned a necklace with a pentacle, bought at a rock concert and never worn because it might upset his mother. In other words, he'd been about as interested in the occult as the average person.

When I left, I hadn't achieved any amazing breakthroughs, but I hadn't learned anything that discounted the Christian-killed-his-sister-in-a-jealous-rage theory, either. A decent start.

I got home in time to make a choice. I could have dinner and read Evans's case files. Or I could go try a karate class. I wasn't hungry, I wasn't ready to read those files, and my body screamed for exercise. So I opted for number two.

As I walked into the community center, I was mentally running through the Marlotte interview as if some new lead would magically leap out. I dimly heard the slam of car doors as children spilled out and shrieked past me.

In my half daze, I walked into the gym and saw a dozen figures dressed in white robes. Small figures.

They were all children.

Before I could retreat, a voice called "Liv?" and there was Gordon Webster, the hardware store owner, in a white robe with a black belt. He walked over, grinning.

"Hey," he said. "Are you joining us?"

I looked around. "I was going to, but I think I'm a little old."

"No, no. It's all ages. We do have one adult— And here she is now."

I turned to see Rose striding down the hall, kids zooming out of her path. Spotting me, she nodded and smiled.

"Olivia," she said. "I didn't know you were taking karate."

"Actually, I was just leaving."

She took off her jacket, showing her uniform underneath, complete with a brown belt. "Stay. I would love an opponent over four feet tall."

Gordon pressed, too, and there wasn't a graceful way to refuse. So I got my lesson. More than my money's worth, given the time Gordon devoted to me, which had a few of the watching parents grumbling.

Afterward, Rose caught up and walked beside me.

"I'm glad to see you taking my advice on self-defense," she said. "Particularly now that you're working alone."

"I know what it might look like, me showing up at your karate lesson, but I'm not trying to get you to play go-between with Gabriel."

"I know."

"You knew what he'd done," I said as we began our walk to Rowan Street. "That's why you told me to make him cookies. You thought it might make him feel guilty."

"It was worth a try. My nephew is a manipulative, scheming, unscrupulous son of a bitch. And those are his good qualities."

I snorted.

"Oh, I'm quite serious," she said. "What Gabriel has accomplished in his life is phenomenal, given the circumstances. The problem is that he knows it. Arrogance is blinding, particularly in the young. When he does make a mistake, he's slow to see it. But he made one with you. He knows that now."

"Good. Maybe he'll think twice before setting up paid interviews with other clients."

Her laugh was so sharp it made me jump.

"Oh, no," she said. "He won't. He shouldn't. He accepts payment for ensuring his clients get a fair shake from the media. There's nothing wrong with that. His mistake was that you are not a normal client. The balance of power in your relationship skews in your favor. You didn't want the interview. He should have retreated or, at the very least, apologized."

"Maybe, but if you expect me to change my mind—"

"I don't. I'm just offering some friendly advice. If you do decide you want to work with him, don't wait until you need him."

"Or he'll know I'm desperate and the power shifts."

"Exactly. He wants this case. Badly. He'll try again and when he does, consider whether you truly mean for this rift to be permanent." She waved for me to cross Main Street. "Now the subject of Gabriel ends. Come over for tea."

"I'd rather not—"

"Did you know that my Internet provider recommends changing my wireless access password every month?"

I glowered at her.

"You'll have tea," she said.

# SIMILITUDE

Veronica watched Rose Walsh walking with the Larsen girl. That was good to see. The tighter the girl was woven into the fabric of Cainsville, the more likely she was to stay.

It was also comforting to see the old families of Cainsville supporting each other. The bonds used to be so much stronger, in the early days, when families found a pleasant hometown and stayed for generations.

When the elders founded Cainsville, they had actively sought to weave *themselves* into its fabric. That was the goal, of course. A lofty one, founded on the very principles of America itself. The great melting pot. Of course, *they* were not quite the sort of old-world immigrants the founding fathers had envisioned, but the principle still held. They would make a new life here, and they would eschew the old tradition of separating themselves from the *boinne-fala*. They would live together in harmony . . . or at least symbiosis.

Part of weaving themselves into that fabric was quite literal. Within the oldest families—the Walshes, the Bowens, and a few others—the old blood was strong enough to produce true powers, as with Rose Walsh and, it seemed, the Larsen girl. Yet it had also had the adverse effect of bringing these gifted individuals to the attention of . . . others.

On thinking that, Veronica instinctively glanced up, but there was no sign of the ravens. They'd retreated. For now. The trick would be keeping them away, convincing the outsiders that the Larsen girl was not her parents—not vulnerable, not unprotected, not weak.

The Walshes would help with that—Rose and Gabriel both—even if they had no idea what exactly they were doing. It came naturally, this recognition of similitude—the instinct to spread wings of protection around one another. And the girl, Veronica feared, would need it.

# CHAPTER FORTY-EIGHT

When we turned onto Rowan, the moon slid from behind the clouds and illuminated a strangely perfect circle of glowing white mushrooms.

Rose quoted, "And I serve the fairy queen, to dew her orbs upon the green."

"*Midsummer Night's Dream* again?"

"Of course." She walked over to the mushrooms. "If it's fairies, it must be Shakespeare. And that"—she pointed—"is a fairy circle."

"Ah." I followed, dew dampening my sneakers.

"You have no idea what a fairy circle is, do you?" She sighed. "Which is shocking for a changeling child."

"What?"

She laughed as she bent beside the mushrooms. "You know what *that* is, then."

"Sure. It's a fairy child left in place of a human one. I stumbled across the Bridget Cleary story in a high school law class."

Rose recited, *"Are you a witch, or are you a fairy, or are you the wife of Michael Cleary?"*

"Her husband burned her to death and was found guilty of manslaughter, not murder, because he claimed she was a changeling."

"And you cannot murder a nonhuman." Rose smiled. "The much-underutilized fairy defense. One that would impress even my nephew."

"So now you're saying that I'm a changeling?"

"Metaphorically speaking, of course. A child stolen from her parents and snuck off to others, who raise her unaware of her true heritage."

Tricked by malicious fairy folk. I wondered what my mother—Lena—would think of that. Was it how she felt?

"Olivia?"

"Sorry." I snapped out of it and nodded at the mushrooms. "What's the story with these?"

"They're considered the dancing place of the fair folk. If you see them, you must hurry on. Do them any harm and you are doomed to misfortune and early death. Dance with them and you'll dance forever, trapped in their circle."

I crouched to look more closely. "There must be a natural explanation for the growth formations."

"Don't be dull, Olivia. There is no graver sin." She began walking again. "Now come. We're having tea, and you're going to tell me what you found in your room."

I looked up sharply.

"Did I mention I have the second sight?" she said.

"No, Grace told you I thought someone broke into my place."

"Perhaps, but how would that explain knowing that something was left in your room?"

"Inference. Or firsthand knowledge."

"You mean I put it there?" Rose laughed. "That would be a trick indeed, considering Grace won't let me set foot on her property. The old bat hates me."

She resumed walking, long strides consuming the sidewalk.

I caught up. "I thought you were friends. I know you gossip."

"No. We trade points of information. When dealing with a bogart, one must be careful."

"Bogart . . . Right. That's a type of brownie."

"You remember. Excellent. Yes, it's a particularly nasty subspecies."

"I don't think she'd appreciate the comparison."

"Didn't I mention that I keep a sprig of hawthorn in my attic to ward off bogarts? Grace hasn't darkened my doorstep in years. If that's not proof, I don't know what is. Of course, it could be the fact that the last time she came over, I threatened to pluck out a hair and fashion a poppet. But I prefer to believe it's the hawthorn."

I laughed.

Rose continued, "She's useful to me, I'm useful to her. As long as that continues, Rowan Street is safe from an old-lady smack down of epic proportions." She turned up her walk. "Come inside, get tea, and tell me what you found."

As it turned out, Rose didn't know that something had been left in my apartment. Grace had told her I suspected a break-in, Rose had guessed that something was left behind and my reaction had confirmed it.

"A con artist mustn't be afraid of being wrong," she said as she set out a plate of ginger snaps. "We must be willing to make guesses, act as if we fully believe them to be true and promptly dismiss them when they aren't."

"I thought you really had the sight."

"I do." She disappeared into the kitchen and returned with the teapot, picking up the conversation as if she'd never left. "But it isn't like a light switch. I can't simply flick it on when I need it. Think of it as . . ."

She walked to a group of vintage photographs, removed one, and brought it over to the table. "Recognize this?"

The photo showed a dumpy old woman in mourning black, with a very recognizable "ghost" behind her. "Abraham Lincoln?"

Rose nodded. "William Mumler's photo of Mary Todd and her dead husband. And this one?" She picked up a second and brought it to me.

"Again, it looks like Lincoln and . . ." I sputtered a laugh. "P. T. Barnum?"

"Correct. Barnum hired someone to create that photo, which he then gave as evidence in Mumler's fraud trial, proving how easily it could be done. Barnum may have believed there was a sucker born every minute, but apparently he didn't think it was fair if the 'sucker' was a grieving relative."

Rose sat across from me. "The second sight is like the ability to see the dead. One cannot simply conjure real ghosts for a photo session."

"Like real fairies?" I said, reaching for a ginger snap.

She waved a finger at me. "You mock, yet you want to know more. Feigning disinterest is fine for teenagers, but you should be beyond that."

Rose poured the tea. "Let me give another analogy, then. My power is like the ability to notice and interpret omens."

My fingers tightened, almost snapping my cookie. She continued without glancing up. "If one could interpret omens and portents, one would presumably have to wait for them to arrive. Like ghosts or the sight. One could not simply conjure them out of the ether." She lifted her gaze to mine. "Can you?"

"W-what?"

"Is the analogy correct? Does the omen need to exist where everyone can see it? Or can one appear to you and only you?"

"I don't know—"

"—what I'm talking about?" Rose sighed deeply and added milk to her tea. "All right. We'll continue this game a little longer. Now, tell me what you found in your apartment."

I showed her the photos of the symbol under my mattress. When I said I had a sample of the powder, she made me retrieve it.

"There was something like it sprinkled outside my door a few days before," I said after I got back, as she opened the paper to reveal the grayish powder within. "I thought I detected a symbol there, too, but I was probably imagining things. Hell, I'm probably imagining the powder, too. It might have just been cigarette ash, and I—"

She lifted a hand. "Don't do that."

"Do what?"

"Qualify and backtrack in an attempt to keep from looking foolish. I'm a professional psychic, Olivia. People come to me and say they've been cursed by their neighbor, possessed by demons, visited by an angel . . . I've heard it all and I never think the worse of anyone for it."

"Never?"

She shrugged. "Demon possession strains the boundaries of credulity, given the sheer number of times it seems to happen. One would really hope demons had better things to do with their time."

She pulled the powder-strewn paper toward her, peered at it, then went to her desk and retrieved a magnifying glass. She took a better look. She rubbed some on her forefinger. She sniffed it. Even tasted it. Then she examined the photos again.

"It's a ward," she said finally. "Very old. Gaelic or Celtic, I believe."

"To ward something off," I said. "What? Evil? Bad luck?"

"Possibly . . . depending on what someone thinks of you."

"Thinks of me?"

"It's a ward *against* you. A magical 'get lost.'"

"An anti–welcoming committee?"

She nodded. "The cards foretold difficulty, which is why I suggested you get a gun. Cainsville has welcomed you, and Cainsville is not a welcoming place. Someone has noticed that and is either envious or concerned."

"Why?"

"As I'm sure you've realized, Cainsville is a peculiar little town. As to the exact depth and nature of its peculiarities?" She shrugged. "Pay attention. That's all I can say. Answers will come when you're ready for them. It's not my place to say more."

"Okay . . ."

"Let's get back to this, shall we?" She poked at the powder again. "Monkshood to warn you that danger is near. Yellow carnation for rejection. Rhododendron telling you to beware."

"In other words, a no-holds-barred 'scram and don't let the door hit you on the way out.' Could it be Grace? She has a key to my apartment."

Rose shook her head. "The only complaint she's made is about your cat, and even then, she's only grumbling. For Grace, that's as close to a seal of endorsement as you'll get."

She looked at the photos again. "Let me think on this and see if the cards will provide direction. In the meantime, I heard that my nephew brought you that gun?"

I nodded.

"Good. Keep it close."


Saturday was my day off. Dr. Evans had e-mailed me the evening before to get my work schedule. He was working on setting up some interviews for the next week. He'd also invited me over Sunday, to talk some more if I wanted. I hadn't given him an answer yet, but I planned to go. Talking to him *did* help.

Having no plans for the day, I decided to sleep in . . . and my phone rang at seven thirty.

I checked the number. A Chicago-area one I didn't recognize. I answered.

"Ms. Lars—" a woman began. She stopped herself. "My apologies. Ms. Jones?"

"Yes . . ."

"This is Dr. Yvonne Escoda. I was contacted by the office of Gabriel Walsh, in regards to your medical files."

After the hospital visit, I'd made an offhand comment to Gabriel that I should really get my old medical records. The conversation hadn't gone any further. Had he placed the call before I fired him? Or after . . .

"Ms. Jones?"

"Sorry. This is just unexpected. Mr. Walsh no longer represents me. When did he call?"

"Yesterday. His admin assistant didn't mention that you were a client. She said you were a friend, and he was doing this as a favor."

Damn it.

Dr. Escoda went on. "Regardless of the circumstances, Mr. Walsh discovered that my father had been your primary physician. He had arranged a meeting at my office this morning to deliver your records to you." She paused. "We do have a file for Eden Larsen. Daughter of Pamela and Todd Larsen. Born 1987."

"That'd be me."

"It ends when you were nearly two. Your parents decided to take you to another physician. I believe they'd moved and our office was no longer convenient. Normally, the file would have been transferred, but there's no record of that."

"So you only have my early file. That's fine."

"No, I'm afraid it isn't. The file we have for Eden Larsen can't be yours. The child in it had spina bifida. If you were her, you'd be in a wheelchair by now, which you are not, as I understand."

"Definitely not. So your father mixed up the records?"

"I . . . I cannot imagine him doing that, but *someone* has made an error."

She went on to assure me that her staff was searching old records for the file that belonged to me. She promised she would contact me as soon as it was found.

# CHAPTER FORTY-NINE

I stood there, holding the phone, feeling . . . pissed. Yes, I was pissed. Unreasonably so, really. I'd only thought in passing of getting my preadoption medical records and had promptly forgotten mentioning it to Gabriel. But now that my files seemed to be lost, I wanted them. Or, at least, I wanted to know that I'd be able to get them if necessary.

When a knock sounded at the door, I walked over and opened it on autopilot. I saw Gabriel and I completely forgot that he wasn't supposed to be there, and all I thought was *thank God*. Gabriel was here, and he'd know what to do about this.

Then I noticed he was holding coffees. Definitely not his usual MO. Which is when I remembered that I'd fired him. In the same moment, I remembered what Dr. Escoda said, about Gabriel setting up an appointment for me to get my medical records. Which is why he was here. To take me to that appointment. To present his peace offering.

"Hey," I said. "Come on in."

He hesitated, as if surprised.

"Dr. Escoda called," I said.

"Ah."

He handed me a coffee. I took a sip. A mocha, made exactly the way I liked it.

Rose had said Gabriel wanted this job. Apparently, he *really* wanted it. There was a moment where I paused and wondered if his eagerness was a tad suspicious. I couldn't see any nefarious motivation for wanting back on the case. Money and the chance to free notorious serial killers was quite enough.

"You'd mentioned wanting those records," Gabriel said. "So I got them. As . . ."

"An apology?"

His lips tightened at the word. "A conciliatory gesture."

"No apology then?"

He said nothing, but his look asked if I really wanted to go there.

"I appreciate your trying to get my records," I said. "Even if the doctor's office apparently has lost them."

"What?"

I explained, then said, "Do records routinely go missing? Should I be concerned?"

"Concerned that it's not a mere clerical error? That someone has purposely hidden your file?" He sat at the dinette. "I don't think so, but I'll see how common this is. If it isn't, there may be grounds for a lawsuit."

"Um, no. I wouldn't sue for a clerical error." At least, I wouldn't as long as I was confident I'd get my trust fund on my next birthday.

"I will investigate in any event," he said. "I also have a lead on Pamela's case."

"Where'd that come from?"

"A gentleman never reveals his sources."

"Which is why I'm not asking one."

He tapped his coffee cup. "I have a friend in the state attorney's office," he said finally.

"You mean a contact you've groomed into thinking he's a friend."

"It was his idea."

I smiled. "I'm sure it was."

"In this case, I provided information that he wanted. Information of negligible value obtained through an informant, not a client. Perfectly legitimate. In return, I gave him a very strict set of parameters on what I was looking for in the Larsen case, and he found something. A friend of Peter Evans reported that Peter had learned something shortly before his death. Something that upset him greatly."

"Which was?"

"I have no idea. It was a comment gathered during initial interviews, and the police didn't pursue it because the friend claimed Peter never actually told him what he learned."

"You think the friend lied?"

"I read the transcript. His language suggests he did know and was waiting for the police to get it out of him."

"Make him talk, so he wouldn't be responsible for spilling his dead friend's secrets."

"Precisely. The detectives failed to see that. They'd made a note to return to it later. Then they arrested the Larsens and the interviews weren't revisited."

"Is the guy still around?"

Gabriel sipped his coffee.

"Okay," I said. "Presumably he's alive, but you aren't going to give me anything that might help me find him myself. I probably still could, given my special new relationship with Peter's father."

"Yes, you could."

I watched the cat travel to his food bowl. Then I looked back at Gabriel. "How much did Lores pay you?"

He sighed.

"I'd like an answer, please."

"It was, as you guessed, not a significant amount. The point, Olivia, is that my clients are often the subject of media interest, with or without their permission. If I know a journalist willing to conduct an unbiased interview, then I do not believe I'm committing any ethical violation of my client's trust by accepting payment for finding that journalist."

"No, but you are if the client makes it *very* clear that she does not want the interview and you push her into it for monetary gain."

"*Not* for monetary gain. You had agreed before changing your mind at the last minute. I have a relationship with Mr. Lores that I was unwilling to endanger by reneging—"

"Just tell me how much."

He hesitated before saying, "Five hundred."

"I want it. Not deducted from my bill. Not put against my laptop. Cash. Preferably twenties."

He looked to see whether I was joking.

"To you, it's nothing. To me, it's more than a week's wages. Give me the money. Stick to the terms of our original agreement. And don't charge me for getting my medical records. Fair?"

He studied me. He didn't seem to be weighing the offer. He just . . . studied me.

"I seem to recall that you have today off," he said finally.

"I do."

"I'll set up an interview with Peter Evans's friend."

"Good. Then we're back in business."

# CHAPTER FIFTY

Gabriel called Peter's old friend, a guy by the name of Josh Gray. He got a busy signal. While he waited to phone back, he suggested something else.

"Pamela has been calling my office," he said. "She's back in prison and would like to see you. She says she has new information, but I fail to see how that's possible, given that she's spent the last twenty years in a cell. She simply wants to see you. I am not averse to the idea."

I said nothing, just sipped my coffee.

"Unless you are . . ." he said.

No. I *wanted* to see her, had all week and felt guilty for staying away. That was the problem.

"Do we have anything to ask her?" I said.

"I could come up with a few questions."

In other words, he knew very well that I might like to see her and was providing the excuse. Damn, the man was full of gifts today.

I found my gaze sliding to the window. Looking for a sign. I shook it off and pulled my attention back.

"We'll do that after we speak to Gray."

Gabriel phoned back. This time, Gray answered. Gabriel introduced himself and said he was investigating the death of

Peter Evans, and Gray hung up on him. Which meant he was about to get an unexpected visitor or two.

Englewood has some decent sections. Gray didn't live in—or even near—any of them.

Gabriel found a monitored lot nearly a mile away, gave the parking attendant a healthy tip to watch the car, and promised to double it if we returned to find the Jag unscathed.

"Would have been cheaper to take a cab," I said.

"I don't take cabs."

I shook my head. Then I stopped. A murder of crows perched on a dead tree. The old rhyme played in my head.

*One for bad news,*
*Two for mirth.*
*Three is a wedding,*
*Four is a birth.*
*Five is for riches,*
*Six is a thief.*
*Seven, a journey,*
*Eight is for grief.*

There were eight crows.

Gabriel noticed me staring at the birds.

"Olivia?"

"Sorry." I yanked my gaze away. "So how do you want to handle the interview?"

We continued on, passing people that I'd have normally crossed the road to avoid—even with a gun in my purse. But they all steered clear. That may have had something to do with the big guy in shades walking at my side.

We reached the walk-up apartment. An unconscious drunk lay on the stoop, his hand extended, fingers poised as if he'd been holding something. Probably his keys. They were long gone. So was everything of value in his apartment by now, I'd bet.

As we climbed the stairs inside, I saw a dead crow on a landing. The hair on the back of my neck prickled, but I kept going.

I'd seen the poppies a few days ago, and Pamela hadn't died. Or had it been a warning that she was in danger? I scowled and rubbed my neck again. That's how superstitions thrive—you see a so-called omen, and when it doesn't come true, you find another event that fits . . . if you ram that square peg into the round hole.

We knocked on Gray's door. A woman answered, and I was glad I'd suggested Gabriel stand back. I'd worked at the shelter long enough to recognize an addict—the haunted expression, the gaunt face, the telltale tracks. Despite the obvious wear and tear on her body, she was decently groomed and had some color in her cheeks. A recovering addict? Either way, she wouldn't respond well to a guy who could pass for DEA.

"Hi," I said, flashing my friendliest smile. "I'm looking for Josh Gray. I'm a friend of his sister, Terri." Gabriel's background check had turned up a half sister in her early twenties.

"The college brat?" The woman looked me up and down. "If she sent you to score from him, Josh don't do that no more."

She started shutting the door. My hand shot out to stop it.

"It's not that. She said he might be getting back into graphic design"—that was his college background—"and I was hoping to hire him."

"I dunno nothing about that."

"Could I speak—?"

"He's not here."

She gave the door a sudden shove and I stumbled back. The door didn't close, though. A big Italian loafer stopped it.

The girlfriend looked down at that shoe, then up at the rest of Gabriel.

"No," she said as she backpedaled. "No, no, no. I don't know nothing. Nothing."

"About what?" he said smoothly, stepping into the apartment.

"You're the guy who called Josh, pretending to be some lawyer."

"Pretending?"

She pointed a trembling finger at him. "You're no lawyer. I know what you are. Josh told me what you guys did to his friend."

"I thought you didn't know anything," Gabriel said.

She ran—straight for the balcony door, which was wide open. I tore after her. She lunged through and yanked it shut behind her. Then she scrambled over the rusted railing and dropped one floor to the ground.

I raced back to Gabriel. "Come on. We need to catch her."

"Do I look as if I'm dressed for an alley chase?"

I glowered at him and started for the door, but he caught my shoulder.

"She'll come back eventually, and we will, too. Perhaps by that time, Mr. Gray will also be home."

"Do you think he bolted after you called?"

"If he was that worried, he wouldn't have left his girlfriend behind. He may have gone to speak to someone after hanging up on me." He pulled his shades down. "We'll return later."

# CHAPTER FIFTY-ONE

'd just stepped out of the building when I saw eight crows on a power line. Not the same ones, I was sure, but there were clearly eight. I kept glancing up, as if my gaze was magnetized.

"What's wrong?" Gabriel asked.

"Nothing."

He peered up at the crows. "Do the birds mean something?"

"Death," I blurted before I could stop myself. I sighed. "Yes, I'm superstitious."

"Crows are a death omen, too?"

The hair on my neck rose. There was something about the way he said it. *Death omen.*

"Only when there're eight of them."

"Then everything's fine, because there are only six."

I looked up. I counted eight out to Gabriel, pointing at each.

"There are only six birds up there, Olivia."

A chill stabbed my gut. I muttered something about one of us needing our eyes checked, then hurried on. Gabriel caught up with me in a few long strides.

"You saw eight, Olivia. Earlier, too, didn't you? I noticed crows in a tree outside the parking lot. You were staring at them."

"I'm tired. Stressed out. We've lost a viable lead—"

He gripped my elbow, turning me to face him. "My aunt is a psychic. Most of what she does is a con, but there's something there, too. Something real. The second sight. Runs in my family, apparently. It passed me, for which I believe I should be grateful. But I know she has it. I've seen her use it. And I've seen how intrigued she is by you."

"We share an interest in spiritualism."

"It's more than that. Last week, you saw poppies, and your mother escaped a potentially fatal stabbing."

"*Escaped*. If poppies are a death omen, she shouldn't have escaped."

"But an omen is a warning, is it not? That's how Rose's powers work. She sees possibilities, nothing preordained."

"I don't—" I shook off his hand. "I don't know. I just . . . I don't want to talk about it."

"Then humor me. Pretend it really is a death omen. Now what?"

"Now what?"

"If you *did* see omens, there would be a reason." He gazed around the street. "What else do you see?"

"Nothing," I mumbled. "That's it. Just the—" I stopped as something caught my eye down the road. A flash, like light reflecting off a window.

"All right," he said. "We'll go that way."

"I never said—"

"I cheated you out of an exhilarating chase down filthy alleys. Let's play follow-the-omens instead."

He started off. I stayed where I was until two guys at the corner began calculating the distance between me and Gabriel. I hurried to catch up with him.

"You lied," I said.

"Undoubtedly. Which particular instance are we talking about?"

"Your aunt told you something about me."

"Only that I should trust your hunches, even when you don't."
He stopped at the corner. "Now which way?"

I felt something tug my attention to the left, and he noticed.

"Excellent. Off we go, then. The game's afoot."

"I don't believe you just said that."

He smiled down at me and picked up his pace.

"Is that . . . ?" I whispered.

I stared at the foot protruding from a pile of moldy card-board. I kept telling myself it was a coincidence. Another passed-out drunk.

Lying facedown.

Covered in cardboard.

Gabriel hauled off the moldy pieces and tossed them aside without so much as a fastidious wipe on his trousers.

When he was done, we were staring at a man with a bullet hole through his back.

Gabriel didn't check for a pulse. There was no need, I suppose, but I did anyway, crouching and pressing my fingers to the man's neck. He was still warm. But dead. Definitely dead. Blue eyes stared at the ground.

Gabriel checked the man's pockets. "No wallet. No cell."

"Robbery then," I said.

Gabriel didn't seem to hear me. He was tapping away at his phone. After a moment, he turned it to face me. On the screen was a photo of the man lying in front of us.

"Josh Gray?" I said.

Gabriel nodded.

"But the killer took his cell phone and wallet . . . ?"

"To delay identification."

"Right." I inhaled and collected my thoughts. "He hung up

on you and came out to call someone without his girlfriend overhearing. Whoever he called told him to wait. He did."

"That's a plausible theory, yes, but—"

"Leave it as a theory until proven otherwise. I know."

I looked around. There was a Dumpster ten feet away. I walked over and climbed up until I could see inside.

"It's less than half full. If you're trying to hide the body, why not dump him in here?"

"Lack of time. Or lack of strength. I could manage it, but it would be difficult, and it would leave me covered with blood."

"Okay, so now we call the police."

I took out my cell. He plucked it from my hand.

"Once the body is discovered, it's only a matter of time before Mr. Gray's girlfriend learns of his fate. Given that she was frightened enough to vault over her balcony, I don't think news of his death will loosen her tongue."

I looked down at Gray. Leaving a man dead in an alley was wrong. But that woman was our only hope of finding out what Peter Evans told Gray twenty-two years ago. Besides, did I really want to get pulled into a murder investigation?

"Should we put him in the bin?" I asked.

Gabriel's brows shot over his shades.

"I just meant . . . Maybe we could buy some time. He hasn't been dead long. Time of death is a vague science. If he's found now, his girlfriend would ID us and we'd be suspects."

"Good thinking."

"I'm surprised you didn't suggest it first."

"I was going to return after I got you safely to the car. But if you're offering to help, that will make the task easier."

So I helped Gabriel Walsh move a body. What consumed my thoughts was not guilt, but how I'd found the corpse in the first place. I'd led Gabriel to a dead body based on omens and intuition, and he was as unperturbed as if we'd stumbled on Gray during a random shortcut.

I didn't know what to make of that.

I remembered Rose asking me if I ever saw omens that weren't really there. I had the answer now. I had a lot of answers now. I'd had them for a while and had just kept pretending otherwise.

Apparently, I could . . . I don't know what exactly. Read the signs? Interpret omens? See portents? Was there a name for such a thing? Where would the ability come from?

I knew the answer to that—from the woman who'd taught me those rhymes and kept a chest of mystical supplies in her bedroom. The woman accused of murdering eight people in occult rituals.

I needed to speak to Pamela again. And I would, in a few hours. For now I had to focus on getting Gray's girlfriend to talk before the cops found his body.

"So how do we do this?" I asked.

"I believe I know a way," Gabriel said. "I'm going to drop you off in a better neighborhood, where you can find lunch. I'll call when things are in place."

"That's very considerate, but I'm not hungry."

"Perhaps not now, but—"

"That tone in my voice a moment ago? Sarcasm. I know you aren't being considerate. You're trying to dump me so I don't see how you get this woman to talk. I'm not hiding in a sandwich shop."

He looked at me over the roof of his car. "I'd really rather you did."

I opened the door. "As the song says, we can't always get what we want."

———

We drove through about ten miles of farmland before Gabriel pulled into a wooded lane marked Private Property. The rutted drive made him wince with each bump. After a couple of hundred feet, the drive widened. It was lined with motorcycles. Big-ass motorcycles.

"First you buy me a mocha. Then you let me help you hide a body. Now you take me to a biker clubhouse. Best. Day. Ever."

His lips tightened. "You're staying in the car."

"Hell, no. This is a once-in-a-lifetime experience."

I reached for the door handle. He smacked down the automatic locks. "This isn't a game, Olivia."

"I'm kidding. But I *did* just move a corpse. I think I can handle this."

"I'm their lawyer. It's a relationship based on mutual respect. I cannot waltz in there with another client."

Damn. Why did he have to make such a good point?

I sighed. "All right."

He hesitated.

"I said all right. Go. I'll wait."

# CLEANUP DUTY

The man looked at the spot where he was supposed to find Josh Gray's body. It was gone.

He peered up and down the alley. Then he walked from one end to the other and checked the GPS coordinates on his phone. This was definitely the place.

He made a call.

"It's not here," he said when his boss answered.

Silence.

"The body," he said. "Gray's—"

"Are you actually telling me this on an unsecured cell line?"

*Yeah, because I don't have a secured one,* he wanted to snap back. He didn't. He apologized. Then he asked what the boss wanted him to do.

"Find it, of course. She didn't drag him out of there."

The line went dead. The man sucked in breath. This was stupid. If you want someone dead, you just kill them. All these layers of complication. First the old man. Now this. He didn't understand it.

The boss said Gunderson's death was a precaution, in case he decided to help the Larsen girl. Which was bullshit—from what he'd read in the paper, there was no way in hell Gunderson was helping the Larsen girl. And how would he anyway? He didn't know anything.

It was just a lame excuse to test the latest "upgrade" to the boss's invention. Now he'd tested it a second time, which left his loyal employee here, trying to move a body that appeared to have . . .

His gaze caught on the Dumpster. He shook his head. No way. The boss was right—the meth-head chick couldn't drag a two-hundred-pound guy, let alone lift him into a bin, which is why he'd been called on cleanup.

And yet . . . well, there wasn't anywhere else to take him, was there?

He put his gloves back on and climbed onto the base of the Dumpster. Then he lifted the lid, peered in, and . . .

Holy shit. How the hell had she done that?

She hadn't. It wasn't possible.

Then who had?

As he took out his phone, a shadow passed overhead and he toppled off the bin, landing on his ass. He fumbled his .45 out and swung it up at . . .

A damned bird. A crow, it looked like. A huge one sitting on the side of the bin.

Had it smelled the body? That was all he needed.

But the bird wasn't looking in at the feast below. It was staring at him.

When he rose, the bird lifted off, almost lazily, but only flew onto a balcony overhead. Then it perched there.

"You think you're getting some of that?" he gestured at the bin. "Not a chance, birdie."

He started to turn back to the bin. That's when he saw the dog. A massive dog, black, with strange reddish-brown eyes. He swallowed and gripped his gun. The dog stared at him a moment, then snorted, turned, and disappeared into the shadows.

Gun raised, he carefully walked over to where he'd seen the dog. It was gone. He peered down the alley. No sign of it. A sigh of relief. He holstered the gun, but kept his jacket open, in case it came back.

He climbed back up and closed the bin. He took out his phone again, then stopped and peered up at the bird. It was still staring at him. He fought a shiver and looked around.

The boss told him not to use the phone. So he shouldn't. He should just leave. Go tell the boss what he'd found. With any luck, he'd decide Mr. Gray could stay right where he was.

One last furtive look at the bird, and the man hurried off.

# CHAPTER FIFTY-TWO

I eyed the forest surrounding the biker clubhouse. I'd been jogging daily since buying sweats, but I'd skipped this morning, which made sitting here even worse. Maybe if I just went for a walk and stayed away from the clubhouse . . .

Yeah. I'd probably step into a bear trap. Gabriel would be pissed if I bled out in his car.

I'd just flipped open my notebook when I heard the rumble of motorcycles. Three were coming up the road. One was that kind with the front wheel that sticks out. Yes, I know nothing about motorcycles. Never met a biker, either. I just hoped Gabriel's window tint was dark enough to hide my gaping.

One wore a full helmet. The second had none. The third wore a small black one without a visor. I'm sure that has a name, too.

The guy with the small helmet looked like a construction worker. Big and burly, but clean shaven with short brown hair. He was dressed in a leather jacket, jeans, and work boots. The helmetless guy riding the bike with the extended front wheel was more what I expected, with shit-kicker boots, a chain looping from his pants, a long graying beard, and a ponytail hanging over the Satan's Saints patch on his jacket.

I cracked down my window as they parked in the row of bikes.

"No, I'm serious," the bearded one said. "Gabe's got a girl in the car."

"Don't call him Gabe," said the guy in the full helmet, his voice muffled. "You know he hates it, which means it's disrespectful."

"Yeah? Well, so is bringing his bitch to the clubhouse."

A sigh. "Gabriel wouldn't do that."

"So who's the blonde in his car?"

Heavy footfalls came closer. A shadow crossed the passenger's window. The guy with the beard peered in.

"Yeah, it's a girl." He shaded his eyes and squinted at me. "Gotta admit, guy has taste. Hot cars. Hot pussy."

"Jesus," muttered the guy who'd defended Gabriel. He had his helmet off, but I couldn't see him behind the others.

When he reached to tug the bearded biker back from the window, I powered it all the way down. Seemed rude not to.

As I did, I got a look at him and . . .

If the guy with the beard and stringy ponytail matched my vision of a biker, this one matched Hollywood's. He couldn't be much older than me. Hazel eyes. Tousled blond hair curling over his collar. A few days of stubble on a chin that I was sure had a cleft when he shaved.

His boots were low-profile Docs, and his leather jacket only had the gang patch on one sleeve. He wore snug, faded jeans and a white T-shirt under his jacket. A blond Marlon Brando, without the broody angst. I'm not normally given to drooling over hot guys— Oh, hell, who am I kidding?

"I'm a client of Gabriel's," I said. "He had to stop by on business and he was stuck with me."

"Holy shit," the bearded biker said, staring at me. "Holy fucking shit!"

The young biker shot him a glare.

Bearded guy waved at me. "Didn't you see the article? The photos? That's Gabe's new client. Todd and Pam Larsen's kid."

He shot me a big smile, but the older one who hadn't spoken eyed me and eased back before stopping himself.

The bearded biker said. "It's an honor to meet you, Miss Larsen."

"Which isn't the name she uses, I'm sure." The young guy extended a hand to me. "Rick."

"Ricky," the bearded biker said, reaching up to ruffle Rick's hair. "Everyone calls him Ricky."

Ricky rolled his eyes.

"Olivia," I said, shaking his hand. "Don't worry. I've been ordered to stay in the car."

"What?" the bearded biker said. "We aren't good enough for Gabe's old lady? Son of a bitch."

The other older guy grumbled something under his breath. Even Ricky's lips compressed in a tight line.

"I'm not Gabriel's girlfriend," I said quickly. "I'm his client. That's one ethical line he wouldn't cross. It doesn't pay well enough."

A whoop of laughter from the bearded biker. "Got a point there."

"He told me to stay out *because* I'm only a client. He said it would be disrespectful if he brought me in."

Ricky nodded. "But if I say it's cool, it's cool. Come on."

I got out and let him lead me down the lane. Ahead was what looked like a cottage, complete with a front porch and chairs. It sprawled off to the rear, making it larger than it appeared from this angle.

"I'll warn you, it might be a disappointment," Ricky said, waving at the clubhouse.

"I'll survive. So, what kind of bike do you ride?" I asked, as if I could tell a Honda from a Harley.

He answered. I didn't quite catch it, maybe because I was focused on that clubhouse door, waiting for Gabriel to barrel out and give me shit.

"You ride?" he asked.

I shook my head. "Never been on one."

"I could fix that." Ricky grinned, as if he was offering to corrupt me in more ways than one.

Whoa. Cute biker was flirting. I guess the "biker" part of that description should have thrown up a big stop sign, but I'd just come out of a relationship with a guy who considered double-parking a walk on the wild side. I was in the mood for a change.

So I flirted back. Nothing overt, but by the time we finished the short walk to the door, the two older men had fallen back behind us, as if giving him space.

Ricky opened the door. Inside it looked like a retreat for business execs who want to get away from the city and pretend they're just regular guys. The walls were wood, as was the floor. There was a stag head on one wall . . . wearing a White Sox cap.

The long bar was rustic but spotless, bottles stacked behind, a few on the top shelf that definitely *were* top shelf, at least a hundred a bottle.

Half of the living space was sofas and comfortable chairs, old and worn, but hardly Goodwill material. The big flat-screen TVs and sound system were the sort I'd see in CEOs' theater rooms.

Tables took up the other half of the room. At one, four guys played poker. At others, guys typed away at laptops, gazes glued to the screen, so intently you'd think they were checking the stock market. Maybe they were.

"Disappointed?" Ricky asked.

"I was hoping for more bullet holes." I pointed at a stag head. "And maybe a rival club member on the wall instead."

"Oh, I think we've had a few hanging from that guy's antlers. But we had to cut them down and let them go."

"Pity."

He grinned. "I thought so."

I pretended to give the room another once-over but concentrated on the occupants this time. The mix was about twenty-sixty-twenty. Twenty percent looked like the old, bearded biker. They were the ones lounging on the sofas and chairs. Sixty percent were more like the one who could pass for a construction worker—mostly clean cut and clean shaven, but burly enough that you knew he didn't sit behind a desk all day. The others, like Ricky, could have pulled off the suit-and-tie look, even if they probably never would outside a courtroom.

There were women, too. They were a little more what I expected. Tight jeans. Tank tops without bras. Evening makeup at noon. Jersey hair. The general vibe varied from "wouldn't look out of place on a corner of 47th" to "could work at a really nice strip club."

The men noticed me, but not in the way I might expect from a roomful of men. Just curiosity, with the occasional nod or smile before turning back to whatever they'd been doing. The women didn't nod and definitely did not smile. I felt like a new lioness walking into a pride, as the others discreetly sharpened their claws. One of the youngest—a blonde at the "really nice strip club" end of the spectrum—even got to her feet, before an older woman tugged her down. As the blonde sat, her gaze went to Ricky, but he wasn't paying attention.

"We'll wait for Gabriel here," he said, pulling out a bar stool for me. "What'll you have?"

"Beer."

He leaned over the bar and plucked a can from a bucket of ice. "Bud okay?"

"Sure."

To be honest, I can't remember the last time I drank beer, and I've probably never had one that didn't come from a micro-brewery. But when flirting with a biker, it didn't seem helpful to admit that.

"I'm sure your situation isn't a topic you like discussing with strangers," Ricky said. "But I just want to say that you were smart to go with Gabriel. I'm guessing he's getting you some money, as he should. You got shafted. Gabriel will fix it."

"He's actually handling other things for me."

Ricky looked surprised.

"Having money is nice," I said. "Having money is not everything."

He leaned over and mock-whispered, "Don't say that too loudly in here."

I smiled and shook my head. "I did say having it is nice. It's just better if you feel you've earned it."

He watched me for a second, then nodded. "Agreed." He took a long drink from his beer.

"Who's your friend, Ricky?"

It was the blonde who'd stood earlier. Up close, I could see past the makeup and realized she was younger than I thought. Maybe twenty. Maybe not even that.

"A client of Gabriel's," Ricky said.

"Gabriel's old lady? You let her in here?"

Ricky's gaze cooled. "I said *client*. One, do you think I'd be having a beer with Gabriel's girl? Two, I can let the pope in here if I want, Lily."

The bearded biker from earlier looked up from the couch

where he'd planted himself. "If you read the papers, Lily-girl, you'd know who she is and you'd keep your mouth shut."

"All right," Ricky said. "That's enough—"

"Shit," one of the men with a laptop said. "She's the Larsen girl. Gabriel repped her mom, didn't he?"

"Larsen?" someone piped in. "You mean the serial killers?"

Lily stared at me like I'd crawled out of the toilet. "Your parents are those freaks?"

Ricky's look made her inch back. "Meribeth? Come get your daughter."

The older woman had been standing since Lily approached us. Now she hurried over and grasped the girl's arm. "I'm sorry, Ricky. She had a couple before she got here."

"Yeah? Well, considering she's eighteen and it's barely noon, I'd say you have a problem there."

The woman scuttled off with her daughter.

Ricky raised his voice a notch. "For anyone who didn't catch that, this is Olivia. She's Gabriel's client, and I invited her in."

He didn't say, "Does anyone have a problem with that?" His tone didn't even imply it. But there was steel in his gaze. Murmurs passed through the room, welcomes for me, and assurances to Ricky that everyone was cool with it. A room full of bikers—most of them older and bigger than Ricky—but when he talked, they listened. Interesting.

Ricky turned back to me, his expression as guileless and friendly as if we hadn't been interrupted. Before he could say a word, though, we were interrupted by a near growl from the other direction.

"Olivia . . ."

I glanced over to see Gabriel bearing down, an older blond man beside him, a door closing behind them. The other man was about fifty, clean cut, and dressed in jeans and a golf shirt.

From the size of his arms, though, I suspected if he ever swung a club, there was someone on the receiving end.

Gabriel was trying very hard not to scowl.

"Told you I wasn't supposed to get out of the car," I whispered to Ricky.

Ricky stepped forward. "Hey, Gabriel. I found Olivia in your Jag. Black car. Sunny day. Didn't seem healthy. I invited her inside. Insisted on it actually."

"Thank you," Gabriel said to Ricky, in a tone that didn't sound terribly grateful. "I believe it's time for us to be going."

"She just got her beer. You want one while you wait?"

Gabriel looked at him. Ricky met his gaze, his expression open, pleasant even, but that steel crept back into his eyes.

Gabriel shot up his sleeve and checked his watch. "Quickly, Olivia."

The older guy in the golf shirt smiled. He murmured something to Gabriel, then gestured at one of the bikers, and the guy nearly fell out of his chair scrambling to come over. Golf shirt was the boss then.

I looked from the boss to Ricky. Noted the blond hair. The similar facial structure, a little softer in the older man.

Biker gang boss. Biker gang boss's son. Okay, that explained things.

Ricky suggested we all move into the back room, which we did, to the disappointment of those who'd decided they were suddenly very thirsty and should hang out closer to the bar.

Gabriel introduced me to the guy in the golf shirt—Don Gallagher—and it took only a few minutes of conversation to confirm that I'd been right about his position and his relationship to Ricky. Gallagher and his son were surprisingly good at making small talk. Maybe I shouldn't say that's surprising. I guess part of me still lives in Kenilworth and always will.

A guy who runs a biker gang is like a Mafia kingpin. He's a businessman. Which doesn't mean he's really a decent, misunderstood guy, only that he's risen high enough that he can have others play thug for him. As for Ricky, his dad proudly told me he was working on an MBA at the University of Chicago. Part-time, Ricky said, because he had responsibilities with the family business.

"We should go," Gabriel said, after Don told his son what Gabriel wanted—someone to persuade Gray's girlfriend to speak to us. "We have that interview."

"Right." I took one last gulp of beer. "We're ready for that, then?"

He nodded. "Don has agreed to provide us with one of his men, who will speak to Mr. Gray's girlfriend before we do."

"I'll handle it," Ricky said.

"There's no need—" Gabriel began.

"I've got errands to run in town, and I can probably persuade her better than any of these guys."

Gabriel didn't like it, but when Don agreed, there was little he could do. He gave Ricky the address and said we'd follow.

# CHAPTER FIFTY-THREE

As we headed out, Ricky walked ahead with me while his father found more he needed to talk to Gabriel about, making them hang back. Ricky mentioned what I'd said about never having been on a bike and offered to rectify that sometime. I said I'd keep that in mind and we bantered a bit before Gabriel caught up and steered me off to the car.

We gave Ricky a head start, since he'd need to speak to Gray's girlfriend before we arrived.

"A word of advice about Ricky . . ." Gabriel said as he swung his car from the end of the drive.

"Is it going to cost me?" I waved off his answer. "Whatever you're going to say, save your breath."

"I overheard him offering you a ride on his motorcycle. I don't believe you understand what that entails."

"Grass, gas, or ass. No one rides for free." I looked over at him. "I've seen the T-shirt."

"I don't think you're taking this seriously, Olivia. Do you know what a one-percenter is?"

I sighed. "Yes, Gabriel. It refers to the portion of bikers who belong to a professional motorcycle club. A gang. Ricky is one. As such, I'm going to guess that the only women who get to ride his bike are also riding *him*. Am I right?"

His mouth tightened as if he didn't appreciate the crass phrasing. "I'm afraid you're under some illusions about Ricky because he does not fit the stereotype."

"Oh, I'm not fooled. He may appear to be the heir to a criminal empire, but he's really an undercover cop, working tirelessly to overthrow his father's evil empire and restore justice and goodness to the land." I glanced over. "Am I close?"

Not even a hint of a smile.

"Oh, please," I said. "I know he's not studying part-time because school interferes with his commitment to Greenpeace. His family business is drugs, with a little murder and mayhem thrown in on the side."

"No, it is not. Mr. Gallagher runs a legitimate motorcycle club and operates a series of auto repair shops. However, he is constantly under suspicion of criminal activity, which means a relationship with his son would not be wise."

"Can we skip this conversation? I really don't think your legal services cover—"

"As representative for both yourself and Don Gallagher, anything between you and his son concerns me. I understand that you're undergoing a great deal of upheaval in your life. You've discovered things about yourself that have thrown your perspective—"

"Stop."

"—and your sense of identity off balance. You aren't who you thought you were and that may lead you to consider reckless—"

"Stop. Really. I only rehired you a few hours ago. Since then, you've done nothing to make me regret that decision. Quit while you're ahead."

"I believe it needs to be said—"

"No, it does not. See this?" I tugged a hank of my hair. "Contrary to popular opinion, blond hair does not feed off brain cells."

"I never suggested—"

"You were about to. Yes, I'm having identity issues. Can't blame me really. Wake up the daughter of respected pillars of Chicago and go to bed as the child of its most notorious serial killers. Maybe I'm making some choices that you think are silly and immature, like insisting on living in a smelly apartment and working at a small-town diner. But if I was single, would I have flirted with a cute biker before all this happened? Absolutely. Would I have done more than flirt? Probably not. Too many complications. Would I do it now? Maybe. Not for a walk on the wild side, but as a conscious decision to try something different. My choice. One that has nothing to do with you."

"Yes, it does, because you are my client and Ricky—"

"God, it's like talking to a cyborg sometimes. You pretend to listen, but really, you've just gone on pause, waiting for me to stop so you can reiterate your original point."

Gabriel's phone rang, saving him from an answer. It was Ricky. Gray's girlfriend was ready for us.

When Gabriel knocked on Josh Gray's door, Ricky answered. He came out and pulled it almost shut behind him.

"Her name's Desiree Barbosa. She should talk, but if she tries to stonewall you, just remind her I'll be back." He walked past with a smile for me and a whispered, "See you later."

As Gabriel pushed open the door, I glanced at him. I'd been sure they weren't resorting to physical violence to persuade Gray's girlfriend. Was I being naive? Telling her that Ricky would come back if she refused to talk sure as hell sounded like a threat.

We found Desiree in the tiny living room. She was on the couch, her legs pulled up. When we walked in, she didn't even tense, just said, "Hey," and waited for us to sit.

As soon as I stepped into that room, I could feel the difference in her. Earlier, it'd been like walking across a carpet in a dry room, her anxiety, her fear, condensing into nervous static-like energy. Now it felt like an island breeze wafting through the room, gentle and warm, telling me to just sit down, relax.

As soon as I felt that, I stiffened, because I'd felt this sensation before, at the shelter. I didn't need omens or signs to understand what it meant.

As we crossed the room, I studied Desiree. Her pupils were dilated, her jaw slack, her eyelids listing, as if struggling to stay awake.

Ricky hadn't threatened her. He'd given her drugs.

My gut tightened, and I glanced at Gabriel. His gaze flitted across Desiree and the look he gave was satisfaction mixed with contempt. He knew. Of course he did. He'd set it up.

We'd known Desiree was a recovering addict. After Gray ran and we showed up, she'd been scared and anxious and alone. Vulnerable. When Gabriel saw that, he'd known exactly how to get her to talk. That's what Ricky meant about telling her he'd come back—he'd given her a hit and promised another if she cooperated.

We'd given drugs to a recovering addict.

I'd just given Gabriel shit for suggesting I was enjoying this walk on the wild side, like a drunken college girl stumbling into a filthy tattoo parlor and letting dirty needles decorate her body with the Chinese symbol for whore. The truth was that I'd been riding a roller coaster of anxiety and adrenaline since Dr. Escoda's call that morning.

And now this.

I sat there, feeling sick and shocked and angry, most of all furious with myself for being such a fool, such a damned fool.

This wasn't a game. It was serious and ugly and I wanted nothing to do with it. And yet, in wanting nothing to do with it, I was a hypocrite. I'd followed Gabriel this far because he got me what I wanted. Now he was, once again, delivering. Was I going to sail out on a wave of righteous indignation?

What would I do to prove that my parents—yes, my *parents*—did not kill anyone?

How far would I go?

Everything in me screamed against this. Yet the deeds had been done, the body hidden, the drugs given, the witness ready to talk. Leaving smacked of hypocrisy and empty self-righteousness. So I stayed.

"That guy says you aren't one of them," Desiree began. "He said you can help if they come for me."

"Yes," Gabriel said. "But I can't help until I understand what's happening."

She snorted. "I don't even understand. It's crazy shit Josh used to tell me when he got high, and I always figured it was just the dope talking. Then he gets a call, and he says it's about that and I was, like, holy fuck, so he wasn't making it up."

"Making what up?" I asked.

"The stuff." She waved her hands. "The crazy shit."

As she gestured, I thought I saw a spot of red on her sleeve. A stain the size of a dime. But when I tried to find it again, I couldn't see it.

"Let's step back," Gabriel said. "You were worried I was some-one else. One of 'them.' Who?"

"The spooks."

We both paused.

"Do you mean ghosts?" I said.

She gave me an "Are you high, chick?" look. "Spooks. You know. The men in black. The alphabet goons."

I glanced at Gabriel.

"Federal agents," he said. "DEA? FBI? CIA?"

"Spooks."

"CIA?"

"That's what I said."

"So Joshua knows something he thinks might make the CIA come after him. Something someone else told him."

"Right. His friend from back when they were kids. The one that got carved up. Supposedly by that couple."

"The Larsens."

She leaned forward. "Only it wasn't really them. They were framed by the spooks."

"The Larsens were framed by the CIA?" I said.

"You're just a baby," she said with a dismissive wave my way. "I was still a little girl, but I remember my parents talking about those murders, and I'd sneak the papers to read about them. I always knew the Larsens couldn't have done it. They weren't more than kids themselves, and anyone could tell they weren't murderers. Then I met Josh, and he told me what really happened. I didn't believe him because he'd only talk about it when he was high. I should have believed him."

"Why did Josh think the CIA had killed Peter Evans?"

"Is that his friend's name? I always forget."

I had to repeat the question before she said, "Because of the secret."

"What secret?"

"What Peter told Josh just before he died."

I doubted Desiree Barbosa was the most articulate woman at the best of times, but this felt like circling a barbed wire fence, seeing my prize on the other side, unable to find a way in.

"And the secret that Peter told Josh about the CIA, which led to his death was . . ."

"About his dad."

"Peter's dad? What about him?"

"Peter found out his dad worked for the spooks. Least, he used to."

"Dr. Evans worked for the CIA? Okay. What else?"

She stared blankly.

"A lot of people work for the CIA," I said. "People don't get killed every time someone finds out."

"But it's supposed to be a secret."

"Did Peter tell Josh *why* his father's old job was a secret?"

"Because he worked for the spooks."

We circled this a few times, but according to Desiree's worldview, it was perfectly logical that the CIA would murder Peter—and his girlfriend—simply because he'd discovered that his dad used to work for them.

"So they killed Peter and Jan and made it look like the Larsens' work."

She shook her head. "Those Larsen kids didn't kill nobody. They were framed. Like I already said."

"Because everybody the Larsens supposedly killed knew a secret about the CIA?"

Another "Are you high?" look at me. I glanced at Gabriel, but he made no move to take over, as if he knew this was the best we could manage. That's what happened when you gave drugs to a potential source.

"Why did the CIA kill the other couples?" I said.

"'Cause that's what spooks do. They kill people. They're real clever, though. They know how to hide it, like murdering a whole bunch of people the same way, so it looks like a serial killer. Then they blame innocent folks."

Gabriel cut in, thanking Desiree for her time and calling Ricky. Seemed he had enough experience with this type of thing to know we weren't getting more out of her.

I wanted to take Desiree aside and try to change her mind. Yes, she'd stumbled, but it wasn't too late to get back on the path. There was no sense arguing, though. Not while she was feeling good and wondering why in hell she'd ever given this up.

So I waited by the door while Gabriel stayed with her.

I hadn't been there long when someone rapped. I opened the door with the chain engaged.

Ricky grinned through the crack. "Hey."

I unlatched the door.

"How'd it go?" he asked as he walked in.

"She talked. Given her condition, I doubt she had much choice in the matter."

He looked at my expression and murmured, "Shit."

He paused, as if he should say something. I waved him into the living room.

"So, I'll, uh, talk to you later?" he said.

When I didn't reply, he said, "How about I get your phone . . .?" He trailed off as he caught my expression. "Or not."

He got three steps away. Then he stopped. Paused. Reached into his pocket and took out a notebook with a pen hooked on the cover. He jotted something on a page and ripped it out.

"*My* number. I know it'll probably go in the nearest trash can, but I'm not walking away without giving it a shot." When I reached out, he held on to the note and met my gaze. "I'm sorry you didn't know what was going on here. I thought you did. You should have."

I nodded, and he released the paper. I tucked it into my pocket as he headed into where Desiree waited.

Gabriel came out almost immediately.

"Ready?" he said.

I gave a curt nod and opened the door.

I'd planned to wait until we got in the car to confront him. I made it as far as the stairwell.

"That was a really shitty thing to do," I said.

"Get answers?"

"You know what I mean. Desiree wasn't that mellow because you hired Ricky to perform stud service. I worked at a clinic and a shelter. I know what people look like when they're high on heroin. You gave drugs to a recovering addict."

"No, I simply asked Don Gallagher to help persuade her to speak to me."

I stopped. I waited for him to turn around. Face me. Confront me. He just kept walking down the stairs. I hurried to catch up.

"You told him to offer her drugs."

"I did not. I explained the situation. If that was the route Ricky chose, it wasn't at my request."

"But you knew what he'd do. You provided drugs to a woman who's trying to turn her life around. It's like seeing someone step onto a ledge and giving her a push."

He stopped now, turning to face me. "That's a little dramatic, don't you think?"

"No, I don't. I've seen women like Desiree. Women who finally get clean. And in my experience—"

"Ah, yes, your experience." Icy sarcasm seeped into his voice. "Your experience, Olivia, is that of a privileged young woman who mingles with the masses for a few hours a week and presumes to understand—"

"Excuse me? I worked my ass off, putting in full-time hours—"

"I mean your work with addicts. I'm presuming you have no training in it. No *personal* experience with addicts."

"No, but—"

"So your time spent with them likely worked out to a few hours a week, in a charity setting, where the addicts would be on their best behavior, saying all the right things, because it was the only way those services would agree to help them. Of those who did stop their drug use, how many do you think stayed clean once they got what they wanted from you?"

"I—"

"Let me tell you a few things about addicts, Olivia. They lie. Consistently. Expertly. Pathologically. They lie to anyone who comes between them and their next high. They'll pretend to quit. They may even actually quit. But it's a sham. At the first opportunity, they will start using again. Anyone who believes their commitment to self-transformation will be disappointed over and over until they finally wise up and stop hoping."

There was no passion in his speech. It was a cold recital of facts without one indication that his words held anything personal. But I knew they did. It was like a wall had slammed down.

When he finished, he continued down the stairs, and I recalled what Dr. Evans had said about Gabriel's mother. I'd suspected she'd been an addict. Now I knew it.

And I knew this wasn't an argument I could win. I remembered Gabriel's expression when he'd walked in and found Desiree high. Satisfaction, yes. But contempt, too. He couldn't look at this and see Desiree Barbosa. He could only see his mother, and nothing I said would change that.

We walked outside. He flipped his shades on.

"If Ricky offered her drugs, clearly she accepted," he said. "No one forced them on her. If she'd been serious about rehabilitating herself, she wouldn't have accepted."

That's how he saw it. She'd been tested. She'd failed. Just as I'm sure his mother had, enough times that he hadn't doubted

Desiree would take the bait. Maybe he was right. Maybe she would have fallen off the wagon anyway, and if we could give her a push to our own advantage, then I shouldn't feel so guilty. But I did.

We walked down the street in silence.

"Can I ask you not to do that again?" I said as we turned the corner. "Not on my case?"

"It was very specific circumstances that I highly doubt would repeat themselves, so the chances of—"

"Can I just ask you not to? Please?"

We were at the next corner before he said, "While I will reiterate that I was not involved in any drugs being given to Ms. Barbosa, I will agree to allow no such thing to happen again on this case without your knowledge."

"Thank you."

# CHAPTER FIFTY-FOUR

We'd been on the road for about ten minutes when I said, "Are we going to discuss what Desiree said? Or are we presuming it's drug-addled crazy talk? I mean, obviously the CIA isn't killing people by posing as serial killers."

"Likely not. It's an intriguing concept, and actually quite brilliant, but it would suggest more creative thought than any government agency is capable of."

"Uh-huh. Okay, well, I also doubt Peter and his girlfriend would be murdered for discovering that his father used to work for the CIA, but do you give any credence to the rumor that Will Evans *did* work for the CIA? That Peter may have, coincidentally or not, discovered it shortly before his death?"

"I'm quite certain it's true. As for whether the discovery was coincidental, that's what we need to find out."

"You really think Evans could have been CIA?"

He didn't answer right away. As he drove, he seemed to be relaxing, the tightness leaving his face.

"I'd be willing to lay a wager on it," he said finally.

"Meaning you know something, because I'm quite sure you don't gamble unless you're guaranteed to win."

He didn't smile, but he flexed his hands on the wheel, losing a little more tension. "Yes, I've heard that William Evans was at one time employed by the CIA. It came up during my initial background checks."

"So it wasn't a secret."

"It isn't something he brings up at cocktail parties, I suspect. But his employment doesn't seem to be a classified matter. I couldn't confirm it at the time, but admittedly, I didn't try very hard because I didn't see the relevance. Now I do, so we will investigate."

We decided to postpone our visit to Pamela. We had a lead and should concentrate on it. That wasn't an easy decision to make. She would have been told we were coming and been looking forward to it. Canceling felt cruel.

But we did have a lead to pursue. And we were starting with a stop at Gabriel's office.

As we walked in, a voice called, "Finally, I've been trying to ring you all day, Gabriel. I realize it's a Saturday, but I told you I'd be working and I'd really like to be able to contact you when I am."

It was the same throaty voice I'd heard whenever I called the office. Gabriel's admin assistant, Lydia.

When I saw the woman sitting behind the reception desk, I had to do a double-take and, for a moment, thought the words were coming from someone else. Whenever I'd pictured the woman on the other end of that sultry voice, I'd imagined someone suitably ornamental, the sexy secretary befitting the successful young lawyer. Instead, I saw a woman old enough to be my grandmother. Small and trim with short, steel-gray hair. She hadn't turned but was still tapping away at her computer.

"Perhaps, Lydia, we could maintain the illusion that I'm in charge of this office, at least when there's a client present."

"Client . . . ?" She turned and saw me. "Oh, I'm so sorry, Mr. Walsh. I"—she waved at a tiny screen—"saw you get out of the car and you seemed to be alone."

"I am not."

"You never bring clients to the office on the weekend."

"So it's my fault. Naturally. Lydia, I'd like to introduce you—"

"Ms. Jones. Of course." She came out from behind the desk. "Please forgive my manners. May I get you a coffee or cold drink?"

I looked at Gabriel. "Are we staying?"

"We are." He turned to Lydia. "We need to conduct research involving your former employers. Don't bother with drinks. You should go enjoy your weekend."

She nodded, and I said good-bye as Gabriel led me through a second door into his office.

Back in high school, I'd had a friend whose father was the kind of guy who never flew business class . . . because he never flew commercial at all. Her family made mine look positively middle-class. Her house had been a twenty-thousand-square-foot ode to modernity, yet her father insisted on having a study that he'd literally had transplanted from a historic manor. I remembered how much I loved that office, like something out of a Victorian novel. Gabriel's reminded me of that, though his actually suited the building.

The walls and floor were wood. The ceiling was decorative plaster, the design so intricate that I could lie on my back and stare at it for hours. And he had the chaise longue for exactly that, though from the looks of the leather, it didn't see much lounging. There was a massive fireplace along one wall, with the faint smell of ashes suggesting that *did* get used. The other three walls were lined with floor-to-ceiling bookcases. It even had a wooden ladder on a track, for reaching books on the top shelf.

That, too, didn't look used—Gabriel would stand head and shoulders above your average Victorian.

Gabriel pulled out the red leather chair behind his wood desk. Then he paused, frowned, and looked around. It took a moment before I realized he was looking for a second chair.

"Lydia must have taken it out," I said.

He shook his head. "I don't see clients in here. I'll pull one in from the meeting room."

As he left, I looked around. He didn't meet clients here? It was certainly impressive enough, and I'd presumed that was the point.

When he rolled in a chair, I said, "You said we're researching Lydia's former employer. She worked for the CIA?"

"For twenty years. Secretary to the Chicago field office special agent in charge."

In thinking Gabriel would hire a pretty young thing, I'd committed an unacceptable misjudgment of character. Would he really waste a decent salary on eye candy? Not when he could hire someone with ten times the experience for the same rate.

"You sent her home," I said. "I'm guessing that means we're about to use access she's given you, and you don't want her to be culpable, should it ever be discovered."

He popped open his laptop. "Not quite. Lydia no longer has access, and even if she did, I doubt she'd betray her previous employer by providing it. She has, however, shown me a few alternate routes to obtain information."

"Back doors?"

He nodded. "Anything Evans did before Peter's death would be at least twenty-two years old. That means it's unlikely to be classified. However, given that my simple background checks did not reveal precisely what he'd worked on, I'm presuming it's something that the CIA would prefer not to post in easily accessible locations."

"Unclassified, but only if you know where to find it."

"Correct."

Gabriel typed and navigated too fast for me to ever replicate his path, but he let me sit there, watching, which surprised me. Hell, after our spat over Desiree, I was surprised he hadn't called it a day and done this on his own. Likewise, he could have insisted I take that lunch break while he visited the Saints' clubhouse.

I could take this as a sign that our partnership had progressed to the point of actual trust. What's that old joke? "A friend helps you move; a real friend helps you move a body." We weren't friends; I knew that. But helping someone hide a body does take a relationship to a whole new level. Maybe it *was* trust. Or as close as we could get.

# CHAPTER FIFTY-FIVE

D r. Will Evans had indeed worked for the CIA. It wasn't a
secret. It wasn't on his résumé, either. Gabriel said that
wasn't unusual. While his position didn't seem to have
been classified, the CIA didn't exactly publish its employee lists.

At first, Gabriel wasn't able to get much more than confirmation that his name appeared on old records. Evans had been
young, just out of grad school, and he'd worked on various
projects as a psychologist.

"What did the CIA use psychologists for in the sixties?" I
asked. "Things like post-traumatic stress? Or was the party line
still 'suck it up and deal'?"

Gabriel didn't answer, just typed in a few search terms. When
the results came in, he frowned. He clicked on one. Skimmed it.
Frowned deeper.

The angle of his laptop was off just enough that I could see
the screen, but couldn't read much.

"Got something?" I said.

"Mind control."

"What?"

He turned the laptop my way. "They did use psychologists
and psychiatrists for therapy, but during the Cold War, they

employed more of them for experimentation. Drugs, behavior modification, and mind control."

I read the article. "*The Manchurian Candidate*? Seriously?"

His frown grew.

"Not a movie buff?" I typed search terms into another browser window. "Huh, it was a book, too. From the fifties. The movie and the book were about a Korean War vet who was brainwashed into becoming the perfect assassin. He'd be 'activated' by seeing the queen of diamonds card. He'd kill someone and forget all about it. Complete fiction. I mean, obviously, right? But not according to that."

I pointed at the other browser window, then scrolled through the Wikipedia entry for *The Manchurian Candidate*. At the bottom, I found a link for Project MKULTRA. I clicked it. I read it.

Another window. Another search, this time pulling up academic references and the proceedings of a joint Senate Select Intelligence and Human Resources committees hearing from the seventies, exposing and detailing MKULTRA.

"Holy shit," I muttered. "Could Evans have been involved . . . ?"

Gabriel took the laptop back and typed. Typed some more. Read and frowned. Typed. Read. Turned the laptop toward me.

There is was, on one of the pages he'd accessed through his back door. Just one reference linking Evans and MKULTRA, but it was enough. We backed up from there and spent the next hour researching the project.

MKULTRA was a code name. It didn't mean anything—it was just an umbrella term for a wide array of CIA mind control projects starting in the fifties.

We got a few bonus history lessons from our research, the kind of thing they don't cover in class. When the U.S. stepped onto the world stage during WWII, the intelligence community realized its intelligence programs were pathetic compared to those of the British. They set about trying to rectify that.

Most of those early projects were more amusing than frightening. That changed after the war, when the CIA realized the potential of psychology to produce the ideal soldier and assassin, and to provide foolproof methods of extracting information from enemy spies. Thus began a decade of experimentation with drugs—particularly LSD—and extreme psychiatric measures like electroshock therapy, sleep therapy, and sensory deprivation.

We could complain about government interference today, but compared to what I read, we'd come a long way. Shrinks subjecting psych patients to treatments that erased their memories permanently. Agents slipping drugs into drinks at bars, inviting people back to parties and spraying LSD in the air. Nothing said it better than a quote I found from George White, an OSS officer heavily involved in the experiments: "I toiled wholeheartedly in the vineyards because it was fun, fun, fun. Where else could a red-blooded American boy lie, kill, cheat, steal, rape, and pillage with the sanction and blessing of the All-Highest?"

That was the crazy, fucked-up piece of American history that was MKULTRA. What did it have to do with William Evans? With the murder of his son? There were no obvious answers here. We had to go deeper.

The only lead we found was the name of Evans's supervisor, Edgar Chandler. He wasn't just Evans's boss at the CIA—he'd been his thesis adviser in school, too. So it seemed that Chandler had worked for the CIA then and brought his prize student along.

While Gabriel made coffee, I continued searching and learned that Evans had been in private practice since Peter was born. Did that mean he'd quit the CIA? Or only pretended to?

The deeper we went, the harder the slog. Finally, we hit a story that hammered home exactly how classified MKULTRA had been in its day.

In 1974, as word of MKULTRA was just beginning to leak, a hungry young Chicago journalist caught a whiff of it and saw a career-making break. As she researched the story, doors were slammed in her face. Colleagues advised her to drop it. CIA representatives *strongly* advised her to drop it. All this only seemed to strengthen her conviction that this story needed to be told. The government was trying to stop her. She would not be stopped.

Except she was. While walking to her car one night, a man approached her in the parking lot. He didn't say a word, but she later provided a perfect description of him to the police. Not surprising, given that his face was the last thing Anita Mosley ever saw.

Her attacker had thrown acid in her eyes, blinding and scarring her for life.

When speculation arose that the man was connected to the CIA, all the local news outlets received a letter from the attacker, claiming he was simply a patriotic American teaching a lesson to a Commie woman reporter. The police never found him to test that claim.

After that, Anita Mosley disappeared from reporting for a while. She might have been scared off, but from everything I read about her, I doubted that was the case. Maybe a significant other urged her to take some time off. Maybe her employer forced her onto disability leave. All I could tell was that she went quiet until the Senate hearing on MKULTRA, and then she reemerged as an authority. That's where I found the connection to Evans's boss, Chandler. She'd mentioned him in an article. Nothing damning, just one name on a list. But it was a start.

"She still lives in Chicago," I said. "Freelance these days, but there's nothing here to suggest she'd like to put MKULTRA behind her. She spoke about it last year at Northwestern."

"She's still angry," Gabriel said. "Certainly understandable, given the circumstances, though it does seem a little . . ."

"Pathetic?" I regretted the word as soon as I said it. Unfair to use against a woman who'd fought so hard and suffered so much. And yet I couldn't help seeing an element of pathos. She'd fought the CIA and lost. By the time she rebounded, the "secret" was common knowledge and she couldn't hurt those who'd wronged her. Yet she wouldn't drop the matter, either, doggedly struggling to keep alive a scandal no one seemed to care about.

Still, it didn't bother me enough to suggest we leave the poor woman alone. She'd chosen to make this her life's work. We'd be foolish not to take advantage.

"She'll see us," Gabriel said when he hung up.

"Really?"

"Are you surprised?" he said. "I doubt anyone other than academics has asked for her expertise in a very long time. She's quite eager to impart it. At a price, of course."

"How much?"

"Five hundred for an hour of her time now, plus an hour of follow-up, if required. Given the usual rate for an expert, it's a bargain."

"It'd be more of a bargain if it was free."

"True. But think of it as a charitable donation to the victim of a tragedy. That should make you feel better."

"Only if I can get a tax write-off."

He shook his head and we left.

# CHAPTER FIFTY-SIX

We met Anita Mosley at a coffee shop. It was a neighborhood of office buildings, meaning the shop was closed on a Saturday. She was at a stone table outside, sitting with military stiffness, hands folded on the table, staring straight ahead as cars zipped past. She was in her early sixties, a trim figure in a stylish pant-suit and perfectly coiffed brown hair, artfully streaked with gray.

"Ms. Mosley?" I asked as we approached.

The shades swung my way.

"Do you want to stay here?" I said. "Or find a shop that's open?"

"The fact that this one is closed is why I chose it. It is public yet not public." Her tone was crisp. "May I ask whom I'm speaking to?"

"Olivia Taylor-Jones."

"Ah. The girl." She turned to Gabriel, as if sensing him there. "And you would be the infamous Gabriel Walsh, I presume."

"I am," he said as we sat.

"Excellent. Now, I have received confirmation that the payment has been wired to my account. Thank you for that, Mr. Walsh. I know it is an inconvenient way to do business, but until the American government sees fit to print bills I can read, I'm stuck with that. Unless I emulate Ray Charles and ask to be paid in singles." A brief, humorless smile. "Which would hardly be more convenient for either of us. Now, I believe it is Ms. Taylor-Jones who wishes the information? You do still go by that name, I presume."

I tensed a little. A reaction I doubted even a sighted person would notice, but she seemed to pick it up.

"I know who you are," she said. "Let me assure you, serial killers hold no fascination for me, and their actions have no bearing on you. I have met monsters, and they all had quite normal parents. I will admit that I find it curious that your investigation would bring you to MKULTRA, but you are being thorough, and I cannot fault that. So Ms. Taylor-Jones, is it?"

"Olivia," I said.

"Thank you. Now let us begin. I can confirm that Dr. William Evans worked for the CIA from 1960 to 1969. He began as a PhD candidate under his adviser, Edgar Chandler, who was also employed by the CIA. Chandler was in charge of several MKULTRA subprojects. His name can be found in the documents turned over to the Senate subcommittee."

"So Dr. Evans was involved in the project?"

"MKULTRA as a whole was huge. Evans's role in it was relatively minor. He started as a graduate student and was still a junior man when he quit shortly before his son was born. Or that's the official line. The matter of secrecy surrounding Evans is twofold. Let's start with part one, the main experiment he was involved in. Have you heard of Operation Midnight Climax?"

"I saw it mentioned in one of the articles, but only in passing."

"The name is proof that the CIA can have a sense of humor. Operation Midnight Climax was a subproject of MKULTRA based in San Francisco, under the auspices of George White.

They realized the best subjects are those unlikely to talk about their experience . . . such as johns who get dosed at a whorehouse."

"Ah."

"At the time, the CIA knew little about the world of hookers. Or about kink. They quickly learned how to exploit human proclivities to their advantage. They eventually opened other whorehouses in Marin County and New York. Yet there's one that can't be found in any of the surrendered documents. Right here, in Chicago. That's where Evans worked. So why hide that one? Because it operated completely off the radar, even within the ranks. In the others, as bad as they were, limits were drawn."

"And the ethics were a little looser at the Chicago house."

"That's the rumor. I can't confirm it. Any evidence has long been shredded and anyone who worked there has kept his mouth shut. I tried to get Evans to talk once. It seemed as if he may have had moral qualms. He politely but firmly shut the door in my face. So my sources have been former subjects—the ones who don't fear for their lives because they're too crazy to know they should."

"Crazy as in reckless or as in . . . ?"

"Certifiably insane. Presumably as a result of what happened in that Chicago whorehouse. That's the beauty of fucking with the human mind. If you break it, that's fine, because the damage covers your tracks. Who's going to believe the paranoid schizophrenic who claims the CIA made him crazy and now they're out to get him?"

"So that's what Evans was involved with before he left the agency."

"*If* he left. That would be the second part. While the record clearly shows that William Evans quit his job with the CIA in 1969, there are suggestions that he did not leave entirely. By the late sixties, most of the MKULTRA experiments had officially been abandoned. The civil rights era meant people were taking a closer look at government powers. Information about the experiments was leaking. It was still years before Gerald Ford appointed a commission to investigate, but things were already coming to an end. Or, as some believe, the CIA was simply pulling the curtain tighter."

"Ostensibly abandoning the projects, to continue them in secret with men like Evans who had apparently left the service."

She nodded. "But that's all speculation. I've pursued it to some degree but this"—she pointed at her glasses—"makes serious investigative journalism very difficult, as I'm sure my attacker knew. So while I can provide you with contacts, this marks the end of where I can take you."

Gabriel wanted to start by interviewing Evans's former boss. "A poor choice," Anita said. "Edgar Chandler will never speak to you." But Gabriel insisted and Anita gave him the information she had on Chandler.

As we were leaving, Anita called me back.

"You're doing this in hopes of proving your parents are innocent," she said. "They aren't. I had friends who covered the case. None of them doubted the Larsens' guilt."

"So you think it's a coincidence that Peter found out about his father shortly before his death."

"I didn't say that. But the likelihood of a connection between MKULTRA and all eight deaths is minimal to nonexistent. You seem like a bright girl. Don't spend your life chasing answers that aren't there."

One could say the same about her. When I looked at her face, lined with bitterness, I realized she knew exactly what she was saying.

"I'll remember that."

"Do. And if you have questions about your parents later, you know where to find me. I may not be much of an investigative reporter these days, but my contact list is extensive."

"Thank you."

# A DROP OF RAIN

Anita sat at the coffee shop table after the lawyer and the girl were gone. She didn't like to hurry off—that seemed as if she was nervous out here, alone. The poor old blind lady. She'd never been that before, and she sure as hell wasn't about to start now, no matter how hard her heart was pounding after that conversation.

They hadn't seemed to notice. That was a blessing. She was getting better at hiding it. Yet even after forty years, it took only the mention of MKULTRA to start her heart racing. Most times these days, though, she was the one mentioning it. Masochism, Blake used to say. Facing her demons, she'd say.

She wished she could tell Blake about the girl and the lawyer. He'd know Walsh. Probably wouldn't have had anything good to say about him, judging by the tidbits Anita picked up in a few quick calls made after Walsh contacted her. Blake had been a civil rights lawyer—he had little patience for young sharks like Walsh. But Blake was gone now, dead four years, and no one had replaced him. No one would.

A footstep crunched on broken concrete, so close that Anita's head shot up. She listened, but no other noises came. Then, when she strained hard enough, the faintest sound of breathing.

"Yes?" she said, snapping with as much impatience—and as little anxiety—as she could manage.

The breathing continued, so close her heart slammed against her chest.

"If someone is there, I fear you'll find this old lady a particularly poor target," she said briskly. "I carry twenty dollars in cash, no credit cards, and no jewelry worth the hassle of hocking it."

She didn't expect that to scare away a would-be mugger, but the street was not completely empty—she'd heard a few people pass since the lawyer and the girl had left. She'd spent enough years with Blake to develop at least a little faith in the human race. They might not be quick to intervene in all cases, but there *were* some advantages to being a blind old lady.

Yet her voice only echoed into silence. Then another shoe-squeak, so loud it seemed deliberate. The breathing moved closer until it was right across the small table from her.

She snatched out her wallet, cursing her trembling fingers as she did. She plucked out the twenty and kept the wallet open.

"As you can see, I spoke the truth. This is all I have. If you insist, you're welcome to it."

Her voice rose as she spoke, taking on an air of desperation. A car whooshed past. Then a second, a loose tailpipe rumbling, and she wanted to leap to her feet, cry out for help, but she knew it would do no good. Drivers would pass oblivious, intent on their destination.

The breathing grew louder, as if he was leaning over the table to take the twenty. Good. Just take it. Please take—

A drop of rain fell on her arm. She swiped it. As she did, she felt something she hadn't felt in forty years. A sensation she'd never forget. Her flesh burning.

Anita screamed. She scrambled up from the seat so fast it toppled over and she fell with it, legs tangling in the bench, taking her down, her hands still raised against her attacker.

Footsteps pounded across the pavement. Hands grabbed her. She fought, screaming.

"Lady!" The voice was young, female. "I gotcha, lady. You're okay."

A male voice, just as young. "Here."

More hands, grabbing her arms to help her up. As she rose from the concrete, her glasses slid off. She tried to grab them, but it was too late.

She heard the boy suck in breath. "Jesus. What—?"

"Don't," the girl whispered to him. A clatter as she snatched up the glasses and pushed them into Anita's hands.

Anita put them on quickly. The chair scraped the concrete. The girl's soft hands helped her into it.

"You're okay," the girl whispered.

"S-someone was here," Anita said. "Did you see him?"

Silence.

"Did you see *anyone*?" she said.

"There was a chick and a guy," the girl said. "Blond chick. Big dude. We passed them."

The lawyer and the girl. Anita's mouth went dry.

"When? Where?"

"Few minutes ago. Down the road. Darnell nearly smacked into the guy coming around the corner. Scared the crap outta him."

The boy grunted. "Dude wasn't *that* big."

The girl chuckled.

"Anyone else?" Anita said. "Anyone running away just now?"

"Nah."

"No, sorry, ma'am."

Anita cursed under her breath. Had she imagined the whole thing? Memories of the acid attack sending her brain into a tailspin?

She brushed her fingers over the spot on her arm and winced with the jolt of pain. No, someone had been here. Someone had warned her. But this time, she wasn't going to be frightened off.

# CHAPTER FIFTY-SEVEN

We decided to drive to Fort Wayne, Indiana, to see Edgar Chandler, Evans's former thesis adviser, and his boss during his years with the CIA.

"Does it do any good to suggest I drop you in Cainsville?" Gabriel asked.

"No."

"May I find a hotel for you in Fort Wayne?"

"No." I glanced over at his profile, dim in the gathering darkness. "Chandler is eighty-six years old. I'm not too worried."

"He's a former CIA agent in possession of potentially damaging information. Someone killed Joshua Gray, and while I'm not convinced the same someone killed Peter Evans and Jan Gunderson, I do believe Gray's death is connected to what Peter told him."

"But you don't think Chandler himself killed Gray. That's why you insisted on getting his contact information. Because he's an old man and you plan to surprise him at night before he has a chance to retreat or get backup."

"That doesn't mean I think the excursion is without risk."

A few more minutes in silence. Then he said, "I'm going to stop by my condo. I should change my clothing."

"Sure. I wouldn't mind a few minutes in a bathroom, if that's okay. Past time to run a brush through my hair."

A pause. A long one.

"Or if you don't want me using *your* bathroom . . ."

"No, no. I was just thinking, we're close to the highway. My apartment is out of the way. I don't really need to change."

"Go. I'll stay in the car."

He shook his head. "I'm fine. If we leave now, we'll be there before midnight, which is preferable."

So Gabriel didn't want me seeing his apartment. Not the inside, at least, since he'd seemed willing to take me as far as the building, meaning he wasn't secretly bankrupt and living in his Jag. Maybe the place was a mess. Hell, given how little I knew of Gabriel's personal life, he could have a wife and kids there. I doubted it, but you never knew. None of my business, though I would have liked to clean up.

Edgar Chandler's house was just outside the Fort Wayne city limits. It wasn't easy to find, and it was past eleven before Gabriel located the long, dark drive with a dimly lit house at the distant end.

There was no way to "sneak" up that lane with the car, so he parked it a quarter mile away. I had my door open and feet on the ground before I realized he hadn't turned off the ignition.

"I should have left you in Cainsville," he said.

I sighed.

"If you were any other client, I would have come alone."

"If I was any other client, I wouldn't be investigating with you in the first place."

"True. However . . ." He stared out into the night. "When I agreed to let you join me, I thought your enthusiasm would end with the first pointless interview. It didn't. That impressed me and might have led me to allow and even encourage your participation when I should not have." He nodded toward the distant house. "Case in point."

"Because I'm the client, so you feel responsible for my safety."

"If something were to happen to you on this investigation, I would feel . . . guilty."

"I know the risks."

"Do you?"

I met his gaze. "Yes. Maybe you should have left me in Cainsville, for your own peace of mind. But I'm here now and you know there's no sense leaving me in the car because I won't stay."

More staring into the night, then without glancing over, he said, "Do you have your gun?"

"Of course. It's in my purse."

"Put it in your pocket."

He opened the door and climbed out.

As we neared the lane, Gabriel caught my shoulder and pointed to the lampposts flanking the drive. The lights were turned off and I couldn't see what was worrying him until he whispered "security cameras." When I squinted, I made out pinpoints of red light just under the lanterns. I followed him across the lawn instead.

Edgar Chandler lived alone. He'd been married, but divorced his wife a half century ago. Two of his three children had predeceased him. The youngest lived in Tucson. Our research suggested Chandler employed a housekeeper/cook, but she lived in the city. He was a man who valued his privacy, even past the age when it was wise to live alone.

The porch lights had been left on, along with one interior light, which illuminated the drawn curtains on a huge bay window. The rest of the house was dark.

Before we reached the porch, Gabriel took out his cell. He

would phone Chandler, tell him why we were here, and ask for ten minutes of his time. Yes, Chandler could call for backup, but it would take more than ten minutes for anyone to arrive.

Gabriel began to dial. Then his chin shot up, eyes narrowing. "What—?"

I barely got the word out before a shadow lunged from the bushes behind Gabriel. I pulled out my gun and started to shout a warning, but Gabriel had the guy on the ground before I could.

I swung my gun behind me. I don't know why. It was as if I'd heard something and reacted before I could process the sound. And on the other end of the barrel? An old man in a housecoat, with a gun aimed at Gabriel.

"Drop the gun now!" I barked.

When he didn't move, I fired into the roses beside him.

"I said, drop it!"

"Oh my," he said. There was no panic in his voice. No fear. "I do believe you mean it. I'm putting my weapon on the ground."

He laid the gun on the porch slowly, as if the movement took effort. I readjusted my grip on the weapon, but my hands were dry and steady. Shock, I think, more than nerves of steel. I probably looked a little ridiculous, poised there like a badass movie cop. No one was laughing, though. Not the old man, straightening now. Not the big guy lying facedown in the grass, his own weapon pointed at the back of his head, a foot on his back. And not the bigger guy pointing that weapon at him.

"Now kick the gun over to me," I said to the old man.

"My dear, I'm eighty-six years old. I cannot 'kick' anything without landing on my posterior and breaking a hip."

"Back away then."

He did. I retrieved the gun. It was a monster—at least .45 caliber. Even I'd fall on my ass if I fired it. I handed the gun to Gabriel and got a curt nod.

"You can consider yourself fired, Anderson," Chandler said to the man on the ground. "I can't have a bodyguard who gets himself thrown ambushing a trespasser."

"I told ya I wanted to get a better look at them first," the man whined. "I couldn't see nothing in the dark."

Chandler turned to me. "As we are now disarmed, I'll ask that your bodyguard releases mine, and allows him to regain some semblance of dignity before I send him slinking into the night."

"He's not my bodyguard. He's my lawyer."

Chandler took another look at Gabriel. "Impressive. May I ask, then, sir . . ." He gestured at Anderson.

Gabriel took his foot off Anderson, gun still pointed at the man. "Go sit on the porch while we speak to your boss." He looked at Chandler. "I haven't met many retired psychiatrists who feel the need for a live-in bodyguard."

Chandler shrugged. "Old age does not accommodate vanity well. With Anderson, I have someone here at all times without the humiliation of requiring a permanent nursemaid."

"Which explains why you met us with guns," I said.

"I'm an elderly man of some means, despite my modest living arrangements. It would not be the first time someone has sought to take advantage of that. I'm presuming, though, that breaking and entering isn't your intent, unless you bring a lawyer in tow, should you be caught." He pursed his lips. "That could be convenient."

"We want to talk about Will Evans."

He blinked, as if caught off guard.

"Dr. William Evans," I said. "He was your—"

"Yes, yes, I know who you mean. I'm simply surprised because I haven't heard that name in a very long time."

"We know you worked for the CIA with Evans—on a classified Chicago-based branch of Operation Midnight Climax."

"Ah. Let me guess your occupation then, my dear. Reporter. Or journalist, as I believe they prefer to be called these days. A young investigative reporter hoping to launch her career by unveiling a secret, sordid part of Chicago's past. May I give you some advice? It's been almost fifty years. No one cares. At best, you'd have a historical interest piece on the city pages. And, in return, you would make enemies you might prefer to avoid."

I turned to Gabriel. "That sounded like a threat."

"Noted." His face was impassive, but a growl escaped in his voice.

I glanced back at Chandler. "How many reporters travel with their lawyers?"

He gave Gabriel another once-over. "I'm still trying to decide if you're joking about that."

"We're not here to grill you on your activities with the CIA," Gabriel said. "At the time, the general public might have taken a prurient interest in Ivy League academics whose forays into understanding human behavior included watching through peepholes in whorehouses. But today it seems more like the premise for a reality television show, and a dull one at that."

"He does sound like a lawyer," Chandler said to me. "Before we go further, then, may I know who I'm addressing?"

"I don't believe that's necessary," Gabriel said.

Chandler sighed. "Definitely a lawyer." He looked over at his bodyguard, sulking on a porch chair. "Take note, Anderson. Size and martial ability do not need to come with a correlating decrease in intelligence." Back to us. "If you *aren't* interested in these stories you've heard about Will Evans, what is your interest?"

"The fact that Dr. Evans worked for the CIA is a matter of public record," Gabriel said. "It is also a matter of public record that he resigned to pursue private practice. However, we have reason to believe his leave-taking was not absolute."

"That he continued with the CIA? He did not."

"You sound very certain of that. I wasn't aware the CIA was such a small agency."

Annoyance flickered in Chandler's expression. He covered it with a nonchalant shrug. "I knew Will very well at the time. If he'd returned to the CIA, I would have known it."

"But you said that you have been out of touch for years."

A tight smile. "Will may not be as old as I am, but he's past retirement age. I doubt he would have returned to the CIA since we last spoke."

"And if he had done so *before* that, he would have told you. Even if it was a classified project."

"I'm sure he would have."

"Perhaps." Gabriel took a slow step forward, making the bodyguard tense. "But I think you're telling the truth—that Evans did not return to the CIA. I think you know this with certainty because, as brilliant as he was, holding down three jobs was more than he could handle."

"Three?"

"His new practice, the CIA, and his work for you."

"My work was for the CIA—"

"Until 1982, when you quit to look after your own company. One that you began in 1970, and is the source of the income that requires you to hire a bodyguard."

"I retired in 1982, young man, and I have no other business—"

"Bryson Pharmaceutical."

"I invested in Bryson Pharmaceutical. I certainly do not own it. If you've found any evidence to suggest otherwise, you need to employ better researchers."

Chandler gestured to his bodyguard. "Anderson? Please escort these young people off my property. If they persist in staying, I will have them know that I contacted the police before we came

out, and they may wish to leave before the authorities arrive."
To Gabriel, "This sort of behavior could result in disbarment."

"Hardly. It's simple trespass, and as we came with the purpose
of interviewing you for a case, our late timing is merely rude. I
suspect I'm as well versed in how to avoid losing my license as
you are in how to avoid being named as the owner of a pharmaceutical company."

With that, Gabriel waved for me to lead the way and we left.

# CHAPTER FIFTY-EIGHT

"Okay," I said when we got into the car. "Did you forget to tell me that Edgar Chandler owns a pharmaceutical company? Or that it's where you believe Evans went to work after he quit the CIA?"

He peeled from the curb. I twisted to peer into the night.

"I don't see the cops, Gabriel. You can slow down."

"I'm hardly concerned about the police. Chandler didn't call them. I'm sure he did phone someone, but likely only to say to send reinforcements if he didn't check back within the hour."

"So why'd we leave?"

"Because I'd accomplished what I came for."

"Dare I ask what that was? Because apparently I wasn't privy to the grand plan."

"I didn't tell you about Chandler because I wanted to confront him myself. I'm better suited to such tactics."

"If you mean physical intimidation, I'll agree that's your thing, not mine. But if you'd told me your reasoning, I'd have let you handle him."

A pause, then a nod, as if this possibility hadn't occurred to him.

"You're going to be so glad when this is over and you can fly solo again, aren't you?"

He made a noise, impossible to make out, but which I'm sure meant "Hell, yes."

"On the topic of partnerships," he said after a moment. "Thank you for covering me with Chandler. Almost allowing Anderson to get the drop on me was an inexcusable error. Had you not been there, I might have had quite a hole through me. Your reflexes are excellent."

"Too many Dirty Harry movies. At least I didn't dare him to make my day. So, what exactly did we just accomplish?"

"I confirmed, by his reaction, my suspicion about the drug company. I had no evidence on that."

"So Evans quits the CIA, using his son's birth as an excuse, and covertly works for Chandler's drug company. Why the secrecy? What do they manufacture?"

"Nothing you could find on the shelves of your local pharmacy. Bryson Pharmaceutical is an export business. Their primary clients are foreign regimes with civil rights laws far laxer than ours."

"Continuing the work from MKULTRA, not for the greater good but for profit."

"Far more sensible, don't you think?"

I shook my head and settled in for the long trip to Cainsville.


The problem with MKULTRA—well, there were lots of problems, morally and ethically—but from a practical standpoint, the problem was that after all that expense and all the risks taken and all the lives altered, the CIA never did achieve its goals. Perhaps there is a lesson in its failure—a testament to the human mind that should come as a relief to anyone who ever worries about things like brainwashing and mind control. In the end, their scientists discovered there was no way to influence human behavior in a reliable fashion.

There were those who believed the answers were still out there, that as many liberties as the CIA took, it was still hamstrung by basic ethics. Had Chandler and Evans seen hints of a breakthrough in their work with MKULTRA? A breakthrough they could better pursue from the private sector? Where they might be able to develop and sell products in countries unfettered by the restrictions of testing and using such products on American citizens?

"So what's the next step?" I asked as we reached the highway.

"To get some sleep. If I recall correctly, your apartment has a sofa."

"It does."

"Then I'll ask you to allow me to stay there tonight, not simply for convenience, but because we have revealed ourselves to Chandler. We didn't identify ourselves, but I suspect he has the means to discover who we are."

"Fine by me. I have tomorrow off, too."

Apparently my sofa turned into a bed. I'd heard of such things, but never seen the marvel of engineering for myself.

"I think the cat likes you," I said as I brought my backup sheets into the living room and found Gabriel sitting on the pulled-out sofa, locking gazes with the cat.

"Come on," I said. "Back to bed, TC."

One brow lifted. "I thought you weren't naming him."

"I didn't. TC. The Cat. It's an acronym."

His lips twitched. "I see." He pulled a .45 from the back of his waistband, then tucked it under the couch.

"You swiped Chandler's gun?" I said.

"No, I merely failed to return it."

I laughed, said good night, and headed to my room.

Before I got into bed, I checked under the mattress, just as

I had the night before. I didn't expect to see anything, but I couldn't go to sleep until I checked. When I saw a piece of folded paper beside the bed, I practically dove to snatch it up.

It was the note Ricky had given me earlier today, his number written on what looked like lecture notes. I started to ball up the page to throw it out. Then I stopped and flipped it over. The biker. The MBA student. Two halves of the whole. His parents were hardly serial killers, but I felt some inkling of kinship there. He'd grown up in gang life. He could escape it if he wanted. He was handsome, charming, obviously intelligent. Yet I didn't get the feeling his MBA was an escape route. He was getting it to secure his position as gang leader. That interested me. *He* interested me.

I fingered the page for another minute, considering. Then I folded it neatly, put it in my wallet, and got ready for bed.

# A MATTER OF TRUST

Gabriel opened the living room window, then closed it again and double-checked the lock. He could have sworn he'd felt a draft coming through earlier, but it seemed fine. He checked the other window. Same thing.

Still, he wasn't satisfied. Olivia's apartment was only three floors up. Easy to scale and break in. He'd done it himself many times, when he'd been younger and much smaller.

She should get a security system. She'd say she couldn't afford it, but he could call in favors, get one for not much more than she'd paid for the gun. He just needed to persuade her that the added security was necessary.

Was it? There were few places safer than Cainsville, if you were the right kind of person. That's what his aunt always said. As for what exactly constituted "the right kind," she was vague on that. It seemed unlikely that Rose would qualify. Even less that he would. But they did. Now Olivia did, too, which should mean she was safe, but . . .

He checked the front door for the third time since she'd gone to bed. It was locked. He knew that. So what was he checking for? He had no idea, only that he felt unsettled. As if something was amiss, and the only way he knew how to deal with that was to keep prowling and listening and checking.

He'd said earlier that he'd feel guilty if something happened to her. He shouldn't—participating in this investigation was entirely her choice. Yet he felt responsible for her and it left him . . . unsettled.

Of course, he had a very good reason for protecting her. A monetary incentive. At the thought, though, he found himself walking faster, pacing the living room, a tickle of something dangerously close to guilt prodding him on. It was like the damned cookies. He hadn't done anything wrong. So why was it bothering him?

It didn't help that the cat kept staring at him.

"I haven't done anything wrong," he murmured as he lowered himself to the armchair.

The cat, surprisingly, did not respond. Gabriel let out a low growl and leaned back. The cat leapt onto the coffee table, sitting right in front of him, staring.

He stared back. He wasn't going to feel guilty about this. James Morgan was the fool who'd made the offer. *Look after Olivia. Keep her safe.* Which is exactly what Gabriel would have done anyway—she was his client—so there was nothing wrong with accepting money for it.

Morgan had come to him, simmering with the kind of shallow, manufactured fury that can only be expressed by someone who's never had any reason to be truly furious about anything. He'd read Lores's article. Clearly Gabriel was taking advantage of his innocent, befuddled fiancée. Gabriel had told him the truth and opined that Morgan should really allow Olivia to pursue this investigation. That she needed answers, and if he truly cared about her, he'd step back and not interfere.

He'd fully expected Morgan to explode. In Olivia, James Morgan would see only a suitable wife. He didn't truly understand her. He certainly didn't love her. Yet Morgan had called a day later and agreed to stay away. He asked only two things of Gabriel, which he would pay for, of course. One, that he look after her. Two, that he lobby on Morgan's behalf, which meant pushing Morgan's suit and telling her that James was there, waiting, whenever she wished to speak to him.

Gabriel had ignored the second part. He wasn't a matchmaking service. He hadn't actually refused the task, but he wouldn't accept payment for it. That was only fair.

So he was taking money for protecting her, yet he wasn't only protecting her because he was taking money for it. Therefore, there was nothing to feel guilty about. Except for the small matter that he and Olivia had that very morning resolved a similar issue over Lores.

If she found out about this . . .

Damn it, why did she need to be so unreasonable? She'd helped him hide a body, for God's sake. She understood necessity. She understood that ethics were in most cases a burden that could be reasonably ignored in pursuit of necessity. She should understand that there was nothing wrong with accepting money for doing something that needed to be done, like getting unbiased media coverage for her or protecting her from harm.

But it wasn't the fact that he'd made the deal with Lores that upset her. It was that he hadn't told her. A silly distinction. Why should she need to know?

Because it was a sign of respect.

He wanted to finish this investigation with Olivia. He might even want to continue their working relationship beyond that. It was still a nascent idea, born when she'd joked earlier that he'd be happy to be rid of her. He wouldn't be.

If she found out about his deal with Morgan, though, their partnership would end. And he had a feeling persistence and concessions wouldn't fix it this time.

He should tell her.

Gabriel looked across the living room at her bedroom door. It could wait. It should—

He rose and walked over. Though there wasn't any light coming from under the door, that didn't mean she was asleep yet. As he leaned in to listen, he accidentally brushed the door and it clicked open.

He put his fingertips against the door as he leaned closer for a better listen. It opened an inch. He reached for the handle to close it, but took a quick look first, to see if she was awake.

She was in bed, sound asleep, covers pulled away. She was facing the other direction, hair fanning over the pillow. She wore an oversized T-shirt and it had bunched up around her thighs, her feet bare, legs bare, and that's when he realized that he wasn't looking through the crack anymore. He was standing in her bedroom, a step past the door.

He backtracked fast. Once outside, he pulled the door shut and retreated to the sofa bed. As he sat on the edge, he felt the cat's stare and looked up to see it on the couch arm.

"I didn't do anything," he murmured.

Nor would he. That was one crime no one could ever accuse him of. He'd never even chased a reluctant conquest. It would be like finding a handful of pennies scattered on the sidewalk and deciding you really must have the one wedged in the crack. Willing partners were plentiful. Besides, seduction might suggest he wanted more than an hour of a woman's time, which he decidedly did not.

He looked back at Olivia's bedroom door. Seduction hadn't been his intention anyway. This was a business relationship. She was a client.

He'd only wanted to talk to her. But the more he thought about it, the more he was convinced such a discussion wasn't necessary—or wise. What if confessing wasn't enough, despite what she claimed?

He should never have agreed to Morgan's offer. While there was—he still believed—nothing wrong with what he'd done, the hassle wasn't worth the payment. Taking care of Olivia was easy enough. She didn't need it, if he was being honest. But working with Morgan? A pain in the ass. The man had left five messages in the last few days, panicked over some newspaper photo of him with another woman. He blamed his mother. Gabriel hadn't bothered getting the details. Obviously Morgan had screwed around, been caught, and now he'd say anything to clear his name.

James Morgan was an idiot. If Gabriel had any doubts on the matter, working with him had erased them. Morgan lost Olivia through his own cowardice and stupidity, and he didn't deserve to get her back. Gabriel had done the right thing. Olivia was better off without him, and given her flirting with Ricky, she knew it.

But there was the possibility she wouldn't see it that way.

He should tell her.

Gabriel stood. Then he sat down again.

Yes, he'd tell her—later. After he'd ended his arrangement with Morgan. That's how he'd fix this. He'd call Morgan in the morning and say he'd changed his mind and wire back his money. Olivia would accept this better if he'd already quit and refunded the retainer. She might not truly understand what it took for him to return money he'd rightfully earned, but she would still appreciate the gesture. It would cement his sincerity, and she would forgive him.

Everything would be fine. He just needed to be patient and handle this properly.

Ignoring the cat, he stripped off his shirt and crawled onto the sofa bed.

# CHAPTER FIFTY-NINE

At 5:30 a.m., I was awakened by a buzzing. I leapt up thinking there were bees in my room, which meant I'd have a visitor—and if I killed the bee, the visit would not be pleasant. It was not, however, an omen, but only my cell phone. Which, I suppose, is a "visit" of sorts.

I picked it up, muttering, "Gabriel," then glowered at the screen, saw Will Evans's number, and remembered that Gabriel was presumably in my living room.

I answered.

"Olivia." My name came out on a sigh of relief. "I am terribly sorry to call you at this hour. I've been trying to wait for a more reasonable one, but I simply couldn't hold out any longer."

"What's wrong?"

"It's come to my attention that you're working with Gabriel Walsh again."

Damn. That was fast.

I moved to the bedroom door to tell Gabriel to keep quiet if he was awake. He wasn't.

He was still on the sofa bed, sprawled on his stomach, head turned to the side. He'd taken off his shirt, but left his pants on, and the sheet was twisted around him as if he'd had a hard time getting comfortable. He was comfortable now, though, and deeply asleep. Also? Very nice to look at in that particular pose, muscular arms and back bare, wavy black hair tousled, long inky lashes against his cheek. Damned nice.

I closed the door. If I was eyeing Gabriel that way, I really should consider giving Ricky a call.

"I know you aren't fond of him—" I began.

"Fond?" A short laugh. "My feelings about Gabriel Walsh do not approach the realm of fond, Olivia. The man terrifies me. There, I've said it." An exhalation. "I know it sounds ridiculous. After all, whatever his reputation, he is still a man of law. An educated man. Presumably a civilized man. I've been trying to remember that, to give him the benefit of the doubt and merely suggest—strongly—that you not work with him. But . . ."

"What is it?"

"I told you I have reasons for distrusting him. I was given those reasons in confidence, which is why I've not done anything more than hint."

"Something about his mother." I lowered my voice. "She was a drug addict, wasn't she?"

"Yes." A pause. "Has he told you what happened to her?"

"We have a professional relationship. He doesn't share anything like that."

"Okay, then. Seanna Walsh was an addict, con artist, petty thief—pickpocket mostly. Never married. There's no father listed on Gabriel's birth certificate. It was just the two of them until Gabriel was fifteen and Seanna left."

"Left?"

"Presumably. Now, if such a thing were to happen under normal circumstances to a fifteen-year-old boy, he would take refuge with a relative, would he not?"

"I guess so."

"Instead he stayed where he was for almost a year, pretending his mother hadn't left. I don't know how he paid the rent, but I doubt it was through a part-time job. Otherwise, he continued living normally, even attending school. Eventually, his aunt Rose discovered Seanna was gone. As soon as Gabriel realized she knew, he ran. She seems to have pursued him for about six months, during which time police records list him as a missing teen. Then she told police he'd been found and the file was closed. She hadn't found him, though. She stopped looking so he would stop running. A few months later, 'Seanna Walsh' rented an apartment again. No one ever saw her, though. Just her teenage son."

And this story was supposed to turn me against Gabriel? How? Because he'd likely been involved in something illegal to support himself? The guy had been abandoned by his drug-addicted mother at fifteen, and he'd made it through *law* school. On his own.

The story explained a few things about Gabriel. Hell, it explained a lot. And it did change my opinion of him, but not in the way Will Evans seemed to expect.

"I don't understand," I said.

"Think about it, Olivia. Do Gabriel's actions make any logical sense? He had an aunt he was apparently close to, who could have easily and happily supported him, yet he refused. He told no one his mother had disappeared. He ran away when his aunt discovered it. Those are not the actions of an abandoned child, and I believe I know why."

"So tell me."

"Seanna was last seen in late September that year. In mid-October, the body of a woman was discovered in an abandoned building several blocks away. The coroner believed she'd died of a drug overdose. The police found evidence to suggest she hadn't died there—she'd been moved to that location. The woman had no identification on her, but her description matches that of Seanna Walsh."

"So the police believed the body was Gabriel's mother and told him—"

"The police never connected the events. The woman was buried as a Jane Doe because Gabriel hadn't reported his mother missing. When his aunt reported *Gabriel* missing, police did not connect the dots back to the Jane Doe. My investigator did."

"You think Gabriel knew his mother was dead?"

"Think about his behavior, Olivia." His voice snapped with impatience now. "Those aren't the actions of an abandoned child. They're the actions of a guilty conscience. Gabriel Walsh gave his mother that overdose, then he hid her body in that building and pretended she was still alive."

"That . . . No, he—"

"—wouldn't do that? She was an addict, Olivia. I'm sure she made his life hell. Gabriel Walsh is an amoral man with clear sociopathic tendencies. Perhaps his mother is to blame, but whatever the reason, he saw her as an obstacle. He rid himself of that obstacle. I have evidence to prove it, and that's why he's trying to frame me for my son's death."

"W-what?"

When Evans started to explain, I was sure either he was crazy or I was still sleeping. Neither possibility completely disappeared as he went on.

When Gabriel first tried to interview him, Evans said he'd looked him up. What he found made him even more curious.

"I'm an old man, Olivia," he said. "Life gets dull after a certain age, and it doesn't take much to pique my curiosity, and a potentially interesting psychological profile always does the trick."

That led him to the missing-person reports, which turned mild curiosity into a full-blown project. Here, presumably, was a boy abandoned by his mother and left on the streets . . . who became a defense attorney. An intriguing case study. So Evans hired an investigator.

"Yes, it sounds borderline obsessive and certainly an invasion of privacy, but I was completely fascinated."

Then he discovered the fate of Seanna Walsh. The investigator gathered enough evidence to make a convincing case that Gabriel was responsible.

"That's when I realized I'd gone too far," Evans said. "That—along with other deeds that the investigator uncovered—convinced me I was dealing with a sociopathic personality. I stopped digging. I refused to see Gabriel Walsh. I hoped he would simply go away. And he seemed to."

"Until now."

"Yes."

Evans believed that when he insisted on seeing me instead of Gabriel this time, Gabriel did some investigating of his own and discovered that Evans knew his darkest secret.

"I'm sure Gabriel had learned that I worked for the CIA long before now. But suddenly it's a matter of great interest to him. Edgar Chandler called me last night and as soon as he described his visitors, I knew it was you two. And I knew what Gabriel was doing. Framing me for my son's death."

"I don't—"

"How did the investigation change course, Olivia? The last I heard, you were pursuing Christian Gunderson as a suspect. Did you discover this new lead? Or did he?"

"It was a joint effort," I lied.

"Was it? And it led to Edgar Chandler?"

No, first to Josh Gray, who wound up dead. Then to Desiree Barbosa, his girlfriend.

Or the woman who *claimed* to be his girlfriend.

Could Desiree have been playing a part? Leading me to Evans with her "secret" about him and the CIA? No. Especially not after all that runaround with the bikers and the drugs. The idea was almost as crazy as Evans's whole "Gabriel Walsh is framing me" theory.

"I did work for the CIA, Olivia. As part of MKULTRA on a classified subproject in Chicago. I'm not proud of what I did. I was young and I naively thought I was helping my country. As soon as I began to doubt that, I left."

"So why would Gabriel frame you? You could do the same to him."

"I don't know what his endgame is. Perhaps simply black-mail. I've heard he's fond of that. Whatever his plan, he's using you. Right now, that's what worries me the most." He paused. "Come to the house, Olivia. I know you don't believe me, but I have the evidence here. I can prove that Gabriel Walsh killed his mother."

# CHAPTER SIXTY

I stood in the living room watching Gabriel sleep. The cat was perched on the back of the sofa again, staring down, as if wondering what this person was doing in his apartment. I could ask myself the same thing.

What was Gabriel Walsh capable of?

A lot. I had no doubt of that.

Was he a sociopath, though?

From what I knew from my experience with Gabriel, he was not incapable of forming relationships. He was just a man who'd learned life was a whole lot safer if you *didn't* form relationships. A survivor, not a sociopath.

Gabriel clearly cared for his aunt, and there was nothing obsessive or unnatural about that. Yes, Rose could be useful, but she seemed to be the one pushing her gifts on him. He was a reluctant recipient, as if she was the one person he didn't want to take anything from. Didn't want to use.

Last night he'd been annoyed because he was worried about putting me in danger. That sounded almost comical when you thought about it. "I'd feel bad if you got hurt and, damn it, I don't want to feel bad." But given what Evans just said, it made sense. Gabriel could form attachments. He just really, really didn't want to.

So had Gabriel killed his mother? No. I remembered his speech when I confronted him about giving drugs to Desiree. That wasn't the reaction of a man who'd dispatched his drug addict mother half a lifetime ago. Seanna's abandonment hurt. Really hurt, even fifteen years later.

So what did I think happened? Yes, his mother was dead. Yes, he knew it. She'd OD'd, probably at home, and he foresaw children's services in his future. So he'd done the same thing we did with Josh Gray when we realized how inconvenient the discovery of his murder would be. Moved the body.

I put the phone on my nightstand and slipped into the living room.

"Gabriel?"

He didn't even twitch. If his back wasn't rising and falling, I might have been worried. I walked over and crouched beside him.

"Gabriel?"

Still nothing.

I touched his shoulder. "Gab—"

His arm shot out, hitting me so hard I toppled onto my ass.

"Oww . . ." I said.

He'd rolled back onto his side, hands clenched, ready to leap up swinging. For a second, he stared up, as if wondering where the groan came from. Then he looked down and saw me on the floor.

"Olivia?"

As I rose, he took in my nightshirt, then glanced down at himself, bare chested, legs wrapped in a sheet. His eyes widened.

"Yes, you're sleeping in my apartment," I said. "On my *sofa*. It was an exciting night, but not that exciting. I'd really hope you'd remember if it had been."

"Wha—?" He blinked, still confused.

He looked . . . young. Very young and very vulnerable. His face relaxed. His expression relaxed. His blue eyes . . . not cold, not empty. Wide and bewildered and, yes, damn it, vulnerable. I looked at him and I felt things I really didn't want to feel about Gabriel Walsh. Not now. Probably not ever.

"You said your friend at the SA's office told you about Joshua Gray?" I said.

He looked up. Met my gaze. Blinked some more. Still confused and sleepy. Good. Pounce before he got his guard up.

"The police report," I said. "The one where Josh said Peter told him a secret just before he died. Do you actually have it? Or did your friend just tell you about it?"

He rubbed his face. "The . . . ? Yes. Sorry. The police report. I have it. Those particular pages, that is. Copies."

"Could I see them?"

"Do you think I missed something?" He sat. "I doubt it, but, yes, you should take a look. It's at my office. Do you want that now or . . . ?" He looked around, still trying to orient himself.

"When we head into the city."

"Okay." He ran a hand through his hair and snarled a yawn.

"Long night. You were dead asleep. That's why I had to poke you. A mistake I will never repeat."

"Sorry."

"Or maybe I should wake you up more often. I bet you haven't apologized that much in the last decade." I turned. "I'll get coffee. Caffeine will help."

"Thanks." He started rising, then looked at the sheet around his legs.

"Don't worry, you're wearing pants," I said.

"Right."

He located his shirt and leaned over to grab it as I headed for the kitchen.

I was measuring grinds into my new coffeemaker when I heard Gabriel. I turned to see him standing in the doorway, watching me. I was—I will point out—perfectly decent, dressed in an oversized T-shirt that hung to midthigh. That was, admittedly though, pretty much all I was wearing.

Gabriel yanked his gaze away.

"Should I get dressed?" I said.

"No, of course—" He stopped. "Perhaps. If you'd be more comfortable."

I turned the coffee making over to him. As I passed, I noticed him watching me again. He looked away fast.

"Oh, and there *is* a reason I woke you up before six," I said. "Dr. Evans called."

Genuine confusion, then he swore. "Chandler contacted him."

"Which you expected, right?"

"That depends." He paused, and I could see him pulling himself back together. When he spoke again, he sounded more like his usual self. "If it required an early morning call, that means he's alarmed by our visit. Perhaps we can use that. What did he say?"

"I'll tell you after I'm dressed."

His hand lifted, as if to tell me not to bother. Then his gaze slipped to my bare legs.

"Yes. You do that. I'll prepare the coffee."

So what did I tell Gabriel? That Evans had called out of concern that we'd joined forces again.

Gabriel sighed. "I should be flattered that he finds me so intimidating, but it's becoming irritating. What does he want?"

"Me to come over right away. He says he has information on you that I need to see."

Gabriel shook his head. No surprise. No consternation. Just that head shake. "I'm sure he does. Some rumor he's dug up and believes himself the first one to do so, which he is not, such being the nature of rumors. All right, then." He paused. "I'm presuming he said to come alone?"

"That's the idea."

"Immediately?"

"Yep."

Now Gabriel did look concerned.

"Yes, I know," I said. "It screams setup."

"It certainly does. However, if that were the case, it would make more sense to invite both of us, since we are clearly both a threat."

"Unless he figures I'll bring you anyway. Or he might really just want to talk. He's seventy years old. I don't think he's going to jump me at the door to silence me."

"Anyone can use a gun, as someone did to silence Joshua Gray."

"You think Evans did it?"

"I have no idea." He paused. "Perhaps he's simply nervous about the pharmacological connection and believes you're the more sympathetic ear. I'll still insist on coming along, though I'll stay outside."

"Not going to argue."

"All right, then. Ms. Mosley's lead can wait. We'll pursue this first."

"Anita has a lead for us?"

"She left a message on my voice mail. Another potential contact, someone she needed to confer with before passing along his name. He was a subject in one of Chandler's experiments. One that Evans participated in. He'd very much like to speak to us, apparently."

I set my coffee cup on the counter. "Shouldn't we do that first? If he can add to the picture, it would help to have that before I visit Evans."

"Perhaps. Evans is waiting, though."

"And it might not hurt to keep him waiting. Let him stew a little. I'll text and say I can't make it right away, but I'll be there by noon." I stood and dumped the rest of my coffee. "Let's go speak to this subject."

He stood. "All right, then. My office is on the way. We'll pick up that police report."

# CHAPTER SIXTY-ONE

I waited on the front stoop while Gabriel brought the car. If he'd left the Jag in front of my apartment overnight, by morning everyone in Cainsville would know he'd stayed over, and that was just awkward.

As I waited, a figure crossed Rowan down at Main Street. He paused, shielding his eyes against the rising sun and then headed in my direction.

It was Patrick, laptop bag slung over his shoulder. I walked to meet him.

"Getting an early start?" I said, waving at his bag.

"The muse is a fickle bitch. Woke me at five. You're up early yourself. I hope that means you're taking Susie's shift. I've been meaning to talk to you. I dug up a few things you might find useful."

As I was saying that I wasn't working today, Gabriel's car rounded the corner.

"Ah, so you *are* working," he said. "Just not at the diner. And you're back with Gabriel. The old folks will be happy to hear it. They were terribly worried, you know."

I was saved from a reply by the purr of the Jag sliding to the corner. I bent to tap the passenger window, but the driver's door was already opening, Gabriel getting out.

"Gabriel," Patrick said. "Good to see you."

Gabriel dipped his chin as he said hello, his shades off. A respectful greeting, like the ones he'd give the town elders.

"Patrick was just telling me he had some research notes," I said. "And I was just going to ask if he has a second to talk about them now."

"Yes, of course." Gabriel waved to my building. "We'll go inside."

"Mmm, better not," Patrick said. "Grace . . . isn't exactly a fan. How about Rose's place?"

"It's a bit early for my aunt." Gabriel's tone was oddly apologetic, as if torn between waking his aunt and offending Patrick. I guess I wasn't the only one who caught those odd vibes from the young writer, the ones that warned to tread carefully around him.

"Oh, I think it'll be fine today," Patrick said. "In fact, I think you're about two seconds from being summoned."

We turned to see Rose in her open doorway. She was wearing a robe and slippers, watching us, as if waiting for a moment to interrupt.

As we walked over, Gabriel said, "You're up early. Do you mind if we come in? Patrick wanted to speak to us, and the curb doesn't quite seem the place to do it."

Rose nodded. Something was bothering her—I didn't need an omen to see that—but Gabriel only apologized for the intrusion as he held the door. Patrick waved me in. Then he paused, hand on the door frame.

"May I?" he asked Rose. "It *is* very early."

"Yes, of course," she said, her tone distracted. "You're always welcome, Patrick. You know that."

He smiled and crossed the threshold.

Rose murmured that she'd make tea. I said that wasn't

necessary, but she insisted and asked Gabriel to help her. They left as Patrick and I headed into Rose's parlor.

"She's seen something," Patrick murmured. "That's what has her up so early, worried about Gabriel. Whatever you two planned for today, you may want to reconsider."

"You believe in it, then?" I said.

"The sight?" His brows shot up. "You might as well ask if I believe in oxygen. I can't see it, but I'm quite certain it's there."

I glanced at him, expecting to see a knowing smile. He was watching me with a very different sort of amusement, the sort reserved for the child who insists there is no such thing as oxygen.

He waved me to a chair. "The sight is one of the manifestations of the old blood. *Bendith y Mamau.*"

The hair on the back of my neck rose. "That's Welsh, right?"

He smiled. "Very good. It means 'the mother's blessing' and is one Welsh name for the fae. The more common one is *Tylwyth Teg*, which translates to the fair folk. In the context of the current conversation, *Bendith y Mamau* seems more appropriate."

I tried to follow what he was saying, but my mind stayed stuck on my first question. "So you know Welsh?"

"Some. It's common enough in Cainsville. It was founded by exiles from the British Isles and hasn't come very far since. You may have noticed that." He lowered his voice to a mock whisper. "Not exactly the most racially diverse town in Illinois."

I looked at Patrick, sitting there, smiling slightly.

*He's playing with me.*

*No, he's not. Look at him, Olivia. Really look. You know there's something—*

A noise in the hall. Gabriel and Rose, talking as they approached. The door swung open, Rose holding it as Gabriel carried the tray.

"I remember MKULTRA," Rose was saying, looking relaxed now. "Mind control." She rolled her eyes. "What rubbish."

"Says the woman with second sight," I murmured.

Gabriel's lips quirked in a smile.

"Apples and oranges." Rose took the teacups and began filling them. "I cannot inflict my sight on anyone. No more than a person who sees omens can force another to see them, too."

I tensed, but Patrick was adding sugar to his tea, and he didn't notice.

"What about hypnosis?" I said to Rose. "You do that."

"Hypnosis merely taps into something already present in the subconscious. At most, it plants an idea. I can use it to help someone who wants to quit smoking; I cannot use it to force someone to quit against her will. That is mind control, and it is beyond the realm of possibility."

"Mmm," Patrick said, stirring his tea. "Beyond the realm of science, I would agree. But the idea of controlling another person is very common in folklore and the occult, everything from fully possessing another person to controlling the risen dead. Even simple spell-craft—incantations, potions, and the like—aims to control behavior. Now, if the CIA's scientists had been more open to *those* explorations, I'd wager they'd have had better luck finding their elixir."

"Sadly, it seems the people we're hunting only practiced the simplest version of behavioral control," I said. "Shutting someone up by putting a bullet through him."

Patrick's lip curled slightly. "How pedestrian. If that's the angle you're pursuing, then I'm not sure my research helps, but if you still want it . . ."

"I do. Please."

Patrick was right. As much as I appreciated his research, I wasn't sure it got us anywhere now.

What he'd found was another Druidic link. Each stone left in the victim's mouths had a small hole through it. At first, they'd been mistaken for amulets, the presumption being that the holes had been carved. Later, they were discovered to be naturally occurring perforation.

Adder stones, Patrick called them. They often had a glassy center, usually flint. Ancient Celts believed that center was the hardened spittle of snakes—or even dragons. Adder stones were , particularly prized by Druids. They were known as *Gloine nan Druidh,* or Druid's Glass, in Scottish Gaelic, and were said to aid in spirit travel.

What did that mean? We had no idea, only that it was a second Druidic link. Patrick said he'd keep digging for more. I told him he didn't need to, but apparently he was having fun chasing this particular mystery.

# MINGLING THE MYSTICAL

**M**ind control. That was an interesting possibility. It couldn't be done by natural means; Patrick was sure of that. Even by unnatural means, it was difficult. One could certainly influence behavior. There were also charms and trances. But their effect was sadly limited. Yet if there was a way to mingle the scientific and the mystical . . . Very intriguing.

Equally intriguing was the fact that Olivia and Gabriel seemed to actually be making headway in their efforts to prove the Larsens innocent. That was unexpected. It was presumed among the *Tylwyth Teg* of Cainsville that the Larsens were in fact guilty, that the ritualistic aspects of the crimes proved they were responsible even if no one quite knew what the ritual was supposed to accomplish.

Was it possible they had been, as the *boinne-fala* would say, *framed*?

Definitely intriguing.

# CHAPTER SIXTY-TWO

Patrick stayed to visit longer with Rose. As we left, I commented to Gabriel that they seemed to know each other well.

Gabriel shrugged. "Well enough. They have similar interests, as you noticed."

"What do you make of him?"

Gabriel looked over, frowning, as we reached the bottom of the steps.

"It's just . . ." I began. "Cainsville seems very old-fashioned in some ways. Respect for elders and all that. But Patrick appears to be exempt. If anything, he seems to be as respected as the elders. Which seems odd for a guy younger than me."

Another frown, deeper now. "Patrick? He's older than I am, Olivia."

"What?"

"Not by much, I presume. But I recall him as a young man when I wasn't more than a teenager. He's definitely older than I am."

I remembered what Patrick said when I commented that he'd seemed young to be published. *I'm older than I look.* Apparently so. That explained a few things.

As we crossed the road, Gabriel said, "Catch," and I turned just in time to see silver flashing toward me.

"I'm driving?" I said as I caught his keys.

"Yes, though those were just for dramatic flourish. Technically, you don't need the keys. As long as they're in the car, you can drive it." He paused. "I probably shouldn't have told you that."

I grinned. "In other words, from now on, whoever gets to the driver's seat first takes the wheel?"

"Unless I refuse to get in the passenger seat."

"Spoilsport." I walked around the Jag and opened the driver's door. "You're serious, though. I get to drive?"

He waggled his cell phone. "I need to check e-mail."

"So I'm actually chauffeuring you."

"Are you arguing?"

I slid in. "Nope. Are we still heading out to interview that MKULTRA subject? Patrick seemed to think Rose had a vision that we shouldn't."

"She did receive a warning. Typically vague, something to do with me, terrible danger, and all that." He climbed into the passenger seat. Then he paused before closing the door. "On second thought, perhaps we should switch places . . ."

"Too late."

I started the engine. He only smiled as if he'd been teasing.

"You don't take the warning seriously, I presume?" I said.

"I do, but a warning only means that I should be alert, and that was all Rose wanted to tell me. Be careful. Danger is in the cards today." He fastened his seat belt and made a show of double-checking.

I made a face at him.

"Go on," he said. "Just keep your foot light until you hit the town limits. Or I'll get blamed, no matter who's driving."

———

There are no stoplights in Cainsville. There are, however, a lot of crosswalks, and you're expected to slow at each. It was still early Sunday morning, but kids were already out, heading to something at the community center.

As I idled waiting for the children to pass, I noticed another gargoyle I hadn't seen before. It was a monkey tucked under a roofline, which would make it completely useless for its original purpose. It was cute, though, peeking out from the shadow as its hands gripped the overhang. Another one to add to my list.

I glanced at Gabriel. He had his head bent as he read his e-mail. He must normally use something to discipline his wavy hair and he obviously hadn't found a substitute in my bathroom, because a chunk of it had fallen forward. He'd taken his sunglasses off to read, blue eyes fixed on his phone. His expression was as intent and serious as ever, but the hair in his face spoiled the effect, and when I looked from him to the monkey, I thought of a boy hunting gargoyles.

Somewhere in Cainsville was a gargoyle with the face of that ten-year-old Gabriel and I wanted to see it. But even as I imagined asking—lightly, teasingly—where it was, I couldn't. Would he want me knowing he'd hunted gargoyles? That he had one modeled after him? No. I didn't think he would. So I waited until the children passed and continued down Main Street. I put my foot down the second we passed the town sign. Gabriel didn't look up from his e-mail, only chuckled and shook his head. I was playing with the acceleration, wishing I had a road more exciting than this flat stretch, when something made my foot pop off the pedal.

Gabriel kept his gaze on his e-mail. "If you thought you saw a cruiser, it's only Marg Wilson's black sedan."

"That's . . . not it."

He looked over, frowning at my tone.

"That billboard there," I said. "What do you see on it?"

He looked from the billboard to me.

"What do *you* see on it?" he asked.

"I asked—"

"Olivia . . ."

I swallowed and adjusted my grip on the wheel. My fingers stuck to the leather, making popping sounds as I pulled them off.

"Poppies," I said. "A bouquet of poppies."

"They're roses," he said quietly.

I tried to see roses, but we were less than a hundred feet from the billboard, the car creeping along, and the flowers were at least ten feet tall. I couldn't mistake them for anything but poppies.

"Pull over," he said.

I shook my head and adjusted my sweaty hands again. "I'm fine. Just . . ." I tried for a laugh. "It's an omen about my driving. Keep going that speed and we'll know what Rose's warning meant."

Gabriel didn't crack a smile. "Pull over, Olivia."

I started to shake my head. Then I saw something else, just past the billboard. I rolled the car onto the shoulder and kept going until I was close enough to be sure.

"Olivia?"

"Do you see the fence there? The wire one with wooden posts?"

"Yes."

"Do you see the bird on the corner post?" I asked.

"Of course."

"What is it?"

"A crow?" He put on his sunglasses and looked again. "No, it seems large for a crow. A raven?"

"Is the tail wedge-shaped or rounded?"

"Wedge. A raven then. Does that mean something?"

"Just that . . . they're practically unheard of around here. And I keep seeing them."

"Maybe it's the same one?"

I thought of the raven outside Niles Gunderson's apartment. I shivered before I could stop myself. Then I started to put the car into drive again. Gabriel pushed the button to turn off the engine.

"I think we should speak to Rose," he said.

"Of course not. I'm just—"

My gaze caught the raven's. It hunched its head down between its shoulders and looked right at me. The words dried up in my throat.

Gabriel opened the door. "Wait here."

I leaned over to stop him, but he was already out of the car, slamming the door behind him. The sound was loud enough that it should have sent the bird flying, but the raven just sat there, staring at me.

My heart pounded so hard my breath caught. I clenched my fists, told myself I was being silly. It was a bird. Just a bird.

*"Ewch i ffwrdd, bran."*

I whispered the words without thinking. My gaze stayed fixed on Gabriel as he bore down on the raven. I wanted to leap from the car. Tell him to come back. Tell him to forget the bird. Just come back. Please come back.

*Don't make a fool of yourself, Olivia.*

The raven fixed its beady eyes on Gabriel. It lifted its wings. Not preparing for flight. Flexing. Crouching. Ready to attack.

I grabbed the door handle. The lock was still engaged, and I had to yank twice. I pushed, ready to call a warning. But Gabriel was already shouting. Telling the bird to scram, waving his arms, and for a second, I saw the little girl in the ruined garden.

*"Ewch i ffwrdd, bran,"* I whispered. "You don't belong here."

The bird lifted off. It didn't make a sound, just flapped its wings and started to rise. As it did, something dropped from its talons. Something red. Floating to the ground.

Gabriel bent as I walked over. He picked up what the raven dropped.

"What is it?" I asked. But I already knew. And when I got there and he put out his hand, I saw what I expected—crushed poppy petals.

"We should speak to Rose," he said.

"About what?" I said, harsher than I intended. "What is she going to tell us?"

He let the petals flutter down. "I don't know." He shook it off, shoulders straightening as he drew himself up. "You said the poppy is a death omen. I might know what it means." He took out his phone and showed it to me. "This is what I was reading when you saw the billboard. It came from a search alert."

It was a news article dated today. The police were searching for Josh Gray following a tip left by his girlfriend, Desiree . . . who'd jumped off a neighboring apartment roof yesterday evening, leaving a suicide note confessing to Gray's murder.

"Desiree?" I said. "That . . . that's not poss—" I stopped as I remembered the drop of blood on her shirt.

"Admittedly, it does seem unlikely," Gabriel said. "She certainly gave no sign that she knew he was dead, much less had murdered him. To maintain that front when she was high would be extremely difficult. But as to why she would confess if she didn't do it . . ." He shrugged. "I have no explanation. It would appear, though, that this *does* explain the death omen."

*No, it doesn't.*

I knew that. Felt that. The omen was not about Gray or Desiree. But there was *something* there, an answer I wasn't seeing.

I remembered Gabriel telling me about Niles Gunderson. I'd

asked him if it seemed strange—Niles's neighbor poisoning him over a poker game.

I'd found two bodies. Two men who might have had answers I needed. Both dead. Both murdered by people completely unconnected to anything I was investigating. For reasons presumably just as unconnected.

It made no sense.

*Yes, it does,* the little voice whispered.

But no matter how hard I racked my brain for a connection, I saw none. I glanced at the poppies again.

*What are you trying to tell me?*

My phone blipped, seeming so loud I jumped. I pulled it from my pocket. There was a voice mail.

"Evans," I said. I lifted the phone and played his message.

"Olivia." Evans's voice was tight, almost breathy. "I just received your text message. I don't think you understand the urgency of the situation. I absolutely must speak to you immediately. Please call me as soon as you receive this message."

I replayed the message on speaker for Gabriel. As I did, I stared at the poppies. When the message ended, I said to Gabriel, "I need to go there. Now."

# CHAPTER SIXTY-THREE

G abriel dropped me off a half mile away. I headed out, slowly, waiting until he was in position at the Evans house. Finally he called to say he was hidden in the yard, with a clear view into Evans's office, where the doctor sat at his desk.

When I arrived, I had my gun in my jacket pocket, my hand resting inside, as casually as possible. The housekeeper answered my knock. As we walked to the office, Mrs. Evans passed and said hello. Seeing them, I relaxed. If anything nefarious was happening here, Evans would have made sure his wife and housekeeper were out of the house.

Evans greeted me, relieved that I'd finally arrived. When he offered coffee, I accepted. I sure as hell wasn't drinking it, though—from everything I'd read on MKULTRA, sneaking drugs into beverages was one of their specialties.

"You said you have proof about Gabriel?" I said as I took the mug.

He nodded and laid a file folder on his desk. "Do you have a strong stomach, Olivia?"

"Strong enough."

He opened the folder. On top was a mug shot of a woman. She looked in her forties, but was probably younger. As with Desiree, you could see the aging effects of drugs—the hard eyes, the thin face. No haunted look, though. This woman stared straight forward, chin up, light blue eyes fixed in a look I knew well.

"Gabriel's mother."

"Yes, Seanna Walsh. And this is the autopsy photo of the woman found in the empty building. I warn you, she'd been there for weeks before she was discovered."

"I know."

The body was not pretty. Decomposed. Scavenged. Naked on a morgue slab.

Was it Seanna Walsh? Given the condition of the body, there was no way to be completely certain without DNA. Still the wavy black hair and the shape of the face and body seemed to fit.

The proof that she'd been moved could be seen on crime scene photos—drag marks in the dirt, the position of the body, haphazardly covered, postmortem bruises.

Evidence of murder? That was tougher. According to the report, the needle had gone in awkwardly, suggesting someone else injected her. Given that Seanna was an experienced drug user, Evans's private eye had said it was unlikely she'd OD'd.

As I read, my gaze kept being pulled to a crow fluttering outside the window. Only one, which should have been fine, but if it was at a window, that was different. Another omen of death.

I clutched the warm coffee mug and struggled to keep my attention on the report, but I kept feeling the pull of that crow. Kept thinking about the poppies by the road.

Was it a warning that I was in danger here? That Evans was plotting something?

Or a warning that I wasn't viewing this evidence with a clear and disinterested mind? I didn't want Gabriel to be guilty. In my gut, I was certain he wasn't because . . .

*Because I trust him.*

Dear God, had I actually just thought that? I *trusted* Gabriel Walsh? The guy I knew was capable of pretty much anything to get what he wanted? The guy who'd already betrayed me once? This was the man I trusted over a respected, elderly psychologist who'd never been anything but helpful?

I liked Evans. In spite of my feelings about shrinks and even in spite of his involvement in MKULTRA, I liked him. I just thought he was mistaken about Gabriel.

I trusted Gabriel. At least in this. There was no rhyme or reason for it. No logic. My gut told me he was not trying to frame Evans. The scheme was too complicated; bringing me into it was too risky.

Evans continued, "I know I said earlier that I wasn't certain of Mr. Walsh's motives, but I'm convinced now that it seems to be blackmail. As I said, I believe he is not unfamiliar with the concept."

When I didn't argue, Evans frowned, leaning forward. "You do know his reputation, don't you, Olivia? You seem to take this all very calmly, which leads me to believe you don't think he's capable of committing a crime."

Sure he was. Lies, deception, threats, blackmail, drugs, assault . . . they were all tools in Gabriel's arsenal. From the way Evans was studying me, I wasn't reacting appropriately.

"Olivia?"

"I-I don't know what to think," I said, injecting as much uncertainty into my voice as I could. "I'm sorry."

"Do you believe he's trying to frame me?" Evans asked. "For the murder of my son?"

"I don't know."

"Do you believe I'm capable of murdering my son?"

My surprise then was genuine. "No, people don't—"

"They do, Olivia."

"But not for something like this. There was a senate hearing on MKULTRA. It's part of history. If your son found out, it wouldn't matter."

"Yes, it would. But not in the way Gabriel seems to think." He folded his hands on the desk. "I am ashamed of that part of my life and would have hated for my son to know about it. That's why his mother and I agreed to keep it a secret."

"So Peter never found out."

"No."

"Actually he did. Peter found out just before he died and he told Josh Gray."

"Who?"

One word. That's all it took. One single syllable and with it, I knew Evans was lying, and I felt a thud in my gut. I'd wanted to believe he had nothing to do with this. Really wanted to believe it, so much that I'd barely dared entertain the possibility.

I'd been wrong.

"Josh Gray," I said. "Peter's best friend."

"I'm afraid I didn't know all my son's friends, and I've forgotten those I did—"

"Josh called you yesterday."

A shot in the dark, but Evans went very still.

"We confirmed the phone records," I lied as I set my coffee on the desk. "By the way, would you try this? It tastes off."

"Wh-what?"

"My coffee. It doesn't taste right."

He looked at my cup and when he did, I could tell he knew exactly what I was talking about, and if I'd entertained any last shred of doubt, it died there. Evans was involved. My coffee was dosed. I was in danger. I tried to keep my breathing steady.

*Where was my gun?*

In my jacket. Which was on the back of my chair. I could get to it if I needed to, but there was no way to do so quickly, not without Evans noticing. My cell phone was in my jeans pocket, which meant there was also no way to discreetly text Gabriel. I had to play this out.

"My coffee tastes wrong," I said. "I think the cream's bad."

A soft exhale of relief. "Oh, of course, I'm sorry. I misheard. I'll get Maria to pour you a fresh cup. Now, about this friend of Peter's, Josh Gray. I'm sure there's been some mistake." He paused, as if considering. "Gabriel told you this, didn't he? About Gray and the phone records."

Before I could answer, the phone rang. He glanced down at the call display. Consternation crossed his face. "I'm sorry, Olivia. I do need to take this."

He rose to carry the cordless phone elsewhere so he could speak privately. I rose, too, leaning over the desk to see who was calling.

*E. Chandler* showed on the base unit call display.

Evans looked startled by my rudeness.

The phone had stopped ringing. He set it back in the base. "I suppose Maria or my wife got it. They'll take a message." He cleared his throat and looked about, as if he'd momentarily forgotten where he was. After a long pause, he lowered himself into his chair. "As we were saying . . ."

The door opened. Evans jumped. Then he let out a breath as the housekeeper walked in. She carried a plate of cookies.

"Thank you, Maria," Evans said. "That's very thoughtful. Before you go, there seems to be a problem with Ms. Jones's coffee. Could you please—?"

Maria dropped the tray. As it clattered to the desk, I noticed something gripped in her hand. My brain didn't have time to fully process the image before I heard the shot.

Evans's face exploded in a shower of blood. As his chair toppled backward, Maria put two more bullets into him.

There was a moment where I didn't react. Couldn't react. I just stood there, frozen in shock.

Evans's housekeeper just *shot* . . . No, that wasn't . . . Couldn't be . . .

But it was. It took only a split-second for the shock to crumble. For me to realize, without a doubt, what had just happened. That Evans's middle-aged housekeeper had shot him. That he was dead. That she was still holding the gun. That I'd witnessed a murder.

I grabbed my jacket from the chair, fumbling to pull out my gun—

Maria pivoted toward me, her face and blouse spattered with blood, her face empty. Again there was a second where my brain just seized up. Her expression was so terrifyingly blank that I couldn't quite comprehend it. Then I saw the gun rise.

I hit the floor as she fired. I'd lost my grip on my jacket, and it lay a few feet away.

I rolled just as Maria fired again. Then I sprang for her legs and knocked them out from under her. The gun went off. Probably dumb luck that the bullet didn't hit me. And that my assailant was double my age and twice my weight. She fell like a rock.

The gun flew from her hand. It sailed across the room. I started to go after it, then stopped.

*That's the gun that killed Evans.*

I couldn't touch it.

I kicked the gun under the desk and went for my own, still in my jacket. Maria scrambled after her gun. I pulled out mine and trained it on her.

"Stop," I said.

It was as if she didn't hear me. She just dropped to her hands and knees, and reached under the desk.

I stepped closer. "I said *stop*!"

Not even a flicker of expression crossed her face. There was a gun pointed right at her, an arm's length away, and she just calmly retrieved her weapon. Then she pushed to her feet.

"Stop," I said. "I swear if you lift that gun—"

She swung it up, right at me and—

I shot her. Point blank. In the chest.

She went down. I stood there, gulping breath.

*I told you to stop. Why the hell didn't you stop?*

I forced myself to close that gap between us. I was sure she was dead, but when I stepped around her, I saw her face, eyes open, lips working, looking confused, as if wondering how she got on the floor.

My hands tightened on my gun, ready to fire again if she reached for hers. She didn't. It was right beside her, and she just lay there, mouth opening and closing.

*Was she dying?*

I swallowed.

*Should I help her?*

I looked at Evans's body, then back at Maria.

*Why?*

*How?*

It made no sense, but I couldn't stop to think about that. Couldn't stop to help her, either. I needed to get out of there.

# CHAPTER SIXTY-FOUR

I kicked Maria's gun out the door while checking back over my shoulder, making sure she wasn't getting up.

"Olivia."

Gabriel came around the corner, Chandler's big .45 in hand. I gave Maria's pistol another kick and he saw it. He bent to scoop it up.

"Don't!" I said. "It was used on Evans. I don't want to leave it where—"

He lifted it by the barrel.

"Or I could have done that."

He caught my arm and tugged me into the living room as he whispered, "Shhh. The wife and housekeeper are still here."

"We don't need to worry about the housekeeper. I . . ." I glanced down at the gun in my hands and swallowed. "I shot her. I think she's dead. Or dying."

He shot me a look. Quizzical. Confused.

"Okay . . ." he said slowly. He straightened. "We'll handle this. We'll say that Evans shot himself, and she walked in—"

"No, she shot Evans."

Full-blown "Huh?" on his face now, and I realized that whatever he'd seen from his post, it wasn't enough to understand what had happened. That's why he'd been bewildered when I said I'd shot the housekeeper. He didn't know why, and that was his reaction. Not horror or shock. Just confusion.

Footsteps sounded in the next room. Mrs. Evans. She must have heard the shots. Yet she didn't seem to be running. Just heading this way.

Gabriel still had hold of my wrist, and his grip tightened as he looked around the living room.

He started shoving me toward the sofa. "Get behind it. I'll handle this."

"Don't hurt—"

I barely got the words out before his frown killed the rest in my throat. Whatever he meant by "handling it," his plan did not involve hurting Evans's innocent wife. I should have known that.

The footsteps continued. He pushed me toward the sofa. I grabbed his wrist and hauled him along behind me.

"I can't—" he began.

Now I tightened my grip, not looking back, just pulling him with me until we were at the sofa. It rested a few feet from the wall. I nudged him in first.

"I won't—" he whispered.

I gave him a shove.

What he'd been trying to say was that he wouldn't fit. Which wasn't exactly true. He could crouch, very awkwardly, behind it, with me beside him. It was the "very awkward part" that bothered him, judging by his glower as I wedged in. Or the indignity of hiding from an elderly woman.

As we squeezed behind the couch, I thought I smelled cat pee and I froze. I don't know why. My heart hammered, and I swore I could smell that acrid urine stink, but then it vanished and I shook off the feeling and pushed in deeper.

Now we waited . . . for Mrs. Evans to walk into the study and see her dead husband and dying housekeeper. I thought of that. The horror of it.

I could spare her. Jump up and say she didn't want to go in there. Pull her out. Force her back.

But I only held my breath and listened to her footsteps as they approached.

"Once she sees the bodies, we'll leave."

I jumped as Gabriel whispered the words at my ear. He squeezed my shoulder, and I'm sure it was more a restraining gesture than a reassuring one, but it felt good, the weight of his hand, the warmth of it, and I realized my heart was pounding.

I unclenched my fists and took a deep breath.

"We'll back out," he whispered. "Move fast. Get outside. Call 911."

I thought of telling him to shush. It really wasn't the time to be talking. But maybe I wasn't the only one a little freaked out.

"It's best if we call," he said. "The wife knows you were here."

I nodded.

"It'll be all right," he whispered. "I'll look after it."

I twisted, saw the concern on his face, and knew that's what he was worried about—that I was going to have to admit I'd shot the housekeeper. He couldn't shield me from that. In that brief moment, mid-crisis, the wall came down, blue eyes clouded, allowing himself, for a moment, to be worried.

"I'll be okay," I said.

The wall swung back up. "Yes, of course you will. Now, *shhh.*"

Right. Because *I* was the one talking.

Mrs. Evans had to be close to the study door. It seemed to take forever, her steps excruciatingly slow.

I heard her shoes squeak as she must have turned in. Yet there was no scream. Not even a gasp. Her steps just continued, as if she'd seen the blood and the bodies and kept going.

*She's in shock.*

Gabriel put a hand on my shoulder. "Follow me," he whispered.

He stood, stooped, ready to duck again as his gaze scanned the room. Then he nodded and exited the other side of the sofa. I followed.

From where we stood, we couldn't see into the study. To get out of the house, though, we had to pass that open door. Gabriel made it two steps before Mrs. Evans said, "I'm here."

Gabriel stopped. His gaze swung back, measuring the distance to the sofa.

"Yes," Mrs. Evans said. "I'm in the study."

She was on the phone. Calling 911, it seemed, her voice dead with shock. I motioned for Gabriel to keep going.

"No, the girl isn't here," Mrs. Evans said. "Just William. He's dead. And Maria. I think she's dead, too." A pause. "There's a lot of blood. She isn't moving."

I stood there, staring toward the study, mentally looping her words. It sounded like a child speaking, the words simple, matter-of-fact. And her tone. There was no tone. Her voice was completely flat.

"No. I don't see a gun." Pause. "Yes. In the desk." Pause. "I will."

Gabriel nearly yanked me off my feet as he dragged me at a jog across the room. As we passed the study door, I glanced in to see Mrs. Evans pulling a gun from the desk drawer. She'd pushed her husband's chair back, his body still draped over it. Pushed it aside as if it was a piece of furniture.

I stutter-stepped as I saw that. I caught a glimpse of her face. Her blank, expressionless face. Just like Maria's.

*That's her husband, the man she must have been married to for almost fifty years, shot dead, and she's shoving his body aside. What the hell is going on here?*

She looked up. She saw me and she gave no reaction. None at all.

When I'd first seen Gabriel without his sunglasses, I'd thought his eyes looked empty. They weren't. Frosted over, yes. Walled off, yes. But not empty. Mrs. Evans's eyes were empty. Blank pools of nothing.

I flashed back to that morning. I heard Rose and Patrick, talking about mind control. That's what I was seeing. As impossible as it seemed, that was the only answer.

I remembered Maria's face when she walked into the study. The way she dropped the tray and fired like a seasoned assassin. A middle-aged woman told to *play* assassin. Triggered by a phone call. From Edgar Chandler.

I started to run. I didn't need Gabriel's help anymore, but he kept his iron-grip on my arm.

Mrs. Evan's shoes thumped on the hardwood. It was a slow thump. Methodical. Just following orders.

*Orders to kill me.* That's what Chandler had been telling her on the phone. The "girl" had escaped and now Mrs. Evans was to make sure I didn't get far.

I looked down at the gun still in my hand. I could kill her first. Easily, I was sure.

The thought barely flitted through my head. If this *was* mind control, then Mrs. Evans wasn't a killer; she was merely the puppet of one.

Maybe I was wrong. Maybe she'd been in on it all, even her son's death. If I'd known that for certain, I could have killed her. Protected myself and Gabriel. But I didn't know. So I kept going.

We made it out of the living room easily. Mrs. Evans was an

old woman and her orders obviously hadn't been "*run* after the girl." Chandler knew the limits of his weapon.

We reached the front hall. The hair prickled on my neck and as I turned, the edge of a shadow crossed on the sidelight.

I yanked Gabriel back as the front door flew open. The young gardener stood there, spade in hand.

I saw the gardener's eyes—those empty eyes—and I heaved Gabriel off balance just as the spade swung at his knees. He twisted. The spade hit his calf instead. It struck with such force that he gasped, leg buckling.

The gardener pulled back for a second swing. I lifted my gun. I heard the shot. Saw the gardener crumple, and for a second I was certain I'd pulled the trigger . . . until a second bullet grazed my shoulder and I stumbled back. Gabriel swung around, gun raised, in time to see Chandler's bodyguard—Anderson—dive to the side, out of sight.

Gabriel started for the door. I caught the back of his jacket as pain ripped through my arm. Gabriel stopped. We couldn't see Anderson, but we knew he was there, and any second now, his gun could swing around the doorway and fire.

Gabriel hustled me along the hall. At the first door, I reached for the handle. Gabriel struck me in the back and I stumbled as a gun fired. I turned to see Mrs. Evans. Gabriel was falling, twisting, his injured leg buckling, blood blossoming. He hit the floor. I fired. I reacted too fast, no time to aim, probably for the best, the bullet hitting Mrs. Evans in the hip, just enough to send her to the floor.

I started to drop beside Gabriel, but he was already rising, pushing me toward that door. I yanked it open, took a step into darkness, and almost tumbled down a flight of stairs. The basement. I started to back out, but Gabriel was at my shoulder, prodding me, whispering, "Go!" between clenched teeth.

I went. He followed.

# CHAPTER SIXTY-FIVE

I felt my way down the stairs, shoulder blazing. By the time I made it to the bottom, my eyes had adjusted to the dim light, and I turned to see Gabriel still near the top, leaning on the rail, slowly descending, hand pressed to his thigh, grimacing with every move.

I started back for him, but he waved me off, emphatically gesturing for me to get into the next room. I stayed where I was but did look around, taking in our surroundings. A basement. Unfinished. Bare walls. Concrete floor.

Light filtered in through distant windows. I jogged to the nearest lit doorway and peered through. It was a laundry room with one window, near the ceiling. I checked the other two rooms—both storage, similar windows.

"Hide," Gabriel said as he hobbled over. "Before—"

I raced back to the stairs. He let out an oath and tried to grab me, but I'd already passed. I wiped blood drops off the steps. Then I hurried back to Gabriel and prodded him into the laundry room. I closed the door most of the way—all the way would seem a clear sign we were in there.

I tried to nudge Gabriel to sit on a pile of sheets, but he caught me instead to get a look at my shoulder. Blood had seeped through and it hurt like hell, but there wasn't a bullet hole, just a shredded line of blood-soaked fabric.

"It's a graze," I whispered. "I'm fine."

I tried to move away, but he caught me again, by the chin this time, lifting my face up to his and studying me. I knocked his hand aside.

"I'm not going into shock, Gabriel."

I looked at him, his hand on the washing machine, his weight all on his right leg. His left one was bleeding at the thigh, where there was a bullet hole, and at the calf, where the spade had sliced clean through his trousers.

"You need—" I began.

"Later. Now, the window. You have to—" He looked at the dryer. "Perfect."

"I know. I checked the options. Can you get up on that?"

"I'm not—"

"I'll help you if you can't, but you're going first. You're hurt worse than me."

"I'm not going—"

"Yes, you are. Now move before—"

"Olivia. Stop. I won't *fit* through that window."

I looked up at it, my heart pounding as I realized he was right. I would barely get through.

I took a deep breath. "Okay, plan B." I fumbled my cell phone from my pocket. "Call for help."

His hand shot out to stop me.

I moved back out of his reach. "I'm not going to be the idiot who lets you bleed out rather than phone 911. It'll be fine. You haven't done anything wrong."

I put a little too much emphasis on "you" and he said, "Neither have you. It was self-defense. Now, get your ass outside. Then call 911."

I dialed my phone.

"Olivia . . ."

I backed up and placed the call, keeping my voice low, in case Chandler's bodyguard picked that moment to open the basement door.

When I hung up, Gabriel said, "Now you're going out that—"

"I'm not leaving you."

"Don't be stupid. I have a gun." He reached into his pocket and pulled out the .45.

"Which will knock you on your ass if you try firing with a bad leg. Sit down before you fall."

"I'm—"

"Sit down."

I walked to the door and peered out. If I strained, I could hear footsteps above. Anderson would search the other rooms first. Then he'd come down here.

When I returned, Gabriel was still standing, leaning against the washing machine. Stubborn bastard.

"So you're staying with me?" he said.

"Yep."

"You may not want to do that."

"Too bad."

"I wouldn't stay for you."

"Probably not."

His mouth opened, as if he'd been prepared for me to disagree. He paused and then said, "I wouldn't. You know I wouldn't."

"Doesn't matter. You're my partner. I watch your back."

He paused. Then he cleared his throat. "What if I've done something that I'm quite certain would make you change your mind about that?"

"About what?"

"Whether we are, indeed, partners. Whether you should stay to watch my back."

I checked out the door again. "If you mean about your mother, I already know."

Silence. I was still peering out the door, listening. After a moment, I backed in and closed it a little more.

"Evans told me," I said, not turning. "He called me here for that. He'd done a background check when you first tried to interview him. An extensive one."

More silence. When I turned, his face was taut, blank.

"You said something about my mother," he said finally. "He told you that she left, I presume?"

"And the rest."

"The rest?"

I backed into the room, flexed my arm, shoulder still aching.

"Evans told me that the police found her body; they just never made the connection. Evans tried to say you gave her the overdose. I think you just moved her, so you wouldn't get sent to children's services. Maybe I'm wrong. Frankly, I don't care. Whatever you did, I'm not leaving you behind."

"Found her body . . . ?"

His tone made me look over, and when I saw his expression, I knew without a doubt that he had not moved Seanna Walsh's body. That he had not killed her. That he'd had no idea his mother was dead.

Shit.

His gaze lifted to mine. "What exactly did Evans say?"

"Nothing. Never mind. I shouldn't have opened my mouth. He was just trying to throw me off the trail."

"What did he say?"

"Never—"

"*Olivia.*"

I met his eyes and saw not anger, but shock. Dread.

"He said they found her body a couple of months after she disappeared. He had photos. Maybe they were doctored. I just . . . I thought that's what you meant. I'm sorry. But I'm not leaving, okay? We need to wait here until the cops arrive."

He was quiet for a moment before shaking his head. "No. We can't do that."

"Yes, it's not the most heroic conclusion but—"

"If we lose Chandler, we lose our explanation for all this. If the police show up, he'll bolt." He moved his leg and grimaced. "Damn it."

A line of sweat trickled down the side of his face. He was in extreme pain. Enough to distract him from any plan except getting me out of here. And having me tell him his mother was dead really hadn't helped.

"Would you sit down?" I said. "Please."

He hesitated, then lowered himself to the sheets. "We need Chandler. He's out there."

"Out where?"

A wave, curt, almost annoyed. "Out there. Watching."

I shook my head. "He phoned in his instructions to Maria. I saw the call display. He's sitting at home, orchestrating all this."

"It was a cell phone. He's here. Keeping his distance but keeping control."

"How do you know that?"

Another flash of annoyance. Or maybe just pain. "Because I know what kind of man he is. He's here, and I would like you to get the hell out that window, so I can go find him."

I cast a pointed look at his leg. "Really?"

He grabbed a sheet and tore off a strip to bind it. "I'll be fine."

"Okay, so if I won't leave, I'm being stupid. If you insist on taking down Chandler when you can barely stand, you're being brave?"

"Olivia . . ."

"How about we call him. See what's what." I lifted my phone.

"I have his home number, not his cell."

"I saw it on the call display."

"And you remember it?"

"Of course. I'm playing detective. The area code was 817. Is that his home number?"

He checked. "No."

I started to dial.

"No," he said, rising. "Let me—"

I shook my head. "I'm the client, remember?"

"I thought you were my partner."

"It varies depending on which best suits my needs."

"As either your lawyer or your partner, I believe I should be privy to your plan."

I told him. He adjusted it. I would have argued on one point, but there wasn't time.

When I called, Chandler's cell rang a few times—I didn't expect him to answer an unknown number. Then it went to voice mail.

"Hello, Dr. Chandler," I said. "This is . . ." I paused. Considered. "Eden Larsen. We need to talk."

# GUINEA PIG

handler listened to the message. Then he smiled. He could hear the desperation in the girl's voice, in the way she'd hesitated, barely able to get the words out. She'd kept her tone clear, trying to be brave, but she was trapped and she knew it. She wanted to negotiate. How quaint.

He summoned Anderson first. Then he phoned the girl back. She answered on the first ring.

"Miss Larsen," he said. "Is that the name you use now?"

"It is."

He gave a soft chuckle. "All right. Let's talk. By that, I presume you mean negotiate."

"I might."

He strained to pick up noise that might suggest where she was hiding. "Admirable, but under the circumstances I don't think you have anything to negotiate *with*."

"Then you wouldn't have returned my call. Technology is amazing, isn't it? We don't have to play cat and mouse, blindly groping around unable to communicate. Likewise, I don't need to play that old ruse where I say I have details of your crimes locked in a safe, to be opened in the event of my death. I can just tell you that I have it right here, in an e-mail, complete with photos of what happened in this house."

He tried not to pause. He wasn't concerned, of course. He'd cleaned up worse messes than this. Still, it annoyed him that he hadn't considered this possibility. He'd been out of the game too long.

He glanced at Anderson, coming out into the yard now. That reminded him what he was supposed to be doing—not chatting with the girl, but using background noise to pinpoint her location. Just keep her talking. She seemed willing enough.

"And Mr. Walsh himself?" Chandler asked.

"Dead, I think. Or dying. Your bodyguard shot him in the thigh. He seemed all right, but after running through the house, I think that bullet nicked the femoral artery. There's a lot of blood. He might still be alive. I can't tell. But if he is, I'd suggest you fix that when you get a chance. Otherwise, you'll need to bargain with both of us, and he's a much tougher negotiator."

"So I've heard."

By God, she was a cold one. Last night, she'd been ready to shoot him to save Walsh. But the moment her lawyer became more burden than help, she'd let him die. Not surprising, given where she came from. He understood now why the Huntsmen had forbidden him to simply remove her from the equation. The restriction rankled, but he dared not defy them. That was beyond dangerous.

The girl continued, "I'm sure your plan isn't to leave me alive, either. Actually, I'm surprised you let me live this long. You knew I was digging for answers. You could have killed me. Instead, you had brainwashed assassins kill Niles Gunderson and Joshua Gray before I could get to them. That seems . . . complicated."

She paused. When she did, he heard the faint sound of a furnace turning on, warming the cool morning. Furnace meant basement.

He motioned to Anderson and mouthed "basement." The bodyguard lumbered off.

Chandler realized the line had stayed quiet. "Miss Larsen?"

"You're not even going to pretend you have no idea who I'm talking about?"

Chandler inwardly cursed. He'd been paying too much attention to that furnace to react properly to her accusation about Gunderson and Gray. He should deny it, and yet . . . Well, he hadn't gotten to where he was by doing what he should. Especially when that instinct to deny was really just his old CIA training. It worked most times, but a smart and independent man also had to know when to give a little. Just a little.

"I know who Mr. Gunderson is," he said carefully. "And I know that Mr. Gray contacted Will, who called me about it. He was concerned. I told him to take care of it. Naturally, I only meant for him to speak to Mr. Gray, and if he did more, that's regrettable, but hardly my fault."

"It was Evans who wanted to get close to me, wasn't it? You disagreed—like when you disagreed with how he wanted to handle Peter's discovery."

"That was unfortunate." Chandler paused. Play the string out a little and then stop it short. Keep the fish on the line while the shark moved in. "I didn't kill Peter, though. Again, I merely told Will to take care of it. When I learned of the deaths, I confronted Will. I knew what had happened. They'd argued and there was an accident. The girl came in. Will panicked and killed her. He denied it, but the fact that he staged the scene to look like the work of your parents sealed the matter."

"How?"

"My dear girl. You do know his field of expertise, do you not? Sociopaths. He followed the murders very closely. Even discussed it with friends on the police force, which is how he knew details that were never made public. He was fascinated by sociopathy. Which is why he was fascinated by you."

A moment of silence as she worked it out. "Because I could, potentially, be what MKULTRA was searching for. The perfect assassin. I have the genes but not the experience. I'm a blank slate for his experiments. And I'm not currently serving a life sentence."

"That is an advantage."

"You let him build a relationship with me, because you were intrigued by his theories. You still are."

"Possibly. Is that what you're offering Miss Larsen? Yourself as a guinea pig?"

"Not sure I have much choice." She went quiet for a moment. "You said Evans denied it. But he ultimately confessed?"

Chandler hesitated only a split-second before smoothly lying. "Yes, he confessed. To me, acting as his doctor, not his friend, though, which meant I wasn't at liberty to reveal it. With his death, that changes. I have proof—"

A gunshot sounded in the basement.

"What the—?" She shrieked. "You—you bastard!"

Chandler smiled. "Calm down, Miss Larsen."

"I'm negotiating with you in good faith, you son of a bitch, and you sent your lackey down here to shoot me. All I have to do is hit the send button. It only takes *one* second."

"It was a mistake," he said smoothly. "I told him—"

"Call him off! If I see his face, I will send this e-mail. I swear it." The line went dead.

# CHAPTER SIXTY-SIX

I hung up. Then I opened the door and peered out. Gabriel was crouched by the foot of the stairs. He waved me over.

As I headed to the steps, a phone started to ring. It came from the body sprawled at the bottom of the stairs. Anderson. Unconscious. Blood seeped from the back of his head. Judging by the way his hair stuck up on one side, I guessed Gabriel had grabbed him by it and cracked his head against the concrete. There was more blood on the steps. Bits of shoe, too. And flesh.

I looked over at Anderson's foot. It was a bloody mess, half of it blown off.

"How'd you manage that?" I whispered to Gabriel.

"I waited behind the stairs and shot his foot through the risers as he came down."

"Smart." I looked around. "Messy, though."

"It's a big gun."

Anderson's phone had stopped ringing. Mine started.

I answered and said to Chandler, "You've called him off?"

A hesitation, then, "Yes, of course. I'm sorry about that, Miss Larsen. I—"

"Whatever. Now, let's negotiate. I want— What the hell? I thought you said you—"

On cue, Gabriel fired his gun. I dropped the phone and fired my own gun, aiming somewhere across the basement. Then I hit the floor, groaning.

"Miss Larsen?" Chandler called from the fallen phone.

I stopped groaning.

"Anderson?"

Silence. Then a curse. I could still hear Chandler's breathing, quickening now, as buttons clicked. He hung up. Anderson's phone began to ring.

I winced as I rubbed my shoulder. "I need to work on my pratfalls."

Gabriel motioned for me to save the commentary and play dead. I did, lying on my back, gun gripped in my hand. Gabriel crossed the room, his left foot dragging now, breath coming ragged. How badly *was* he hurt? Too badly to play this game much longer.

*Too badly to finish it?* I hoped not. Really hoped not.

A few minutes later, the basement door creaked open. A long pause. I imagined Chandler peering through. A curse as he saw Anderson's fallen body. Then a louder one as he saw me lying several feet away. He started down the steps. I counted them off.

Four, five, six . . .

"Stop," Gabriel said. He didn't bark it. Barely even raised his voice. Just a calm and steady, "Stop."

I sat up, gun aimed.

"You know the routine," I said. "Drop the gun. Don't bother backing away this time. Just drop it over the side of the steps."

He paused. Then he started to raise his gun. Gabriel fired, the bullet passing close enough to make Chandler lose his footing and tumble down the stairs, gasping, gun falling.

"Or we can do it like that," I said as I walked over to where he lay, moaning as he struggled to get up. "I'd stay down there.

I'm sure you broke something. The cops are on their way, and lucky for you, they're bringing an ambulance. Unluckily, yours will be going straight to a prison hospital."

Chandler managed to sit, grimacing at the pain. "You don't want to do that, Miss Larsen."

"Oh, I'm pretty sure I do."

"No, you do not. You have no idea what you've gotten involved with. What you've stirred up. I can help you."

"Right. Let me think about that . . . No."

"You're a child," he said. "A silly little girl who has mistaken being glib for being clever." He turned to Gabriel. "There's opportunity here, boy. I've heard you appreciate opportunity."

Gabriel didn't reply.

"At least hear me out," Chandler said. "Call the police and tell them it was a mistake. Listen to my offer—"

"Like Ms. Jones, I am not interested."

"Then you are a fool, boy."

"Perhaps." Gabriel glanced up at the door above and I heard faint voices. "I believe we have company. Olivia? It's best if a woman's voice hails them."

Before I could shout, Chandler grabbed my ankle. I kicked him off and backed away.

"Reconsider, Miss Larsen," he said. "You have no idea what you've—"

"We're down here!" I shouted. "In the basement."

"We should back out of their line of fire," Gabriel said, raising his voice to be heard over Chandler's protests and proclamations of doom.

We moved to the side and readied our guns, just in case whoever was at the door wasn't who we'd invited. But when it opened, it was indeed the police. We lowered our weapons to the floor and lifted our hands.

"You've made a very big mistake, Miss Larsen," Chandler hissed as Gabriel shouted up an explanation. "Do you think Cainsville will protect you?"

I glanced over sharply. "Cainsville? What does Cainsville have to do with—?"

"You'll find out." Chandler smiled. "The hounds will come to Cainsville and when they do, you'll wish you'd made a very different choice today."

It wasn't long after the police arrived before I did begin to wish I hadn't been so quick to call them. When you're trapped in a basement with gun-wielding mind-controlled assassins at every turn, it's easy to think, *Damn the consequences—just get me out of here!* The consequence, as it turns out, was that the daughter of Pamela and Todd Larsen had been found in a house full of dying people.

Within about fifteen minutes, I was convinced I'd be joining my parents in jail. That's as long as it took for the paramedics to wrap Gabriel's leg, and for him to hobble back and handle things for me.

The evidence was clearly on my side. We'd documented every step, including taping my conversation—I'd put Chandler on speaker and recorded with Gabriel's phone. We hadn't touched the trigger of the gun that killed Evans, leaving only Maria's fingerprints. We expected to find drugs in my coffee, further supporting my story. And there were no actual deaths to lay at our feet. Mrs. Evans, the gardener, and Anderson were still alive. Even Maria had survived—for now, though she was being rushed into surgery in critical condition. Mrs. Evans and the gardener had no idea what was going on, and I was sure tests would reveal drugs in their systems, too. As for Anderson, he'd started ratting out his boss the minute he woke up to find himself with half a foot.

Still, it was messy. Really messy. And we weren't even saying the words "mind control," instead sticking with "they seemed to be drugged." We weren't mentioning Niles Gunderson and Josh Gray, either. If Anderson wanted to pin those on his boss, that was his choice; we wouldn't muddy the waters.

As for Chandler, he still blamed Will Evans for everything. Naturally. Dead men don't tell tales—or refute accusations. The truth would come out at trial. All that mattered was that my question had been answered. My parents hadn't killed Peter Evans and Jan Gunderson.

Did that mean they were innocent of all charges? Not necessarily. But they *could* be. It was a start.

# CHAPTER SIXTY-SEVEN

I sat in the waiting room and tried to keep my hospital anxiety at bay. The paramedics had cleaned my shoulder—a deep graze that would hurt like hell for a while. Gabriel's leg, though, had needed a hospital visit.

Had they known the man, they'd have realized that the only sure way to get him there would have been to tie him to a stretcher. But no, they trusted that Gabriel was a responsible adult and would seek immediate medical attention. Which meant that it was up to me to get him to a hospital, and as long as he wasn't bleeding out, he didn't see the rush.

First, he had to make sure I wasn't going to be arrested. Then he had to contact the media himself and invite those of his choosing to a late-afternoon press conference. Then he needed Lydia manning the phones, which required stopping at the office to explain the situation.

I let him get there before threatening to induce bleeding if that would get him to the hospital. Lydia helped me cajole and bully him back into the car.

Now I was in the waiting room . . . waiting. While reminding myself that if a guy took a bullet helping me, I really shouldn't dump him at the front door and flee.

I sat near a window, legs pulled up, enjoying the midday sun. When raindrops tapped against the glass, they startled me, and I looked out to see the sun still shining despite the sudden shower.

*Rain on a sunny day. That's good luck.*

I smiled. I could use some luck.

As for whether I could truly read omens, I knew only that things had changed. That I had changed. I didn't feel overwhelmed by sights and sounds and smells anymore. I understood it was information my brain needed to process. I was aware of stimuli there, tickling the edges of awareness, but it didn't bother me the way it had.

I'd changed in other ways, too. Maybe I was still changing. I knew one thing—I wasn't hiding anymore. I wasn't going to start calling myself Eden Larsen, but I wasn't going to pretend I'd never *been* Eden Larsen.

Gabriel stepped from the back room, looking annoyed, as if the visit had been a dreadful inconvenience. When he saw me, the scowl smoothed out.

"Everything okay?" I asked.

"They said I need this." He nodded down at a cane.

"And the fact that you took it suggests walking is more painful than you let on."

He held the door for me. "I'll use it for a few days."

A woman bumped into him, so intent on texting that she just kept walking.

"No, no, don't apologize," I said. "Really. It's okay."

Gabriel gave a half smile.

"Yes, I'm a whole lot braver when they can't hear me," I said.

"We'll work on that."

As we stepped out, I spotted a child standing in the ambulance lane. A dark-haired boy no more than three, frantically looking about.

I glanced back at the woman who'd bumped into Gabriel, still visible through the window, still texting.

"Are you looking for your mommy?" I called to the boy.

He nodded, solemn faced.

I put out my hand. He didn't take it but let me lead him into the hospital. Gabriel followed. When we got to the waiting room, the boy let out a breath of relief and ran to the woman. She shot him a glare of annoyance, gestured to a chair, and told him to be quiet.

"Bitch." I looked at Gabriel. "I'm ready to say that to her face now."

"It wouldn't do any good," he said.

I was holding the door when I realized he was still inside, watching the little boy. He noticed me and strode out.

We were at the car before he spoke. Even then he cleared his throat twice—pausing for a few moments after the first time, as if reconsidering. When we were in the car, he cleared it again and said, "At Evans's house. You said he had photos of my mother."

"Or someone he claimed was your mother. I wouldn't know, of course, and I suspect it was just a lure to get me there—"

"Olivia?"

I glanced over.

"You don't need to make this easier for me. If he knew about my mother, he knows about my past. I'm presuming he hired an investigator. I'm presuming he told you what that investigator discovered."

"He really didn't say—"

"Olivia." He waited again for me to meet his eyes. "I would like to know what he told you, in case there are any lies that need correcting."

"Like I said, he claimed you killed your mother, which I didn't believe. I thought she OD'd, and you hid the body to avoid going to children's services. From your reaction earlier, I know that's not true, either."

"And the rest?"

"He said that you pretended she was alive and lived on your own."

He nodded. He put his sunglasses on, despite the dark parking garage, and faced forward, starting the car.

"I'm sorry," I said. "It was completely unsolicited information, and I know you'd rather I hadn't heard, but I can promise that I will never pass it on."

"It's a matter of record, if one digs deeply enough. I'm not ashamed of it."

"You don't advertise it, either. Nor will I."

"Thank you." He started to back the car from the spot. Then he looked over. "And thank you for not believing I killed her."

I nodded and waited for him to finish backing out. He didn't, just let the car idle there.

"The police will have the photos," he said. "I'll need to see them."

"You will. And if you want company . . ." I felt my cheeks flush and was glad for the semidark. "Not to presume, of course. I just meant that someone should go with you. I'd be happy to, but you'd probably prefer Rose."

"No. You've already seen the pictures, so that would be easiest." He cleared his throat. "You should be there anyway, to confirm they're the ones Evans showed you."

"You're right," I said. "Just set up a time, and we'll do that."

He nodded and backed the car out.

We didn't speak anymore of Gabriel's mother. We had another parental issue to tackle. I needed to see Pamela. To tell her what had happened, what we'd found.

When we arrived at the jail, Gabriel asked me to wait in the car for a moment. He had another call to make. A *very* private one, apparently, because he didn't even take out his phone until he'd walked several cars away. He wasn't gone more than a couple of minutes before coming back for me.

We were about a dozen steps inside the prison doors when Gabriel's phone rang. He checked the screen and frowned.

"Blocked," he murmured. He started to put the phone back into his pocket, then hesitated and answered. "Gabriel Walsh."

A voice replied. I could only catch the sound of it, no words.

Gabriel's frown deepened into a scowl. He waved at me, telling me to stay put while he took the call outside.

"I believe my message was very clear," Gabriel said. "Our business is at an end. I wish to return your—"

The heavy doors cut his voice short. A few minutes later, he came back. I couldn't read anything in his expression. He just limped in, motioning for us to carry on. It wasn't until he was through the next set of doors that he paused. He looked around, as if confused. Then he took off his sunglasses.

"That helps," I said.

He only grunted, his gaze distant.

"Having second thoughts about this visit?" I asked.

"Of course not. Pamela should hear the news from you."

We got another few feet before he stopped and turned to me. "We need to talk."

"Change of script?" I said.

He frowned.

"For speaking to Pamela," I said. "You want to change what we discussed."

"No, no. This is—" He shook his head and resumed walking before continuing, "Did *you* want to change anything? I understand this will be difficult. If there's anything you want to discuss, now is the time."

*Will you tell me what you really think? Did my parents kill those other three couples? Am I chasing a fantasy?*

*Is there a chance they're innocent? Or could Todd Larsen have done it alone? Could Pamela be innocent?*

*I'd like your professional opinion. No, I'd like your personal opinion, Gabriel, and I'd like your advice, and I know I can't ask for either, because you'll only give me the professional line — how you have no opinion as to their guilt or innocence and pursuing this matter further is entirely up to me.*

He looked over. "Olivia?"

"Let's do this."


We reached the visiting room. Pamela was already there when we arrived. Her eyes lit up when she caught sight of me.

Dr. Evans had told me to be wary of Pamela. To remember that I could be dealing with a sociopath who would show me whatever facade would get her what she wanted. When he'd said it, I'd looked back on my encounters with Pamela and wondered if I'd already seen proof of that.

But her anticipation and delight as I walked through that door wasn't feigned. She loved me. I might wish she didn't, but that wouldn't change the truth of what I saw in her face.

I saw more, too, as I walked in. I saw the pale, faint lines around her mouth and eyes, and I knew she hadn't fully recovered from the attack. She was still in pain, maybe not sleeping, and I wanted to back out and demand to get a doctor and make sure she was still being treated. Make sure she was healthy and comfortable and safe.

I'd loved Pamela Larsen once. Adored her. That doesn't go away. It can't, even when you think it should. Like my feelings for Lena Taylor. Or for James. However much they'd hurt me, I still loved them.

I should have raced in to tell Pamela the news. Seen her face light up with hope. Hugged her as we celebrated. While I could imagine the scene playing out in a TV movie—heartwarming and heartrending at the same time—I could not imagine myself in it.

"You were right," I said to Pamela. "You didn't kill Peter Evans and Jan Gunderson."

She went still. Stared. "You . . . you found . . ."

"There's another man in custody," I said. "I'm sure they'll tell you about it soon. His name is Edgar Chandler. He claims William Evans confessed to killing his son and Jan Gunderson years ago. Unfortunately, Evans is now dead and Chandler will likely be charged with his murder. But whether Evans did it or Chandler did it, that should clear you and . . . and my father."

She collapsed then, her shoulders falling as she slumped forward, eyes filling. "Oh my God. All these years . . . And you . . ." She reached out and clenched my hands so tight it hurt. "So many people tried, and *you* did it."

"Not alone," I said, with a glance toward Gabriel.

Her gaze flitted his way. She went still. Then she inhaled and looked at him.

"Thank you, Gabriel."

She tried to be gracious, but I could tell the words hurt almost as much as that knife wound in her side.

"There will be an appeal now, naturally," Gabriel said.

"And I suppose you want it." She glanced at me. "You haven't promised him anything, have you, Olivia? I know the Taylor-Jones family has money, but—"

"Olivia has not offered to pay for your appeal," Gabriel said. "Nor would I allow her to. I have no expectation of representing you."

She released my hands and eyed him to see if he was bluffing. The fact that she even bothered trying proved she didn't know him very well.

I continued, "Finding another killer for two of the victims is a good start, but . . ."

"It's two of eight," she said, turning back to me. "Only a quarter of the way there."

"And having Chandler say that Evans copied the earlier crimes doesn't help. It's unlikely he killed all eight, which is what we were hoping for—a single killer. This complicates things." I paused. "It further complicates things because you asked me to investigate those two. *Specifically* those two."

She paused, as if processing my meaning. Then she shook her head. "I picked them because they didn't fit the timing pattern. It was a place to start." She met my gaze. "I didn't kill anyone."

"But it could have been my father."

"What? No." She clutched my hands again. "That's not the way to go, Olivia. My lawyers wanted to use that angle, to raise the possibility that your father acted alone. I refused because I have no doubt—*no* doubt—that he isn't responsible. If you're even entertaining the idea, you need to see him. Either way, you need to see him." A wistful smile. "You loved your mommy, but you were Daddy's girl."

*Just like at home, with my other parents.*

I pulled back. "I'll see what I can do. In the meantime, I'll be watching the Chandler case, and looking for a connection to the other victims. You also need to think of anything else I can use. I'm sure you've done that a million times in the last twenty years, but I'm going to need more."

"I'll put together everything I can."

I stayed for a little longer, just talking. Then the guard came to say our time was up. As Pamela rose, I said, "One more thing.

I'm trying to get my medical records. Do you remember who I saw after Dr. Escoda?"

"Escoda?"

I spelled it. She said the name didn't ring a bell.

"You should ask your father," she said. "He took you to most of your appointments, and he has a much better memory for dates and names. Is something wrong?"

"No, just checking."

"So you're all right?" she asked, waving off the guard's attempts to lead her away.

"I am." I walked over and tried to give her a hug, but the guard wouldn't let me. I stood there as she walked away, looking over her shoulder, watching me until the door closed between us.

# CHAPTER SIXTY-EIGHT

That evening I was sitting in my favorite Chicago restaurant, attacking a T-bone like it was my last meal. Dinner was Gabriel's treat. A celebration. I could argue—and had—that he should be resting, but that was like jumping in front of a train and ordering it to stop. He had his cane, and that was the only concession he'd make.

As this was a celebration, the subject of our investigation was off-limits. Gabriel wasn't just paying, he was entertaining, too, and spent the meal regaling me with past cases. I listened to his stories and I ate my dinner and I drank my wine and I was happy.

I shouldn't have been happy. I should have been traumatized, curled up in a corner, reliving the ordeal at the Evans's house. I'd shot two people. Maybe in a few days that would hit me, but for now, I only regretted that it had to happen.

"Have I made legal life sound exciting?" Gabriel asked as he refilled my wineglass.

"You have."

"Good. Because I have a proposition to make."

"Really?" I waved at the bottle. "So that's why you're plying me with wine."

His eyes glittered, and he opened his mouth to say something. Then he shook his head, smiled, and eased back in his seat.

"Rest assured, it's not that sort of proposition. It's a job offer. You proved an apt investigator. I'd like you to continue in that capacity. Particularly if you promise to do all the online research."

"You're too kind. Tell me more."

"You'd do the research mostly from your apartment—I'll set you up with proper Internet. You'd still need to come into Chicago to discuss cases and conduct interviews. While I can't provide you with an office, I'm sure we could set up a desk with Lydia for when you're in town. I can't offer full-time hours, but the pay would be sufficient for you to quit the diner."

"I don't want to quit the diner."

He fixed me with a look. "Don't tell me you enjoy waiting tables, Olivia."

"I don't. I hate it."

He pulled back then, gaze cooling. "You aren't intrigued by my offer?"

"Oh, I'm very intrigued. But the part I don't like? Having you as my sole source of income. If you do something I don't agree with, I can't argue. If you ask me to do something I don't want to, I can't argue."

His gaze thawed. A faint smile. "I'd be fine with that."

"I'm sure you would."

"And the rest of the offer?"

"Sounds great. If we can work it around my job at the diner."

His fingers tapped the table. "All right," he said finally. "We'll see how it goes. But you may lose better-paying hours with me if we need to work around your diner schedule."

"I'll survive. So when do I start?"

"Tomorrow is a holiday so perhaps Wednesday, if you can. I

have a case . . ." He trailed off. More table-tapping. It seemed like annoyance now, his frown growing.

"What's wrong?"

He shook his head. "Just something we ought to take care of first. We need to . . ." A wave. "Talk."

"Go ahead."

"Not now. This is our celebration dinner. You said you're going back tomorrow? To your parents' home?"

My parents' home. Not "my home" anymore. I liked the sound of that. It felt right. "I am. My mother isn't back yet, but I've decided I'm being silly, leaving a perfectly good wardrobe there."

"Come by the office Wednesday morning then. We'll talk. Get this"—another wave—"other business out of the way. Then we'll set you up for work." Another few taps. Then he shook it off and picked up his barely touched wine. "A toast. To our next investigation."

I lifted my glass. "May it go as well as the first. With fewer bullet holes."

Gabriel laughed, quite possibly for the first time since I'd met him.


The next morning, I was up early. I couldn't sleep in. I was still riding high from yesterday's adrenaline rush.

I wasn't the only one awake. I grabbed my phone to head out for a walk and discovered that Gabriel had texted me nearly an hour before, saying he needed me at his office by ten Wednesday morning. We'd already decided that last night. I could blame his forgetfulness on the wine, but he'd barely touched his. I think he was really checking to see if *I'd* had too much wine when I agreed to work for him.

I texted back that I'd be there and that I hoped he was using the cane. He replied that he no longer needed it. I responded with "Bullshit." He merely replied that he'd see me at ten. Without the cane, I supposed. We'd need to work on that.

I smiled as I put the phone away. I was looking forward to working with Gabriel. In fact, the prospect was one thing that had me unable to sleep. Was I just excited to be doing work I really enjoyed? Or was I also a little bit happy to have the excuse to keep in touch with Gabriel?

Yes, I won't deny it. Gabriel and I had shared something yesterday, something terrifying and life-changing, something that would transform our relationship. And afterward, he'd taken me out, just the two of us, for an intimate dinner, during which he'd propositioned me . . . with a job offer.

There was no need to worry that I was falling for Gabriel because any interest was clearly not reciprocated. Which was good. It was safe.

I could enjoy his company and not worry about it turning into more, because if it did, I'd get hurt. There was no question of that. Gabriel may have opened up a little, but that wall was still impenetrable. Life had taught him that people were resources to be exploited and used. That's what I saw in his eyes. That was the emptiness. An inability to form the kind of basic human connection I'd need from a lover. Maybe someone, someday could break through, but I wasn't naive enough—or arrogant enough—to think it would be me. I'd gotten closer than most and that was enough. It had to be.

By the time I reached the park, my ebullient mood had begun to fade. Maybe it was thoughts of Gabriel, of his childhood, his youth. Which bled into thoughts of my own family and my life, and all those tangled threads. I'd taken the first steps toward unraveling them this morning. I'd told Howard I was coming home later today to collect my things. Ten minutes after I hung up, I got a near-panicked call from my mother. What did I mean I was getting my things? Was I moving out? Was I angry with her?

I could have laughed. I think I might have. It was as if she honestly couldn't imagine why I'd be put out by her behavior over the last few weeks. The sad truth is that I wasn't surprised she couldn't. In her own way, she's as self-centered as Gabriel. Maybe that's why I understand him so well. But there's a difference, too. Gabriel might always have his own best interests at heart, but he expects everyone else to do the same for themselves. To him, we are all the center of our own universes. My mother sees herself as the sun, the rest of us revolving around her.

Do I hate her for that? No. I think in her own way she's as much a victim of her upbringing as Gabriel. The very fact that she didn't expect me to move out proved that ultimately nothing had changed between us. My mother loved me as best she could. There was comfort in that.

I was also ready to deal with the problem of Todd Larsen. I would go see him as soon as Gabriel could arrange it. This wasn't easy for me. I knew from Pamela—and my returning memories—how close we'd been and I feared how much of that was tangled up in my love for my dad.

It would be harder now, too, seeing Todd when I knew he might be innocent. *Might be.* Perhaps I should have more conviction than that. I wish I did. But there was still a long road to travel before I could reach that conclusion. Some questions had been answered, but so many more had been raised.

A shadow passed overhead. I looked up quickly, tensing, but it was only a hawk. It circled once and flew off, but I kept staring up, thinking about ravens now. Ravens and owls and signs and portents. There was more going on here. So much more, and that was one puzzle I hadn't even begun to unravel. I wasn't sure where to start.

I was about to sit down when I stopped. Someone was watching me. I could feel it, the hairs on the back of my neck rising. I glanced slowly over my shoulder and—

There was a dog beyond the park fence. Standing in the shadows. A massive dog, the size of a small pony, with thick curling black fur and eyes—

Red eyes.

I swallowed and blinked, and when I looked again, I could see the eyes weren't red, but a rich mahogany brown, reddish when the light hit them just right.

The dog was staring at me. Staring right at me, gaze fixed on mine.

I heard Chandler's voice.

*The hounds will come to Cainsville and when they do, you'll wish you'd made a very different choice today.*

At a sound to my left, I glanced over sharply. Nothing. I turned back toward the dog, lifting my phone to get a picture . . .

But there was nothing there. The hound was gone. I was alone in the park again.

## ACKNOWLEDGEMENTS

Starting a new series is a terrifying and exciting endeavor. I've done it before, but I always had my Otherworld books to fall back on. This time, my safety net is gone. Yet my support group stayed in place, there to guide me through the transition and catch me when I stumbled, and I cannot express how grateful I am for that.

Thanks to my agent, Helen Heller, who didn't panic when I said I wanted to end a successful series and start something new, but said "Go for it," and supported me every step of the way. Thanks to Anne Collins of Random House Canada and Antonia Hodgson of Little, Brown UK, for doing the same. Thanks to Dutton U.S. for being equally supportive, and to Jess Horvath, for coming onboard as my new U.S. editor.

Finally, if you're an Otherworld reader, thanks for giving this one a try. Welcome to Cainsville. I hope you enjoy your stay as much as I did.